MICHAEL BERES
CHERNOBYL
MURDERS

PRESS®

Medallion Press, Inc.
Printed in USA

MICHAEL BERES
CHERNOBYL MURDERS

"A recent article in *Publishers Weekly* talked about how the current White House does not like that the publisher of this book has used the presidential seal on the cover because there are several bullet holes. I applaud Medallion Press for standing firm on its use of the artwork for this timely work of fiction. The novel is all about conspiracies, presidential assignations, and covert operations. Beres has written a very tense nail-biting thriller that is filled with several well fleshed out characters in tense situations. Beres sums up the discontent voters have for all politicians in this country very well in a few short sentences. THE PRESIDENT'S NEMESIS is a great political thriller."

—Gary Roen, Midwest Book Review

"Michael Beres has written a suspenseful novel that delves into paranoia as Stanley Johnson becomes involved in a convoluted plot to assassinate the President. Readers will enjoy Johnson's plunge into madness as people and events beyond his control begin to take over his life. Beres' plotting is brisk and full of twist and turns. Fans of Stephen King and Dean Koontz may want to check out this great beach read."

—Bob at jabberwocky.booksense.com

Accolades and reviews for *Final Stroke*:

"From Naples, Florida to Chicago, Illinois, conspiracies abound in FINAL STROKE. Author Michael Beres terrifyingly captures the paralysis and helplessness the infirm must deal with every day of their lives. Scary stuff."

—Julie Hyzy, author of *Deadly Blessings* and *Deadly Interest*

"Michael Beres skillfully leads us into the fragmented, frustrating world of the injured brain, giving us an engrossing story that blends violence with compassion, and an outcome that suggests hope is something worth clinging to."

—David J. Walker, Edgar-nominated author of many novels, including the *Wild Onion, Ltd.* series

"The Investigation by the Babes and the Feds domestic spying take a back seat to the deep look into recovering stroke victims. The communications between the Babes is incredible especially the patience of both as it must be frustrating to not be able to say what you mean to the transmitter and to the receiver. Although there is perhaps too much going on in the background (though not explored to any intruding depth), readers will appreciated this character driven whodunit starring a unique pairing of an amateur sleuth and a left brain stroke former cop."

—Harriet Klausner, The Midwest Book Review

Published 2008 by Medallion Press, Inc.

The MEDALLION PRESS LOGO
is a registered tradmark of Medallion Press, Inc.

Printed in the United States of America
Typeset in Minion Pro

Library of Congress Cataloging-in-Publication Data

Beres, Michael.
  Chernobyl murders / Michael Beres.
    p. cm.
  ISBN 978-1-933836-29-4 (alk. paper)
  1. Chernobyl Nuclear Accident, Chornobyl, Ukraine, 1986 Fiction. 2. Ukraine--Fiction. I. Title.
  PS3602.E7516C47 2008
  813'.6--dc22
                        2008009011

10 9 8 7 6 5 4 3 2 1
First Edition

DEDICATION:

To Chernobyl survivors and their families.

"Now I am become Death, the destroyer of worlds."

—Bhagavad-Gita, Hindu Scripture, quoted by
J. Robert Oppenheimer, 1945

"I don't know what I should talk about—about death or about love? Or are they the same? Which one should I talk about?"

—Wife of Chernobyl Fireman, in *Voices from Chernobyl*,
Svetlana Alexievich (1987)

CHAPTER 1

Present Day
Kiev, Ukraine

Kiev is unusually warm for May as a noon crowd thickens with workers on their lunch break. Some carry lunches wrapped in newspaper as they weave in and out of tourists studying brochures and shoppers carrying parcels. The workers move quickly downhill on Khreshchatik Boulevard like rivulets of water eager to reach the cool river bottom of the ancient valley. They flood onto European Square like conquering Mongol hordes, taking tourists and shoppers with them into the park, where food vendors wait in the shade of chestnut trees. Ignoring pedestrian underpasses, the crowd tightens a tourniquet on the flow of traffic. A person monitoring a spy satellite might conclude something in the city has resulted in panic, but it is simply hunger.

Queues at food vendors extend into the hot sun on the square. Slavs with frowning broad faces lean sideways to study the length of queues. These workers from downtown hotels, museums, and shops wear faded cotton coveralls and dresses of nonprofessionals. Although tulips bloom in European Square, locals scowl as they curse the current Eurasian heat wave.

On the other hand, thin-faced non-Slav tourists in casual dress

1

wear grins. It is as if the Carpathians ruled out smiling for anyone born east of its slopes. Perhaps it has to do with the Great War,
the reign of Stalin, and other more recent terrors. Sordid headlines
of war and global climate change all around them, yet Americans,
British, and Hungarians with money to spend put on contemporary
"happy faces," while Ukrainians, Russians, Belarussians, Czechs,
and Serbs insist on misery. The climate going to hell. Unchecked
fundamentalism stretching its talons across the Black Sea to con-
vert cathedrals into mosques. Who knows how many causes can be
blamed for traditional Eastern European melancholy?

But here is a contrast. At the wide entrance to the park, an older
man sits alone on a bench. Even though his face is thin and he wears
a baseball cap typical of a tourist, he does not smile. Most park
benches face south into the sun, or west to provide a view of the
tree-lined boulevard. The bench on which the older man sits seems
the only one facing away from cheerfulness and into a four-foot wall
put up to block side-street construction. The construction continues, machinery buzzing and clanking despite the noon hour.

It is difficult to tell the age of the man facing the construction
wall. He wears slacks and, despite the heat, a sports coat and a red,
white, and green tie. The white emblem above the beak of his black
baseball cap reads, "Sox." The man's sharp nose is prominent, his
narrow face deeply lined. A pair of frowning native Kievians, white-
uniformed young women carrying lunch sacks, comment on his age
as they pass. One saying from behind he looked younger in his cap;
the other commenting on his face. "A man who has lived a hard
life," she says. "You can always tell."

The older man turns to watch the young women depart, nods,
then looks back to the construction wall. A younger man, who
has been leaning against the wall observing construction on the
other side, turns and stares at the older man. The younger man

2

is in his thirties, tall, shaved bald, and wearing dark sunglasses. After a moment the younger man approaches the bench, smiling as the older man slides over to make room. The younger man wears khaki slacks, carries his jacket, and does not wear a tie. He raises his sunglasses for a moment and glances down at a tour guidebook he carries. He speaks, his voice loud enough to be heard over traffic and the construction.

"It says before the fall of the Soviet Union this was called Lenkomsomol Square. I beg your pardon, but do you happen to know the meaning of *Lenkomsomol*?"

The question is in Ukrainian, and the older man answers in Ukrainian. "It's a shortened version of Lenin Komsomol, or Lenin Youth League. They changed the name some time ago." The older man motions with his hand beyond the construction wall. "Over there the Ukrainian House used to be the Lenin Museum."

"My first trip to Kiev," says the younger man. "I hope I didn't interrupt your lunch break."

"Not at all," says the older man. "As you can see, I'm not eating. I can't make out your accent. Is it Russian?"

"I'd call it *goulash*," says the younger man, smiling. "A mixture of several languages. Hungarian, English, Russian ... even some German."

The older man studies the younger man several seconds before responding. "You speak Ukrainian well. Coincidentally, besides Ukrainian, I also know Hungarian, Russian, and, more recently, English."

The two men consider one another several seconds before the younger man continues. "Are you from Kiev?"

"I currently live in Chicago, Illinois, in the United States."

"I can see from your cap. Are the Sox white in Chicago?"

"Yes."

"I wasn't sure if they were white or red. But regarding Kiev, is this a return visit?"

After a pause the older man says, "I lived here many years ago. The mood was completely different then."

"How so?"

"A state of panic. And I don't mean the rush to queue up for lunch."

The younger man raises a hand to shade his eyes and looks more closely at the older man. "Surely you're not speaking of the war. You're not old enough to have served in the war."

"No, another time when people faced uncertainty and shorter lives for their children."

"Of course," says the younger man. "You're speaking of Chernobyl. You say you lived here then? Have you visited Chernobyl?"

"I could have gone today if I'd wanted," says the older man, turning to look north, staring up at the sky beyond the buildings. "The last time I saw the plant was before the accident. Those who came with me to Kiev on this trip insisted I join them, but I turned them down. I need to keep alive my memories of happier times. Visiting the sarcophagus would be like visiting the graves of loved ones. Did you know lunch is brought in with the tour rather than being cooked in the exclusion zone?"

"I'd heard," says the younger man. "My tour book suggests a visit to the Chernobyl Museum a few blocks from here. It says many who wish to tour the plant and the exclusion zone decide not to go after a visit to the museum. It must have been chaos after the explosion. Everyone running about in a state of panic, the drunken peasants from the north causing most of the trouble, I suppose . . ."

"I blame officials for the panic," says the older man. "In their search for scapegoats, they became murderers."

The younger man rubs his chin with one hand. "Tell me, do you think Chernobyl really was an accident as they say?"

"You're not the first, nor will you be the last to pose the question. History loves conspiracy. Facts hide in the mists of time. If you're going to ask if I think there was a conspiracy to cause the Chernobyl explosion, which I know is your purpose, you'd better hurry."

The younger man glances about. "Why?"

"Because one of these days it will be time for me to put my violin back in its case. When I do, my strings will be silent."

The younger man smiles. "You're a smart one."

"Not as smart as I could have been, especially back then."

"When do your friends return from Chernobyl?"

"The bus arrives at the Chernobyl Museum at seven."

"I assume you'll dine somewhere in the city when they return. I also assume you are staying at one of the nearby hotels. Perhaps the Dnipro across the square . . ."

The older man interrupts. "It used to be called the Hotel Dnieper, same as the river. The locals use the Ukrainian spelling. Many things have changed names since I was last in Kiev."

"Everything changes," says the younger man. "Especially the weather. I don't recall it ever being this hot in Kiev in May."

"You said this was your first trip to Kiev."

The younger man smiles, takes out a handkerchief, and dabs his bare head. "Many believe the Earth Mother is in the process of kicking our asses off her planet. First we have ice-age winters, now we have a tropical spring. Some locals say Chernobyl, as well as climate change, are ongoing signs from God. He's weary of our fiddling in his business."

The older man turns and simply stares at the younger man without comment.

"This weather," explains the younger man, putting his handkerchief away. "God sending the Earth Mother to retaliate for our having messed with the planet. It's a record temperature for early May. This morning the war veterans sweated their balls off during their patriotic march."

The older man turns back to the construction wall, above which a cloud of dust has risen. "I believe you were going to suggest a restaurant."

"I suppose, since you skipped lunch, you will be quite hungry by dinnertime. It's the restaurant in Casino Budapest. I dined there last night. Excellent cuisine as well as entertainment. Not far from here at Leontovicha Number Three. Don't worry about mixed company. The strip club isn't connected to the restaurant. The entertainment in the restaurant is strictly musical."

"How do you know I haven't already eaten lunch?" asks the older man. "And how do you know I won't want to enjoy a striptease show while I eat?" When the younger man does not answer, the older man continues. "Will I see you or another representative from your agency at dinner tonight?"

The younger man shakes his head sadly as he stands. "Casino Budapest has an excellent restaurant. I may dine there myself again tonight." He points to the older man's chest. "Perhaps your tie prompted my suggestion. The colors of the Hungarian flag."

"The Italian and Bulgarian flags also use these colors, only in different order."

The younger man smiles and begins walking away. "You know your flags. Now, if you'll excuse me, I'm headed for the Ukrainian House exhibition center. It used to be called Lenin's Museum, you know."

After the younger man is gone, the older man takes off his Sox cap, raises one arm to wipe his forehead with his jacket sleeve, and puts his cap back on. He stares above the construction wall at its north end. Beyond the layered clouds of dust between buildings, he can see storm clouds gathered on the horizon. For a moment, the look on the older man's face freezes in an expression of terror and panic, and he stands. But soon his expression calms, he straightens his tie, and begins walking, crossing the square with a cabal of pedestrians who have managed to stall the flow of traffic.

The older man heads west up Khreshchatik. As he walks, he glances at his watch. Because of the plethora of Western gear sold in shops along the boulevard, his Chicago White Sox baseball cap does not give him away. He could be a Kievian businessman heading back to work after a lunch break across the square in the park. The older man blends into the crowd on the shaded side of the boulevard. Some distance behind him, also blending into the crowd walking beneath chestnut trees in full bloom, is the younger man with shaved head and sunglasses, who now wears his jacket despite earlier complaints about the heat. The younger man pauses at a kiosk to purchase a newspaper, quickly scans headlines chronicling unusual weather patterns throughout the world, tucks the newspaper beneath his arm, and continues following the man in the White Sox cap and the red, white, and green tie.

In the ghost town of Pripyat, near the decommissioned Chernobyl Nuclear Power Plant, a storm threatens. Because of the dark sky and windblown dust in deserted streets, the tour directress, Lyudmilla Nashivankin, has the driver of the van stop beside an apartment building where they will be shielded from the wind and not encounter so much dust. It is rare, especially in the spring, to have a storm during a tour. Tours are cancelled when storms are predicted, and most likely this one is an anomaly of the early heat wave and will soon blow over.

So as not to alarm the tourists, Lyudmilla checks the radiation monitor in the front pocket of her coveralls discreetly and observes Anton, the van driver, already closing the van's outside vents and adjusting the air-conditioning without being asked. She and Anton are well aware of hot spots between buildings. The threat posed by wind-whipped dust was part of their training.

"Soon it will rain a little," says Anton in Ukrainian. "The dust will settle."

Although everyone on the tour wears off-white coveralls and there are face masks for each stored in the van, Lyudmilla knows these are mostly for show.

"I hope it rains soon," announces Lyudmilla in English, the primary language of members on this tour. "We should want to exit the van and listen to the silence of Pripyat." She shrugs her shoulders. "But if not, we will view Pripyat from inside and imagine the silence."

Ahead of the van, dust blows between buildings and across the road. The row of apartment buildings, up to sixteen stories tall, stretches several blocks. If one observed only the upper floors, one would think this was part of a city alive with people. However, on closer inspection, one can see most window glass is gone, and here and there the shredded remnant of a drapery flaps in the wind. At ground level, abandonment is more obvious. Trees, bushes, and weeds have overgrown sidewalks and walkways. The outside lane of the once-wide street is overgrown. Larger trees, having gone wild without being trimmed for decades, hide first- and second-story windows, the trees sending branches into the apartments as if to reside there.

Lyudmilla points ahead of the van to a clearing on the opposite side of the street across from the apartment complex. "See the Ferris wheel in the distance? It was part of the May Day celebration coming five days after April 26 in 1986. Local people called it a devil's wheel prior to the accident. Now the name has more serious meaning."

Several tourists nod. A young woman and man in their twenties sitting behind the driver hold hands and look to one another. They do not smile. Rather, they briefly tighten their lips as if to silently acknowledge something poignant. The young woman has dark brown hair brushed out straight cascading down onto her coveralls. Her eyes are large and, upon close examination, which the young man is obviously doing, are greenish-gray in color.

Lyudmilla continues speaking. "This is why Anton and I came to Pripyat first instead of the sarcophagus. We wished to be here before the storm so we could hear the silence, then we could have stayed in the van at the sarcophagus. But now, who knows?"

Lyudmilla sits down in the front seat on the right side of the van to watch the storm. She turns and smiles reassuringly across the narrow aisle to the young couple sitting behind Anton. The woman is in the aisle seat, the man in the window seat. They are American, as are several others on the tour. Lyudmilla admires the fine pale skin of the young woman. She studies the woman's eyes, noting the shade of eye shadow, wondering how it would look on her. The lower-level cosmetic shop at Independence Square must certainly carry the shade.

"This storm will blow over, I think," says Anton in English over his shoulder.

Lyudmilla nods agreement. The young man smiles at Lyudmilla. It is a pleasant smile. She has seen other African Americans on the tour, but not many, and especially not this young. The shade of the young man's skin is comfortable, like honey or bread toasted to perfection. The man is tall, his shoulders wide, his dark slacks showing at his ankles because the coveralls are too short for him.

9

Lyudmilla became fond of the couple early in the tour. While observing photographs of Chernobyl victims, the young woman began weeping. Lyudmilla can still picture the way the tall young man with his strong arms and hands held onto the young woman. Lyudmilla assumes they are not married because they signed up for the tour separately, whereas a married couple could have used a single sign-up form. Although she cannot recall their names at the moment, Lyudmilla recalls the young woman touching a particular photograph in the museum before she began weeping. Not one of the many firemen, but rather a reactor worker who died a few days after the accident in Moscow. She recalls wondering whether the young woman was related to the victim in the photograph and was going to ask about this, but the German tourists, whom she has seated at the rear of the van, had interrupted at that point and carried on with questions for what seemed hours.

Outside the wind is dying down, but it is not raining. "The weather front," announces Anton over his shoulder. "It will blow over in a few minutes."

Across the aisle from Lyudmilla, the young man puts his arm around the young woman's shoulder. The young woman's pale skin goes well with her greenish-gray eyes. Her skin also contrasts nicely with the hand of the young man. The two lean close and speak quietly.

"Reminds me of a black-and-white movie about nuclear war," says the young man.

The young woman pulls his hand from her shoulder to her mouth, kisses it. "Like *On the Beach* where the submarine parks in San Francisco Bay, and they look through the periscope at empty streets. Except for being overgrown, it's like people simply disappeared one day."

"I was thinking of *Fail-Safe*," says the young man. "But in that movie the people are in the city when it gets nuked."

The young woman points out the van's windshield. "I can't help wondering what apartment they lived in."

Lyudmilla, who has been listening in, stands in the aisle, pushes her hands into the deep pockets of her coveralls, and speaks to all the passengers. "In some apartments letters were found. Children, prompted by teachers, wrote letters to their homes, saying good-bye. School was in session in Pripyat that Saturday, and teachers must have been aware of the explosion occurring a little after one in the morning. Even though evacuation had not yet begun, teachers may have guessed the seriousness of the situation. This was the exception. In most cases residents assumed they would be gone only a few days. So much was left behind. Over the years, and even though they are not supposed to be in the exclusion zone, looters have done their damage. You will notice most window glass and doors have been removed. This allows outside air to flow freely in the buildings so radiation hot spots will not accumulate."

Lyudmilla holds one pocket out wide to check her radiation monitor again, then pulls her hand from her pocket and points up the street. "The shorter building near the Ferris wheel was an indoor swimming pool. There were many schools and kindergartens. Inside these, lesson plans and children's drawings still hang on walls."

A man speaks loudly with a German accent from the back of the van. "You said how many lived here?"

"Approximately forty thousand men, women, and children lived in Pripyat. Although we call it a town, many considered it a city. Most worked at the Chernobyl plant, as I said, but some worked at the radio factory."

"Is the radio factory still in operation?" asks the German man.

"The factory was here in Pripyat," says Lyudmilla. "Nothing is in operation in Pripyat."

"The wind is less," announces Anton. "I shall drive to the May Day carnival site, and there we can open windows and listen to silence. Next we go to the sarcophagus, where we will be able to get out and listen to silence there."

Lyudmilla sits down, Anton puts the van in gear, and they drive slowly down the street.

The front has passed, the air has freshened and cooled, and the sun is out as the tourists in their off-white coveralls exit the van at the sarcophagus observation platform. Because construction is in progress on the new sarcophagus, it is not as quiet here as it was when they opened the windows of the van at the carnival site. A crane is running, lifting a shiny rectangular section to be fitted onto the structure going up around the perimeter of the old sarcophagus. The old sarcophagus is gray, like a tombstone, making the new sections surrounding the base into a necklace in the sun.

Lyudmilla stands at the railing at the front of the observation platform. She has taken a radiation measurement, which she announces to be a safe three hundred micro-roentgens per hour. In the distance, where the core of Chernobyl number four is buried beneath tons of concrete and steel, the crane suddenly stops running, and it is deathly silent.

"Don't worry," says Lyudmilla. "The workers have simply reached the end of their shift at the site."

She points to the base of the sarcophagus in the distance. "See the movement at the cab of the crane? The shift is changing. Workers can only be in certain locations for short periods."

"How short and how many roentgens?" asks the German man, his voice booming in the silence.

12

"I am not a technician," answers Lyudmilla. "You will be able to ask technical questions at the lecture after our lunch back at the Slavutych Visitor Center outside the inner zone. Please save your questions for then. For now we should board the van because our lunch will be waiting. Our last stops will be the red forest and the vehicle graveyard, where is located equipment used during the initial work at the site. These include helicopters, fire trucks, and countless other vehicles."

As they walk to the van, Lyudmilla stays close behind the young American couple and listens in to their conversation.

"I can understand why your father didn't want to come with us," says the young man.

"He's not really my father, Michael."

The young man turns with a puzzled look. "But you call him Dad."

"I know," says the young woman, turning to smile up at the young man. "And he is."

Lyudmilla almost runs into them when they suddenly stop walking. She steps to one side but continues listening in.

"This must be part of the puzzle," says Michael. He looks back at the necklaced sarcophagus. "This entire place is a puzzle."

The young woman smiles and pokes him in the ribs.

He laughs and pokes her back.

Their laughter breaks the stagnant silence. Lyudmilla has turned to watch the others climbing into the van. An older woman whose coveralls are much too large for her frowns and shakes her head at the young couple. But Lyudmilla pays the older woman no mind. Suddenly her thoughts are elsewhere. She is with Vitaly. They are basking in the sun at a Black Sea resort. It is 1991. The union has fallen, and although most resort visitors don't seem to know whether to celebrate or despair, she and Vitaly chose to celebrate because they are young and in love. If only Vitaly were here with her today. If only they were young and in love again. Perhaps they could at least be in love again. She recalls their bitter argument before this shift of duty. Vitaly most likely at home brooding all week . . . if he is home.

Before getting into the van, the inquisitive German man questions Lyudmilla. "The Belarus border is how far from here?"

"Fifteen kilometers," answers Lyudmilla.

The German climbs into the van but keeps talking. "It was the Bel-o-russian Republic back then. They received the worst of the radiation because of the winds. Perhaps it is part of the reason they changed the name to Belarus. There is confusion regarding the spelling. Some say they are Bel-a-russians with a letter *A*, while others retain the old spelling with an *O*. And sometimes, like in your brochure for the tour, they can't make up their minds how many *S*'s are in the word. It makes one wonder whether the radiation is still having an effect, knocking letters about in the name of the people to the north."

The German chuckles at his cleverness, but no one else seems amused.

After everyone is back in the van and it drives down the road where weeds emerge from cracks in the pavement, the crane at the sarcophagus starts up again. A new shift of workers has returned to their duty, attempting to permanently entomb the Chernobyl mistakes of the past.

Back in Pripyat all is silent. The sun is out, the dust has settled, and the ghosts of the past assemble. Inside a kindergarten, a tattered poster shows children doing exercises. Inside the lobby of an abandoned movie theater, banners prepared for the 1986 May Day celebration lie scattered on the floor. One of the banners is stretched across the floor. Its faded red has Russian lettering saying, "The Party of Lenin Will Lead Us to the Triumph of Communism."

Out on the overgrown boulevard, streetlights, which will never light again, resemble skinny guards with crooked necks. A hotel of several stories has a sign with raised letters on its roof. Several letters are teetering, but it can still be read. "Hotel Polissia." An overturned child's tricycle in an overgrown school playground has a small tree growing up through its spokes.

In front of one apartment building, a pair of wolves walks along the street. One wolf turns up an overgrown walkway and heads for the open doorway to the building. The wolf stares inside, then, as if knowing the danger, turns quickly to catch up to its companion, and the two trot off into the late-afternoon sun and head for the pine forest in the distance.

Inside the building, the doors to the elevator in the lobby have been pried off and lie on the floor. A bird flies in the front door and up the elevator shaft. In a hallway on an upper floor of the building, someone has chiseled, "Good-bye forever," in Ukrainian, in Russian, and in English on the plaster wall. Inside an apartment, tattered family photographs barely hang onto a wall from which plaster has peeled away. Other photographs lie on the floor, half-covered with debris.

Outside the window of the apartment is a view of Pripyat with its many buildings and streets and ghosts. In the distance, along a main boulevard, the two wolves have captured a small animal in the weeds and take turns tearing it apart. Farther away beyond the pine forest, but not far enough, the weathered towers of the Chernobyl Nuclear Power Plant (once known as the V. I. Lenin Nuclear Power Station) are clearly visible.

Because of the setting sun, the old sarcophagus with its new construction blends into the earth, making the mound that was once reactor number four small and meaningless, like the raised soil of a grave. But suddenly, as the sun settles into the horizon, nature performs one of her tricks, turning the necklace of new construction into a crimson choke chain. Two decades earlier, when the chains of Marxist-Leninist social order hung by a thread, little was known of the terror and violence generated by vindictive men behind the veil of disaster.

CHAPTER
2

August 1985
Far Western Frontier, Ukraine Republic, USSR

Detective Lazlo Horvath, known as the Gypsy by his Kiev militia comrades, sat on a wooden bench in a hole in the ground. Above his head, at the top of the shaft, a wooden trapdoor held up with a stick partially blocked daylight. It was cool in the hole, so much cooler than in the relentless sun aboveground.

Lazlo took a deep breath, nostrils tingling from dampness and the smell of wine-soaked wood. The absence of his shoulder holster and his Makarov 9mm pistol was noticeable. He felt unconstrained and at peace, a bear gone into hibernation in summer instead of winter. The sweet, cool air made breathing easier, and he wondered if inhaling it could recapture his youth. Unlike Kiev's polluted air, this was country air, the air of the plateau adjoining the northern Carpathian range where he was born and raised. Compared to the congestion in Kiev five hundred kilometers to the east, the plateau was paradise. Breathing cool underground air by day and sleeping beneath the stars by night made life as a detective in Kiev a bizarre fantasy, an old silent film in which everyone runs about bumping into one another.

Lazlo closed his eyes, imagined the plateau's altitude superimposed upon Kiev's valley, imagined himself floating a hundred meters above the city. Detective Lazlo Horvath on a flying carpet, which suddenly shifts sideways, veering dangerously close to the statue of Saint Vladimir. Lazlo performs a gymkhana move to avoid being poked in the ass by Saint Vladimir's bronze crucifix. Saint Vladimir, who performed baptisms in the Dnieper River, is getting even with the Gypsy for his years away from church.

When Lazlo opened his eyes and laughed aloud, earthen walls reinforced with decaying timber absorbed the sound, making the laugh resemble a series of belches from too much Russian beer. But he was not light-headed from beer. Red wine had been today's drink. And this was no ordinary hole in the ground. This hole was the wine cellar in the yard of the family farm. It had been dug into the plateau decades earlier. He was far away from Kiev on the Ulyanov collective near the village of Kisbor twenty-five kilometers from the Czech border. He and his brother and his brother's family were spending their August holiday with Cousin Bela, who now ran the farm in this Hungarian-speaking district that, before the war, had been part of Czechoslovakia. Yesterday had been a family reunion of sorts when U.S. Cousin Andrew Zukor and his wife visited. A brief visit because of the Soviet security proviso insisting all foreigners return before nightfall to the Intourest hotel in Uzhgorod.

After awakening from the momentary dream and realizing where he was, Lazlo recalled his bloodcurdling fear of the wine cellar when he was a boy. He had been five or six when his father first sent him into the cellar for dinner wine. At the time he was certain the dead from the nearby cemetery would tunnel in and get him. So long ago when his mother and father were alive. Now they rested in the cemetery, and he wondered if they were aware of him, their detective son unearthing childhood terrors. And in another cemetery on the other side of the mountains, someone else might be aware of him down here. The deserter who gave up the name Gypsy when Lazlo's trembling finger pressed the trigger of his rifle many years before he ever thought of joining the militia.

To drive the adversity of his youthful army years from his mind, Lazlo envisioned his small corner cubicle at Kiev Militia Headquarters. He wears his old, worn shoulder holster and his scratched Makarov. Down the narrow walkway between cubicles, Chief Investigator Chkalov sits in his office. Chkalov's fat face smiles as he piles on yet another case because of the Gypsy's bachelor status.

Which was worse? Rehashing a terrible past episode from the army, or anticipating his future return to duties in Kiev? The wooden ladder at the entrance to the wine cellar answered his question by giving off a loud creak. It was better to live in the present. He looked up to see bare legs and feet encased in red canvas sneakers descending the ladder. The legs coming down were those of his younger brother, Mihaly, who had, a few minutes earlier, left the hole to relieve himself.

Mihaly stood in the shaft of light from the entrance, fastening a button on his shorts. He spoke in Hungarian. "I can't see a damn thing after being out there. The heat is unbearable. I don't see how Nina and the girls can stand it in the house. I thought they'd be in the yard." Mihaly shaded his eyes with his hand. "Laz? Are you here?"

"I dozed off for a moment."

"It's the wine," said Mihaly. "All these beautiful barrels of wine." Mihaly did what looked like a quick *czardas* step, which raised dust on the dirt floor. "This holiday should go on forever."

"If we keep drinking like this, we'll be minus our livers," said Lazlo.

"We hardly drank yesterday when Cousin Andrew was here. He and his wife and their bottled water." Mihaly ran in place, raising more dust. "We'll burn off the alcohol. How about a run, Laz? We'll become health-conscious like our American cousin. And when we come back, we'll down a keg before dinner."

"You run if you like. You're younger."

Mihaly stooped down, began retying the laces on his red sneakers. "What do a few years mean, Laz? You're only forty-one."

"Forty-three. I'm older than my gun."

"What does your gun have to do with it?"

"It's a scratched and worn antique from the fifties only a gun collector could love."

"Okay, so you're forty-three. Lots of rock stars swooned over by teenaged girls are in their forties. What's important is how you project yourself to others."

Lazlo stared at Mihaly's sneakers. "Do red shoes make you feel younger?"

"Of course," said Mihaly. "If I wore them to work, my boss would bleed from his eyes. He's the one who made the engineers get their Party cards. The bastard is always lecturing, using worn-out phrases like saying our mother's milk hasn't dried on our lips."

Mihaly finished tying his laces and stood up. "I used Uncle Sandor's Hungarian phrase on him once. 'Your feet are still in your mother.' Only I said it in Hungarian, telling him it was simply a translation of the mother's milk phrase. He believed it. Chief engineer because he's a Party boss. Doesn't know the unit the way he should. But he is strict."

"I suppose a chief engineer at a nuclear plant has to be strict."

Mihaly walked slowly out of the shaft of light, bent his head because of the low ceiling, and sat down on the bench beside Lazlo. "Strict, but not in the right areas or at the right times."

"What do you mean?"

Mihaly slapped Lazlo on the knee. "Hey, we're on holiday.

20

We're not supposed to talk about work. Cousin Andrew did enough yesterday. I ask him if he thinks anything positive will come of the Gorbachev-Reagan summit, and all he wants to do is talk about my work at Chernobyl. In any case, we were discussing my shoes. How do you like them?"

"The color is patriotic, Mihaly. Did you pick them out yourself?"

"Yes. Czech shoes. Better made. But there was no choice of color. Someone at the Purchasing Ministry likes red, so we get red. It's as bad as those idiotic two-for-one sales. A few weeks ago Nina had to buy a useless pink vinyl belt in order to get a purse she wanted. Capitalist businessmen should take lessons from us. Red shoes, take them or leave them. Just give us your twenty rubles."

"Perhaps," said Lazlo, "they shipped reds to Kiev, whites to Moscow, blacks to Minsk, and so forth. This way they can keep track of who's who in our so-called union by simply looking at our feet."

Mihaly laughed. "And if I try to cross the western frontier, they'll know by the color of my shoes where to shoot me."

"Where would that be?"

"In the head, of course. If I wore white shoes, I'd be a Muscovite, and they'd shoot me in the ass, thinking my brain was there."

Lazlo laughed with Mihaly, but in his mind was an image of a young man shot in the head, a boy, the deserter.

Suddenly there was a shadow at the entrance. "You two still down there?" It was Mihaly's wife, Nina.

"Yes, my sweet," said Mihaly.

"You can come out any time," said Nina.

"But we like it here," said Mihaly. "If there were a nuclear war, we'd be in the best possible place."

"Not a nuclear war," said Nina. "An explosion in your stomachs. You two in the wine cellar is like putting wolves in the chicken coop. We're eating in the yard tonight. After you move the table into the shade, you can build a fire in the pit to roast the chickens your hard-working cousin so graciously provided."

"Healthy Andrew and his wife have returned with healthy American chickens?"

"Not Andrew and his wife. Their visa allowed only one visit. Now come out of there."

"Ah," said Mihaly, after Nina had gone from the entrance. "The sound of my sweet, innocent bride."

"Do I detect sarcasm?" asked Lazlo.

"Well, Nina isn't exactly an innocent bride anymore. We have two daughters to prove it."

As if prompted by Mihaly's mention of his two daughters, Lazlo could hear Anna and Ilonka calling to their mother, their high-pitched screams to "*Mommychka!*" coming into the dark wine cellar like the chirping of crickets.

Lazlo thought about Nina, how she looked before she became "*Mommychka*" to Anna and Ilonka, how she looked when he stood up at the wedding. Nina, the girl become woman, the white flowing dress cinched in at her slender waist, her hips and bosom giving the wedding dress a shape he could not forget. Her voice, pure and feminine, repeating the vows. And he, Lazlo, the older brother, the bachelor brother, standing to the side and, though he never told Mihaly, becoming infatuated, falling in love with Mihaly's bride.

Lazlo closed his eyes to form an image of Nina in the yard in a thin cotton dress, a hot breeze rippling the dress about her thighs. Nina reaching up to brush her dark brown hair from her eyes. And what was it Mihaly had said? Not innocent anymore?

"Mihaly?"

"What is it?"

"Shall we have another glass before we go out into the sun?"

"Yes, another glass."

While Mihaly took their glasses and began filling them at today's newly tapped keg, Lazlo vowed he would ask Mihaly if everything was well between him and Nina. Tonight, when they were alone again, he would, like a proper big brother, provide an ear for his younger brother. And perhaps he would finally tell Mihaly his secret from the army. Being put in the situation of having to kill another boy his age simply because he could speak Hungarian. He and Viktor assigned in 1963 to arrest deserters near the Hungarian and Romanian borders. Boys assigned to hunt down boys who deserted their ground-forces draft obligation. Boys killing boys because their officers were still angry with Khrushchev and his Cuban missile fiasco.

Mihaly handed him a full glass of wine and stood near the entrance to the cellar, holding his glass high in the shaft of light from above. "To our holiday, may it last forever."

They drank.

Mihaly continued standing, held his glass up again. "To this hole in the ground. It hid our parents from the Germans so we could be here today."

After drinking again, Lazlo stood and gave his own toast. "To you and your beautiful girls. Nina, Anna, and little Ilonka."

By standing, Lazlo had positioned himself with Mihaly between him and the entrance to the cellar. He could see Mihaly's face profiled against the shaft of light, and it reminded him of a wedding photograph of their father—sharp nose, small chin, sloping forehead. A stern face pausing, waiting before drinking the toast, not knowing his profile was so revealing.

"Ah," said Mihaly, finally taking a drink. "The nectar of our homeland. The best wine in the world. Shall we go up into the heat of the world?"

Lazlo had not finished his entire glass, so he took it with him.

While climbing the ladder into the white heat of day, his thoughts returned to Nina and how she would move about the table in the yard, serving dinner beneath the shade trees. If he could watch her movements without concern for what she or others might think, if he could be alone with her beneath the stars through the night, then this would be Eden.

Unfortunately it was not true. He was a forty-three-year-old detective in the Kiev militia who, having been unsuccessful in his relationships with women, lusted after his brother's young wife each year while on holiday. Perhaps it would have been better if he had married years ago. Perhaps he should marry now. But who would have him? Tamara Petrov, perhaps? He tried to imagine Tamara as a bride, her long black hair showing through the veil, bracelets and earrings jingling as she walks up a church aisle. If anything, Tamara would demand a church ceremony, not because she is religious, but because it would go against the mandated state ceremony. But enough—neither he nor Tamara were interested in marriage. He was at home in his cubicle at Kiev Militia Headquarters, while Tamara was at home in her cluttered literary review office or at Club Ukrainka, somewhat of a wine cellar in its own way. A wine cellar in central Kiev where artists and composers and writers went to drink and talk, but mostly to drink. A cellar he often visited after a late shift in order to share part of his evening with Tamara.

Here, on holiday, there were no women for a lonely militia detective. Here there was only Nina. At the top of the ladder, the heat of the sun on his head was like hellfire. Even if Nina was in the yard, he could not see her because the sunlight, like a nuclear bomb, had momentarily blinded him.

That evening after dinner, everyone else watched television while Lazlo and Mihaly listened to music on Cousin Bela's record player. Some of the records were very old, from when Lazlo was a boy and Mihaly hadn't yet been born. The scratchy sounds of the Lakatos Gypsy Orchestra filled the house, Lazlo and Mihaly sang, and the children promptly fell asleep. After they were chased from the house, Lazlo and Mihaly spread a blanket in the yard and reclined beneath the stars. It was a clear, moonless night, the trees in the yard forming grotesque shadows upon the blanket of stars. The lights had just gone off in the house, and now the only artificial light came from the village two kilometers away. Because the farmhouse sat atop a hill, only the tallest streetlights and a few lights in the upper windows of village houses were visible. A pair of dogs barked in the village. Otherwise it was silent and deathly still, like the graveyard up the road.

"Lights are all off," said Mihaly. "But Bela hasn't started yet. Snores like his father. Remember Sunday dinners when we were kids? After we finished eating, Uncle Sandor would fall asleep beneath the chestnut tree."

"We thought he'd shake the chestnuts down on himself," said Lazlo.

"And when he awoke, he refused to believe he'd been so loud. He thought everyone was playing a joke on him. Not funny, though, since asthma eventually killed him. I suppose Bela inherited his father's snoring. I wonder why he hasn't started yet."

"Give him time," said Lazlo.

"Did you think we'd ever come back here, Laz? I remember at Mother's funeral thinking it would be the last time I ever saw the place. And now here we are, sleeping out back like boys. We sold Bela the house for a good price when Mother died."

"If we hadn't sold it to him, he'd still be living with his in-laws, and the collective would have taken it over."

"What do you think of Mariska, Laz? One baby and she already looks old, especially in those dark dresses and farmer shoes. What a contrast to Cousin Andrew's wife."

"Shoes and dresses don't make a woman, Mihaly. Perhaps in bed things are different."

"It's the reason Bela's not snoring." Mihaly began laughing. "He can't because his mouth is full of breast."

Lazlo tried to control himself, but Mihaly's laughter was contagious.

"And later," said Mihaly. "Later, when he *is* snoring . . . listen, stop laughing." Mihaly whispered, "Later, she has Bela's *kielbasa* in her mouth, and he really gets going."

Lazlo and Mihaly both laughed, both began coughing while they tried to contain their laughter. Finally they climbed down into the wine cellar and laughed like a pair of crazy old women in their hole in the ground. When they finished laughing, they groped about in the dark until they found one-liter glass jars on a shelf. They wiped dust from the jars with their shirts.

"Enough to last the night," said Mihaly as the wine gurgled into the first jar.

After filling both jars, they climbed out of the cellar and went back to their blanket. They spoke of Bela's hard work keeping up the farm. They spoke of Mariska's fortune-telling games with the children. They reminisced about the old days on the farm. Lazlo spoke of bedtime stories in which their father said he'd lived with Gypsies when he was a boy. Mihaly, who had not been born until Lazlo was eleven, said he couldn't recall the stories, but he did recall their mother not wanting their father to ever mention Gypsies.

While Lazlo and Mihaly nostalgically recalled their reflections in their mother's chicken soup, the sound of Bela's snoring came from the house. As Bela snored louder, Lazlo and Mihaly laughed harder, Mihaly keeping the joke alive by describing moves on the part of Mariska to keep Bela snorting. Finally, a light went on and off in the house, Bela stopped snoring, and Lazlo and Mihaly quieted down, clearing their throats and sipping wine.

"How are things in Kiev?" asked Mihaly.

"The usual summer heat and traffic. The greenery helps. It must have been beautiful before humans arrived, a jungle river valley. What about you, Mihaly? How are things in Pripyat?"

"Flat and boring," said Mihaly.

"When you got your job, you described the landscape as gently rolling grassland."

Mihaly laughed. "Gently rolling. Another term for flat."

"A good place for soccer," said Lazlo.

"If one has time."

"You said your team was as good as Kiev's Dynamo."

"No more soccer. Our work schedule is erratic, the hours too long. Sometimes, even in summer, I never see the light of day. On my way home on the bus at night, all I see out the window is darkness. Did I ever tell you how the Chernobyl area got its name?"

"Tell me again."

"It's named after a wild grass called wormwood. This wormwood, or Chernobyl grass, was originally named after a star mentioned in the Bible. In the Apocalypse, the Chernobyl star fell to earth and made the land foul. So there you have it, Laz. I live in a gently rolling landscape overrun by foul grass named after a fallen star. Luckily the grass hasn't yet made it into our nine-square-meter-per-person apartment in scenic downtown Pripyat. A few rolling hills away from Chernobyl on one side, the Pripyat marshes on the other, the Belorussian border up the road, and illiterate farmers everywhere else. What I'd really like is a car to get away on trips.

I've been saving and I could probably get a Zaporozhets or Moskv-ich, but I'd prefer a Volga."

"My turd-green militia Zhiguli isn't bad," said Lazlo.

"Italian design," said Mihaly. "An old Fiat. Volgas are the only well-built Soviet cars. Everything else is junk, even Chaikas and Zils. We save our money to buy junk, and the KGB drives Volgas. In my office at the plant, I have a photograph of a Chevrolet Impala . . . gorgeous."

The wine was beginning to have its effect. Lazlo could feel within him an intense desire to take his turn complaining about his fate. It was in their blood to be melancholy. Brother complaining to brother. Yesterday their American cousin had been here; now they were alone.

"Once you get your Volga, all will be complete, Mihaly. You have everything else . . . successful career, beautiful wife, children. Not like me."

"What's wrong with you?" asked Mihaly. "You make it sound like you're a failure."

Lazlo took a gulp of wine. "Still a detective after twenty years. Living in an apartment alone. It's always needed a woman's touch. But there will be no woman by my side as I enter middle age, then old age. No children or grandchildren to visit me in the pensioner home or to decorate my grave."

Mihaly rubbed Lazlo's shoulder. "Goddamn, Laz. You're only forty-three. You've got half your life ahead of you. And you've got us. We're your family. I only wish we lived closer to Kiev so we could see you more often. Nina and the girls love you."

Lazlo imagined Nina in bed, the nightgown caressing her hips and breasts, her hair spread on the pillow. Then he imagined his nieces, Anna and Ilonka, their faces content with the innocent dreams of youth.

"And I love them," said Lazlo.

He and Mihaly toasted the stars, the old house, the lights of the village, their futures.

But something bothered Lazlo. Something about the way Mihaly did not seem as close to Nina on this trip. The more Lazlo drank, the more this disturbed him. Then, in the midst of a nostalgic conversation about the university in Kiev they each attended in their own time, Mihaly confessed he sometimes wished he had never married.

"Why?" asked Lazlo. "Why should you want anything different after all I've said about the goddamned life of a bachelor?"

"Being tied down, I suppose. My job, my family, the pressures from both sides."

"Your job I can understand," said Lazlo. "But what pressure could Nina and the girls cause?"

"I don't know, Laz. I'm sorry I brought it up."

"Is it Nina? Is something wrong between you and Nina?" When Lazlo said this, he had a split-second thought, a flash in which Nina and he were bride and groom. And this made him feel foolish.

He had expected an immediate negative reply from Mihaly, but there was a long pause before Mihaly finally said, "No, nothing between me and Nina."

As Lazlo and Mihaly finished their jars of wine, the conversation became disjointed. Before falling asleep, Lazlo remembered part of it, Mihaly muttering something about Chernobyl. In order to remember to ask Mihaly about it the next day, he repeated over and over to himself. *What's wrong at Chernobyl? What's wrong at Chernobyl?* Then the stars blinked out.

The following day, Lazlo and Mihaly ate a late breakfast, went for a walk into the village, came back for lunch, and napped in the yard. Nina and Mariska went to the market while Cousin Bela fulfilled his duties on the collective.

When Lazlo awoke from his nap he watched his nieces, Anna and Ilonka, playing with Bela and Mariska's baby girl. His nieces took the baby's chair and stools for themselves to the closed wine-cellar entrance and placed sticks and stones on it in patterns, making the elevated trapdoor into an imaginary dining-room table. With its lid closed, the entry to the wine cellar looked simply like a box placed in the yard. Or like one of the mock coffins used as markers in the nearby cemetery. Perhaps this was what the German troops thought when they marched through. Lazlo recalled the story. How his mother feared the Germans would discover her husband's Gypsy heritage and take him away. How his parents had gone into the wine cellar just as the helmets of the troops became visible, advancing up the hill.

But there was no war now, no need to concern himself with the outside world. The children were at play, and all was peaceful. Here, on the farm, there were no cars or trucks or scooters, no Aeroflot jets climbing overhead, no questioning of paranoid citizens who would deny the existence of their parents, so great was their fear of the militia. No Chief Investigator Chkalov or Deputy Chief Investigator Lysenko. The only place he missed being in Kiev was Club Ukrainka, where he would go to see Tamara, the woman who helped him forget age and unfulfilled desire.

The make-believe table being set by his nieces reminded Lazlo of his plan to ask Tamara to his apartment, where he would prepare a Hungarian dish for her, one like his mother cooked here on the farm when he was a boy full of anticipation for the future.

Lazlo and Mihaly did not go into the wine cellar again until late afternoon. After Nina and Mariska returned from the market and the girls were napping, they decided their systems were properly recovered and they could enjoy a glass or two before dinner. Because they had slept, and afterward others were about, Lazlo saved the question concerning Chernobyl for the seclusion of the wine cellar.

"What's wrong at Chernobyl, Mihaly?"

When Mihaly did not answer, Lazlo pressed him. "Something's wrong, Mihaly. Something's been on your mind this entire holiday. I'm your brother, and we're in the wine cellar. No one will hear. Yesterday I told you about my bastard chief. Today you'll tell me what's wrong at Chernobyl."

Mihaly took a gulp of wine. "The situation is out of control. Fucked because of an insane policy."

"What kind of policy?"

"It's hard to discuss without getting technical, or emotional."

"So, don't get technical or emotional. But tell me about it before I bust one of these kegs over your head."

Mihaly laughed, sipped his wine, bent forward with his elbows on his knees. "Okay, Laz. I'll cut through the technical shit. During the past year, I've gotten bits of information, not from a single source, but from many sources. From engineers and safety inspectors at other plants. Many believe the power plants at Chernobyl are being put through unnecessary experiments. Tests to find out how far the system can be pushed."

"Who's doing these experiments?"

"The chief engineers and the plant manager. They're playing with fire. It's like prodding a sleeping demon. You never know when she might turn on you."

"How dangerous is it? Could people be killed?"

"Oh, yes," said Mihaly. "If there were an accident like the one they had at Three Mile Island in America, there would definitely be casualties. Our reactors are naked. We don't have the containment vessels they had at Three Mile Island."

"But if this is true, why haven't higher authorities stopped it?"

"I don't know. Maybe it's the distance from Moscow. Or maybe, somewhere in Moscow, there's an official perfectly willing to let the experiments go on."

"Why would an official in Moscow want to endanger lives?"

"By pushing for testing at Chernobyl, Moscow officials might learn the limits of their designs without putting their own lives at risk. Citizens of the Ukraine are more expendable than the citizens to the north and east. The power from our plant stays mostly in the Ukraine, with some going to Bulgaria, Poland, and Romania. None of the power from our RBMK-1000s goes to the Russian Republic."

"But to risk lives . . ."

"Consider the perspective of a Moscow official," said Mihaly. "Or even the Party secretary at our plant. He's a transplanted Russian. He hasn't ordered something wrong to be done. He's simply turned his back on the enthusiasm of managers and chief engineers to meet higher quotas. In the bureaucratic mind, there could be benefits from an accident."

"What benefits?"

"You send in observers from other plants and from industry so they'll learn, without speculation, what actually happens in the event of a nuclear accident. The loss of millions in war did a lot to make the union strong. With this kind of thinking carried to its extreme, who knows what advantages can be dreamed up? We'd learn about radioactive fallout and its effects on humans. We'd be able to see the effects on people and local government and medical facilities. We'd be able to extrapolate these data to create models of nuclear accidents and nuclear war."

"Mihaly, this is insane!"

"You told me to get it out of my system, Laz. I'm simply telling you about my speculation. The safety at the plant is failing, and everyone aware of it is trying to come up with a reason. Can you think of a sane reason to reduce safety standards?" Mihaly took a gulp of wine. "Maybe I'm too close to the situation. Maybe it's the pressure making me come up with crazy theories."

"I'm not trying to talk you out of it, Mihaly. If you really think there's a problem, if safety has taken a back seat, quit your job, get transferred."

"I'm going to apply for a transfer," said Mihaly. "That's why I've told you . . . to convince myself to go through with it. They've got too many working at the plant as it is. Too many cooks in the she-demon's kitchen. When I complained about an upcoming test, my chief said to tell my men if things aren't done right, they'll have to turn in their Party cards. When I reminded him the men under me don't have Party cards, he jokes they should get them so if something goes wrong, they'll have cards to turn in. He's more concerned about minor things, like workers smoking hashish in the locker room. When I complained about the printout for reactor conditions being too far from the control room to do us any good in an emergency, he said to use one of my men as a runner to bring the printout to the control room. He's gotten things upside down."

"Mihaly, if you're thinking of revealing this to anyone else, forget it. Do whatever seems reasonable to point out obvious safety flaws. But don't draw attention to yourself. Don't get labeled a counter-revolutionary by questioning the system. Whatever you do, don't mention conspiracy. Without mountains of documentation, no one will believe you. You'll be fired, and then there will be documentation, all of it against you, against your character. The KGB will be up your ass. You'll be fucked! Don't even think of telling anyone else. If you can't get a transfer, quit. I'll see about getting you a job in Kiev. You and Nina and the girls can move in with me. You can have my apartment. Tell me you'll get out of there, Mihaly!"

"I'll get out," said Mihaly, gulping down more wine. "I would have told you about this yesterday if Cousin Andrew hadn't been here. Hiding Bela's shortwave radio before Andrew and his wife arrived brought back the old fears from my university days. I'm glad we're alone and it's off my chest. As brothers, we should be honest with one another."

After drinking to secrecy, Lazlo and Mihaly hugged in the darkness of the wine cellar as if they were the last two souls on earth. While they hugged, Lazlo promised himself he would someday be honest with Mihaly and tell about the killing of the deserter. Someday soon.

CHAPTER 3

Morning dew weighed heavily on late-summer foliage along the Pripyat to Chernobyl Road. At the gate of the nuclear facility operated by the Ministry of Energy, a guard inspected a car waiting to get in. The few employees who commuted by car had to stop at the main gate for identification and sometimes a look into the luggage compartment. Buses passed more quickly because a guard assigned to each bus checked identification and inspected briefcases and lunch containers while the bus was in transit.

When entering the main gate, the first buildings one saw were laboratory buildings, including the low-level counting laboratory operated by the Department of Industrial Safety. Incoming buses stopped here first. The building, set back from the road, was inside another fence and inspection gate. This inner fence was not capped with barbed wire like the main fence. Its purpose was to keep out stray animals or ignorant maintenance workers who might bring unwanted radiation into the building. If there were a "spill" of nuclear material at Chernobyl, however small, and if some of it were to contaminate the low-level laboratory, it would put them out of business. Recently, the head of safety at the plant had ordered low-level laboratory personnel to take their pocket dosimeters home with them in the unlikely event they picked up radiation on the bus or elsewhere. Along with the written order was a strongly worded message saying the measure was experimental and anyone generating unfounded rumors would be dealt with severely.

The low-level laboratory housed a monitoring system to analyze samples from numerous locations surrounding Chernobyl, as well as samples from all over the Ukraine. The equipment here could detect radiation levels so small, background radiation caused by cosmic rays from outer space had to be shielded out using steel vaults. Within the vaults, samples were analyzed by counting ionizing particles of radiation through the use of ionization chambers commonly called Geiger counters.

The building had two upper floors, a basement, and a sub-basement. The upper floors contained offices for engineers and scientists, laboratories for converting samples into gases to be put into Geiger tubes, and computer equipment to analyze data. The electronic counting equipment and the vaults, referred to as "tombs" by technicians, were below ground in the windowless basement and sub-basement. The technicians called themselves "moles."

Juli Popovics was a mole. Like many technicians who worked in the sub-basement, she was well acquainted with radioactivity and its terminology. Strontium, half-lives, and the characteristics of radionuclides such as krypton-85 and cesium-137 were second nature to her. Although the advertised reason for the low-level counting lab was safety, she knew it had another purpose. Scrubbers were installed on site to camouflage the extent to which reactor fuel was reprocessed before dangerous fission products had a chance to decay. Few technicians at Chernobyl were aware the Americans and British had developed a way to measure radionuclide off-gassing and use the measurements to estimate weapons-grade fuel reprocessing.

The only reason Juli knew of these techniques was because of another technician named Aleksandra Yasinsky.

Juli and Aleksandra graduated university together and came to work at Chernobyl and live in Pripyat the same year. Aleksandra was a dear friend, but she was also an activist. Aleksandra kept charts in her desk showing ongoing increases of radioactive noble gases based on air samples taken outside the plant. Aleksandra said scientists throughout the world would someday have to answer for increases caused by nuclear production. Aleksandra thought she was helping by keeping the charts. The plant manager, notified by plant security, felt differently. One day Aleksandra was at work; the next day she was gone. According to the fabricated story, Aleksandra had transferred to the Balakovsky power plant. But Juli knew Aleksandra no longer worked for the Ministry of Energy because on a visit to Moscow, she had met with Aleksandra's mother, who broke down in tears when asked about her daughter.

Each morning, before going downstairs where she once worked side by side with her friend Aleksandra, Juli paused at the windows inside the building entrance near the dosimeter rack. After dropping off her dosimeter and picking up a recharged one, she looked back outside to memorize weather conditions before descending into her hole. At lunchtime, when she came out of her hole, she immediately looked out the window again to see how the weather might have changed. After lunch she repeated the process, looking forward to the end of the shift. In winter, however, after being in the fluorescent-lit basement all day, the darkness outside became an even deeper hole, a hole into which she, like Aleksandra, would someday disappear.

Last winter had been terrible. Sergey broke off their year-long engagement. Then, a week later, her father died, and she took the train to Moscow on funeral leave. Her mother, to whom she had never been close except when she was a very small Muscovite, was especially cold. It was during this trip she discovered Aleksandra was missing. It was during this trip she felt closer to Aleksandra's mother than to her own mother. After the trip to Moscow last winter, Juli returned to the loneliest time in her life. Each night, as she left the building, the demon darkness drained her, emptied her of purpose the way the gurgling vacuum pumps in the main-floor labs sucked air from the Geiger tubes.

But spring came as it always does, and darkness no longer awaited her after work. In spring she moved in with Marina. Having Marina for a roommate was like having the sister she'd always wanted. On days off they shopped together, waiting in lines, giggling like schoolgirls. Evenings they'd lie awake late into the night, talking about the future, which of course always included wealthy men who would give them the lives they deserved. The lonely nights were when Marina was out with her boyfriend, Vasily. This was how spring went. Then in summer, Juli met Mihaly.

Mihaly was slender with dark hair and eyes. He reminded Juli of her father when she was a little girl. Small chin, thin nose, forehead sloping back to his hairline. Like her father, Mihaly was Hungarian. Although they simply rode the bus home from work together during June, Juli knew she had fallen in love the very first day when they sat together and spoke in Hungarian, keeping their voices low so others would not overhear them. Russian was the official language at the facility. Ukrainian was looked down upon. Hungarian was barbaric.

On a warm July day, Mihaly got off at Juli's stop so he could walk her home. On a hot August day, he came to her apartment. They sipped wine and made love. The next time Mihaly came to her apartment, he told her he was married and had two daughters. Juli didn't want to hurt Mihaly or his wife and daughters. She kept trying to convince herself she needed Mihaly only for the moment. Another man would appear, and Mihaly would remain a good friend. But now, after he'd been gone three weeks on summer holiday, she knew differently.

When Juli paused at the entrance to the laboratory building before going down the stairs, she looked out to the southeast where the red and white reactor stacks pierced the sky. Today was Monday, and she knew Mihaly was back to work, had taken the earlier bus as usual. Tonight, after a three-week absence, he would catch her bus and she would see him again.

By applying herself to her work, Juli made the morning go by quickly. She turned off the overnight counters, did her calculations, removed the counting tubes from the tombs, and sent them up the dumbwaiter to be refilled with fresh samples. After lunch, she would busy herself again—new samples into the tombs, voltages set, samples logged, tombs closed, overnight counts started. But for now, the moles were out of their hole for lunch.

Juli sat alone at a table near the windows until a lab technician who worked on the main floor joined her. The technician's name was Natalya, a plump girl with a loud voice. Juli might have gotten up to leave, but it was obvious she had just started eating.

Natalya placed a large brown bag on the table and began emptying out food, making their table look like a table at a street market. Bread, cheese, two tomatoes, a large cucumber, cookies, cake. Besides speaking in a loud voice, Natalya spoke with her mouth full, which resulted in the occasional flight of a crumb of food across the table.

"I'm so hungry," said Natalya. "Even if my work is not strenuous, I still get hungry as a bear. You have so little, Juli. A simple sandwich, and look at my lunch. I went across the Belorussian border to shop at farm markets and bought too much. One of these days, for sure, I'm going on a strict diet before I explode." Natalya swung her arms outward to portray the great explosion. "Perhaps I should try one of those American movie-star diets. Did I tell you the Odessa Bookstore on the north side of town has a stock of American magazines?"

"No," said Juli. "What kinds of magazines?"

"Celebrity magazines," said Natalya. "I can't bring them to work anymore. The chief technician says they're distracting. She caught me looking at Bruce Springsteen. The Frank Sinatra of the eighties. Am I right?"

"Each generation has its idols."

"So, who is your idol, dear Juli?"

"I don't have an idol."

"What about your boyfriend? Couldn't he be considered your idol?"

"I don't have a boyfriend."

"No? A pretty girl like you with no boyfriend? It's shameful we have boys around here instead of men. The real men are married. Here, when the boys aren't drinking vodka, they hover over their books and calculators. I prefer older men. I'm waiting for a widower who needs a helpmate to cook meals and send him off to work so I can relax." Natalya sighed. "But if I'm home all day watching television and reading magazines, I'll eat myself into an early grave. You're lucky to have been born thin, Juli. All the women in my family are heavy. None of the diets I've tried do any good. So I might as well enjoy it while I can."

They ate, silent except for explosive crunches as Natalya munched her cucumber. After she finished that, Natalya polished off the cookies and cake. Then she leaned across the table and whispered.

"Did you hear the latest joke circulating up here?"

"Here" meant the main floor, as opposed to the basement or sub-basement. Gossip from the facility entered the building by way of the main floor, where workers had contact with drivers who brought in samples and reactor personnel who sometimes visited. Juli leaned close to Natalya, hoping the joke would not be overheard. Even Natalya's whispering was loud.

"Is it the one," asked Juli, "about the reactor inspector who wears gloves even in the summer?"

"This joke is much better," said Natalya. "The head of the SSNI in Moscow receives an invitation for delegations of Soviet reactor safety engineers to visit U.S. facilities and study reactor safety principles. The U.S. official says they can visit any reactor they like in the United States. The SSNI head makes his selections and, a few days later, hands his list to the U.S. official. 'Everything looks fine except for one thing,' says the U.S. official. 'What?' asks the SSNI head. 'You've said you wish to send your Chernobyl engineering staff to Three Mile Island. Don't you realize,' asks the U.S. official, 'we had an accident there in the seventies?' 'Of course,' says the SSNI head. 'But Three Mile Island is more than adequate for Chernobyl engineers, because at Three Mile Island you had only one accident!'"

Natalya laughed so hard Juli thought she would tip over backward in her chair. Several people at other tables turned and smiled. At one table, a man Juli had never seen before took out a notebook, wrote something in it, then put the notebook back in the pocket of his lab coat.

For a moment Juli considered warning Natalya about the recent memo condemning "malicious gossipmongering." But Natalya would probably say something worse. Besides, the joke would spread throughout the facility by quitting time. Better to let the matter rest despite the man in the lab coat.

"Funny, yes?" said Natalya.

"Yes," said Juli. "But now I've got to get back to work."

As she left the cafeteria, Juli noticed the man in the lab coat tug at his earlobe. And while going down the stairs to the basement, she wondered if Natalya might be part of the head office's underground network. If the joke was a test, it wouldn't work because, since Aleksandra's disappearance, Juli never repeated these jokes to anyone, except Mihaly.

All afternoon, while inserting Geiger tubes of various sizes into the tombs, Juli imagined each symbolized a night she and Mihaly would spend together. By the time she finished work, she had accumulated over fifty nights with Mihaly, fifty nights she wished might come true.

Juli rushed from the locker room in the basement so she could be first at the bus stop. She stood alone in the sun while others waited in the shade of the building. Being first in line guaranteed entry into the first bus for Pripyat, the bus she and Mihaly always took. As the bus approached in a shimmer of heat, she wondered if it was full, if it would pass by like it once had with Mihaly onboard. No. Mihaly would make up an excuse, tell the driver he had business at the low-level laboratory, and get off. But what if Mihaly was not on the first bus?

When the bus wheezed to a stop, Juli got on, walked slowly down the aisle, but did not see Mihaly. For an instant she imagined what had happened. Mihaly on holiday with his family at his boyhood home near the Czech border, reminders of his duties as father and husband everywhere. Mihaly taking another bus so he would not have to face her. Then a newspaper lowered at the back of the bus, and Mihaly, looking like a boy who has done something deliciously evil, grinned at her. She closed her lips tightly to keep from laughing, walked to the back of the bus, and sat next to Mihaly so abruptly he barely had time to remove his briefcase.

A few seats ahead, Juli saw a woman turn to look at her. The seat next to the woman was empty. Juli took a section of Mihaly's newspaper, and they both held newspapers up before them. When the bus was through the gate, moving along on the road to Pripyat, the noise of the rear engine allowed them to speak without being overhead. They spoke softly in Hungarian.

"How are things on the farm?" asked Juli.

"Fine," said Mihaly. "How are things here?"

"The usual. No radiation releases."

"Good. How about the weather?"

"Hot and dry."

"Same as the farm, hot and dry except for all the wine my brother and I drank."

"Is your family well?"

"Yes. How about yours?"

"Don't be cute. You know I have no family here."

"What about the grass, then? Has it taken over?"

"The other day in the courtyard, it grabbed my ankles and dragged me into the bushes."

Mihaly rattled his newspaper section and made an evil smile. "And what did the naughty grass do to you in the bushes?"

"I can't tell you. There's a crackdown on gossipmongering."

"If you don't tell, I'll brood like my bachelor brother."

After making sure her newspaper section shielded them, Juli turned and softly bit Mihaly's ear. They kissed, and her arms grew tired holding up the newspaper.

Before the bus entered Pripyat, the guard finally made his way to the back. After checking their identity cards, the guard returned to the front of the bus, and Juli and Mihaly left the newspapers in their laps. Beneath the newspapers they touched one another gently. Because Juli had changed into shorts, Mihaly was able to caress her intimately.

"Will you get off at my stop tonight, Mihaly?"

"I can't, not on my first day back. Is your roommate still working at the department store Wednesday evenings?"

"Yes."

"Good. I missed you, Juli. I'm not joking."

"It's hard to tell when you are and when you aren't."

"It's my protection. I can make up the world as I go along."

"Am I in this made-up world?"

"You and me and the wild grass."

"Where is everyone else?"

"A parallel world. I've left a duplicate of myself there."

Juli tickled Mihaly on his inner thigh, and he coughed to cover his laughter.

"Not tonight, then?" she asked. "Not even a walk?"

"Wednesday. I'll arrange a late night Wednesday."

Before the bus reached her stop, Juli told Mihaly the joke Natalya had screamed in her face at lunch. Mihaly nodded. "I heard it this afternoon, but I didn't want to ruin it for you. It's all over the facility. The engineers added a new ending. After Chernobyl's engineers leave for the United States, *Pravda*'s diplomacy page features the story. The headline reads, 'Chernobyl Engineers Permitted Inside Three Mile Island Containment Building for Firsthand Look.'"

The bus was at Juli's stop. When she got off and looked back, Mihaly grinned at her with his eyes crossed and his nose pressed to the bus window.

CHAPTER 4

Major Grigor Komarov of Branch Office 215 of the Special Department of the Soviet Committee of State Security—the KGB—stood at his office window. He admired Kiev's greenery, dark and thick beneath the morning sky. Because his window faced west, the window was relatively clear. This afternoon, with the sun in the west, streaks left by inept window washers and the previous evening's rain would glare like graffiti. He stared at the horizon in the direction of the GDR and East Berlin a thousand kilometers away, where he was stationed before being sent to Kiev. Major Komarov had fond memories of his years in East Berlin, years replete with hard work and hard play. And the women . . . ah, those fine German women.

A blonde walking below on the boulevard triggered Komarov's memory of an especially fine woman, a blonde named Gretchen he had used several times to compromise Western diplomats. Beautiful Gretchen, the most productive KGB operative in Berlin. But this was long ago when he was younger. Long ago when using Romeo agents for sexual blackmail was still effective. In the modern liberated world of Western decadence, the blackmailed chap simply asks for extra copies of the photographs for his friends.

In the old days, male Romeo agents seduced secretaries of embassy officials, while female Romeo agents seduced the officials themselves. Agents like Gretchen who could turn a penis into a Siberian fencepost. Of course some Romeo agents, Komarov wished he could forget. Not only the men. He hated men who became Romeos. But there was a woman named Barbara, half-Russian half-Hungarian. If only he could forget the humiliation suffered because of the dark-haired witch during his first week of field training. If only the new recruit had been intelligent enough to realize Barbara's seduction was a traditional "safe" house hazing in which veteran agents bust through the door when the newcomer's trousers are down around his ankles.

To help him forget the hazing incident, Komarov took out his wallet, carefully opened the "secret" compartment behind the bills, and removed a tattered photograph. This was Gretchen. Nothing else remained of Gretchen because, back in the GDR, after he'd gotten beyond being a fresh recruit, he'd used Gretchen as a stepping-stone. He had not wanted to do it. He had agonized over it. But it was necessary. Whereas he wished he could have killed Barbara the Hungarian, he had instead killed Gretchen.

All plans consist of logical steps. In order to create a trail of evidence leading to Captain Sherbitsky, who had been in a high position in the GDR for a decade, two comrades needed to be eliminated. First, a fellow agent named Pudkov; next, Gretchen. Finally, by hunting down and killing Sherbitsky, Komarov gained admiration from his superiors. The fabrication of a double homicide fueled by jealousy, and the successful capital punishment of the pseudo murderer, created the atmosphere leading to Komarov's captaincy a year later.

Komarov kissed Gretchen's photograph, feeling the warmth of it and smelling the leather from his wallet. After returning the photograph to his wallet and the wallet to his pocket, he looked out the window again. He leaned forward, facing north instead of west. Here, a hundred kilometers away, beyond the widening of the Dnieper River, lay the Chernobyl Nuclear Facility operated by the Ministry of Energy. Since his transfer to Kiev ten years earlier, counterintelligence at Chernobyl had been his assignment. Instead of recruiting Westerners, instead of the hard work and hard play of his Berlin years, his work now consisted of monitoring hundreds of workers and thousands of relatives and friends of workers at Chernobyl. Each month he reported his findings to Deputy Chairman Dumenko, head of KGB operations in the Ukraine. Dumenko was Komarov's link to Moscow. Dumenko's position was one Komarov felt he deserved after his years of loyal service—a position of authority instead of playing nursemaid to a bunch of technical types at the Chernobyl facility.

Although his position in Kiev was a reward for years of GDR service, although even he at first valued the position, at age forty-five he felt stagnant. Was it time for the ruthless Komarov, who had created and solved the Sherbitsky crime so efficiently, to come out of hiding?

The phone rang and Komarov left the window to answer it. Captain Azef from two floors below said his weekly report from Chernobyl was ready. He told Azef to bring the report to his office in five minutes.

Back at the window, Komarov lit a cigarette. When Captain Azef arrived, he would, as usual, comment on the view. Komarov's window faced the length of Boulevard Shevchenko as it exited the city and continued northwest over the hills. Up and down went Boulevard Shevchenko, up and down like life. In Berlin, after becoming captain, Komarov had played hard, meeting many women without his wife's knowledge. Now he only drank hard, the vodka bottle dominating yet giving him solace. It helped him forget his son, recently ejected from university, was a lover of men disguised as a would-be artist. It helped him forget his wife, who catered to their son, was interested only in social position and fashions of the West.

His climb into the bottle had unearthed past dreams of success. The Sherbitsky affair had served him well. But how could he create a modern plan with national implications? A plan to garner the prestige needed to take over Dumenko's chairmanship? He was forty-five years old, his wife and son were foreign to him, he drank too much, and time was running out.

He coughed several times, turned from the window, and coughed repeatedly into his handkerchief. He put his cigarette out angrily amid dozens of others in the ashtray. There was a knock at the door.

"Come in!" he shouted and coughed again after he sat at his desk.

The stack of folders Captain Azef placed on Komarov's desk was formidable, and Azef was short, only his smiling face and bald head visible above the documents after he sat down.

"How are you this fine morning, Major?"

"As well as can be expected, Captain."

"I heard your cough." Azef glanced at the ashtray. "The cigarettes do not help?"

"A difficult habit to overcome," said Komarov, glaring at Azef.

"Sorry, Major. You said to remind you from time to time about the need to reduce the number of cigarettes."

"I don't smoke when we're in the car anymore."

"But you seem to make up for it here. I'm simply trying to be helpful."

"Helpful," said Komarov. "Get on with the report."

Because the summer holiday season was ending, there was an extensive summary of where personnel had traveled. Many visited

Black Sea resorts to turn their skin to leather. Some returned to villages where they had grown up. A handful crossed the frontier, but these were officials of the Ministry of Energy whose whereabouts were monitored by the committee office.

Another summary listed unusual absences from work. In the fall this list would lengthen with illnesses, but now, in warm weather, there were few unplanned absences. The list included two pregnancies, an appendectomy, a gall-bladder operation, a death due to an automobile accident, and a hospitalization for lung cancer. The mention of lung cancer made Komarov think of the cigarette pack in his shirt pocket. He fought the urge to light up and concentrated on Azef's report.

The last unplanned absence was for an engineer who suddenly went mad, telling everyone reactor unit one, to which he was assigned, was going to blow up. The engineer referred to a 1982 accident during his outburst, a minor accident that was supposed to be secret. The engineer stayed home and refused to return to work. Eventually, the Institute for Mental Health took him away. Komarov knew this meant confinement for several years. There was nothing for the KGB to do in the matter except to continue monitoring the man's co-workers.

The report from agents at post offices and telephone exchanges was routine. No questionable letters or telephone calls. Of course, during the holiday season, with staff being short-handed, less than five percent of calls and letters had been examined.

"We should increase our monitoring here," said Komarov.

Azef nodded. "I contacted Captain Putna at the PK."

"I want the next report back up to ten percent."

"Yes, Major. I told Putna ten percent."

"Good," said Komarov, somewhat angrily.

The summary of rumor and gossip was more interesting. An

electrician at the facility told co-workers, ever since he began working near the reactors, his hair had begun to quickly turn gray. Because the man's hair was indeed turning gray, news spread quickly. But finally, the man's superior determined the man had been coloring his hair for years and suddenly stopped.

The engineer going mad and claiming unit one was going to explode caused several spin-off rumors. One claimed the Ministry of Energy in Moscow had, for some reason, decided to experiment with safety limits at Chernobyl. Chief engineers met this rumor with denial and disciplinary action. Next was a rumor claiming chief engineers were technically unqualified. This rumor died out on its own after a time because it was viewed as reactionary.

Each week the report contained new jokes circulating. Last week's big joke had been about eating the food in the cafeteria. It was okay to eat there, the joke went, as long as you shit in a lead box. This week's joke dealt with nuclear engineers being sent on a fact-finding tour of U.S. reactors. Engineers were going to Three Mile Island in order to model safety at their own facility after the safety procedures at a reactor with a stellar record. Only one accident!

"Our internal agents overheard several persons exchanging the joke firsthand," said Azef, handing Komarov a list of names.

The last summary in the report on Chernobyl personnel was Captain Azef's favorite. Azef took delight in detailing sexual relationships among facility personnel. Because of his own son's sexual orientation, Komarov was glad to hear there were no new reports of homosexual encounters in the locker rooms.

Azef handed over a list of couples allegedly having affairs. The list contained details of four relationships.

"You will notice," said Azef, "one of the women appears on this list, as well as on the one concerning the new joke."

"I can read," said Komarov.

"And you will also notice the man she is servicing is married."

"Perhaps he is servicing her."

Azef laughed. "Very good, Major. In any case, because he is a senior engineer and she has appeared on two lists this week, I've taken the initiative to retrieve their files."

Komarov opened the files and scanned the personal summary sheet for each. Juli Popovics, lab technician at the low-level laboratory. Mihaly Horvath, senior reactor control engineer. Both residents of Pripyat. But unless they wished to live in one of the backward villages and suck salt pork, workers at Chernobyl had only two choices of where to live, either in the town of Chernobyl or the larger, more modern town of Pripyat. And then the file reminded Komarov of two other interesting facts. Both had Hungarian lineage, and Mihaly Horvath's brother was Detective Lazlo Horvath of the Kiev militia. Komarov closed the folders.

"What do you suggest?" asked Azef.

"Put both under operational observation."

Azef took a notebook from his pocket. "Anything else?"

"Arrange for Engineer Horvath's wife to discreetly find out about the affair. You knew it's what I would order, didn't you, Captain?"

"Yes, Major."

But Captain Azef did not know everything, did not know a directive had come from Deputy Chairman Dumenko's office at KGB headquarters in Moscow to be read only by Komarov. The directive had instructed him to watch for rumors of inadequate safety at Chernobyl and to act accordingly to squelch the rumors. The directive also said to watch for the possibility of U.S. intelligence involvement. No reason was needed for an order from Moscow. Perhaps sabotage or foreign intelligence played a part. Despite Gorbachev's new policies of openness, Komarov felt the real powers in Moscow were intact. Unknown to Azef, Komarov had passed along the name of an American, one Andrew Zukor, who had visited Mihaly Horvath and his brother, Detective Lazlo Horvath, during the summer. He gave the name to Major Dmitry Struyev here in Kiev. Struyev was a member of Directorate T and was interested in any Americans visiting the Soviet Union. Not only to keep track of them, but to use their presence for counterespionage if possible.

After Azef was gone, Komarov returned to the window. He stared out at the horizon to the west and thought again about the days in East Berlin. He recalled his knowledge of deep-cover operations. Projects to provoke American firearms organizations and turn them against their government. Projects to discredit U.S. presidents, including Ford and Carter. He had taken part in trying to compromise a U.S. diplomat in order to discredit Carter's hawk advisor, Brzezinski. He knew about past projects involving U-2 spy planes and attempts to discredit Martin Luther King Jr., and even a more recent project with the Bulgarians to do something about the pope, who was causing trouble in Poland. But once he was transferred to Kiev, he felt cut off. Although he'd been aware of newer projects concerning Ronald Reagan and electrical sabotage on the U.S. East Coast and negative AIDS propaganda, he remained cut off from active measures once he moved to the Ukraine. Perhaps this is why he relished his time in East Berlin. Some time ago he had tried to share these feelings with Major Struyev, who maintained an office one floor down. But because he was an operative of Directorate T, Struyev would share nothing. Struyev was an old hard-liner, older than Komarov, with more secrets than Komarov. Struyev would go to his grave with his secrets.

Komarov reached into his pocket, pulled out a cigarette, and lit it. He imagined Azef wagging a finger at him. When he thought of how Azef seemed to have all the answers and all the right files, he wondered if he was becoming paranoid, if he was becoming fearful of his assistant vying for his position. But what was paranoia except the drive for power, the need to be on top? Long ago Komarov concluded all truly powerful men had advanced because of paranoia, not in spite of it. Even Lenin.

Komarov sat at his desk and placed his lighted cigarette in the ashtray. He took out his keys, unlocked a side drawer, and opened it. Inside the drawer was his Walther 9mm West German automatic in its shoulder holster. The pistol was atop a notebook listing secret sources and informants throughout the years. He hadn't used the pistol in years, and the notebook was long out of date, many of the persons having moved, or died.

He pulled the drawer out farther, reached into the cave of the drawer, and felt the fluted handle of the knife he knew would be there. He retrieved the knife, placed it on the desk, then closed and locked the drawer.

It was an antique German knife, not a war souvenir, a knife made before the war, before swastikas. It was nearly as long as his hand, and with the single blade unfolded from the handle, it was two hands long. The handle was inlaid with alabaster gone pale over the years. The knife was a souvenir given him by the deputy chairman of the East Berlin branch office as a memento of his success in the Sherbitsky affair. The knife had belonged to Captain Sherbitsky and was determined by the investigation to be the knife used by Sherbitsky to kill beautiful Gretchen and Agent Pudkov.

Every time Komarov touched the knife, he again felt the thrill of the case. How ironic the knife was presented as a reward to the creator of the Sherbitsky affair. Komarov rubbed his thumb back and forth on the alabaster handle, recalling the praise, the medal, and his elevation to captain, then major. But the knife, like him, had become a relic in the back of a drawer.

Komarov held the knife in both hands and slowly unfolded the blade. He wiped skin oil from his forehead—his receding hairline apparent—and applied the oil evenly to the blade with his fingers. He shined the blade on his trouser leg, carefully, because the blade was as sharp as it was when he pushed it deep into Gretchen's abdomen while, at the same time, caressing her and staring into her eyes.

It happened at the "safe" house outside Berlin. Agent Pudkov, a devilishly handsome recruit, was using the "safe" house to rendezvous with Gretchen. Komarov had opened the door noisily. They were naked and quickly pulled a blanket about them. Komarov feigned surprise, then smiled, saying he would wait in the hall, saying he would be next to share a bed with Gretchen. And he did wait. He waited until Pudkov came into the hall. The knife entered the flesh of Pudkov's neck smoothly, the passion of a few moments before draining his blood quickly. Komarov held his hand over Pudkov's mouth as he died and left him on the floor.

In the bedroom Komarov kept his hands behind him so Gretchen would not see his gloves and the bloodied knife. When he got into bed, Gretchen complained about his rough uniform and boots. But she smiled when he spread her legs, touching her intimately with his leather-gloved hand. While she searched his eyes, staring at him without blinking, without shame, he thought of Barbara the Hungarian, who'd humiliated him. Pushing the knife home with his right hand, Komarov felt Gretchen's legs close about the fingers of his left hand like a vise for a moment until the twisting of the knife drew the strength from her. Then he closed her eyes and slit her throat.

At his desk Komarov held the knife the way he'd held it when he ended Gretchen's short but active life. Underhanded, his thumb along the length of its handle. He thought of the two ways smokers held their cigarettes. Between the two first fingers—western—or between finger and thumb—continental. The grip he used with his knife was elegant, just as the Sherbitsky affair was elegant. Even the bullet through Sherbitsky's head was elegant. A shot from the front, a shot proving he had defended himself from the murderer. A shot fired in the woods several kilometers from the "safe" house at a man on the run.

After killing Sherbitsky and returning the knife to its rightful owner, the investigation commenced. It was an investigation accompanied by the incessant weeping of Sherbitsky's widow. In the end, when Sherbitsky's known hotheadedness and jealousy were revealed, the case became so clear-cut even Komarov, while testifying, was able to momentarily suspend his true knowledge and feelings. At the time he wondered if this ability to create, in his mind, an alternate reality was a sign of instability or schizophrenia. But this was not the case. Temporary alteration of reality was simply a method to survive the hearings unscathed. After all, he had killed a senior officer, and this killing had to be rigorously justified.

Recently, whenever Komarov thought of the Sherbitsky affair, he felt in a festive mood, but he could share the mood with only one friend, a friend who was not here because he dare not bring a bottle to his office. He saved his friend for evenings alone. In summer and most of the spring and fall, he spent evenings on the back porch of his house. Even when cold weather drove him indoors, even with his wife in the same room, he was alone with his friend because, while she watched her television, he would wall himself in and dream of success and triumph.

The cigarette in the ashtray had smoldered down to a couple of centimeters. He took one last suck on it and smashed it out. He folded the knife blade into its alabaster handle and put it into his inside jacket pocket, where it rested reassuringly against his chest. Finally, he reopened the Chernobyl personnel report Azef left on his desk and began studying it.

CHAPTER 5

February 1986

During the cold war, some KGB agents worked in post offices. They were part of the PK Service operational branch, short for *Perlyustratsiya Korespondentsii*, a term rarely used except within the walls of KGB branch offices. Even the abbreviation *PK* was not widely known because PK agents were supposed to be viewed, by the public, as ordinary postal workers. In back rooms of selected post offices across the Soviet Union, PK agents spent their days opening mail, reading it, making notes or copies as necessary, then resealing the mail, and passing it on to the real postal workers, whose job was to transport the mail to its rightful owners.

The postal service was busy during the months of December and January. Religious holidays revolving around the birth, two thousand years earlier, of a boy child in the Middle East had created a season of familial joy and letter writing. Yet, a few weeks into the 1986 new year, with continued cold war quibbling and shortages at the markets, the Soviet people settled in, bracing themselves against the winter winds. No matter how much talk of love and peace took place during the holidays, no matter how much talk of a new openness in the Soviet Union, it seemed the world's fate was in the hands of irrational forces. Even the deaths of seven astronauts in the United States in late January reinforced the depression as winter settled in.

On the first Monday in February, in a small, windowless back room of the Pripyat post office, PK agents Pavel and Nikolai went through the morning mail presorted for them and passed through a slot in the wall by legitimate postal workers. Pavel and Nikolai were trained in languages, one fluent in Hungarian, and the other in Ukrainian. But they always used their Russian mother tongue as they sat across from one another at a long table opening-reading-resealing, opening-reading-resealing. The room was warm and humid because of the small electric steamer on the table.

"No more letters to Saint Nick," said Pavel.

"The season to be jolly is over," said Nikolai.

Open-read-reseal. Open-read-reseal.

"Several mentions of the American astronauts," said Pavel. "From the looks of the explosion on television it must have been instantaneous. Do you think they felt anything?"

"They must have felt something," said Nikolai. "Perhaps like a blow to the head."

"Americans advertise everything," said Pavel. "Even failures."

"An odd practice," said Nikolai.

Open-read-reseal.

"Ah," said Pavel. "Here's another letter to Mihaly Horvath."

"He's under observation," said Nikolai. "You'll have to copy it."

Pavel glared at Nikolai. "I know. I'm not an idiot."

"I didn't mean to imply you were an idiot, Pavel."

"Then why must you always remind me of the obvious?"

"I don't know," said Nikolai. "Perhaps I'm tired of reading the same things over and over. 'How is everything there?' 'All is fine here.' 'How were your holidays?' 'Our holiday was joyful, and all are in good health.' It's enough to drive one mad! Don't these people have any imagination?"

They both laughed, the outburst designed to relieve boredom.

"So," said Nikolai, "what does Mihaly Horvath's brother say today?"

"Again," said Pavel, "he refers to a matter they spoke of last summer at the farm. Detective Horvath pressing his brother about some kind of decision, just as he has in previous letters. He implies everything will not be well if his brother does not act."

Pavel turned to the second page of the letter. "Here's something." He raised the pitch of his voice slightly as he always did when translating a letter. "'Mihaly, I'm sorry I was unable to visit during the holiday season. Things were busy in Kiev and I had to remain on duty. But I'll make up for it and be able to see you and Nina and the girls the third Sunday in February. I'll drive up in the morning and should be there by noon. Perhaps you can tell me of your decision in the matter we discussed. Tell Nina not to cook anything special . . .' And it goes on."

"What do you suppose this 'matter' is?" asked Nikolai.

"I don't know," said Pavel. "But since Mihaly Horvath is under operational observation, and his militia detective brother has been worried about something since summer, Captain Putna and Major Komarov will be interested."

"By now," said Nikolai, "Detective Horvath must also be under operational observation."

"It could be related to the Gypsy Moth Captain Putna told us to watch for," said Pavel.

"Why would it have anything to do with the Gypsy Moth? It's nothing but a code word, and it wasn't mentioned in the letter."

Pavel touched his finger to his temple. "I was thinking. Horvath is a Hungarian name. Gypsies have connections to Hungarians.

And last summer, remember the letter in which they spoke of the visit of their cousin, Andrew Zukor, the American? Consider the gypsy moth insect, the one causing problems in America since its introduction last century. I read about it in *Entomological Study of . . .*"

"What are you talking about?" asked Nikolai.

"I'm talking about the American cousin of the Horvaths," said Pavel. "I'm talking about letters to Detective Horvath last year in which Andrew Zukor told of plans to visit the Horvaths during their summer holiday. This could be a Gypsy Moth connection."

"A weak connection at best," said Nikolai. "We could mention it in our report to Captain Putna. But I think it best if we wait and see if there is another letter from the American cousin. You know how the captain feels about unfounded speculation. In the meantime we'll copy all letters to or from the Horvaths."

"Challenging idea," said Pavel, floating the letter like a giant flake of snow into the COPY tray at the corner of the table.

The sky was overcast, snow covering the rolling farmland in virgin white. Although the drive to Pripyat was slow, it gave Lazlo time to think. As he passed through a village, he saw two boys heaving snowballs at one another. Even though he and Mihaly were eleven years apart and were never really young boys together, he was reminded of quiet winters on the farm. Quiet winters before he went into the army to fulfill his draft obligation, before the hazing in camp, before the assignment to arrest the deserter near the Romanian border. Boys killing boys.

The snow covering the hilly road forced Lazlo to continually shift up and down through the gears in order to maintain his speed. The Zhiguli's transmission whined, its engine sputtered and coughed, and snow packed into the wheel wells rubbed against the tires. Because his tires were small and almost treadless, he could not maintain the speed of a Volga, which passed him, its fat tires lifting packed snow onto his windshield. If he had a Volga, or newer tires, he'd get to Pripyat sooner. But a mere detective in the Kiev militia was lucky to have any car to drive on his day off, even a three-year-old Zhiguli in need of tires and, from the new sound he was hearing, a muffler or exhaust pipe.

The use of the car provided some freedom, but also meant he was on call, day and night, for every type of crime, from the most mundane theft to murder. Lazlo recalled the day, several years earlier, when Chief Investigator Chkalov told him he was free to use a militia car for personal business instead of turning it in to the garage after each shift. He also recalled the day three years ago when Chkalov handed him the keys to the then-new Zhiguli.

As Lazlo shifted madly through the gears, most likely taking months of life from the transmission, he glanced at his keys swinging from the ignition and recalled the conversation with Chkalov on the day he received the keys to the new Zhiguli.

"You have been with the militia for many years, Detective Horvath. Your service has been loyal, and you have proven your detection skills. Although it is not a promotion, the receipt of a new car is an honor."

"I realize this," said Lazlo. "And I appreciate it."

"Many other detectives do not respond as consistently as you. Perhaps because you do not have family matters to attend to. The woman murdered near the post office in Kalinin Square, for example. If you had not arrived at the scene before dawn to have the area cordoned off, street cleaners would have flushed the shell casings down the sewer. Timing. It's all a matter of efficient response."

"Thank you, sir."

"And your translations of Hungarian material have also proved valuable," said Chkalov. "When you joined the detectives, pessimists questioned whether an officer from the western frontier could be trusted. Despite your comrades still calling you by the pet name Gypsy, you have proven yourself worthy."

"I appreciate your comments, sir."

"By the way, Detective Horvath. Why do you think the name Gypsy has endured so many years?"

"It's an affectionate name. I've not tried to discourage its use."

"Well," said Chkalov, his tone becoming heavier, "perhaps you should discourage it. Gypsy could imply you'd wander off. We wouldn't want you making off with the militia's shiny new Zhiguli."

Chkalov had laughed then, his chair squeaking as his chest heaved. "I'm joking, Detective Horvath. I know a man of your stature would not run away. There's too much for you here in Kiev. Your position, wine and women, and even Gypsy orchestras playing in the clubs. Not as many Gypsy orchestras as in Budapest, but enough. Of course, the Gypsy culture is nothing more than nostalgia, even for you. And now Hungarian is a second language to you. You are a true Soviet citizen, Detective Horvath."

But Chkalov was unaware of many things. After the holiday at the farm last August, speaking Russian again had been difficult. If it weren't for his brother, Mihaly, and his family, Lazlo would like nothing better than to leave the Soviet Union. If only Chkalov knew how much all the detectives at the Kiev station hated to sit through his long-winded sessions ranging from syrupy praise to chest-pounding nationalism. Very few knew how Lazlo came by the name Gypsy, not even Chkalov.

The keys dangling from the ignition of the Zhiguli rang out as the wheels hit a series of holes hidden beneath the snow. Lazlo held the jittering steering wheel tightly and drove on. To the north, where

Mihaly and Nina and the girls awaited him, the sky was dark.

When Lazlo neared Pripyat, he could see evidence of the Chernobyl Nuclear Facility to his right. A tall fence paralleling the road, warning signs threatening trespassers, high-tension towers leading away from the facility. It had stopped snowing, and where the road crested a hill, he saw the red-and-white-banded reactor stacks and the rectangular-shaped buildings in the river valley. The buildings resembled a string of coffins. The high-tension towers leading away from the buildings became a line of mourners waiting to pay their respects.

If something was wrong at Chernobyl, as Mihaly had implied last summer, perhaps the denials in letters and phone calls were because he feared the mail was being read and phone calls overheard. Today they would finally be face to face.

The road came to a T. When Lazlo stopped, he could see the entry gate to the Chernobyl Facility to his right. A black Volga was parked outside the gate and a man in a dark hat and coat stood talking to a uniformed guard. It was the same Volga that had passed him earlier.

Lazlo turned left on the road to Pripyat and looked into the rearview mirror. The man from the Volga glanced his way. Although there was no way to be certain, Lazlo knew the man could be KGB. But even if it was KGB, the suspicious nature of their agents made them glance at any car driving past on a snowy Sunday. Driving the last few kilometers to Pripyat, he watched the mirror but did not see the Volga.

"If the KGB is watching you," said Mihaly, "I can understand why. It's your letters. I kept telling you everything was fine. Why didn't you believe me?"

Lazlo was alone with Mihaly, an after-dinner walk in the small park outside the apartment complex. They walked among abandoned playground equipment, looking down and listening as their boots creaked in the snow. They spoke in Hungarian.

"I carefully phrased the letters," said Lazlo. "Anyone reading them would assume it was a personal matter. And I didn't say the KGB was watching me. I simply told you about a car I saw on my way here. You're the one who started it back in August, talking about Chernobyl."

Mihaly nodded. "I suppose you needed reassurances after what I said."

"You had me picturing Gorbachev trying to win propaganda points by blowing up a reactor, then showing how compassionate he is."

"I'm sorry, Laz. Last summer it was the wine. My letters were the truth. Everything's fine. Simply occasional problems to be solved and tests to be run. On holiday I made a mistake with my big mouth. You asked me about something else, and I used Chernobyl to cover it up."

Mihaly turned to him. "I'm an ordinary man, Laz. I have ordinary faults and weaknesses and feelings. I've let my emotions get in the way of reason."

"Is it about Nina?"

Mihaly looked away. "Nothing's wrong with Nina. It's me, Laz. You're the only one I can talk to. I should have told you last summer, but I was a coward. I've . . . been seeing another woman."

They stopped at a series of interconnected wooden platforms designed for children to climb in better weather. Mihaly sat on a low platform even though it was covered with snow. Lazlo stood above Mihaly. He wanted to scream. He was aware of having left his Makarov and shoulder holster locked in the Zhiguli. He wanted to tell Mihaly he had experience killing another man. Blood spurting from a boy's face momentarily blurred his vision . . .

Mihaly looked up. "I'm still seeing her, Laz. I'm still seeing her, and I feel guilty as hell."

"You should feel guilty!"

"She works at Chernobyl," said Mihaly. "She's from another division. I didn't seek her out. We simply met on occasion."

"An occasional fuck?"

"It's not her fault or my fault. It simply happened."

"I hear this all the time from criminals! Nothing simply happens!"

"I understand your anger, Laz. In a way I welcome it."

"You welcome it? A boy being scolded? You're a man with responsibilities to a family!"

"I don't expect you to understand. But I want you to know I still love Nina and the girls."

Lazlo felt dizzy and braced himself against a vertical section of the playground equipment.

Mihaly looked down. "Please believe me, Laz. Juli is also sensitive to my family. We've discussed ending our relationship. But we keep putting it off. I felt if I told you, I'd gather courage to end it. I still love Nina. Nothing . . . no, I can't say nothing has changed." Mihaly looked up. There were tears in his eyes. "Everything has changed, Laz. It's tearing me apart. All I can think about is Nina finding out. Sometimes I think she's already found out because of the way she acts. But it can't be. She must be reacting to the way I act . . ."

"Next time you're with this lover of yours . . . what was her name?"

"Juli."

"Next time you're with this Juli, you think of me! Think of

your old brother because he's going to tell you something he never thought he'd tell anyone. It's about Nina. It's about my feelings. It's about sibling jealousy and envy and unfulfilled desire. When you're at the market with Nina, don't you see other men and even women looking at her? What the hell do you think it means, Mihaly? She doesn't have a deformity, does she? I guess not! Perhaps it's beauty. And not just a pretty face or a slender figure. It's the way she carries herself, the way she acts around those she loves. I've seen it, Mihaly. I've seen the way she acts when she's with you. You should look in a mirror when you're with her!"

"Am I looking in a mirror now, Laz? Are you my reflection?"

"What do you mean?"

"Nina. If you wanted her so much, why didn't you marry her?"

Lazlo reached out, saw his gloved hand open before Mihaly's neck.

"Are you going to choke me, Laz?"

"I've killed before!" As soon as he said it, Lazlo wished he could take it back. His hand, inches from Mihaly's neck, was shaking.

"What did you say?"

Lazlo pulled his hand back. "It would be better to use my belt on you because you're still a boy."

Mihaly stood up. "I deserve it. But you don't know her, Laz. You can't know how it is. Just like with me and Nina, you see everything from the outside."

They started walking again, Mihaly kicking snow up in front of him.

"She's Hungarian," said Mihaly. "In a lot of ways, she's like Nina. I know. Don't say it. Let me finish. It started last summer after she broke up with her boyfriend and her father died. She was alone when we met on the bus and realized we both spoke Hungarian. For a long time it's what we did, speaking to one another in Hungarian on the bus. But then I walked her home."

"I have one question I'd like you to answer truthfully, Mihaly. And when you do . . . even if you don't tell me the truth . . . when you answer this question honestly to yourself, you'll know about guilt. You'll know whose fault it was."

"What's the question?" asked Mihaly quietly.

"When did you tell her you had a family? Think about it, Mihaly. Not when you might have hinted it. When did you actually say, 'Look, babycakes, I forgot to tell you, I've got this good-looking wife and two little girls to bring up?'"

They walked in silence for a while. Then Mihaly stopped.

"It was afterward. It was after I went to her apartment the first time."

"And," said Lazlo, "I don't suppose she had a rope around your neck."

"No, she didn't."

"Did she wear an evening gown on the bus so your hormones got the best of you?"

Mihaly began looking angry. "She's not that kind of woman. She's attractive, yes. But it was a combination of things . . . her being Hungarian, her loneliness, both of us wanting to talk with someone after work about something other than work. I should have tape-recorded the entire affair to satisfy your curiosity."

"Perhaps you should have, Mihaly. But would you have been able to afford all the tapes and batteries?"

Mihaly sighed, and they walked back to the apartment in silence.

During the remainder of the visit, Lazlo and Mihaly played with Anna and little Ilonka. Lazlo fought to remain cheerful. But each time he looked at Nina, he felt his anger grow. He was angry with

Mihaly for being able to put on the act of faithful and loving husband. He was angry with himself for not being able to put on a cheerful act.

Nina must have sensed his anger because, while Mihaly gave horseback rides on the floor, Nina sat beside Lazlo on the sofa and asked if something was wrong.

"Nothing is wrong, Nina. You know how it is, these moods I get into . . ."

She sat close to him, placed her hand on his. "I know. Mihaly is sometimes like this. He says it's in his blood. One minute he's joking . . . the next minute he's brooding. I ask him what he thinks about when he broods, and he says it's nothing. Are you the same, Laz?"

Nina's hand was soft and warm. He could smell the sweetness escaping from the V-neck of her dress. The sofa sagged, and Nina's hip pressed against his. He held her hand with both his hands, looked into her eyes, and said, "We Horvaths are very moody." But as he said it, he felt his breath quicken because what he'd wanted to say, what he'd imagined saying in a different place, in a different time, was that he loved Nina and wanted to hold her, smother her with kisses, protect her from ever being hurt by anyone or anything.

As if she could read his mind, as if she wanted him as much as he wanted her, as if Mihaly was not whinnying and the girls not giggling on the floor, Nina smiled at him.

"You're blushing, Lazlo. I've said something to make you blush."

"Am I?"

"Yes. Is brooding a private thing? A secret between you and your brother, the horse?"

"Perhaps it is. We want to be morose until someone points it out. Then we deny it. Father was the same way."

"And your mother?"

"She was kind and gentle and cheerful. A lot like you."

Nina smiled and slowly withdrew her hand. She touched his cheek.

"You're a good brother-in-law, Laz. And now I'm blushing." She stood, stepped over little Ilonka, who had just rolled from her father's back, and went to the kitchenette.

"Who wants cake?" called Nina.

The girls screamed, "Me! Me!"

Mihaly whinnied.

Lazlo nodded, staring at Nina who glanced back to him and seemed, for an instant, to brood as she went to the refrigerator.

"The cake is fresh, but the milk's sour again," said Nina behind the open refrigerator door. "Not like on the farm where they have their own cow."

Mihaly mooed, and the girls laughed.

"All right," said Nina, "I'll make tea."

After dark Nina looked outside, saying the lights on the Chernobyl towers in the distance were almost invisible because of the snow. She asked Lazlo if he wanted to stay overnight. He thought about how it would be to sleep in the same apartment with the sounds of Nina and Mihaly turning discreetly beneath the blankets. He thought about how depressed he would be early in the morning, driving back to Kiev. He said no, and Nina, the perfect woman, smiled at him, made strong tea for his drive back to Kiev, kissed him good-bye gently when it was time to go, linked arms with her husband, and waved to Lazlo from the doorway.

The long drive in the dark back to Kiev was filled with images of Nina, the woman who, if she belonged to Lazlo instead of Mihaly, would never have to worry about his fidelity. Halfway to Kiev, snow danced in the headlights like millions of shooting stars whose wishes were doomed to failure. When the snowflakes turned into blurred streaks of light, he realized he was weeping. Was he weeping for Nina and the girls and what Mihaly had done? Or was he weeping because he was going back to his lonely apartment in Kiev? Perhaps he was weeping for the Gypsy who had hidden a pistol in his violin case should the boys recruited to arrest deserters come for him.

A snowy day in the eastern Carpathian foothills along the Romanian border. Lazlo and Viktor leave the army truck with their rifles and trudge through the snow to the farm village while the driver waits for them on the main road. He and Viktor are only nineteen; the driver, twenty-one. All three have undergone hazing together, Ukrainian recruits shipped to the Russian camp where Russian soldiers had their way with them. One nightmarish session consisted of putting a wig backwards on Viktor, painting a face on the back of his shaved head, painting breasts on his bony shoulder blades, and forcing Lazlo down onto Viktor.

A snowy day in the eastern Carpathian foothills in 1963. Russian officers are angry because of Khrushchev's 1962 Cuban missile fiasco. Sometimes they take out their anger on Ukrainian recruits. Lazlo and Viktor are chosen for deserter duty because they both speak Hungarian and the area in which the deserter's family lives is Hungarian speaking.

A snowy day in the eastern Carpathian foothills. He and Viktor hear a violin playing as they approach the farmhouse, a sad solo not badly done. The deserter's file back in the truck indicates he comes from a family of violinists. He and Viktor hope the deserter is not there. He has hidden and will come out later so he can stay the winter and help with spring planting. Deserters are common. Many are forgotten. When Viktor knocks, the violin stops playing. But instead of a parent or grandparent answering, the deserter himself, with violin in hand, answers the door.

A snowy day in the Carpathian foothills. Mother and sister are also in the house. The sister, perhaps sixteen, pleads as the deserter gives himself up. He asks to bring his violin. He retrieves the violin case, reaches inside, turns with a pistol, and shoots Viktor in the chest.

A snowy day. Viktor falling back through the open door. The pistol turning toward Lazlo. The eyes of the deserter determined. Lazlo's rifle already aimed. The struggle to release the safety and pull the trigger moves the rifle too high. The bullet explodes the deserter's face, and the women scream. Blood streaks the snow as Lazlo and the driver drag Viktor and the deserter to the truck. Both are alive, but they die while the truck speeds to the nearest hospital.

When Lazlo visits the farmhouse again with his captain, the deserter's father is home. He gives them the violin to bury with his son, saying villagers called his son Gypsy. The mother is in another room, having wept for days. The daughter stares at Lazlo with dark eyes like those of her brother. Only sixteen, yet she has become a woman. Except for the visit with his captain to the village to confirm what happened, there is no further investigation. Back at camp, Lazlo's comrades baptize him with the name Gypsy, insisting the name migrated from the deserter's soul to his soul when he avenged the death of his friend Viktor.

A snowy day much like this snowy night. But he is no longer a young man. It is too late for him. He had wanted to tell Mihaly this today. He had wanted to say to Mihaly he should be happy he has a wife in whose eyes he can gaze without seeing the eyes of the deserter's sister.

As Lazlo drove into Kiev and along Boulevard Shevchenko, streetlights on new fallen snow made it seem like daylight. Although the hour was late, he decided not to go to his apartment. Instead, he drove to the central city to visit Club Ukrainka, where he would drink wine with artists, composers, and writers. If he were fortunate, Tamara would be there. Tamara, the editor of the literary review, his true friend for so many of his years in Kiev, the last woman who had slept with him and comforted him in his loneliness and melancholy. A woman who did not remind him of the past.

When he entered Club Ukrainka, he could hear a single saxophone playing a sad song in a minor key, a song which, if played on a violin, could have been one of the Gypsy *primas* played by Lakatos and his Gypsy Orchestra, a Gypsy violin crying in the night the way he had cried on his way back to Kiev.

Layers of overcoats hung on the hooks near the entrance. He could smell wet wool along with disinfectant from the single washroom. Since his last visit to the club, someone had crossed out the sign "Men and Women" on the door and replaced it with a scrawled "Czars and Czarinas." The smells in the club entrance reminded him of a farm. Yes, a farm in winter, coming in from the wet cold while his mother cleans walls and floors, while his mother washes his baby brother's diapers in a tub in the kitchen.

He entered the main room of the club where the shine of the saxophone pierced the smoky air. Tamara sat at a corner table with two bearded men. Her black hair gleamed in the light from the candle on the table. Long silver earrings glittered at the sides of her face. When she saw him, she raised her eyebrows and said something to the two bearded men, who immediately left the table.

Lovely Tamara sat with her hands folded and mouthed the word "Gypsy" with her red, red lips as the saxophone cried. When Lazlo approached the table, he sensed the heat of the room and recalled the heat of Tamara's body against his. For an instant he felt himself more of a betrayer than his brother.

CHAPTER 6

On Wednesday nights Juli's roommate, Marina, worked late, allowing Mihaly to visit. Every week, as Wednesday approached, Juli's guilt increased, making her think of it as their last rendezvous. But as soon as Mihaly left her apartment, she would begin looking forward to the following Wednesday. Sometimes she imagined she had gone to medical school as her father wished instead of becoming a Chernobyl technician and meeting Mihaly.

While waiting for the bus to Pripyat, Juli recalled the previous winter. Her father had died, Sergey had broken off their engagement, and it had been miserably cold. This winter, while waiting at the stop outside the low-level laboratory building, it seemed much milder. She stared at the stars visible above the Chernobyl towers, wishing they could provide an answer.

Mihaly's birthday had been on the weekend. The previous Wednesday he wondered aloud what kind of gift she could possibly give him. Not something from a shop. Not something he would need to hide. In the locker room before leaving the building, she had stuffed her blouse and brassiere into her purse and worn only slacks beneath her fur coat. She could feel fingers of air slipping beneath the coat. The sound of the bus coming over the hill excited her, and she wondered if this was how a prostitute felt. For a moment she thought she might have made a mistake. The bus was coming, and it was too late to run back to the building. But if she made a fool of herself, so what? Her father was dead. Life was short.

When she sat next to Mihaly and the bus lurched forward, he decided to warm his hands beneath her coat. Her surprise for him caused a quick intake of breath. Then, during the bus ride, he whispered a description of what would happen when they arrived at the apartment.

"We'll go onto the snow-covered balcony in the dark. I'll kneel in the snow, and you'll wrap your coat around me. If anyone watches from the ground or another apartment, you'll appear alone, a woman looking up to the stars. The balcony railing will conceal me, allowing me to work. Afterward I'll carry you inside, where we'll travel to another world."

When the plan whispered on the bus was finished, they rested in bed, Mihaly's arm cradling her head on his chest. She could hear his heartbeat finally slowing to normal rhythm.

"I almost didn't make it tonight," said Mihaly.

Juli kissed his chest. "You did fine."

Mihaly laughed. "I meant, something happened, and I almost missed the bus. A valve solenoid had to be replaced."

Juli lifted her head from Mihaly's chest. "Was the fix done before you left?"

"I stayed to watch the electrician install and test the new solenoid. Not part of normal procedure, but necessary. All the engineers agreed to take up the slack when they cut the number of safety inspectors."

"Isn't that risky?" asked Juli. "Depending on the loyalty of the engineers to plug holes in the safety program?"

"Of course," said Mihaly. "But in the bureaucratic mind, transferring personnel to new units so they can be brought on-line sooner outweighs the risk."

"Do you still think the risky tests are being done at Chernobyl rather than the other reactors?"

"I don't know what to think. The maintenance shutdown and low power test wasn't supposed to be until summer on our unit, but now they want it done before May Day. They'll invite visitors from all over the union so the chief can show off. A piece of cake, as they say in America. During the test, he'll give his speech to visitors in the control room about how the plant is simply a giant steam bath, nothing but hot water. During his speech, the informants among us will watch to be certain everyone in the control room laughs appropriately, and if someone doesn't laugh . . ."

Juli touched Mihaly's lips with her fingertip. "If someone doesn't laugh, will the KGB be informed?"

"Who knows?" said Mihaly. "There are more strangers snooping around. Maybe the KGB is waiting for something to happen so they can cover it up."

"Do you still wonder about your cousin possibly being an agent?"

"Yes, he kept asking about Chernobyl. He tried to get me alone. He implied there might be something in it for me if I spoke openly. He said the KGB followed him when he visited Budapest. Luckily Laz was at the farm, and our cousin only spent the day."

"What is your cousin's name?"

"Zukor, Andrew."

"And you really think he was after something?"

"At the time I thought so. He alluded to the 1982 accident on unit one, and it's supposed to be secret. He asked about the bunker beneath the administration building like he already knew about it. He even discussed fuel reprocessing, which both of us know is strictly off-limits."

Juli thought for a moment. "Aleksandra talked about reprocessing and scrubbers."

"Or lack of scrubbers," said Mihaly. "Rather than being worried about her opinions concerning scrubbers, I think ministry officials had bigger fish."

"Her radionuclide charts?"

"Yes," said Mihaly. "The possibility of her telling someone about ongoing background radiation increases pissed them off."

"Who could she tell? The Ukrainian Writers' Union? Aleksandra had nothing to do with the stories in their journal."

"I know. If she had, she would have disappeared sooner." Mihaly placed his hand on Juli's head. "She was your friend, and they treated her like shit."

Juli thought about Aleksandra and wondered what Mihaly was thinking. *Insane, the system ignores possible problems while heroes like Aleksandra are made to disappear.*

Finally, Juli said, "The energy ministries have been degrading the environment to produce energy for years. And for what? So they can make cheap, ill-fitting shoes."

Mihaly pulled her to him and kissed her. "You're the one person I can discuss these things with."

"How touching," said Juli. "Chernobyl is part of our relationship."

Mihaly tickled her tummy. "Aha. A reaction gone wild. Radiation levels increasing, but where's it coming from?" Mihaly tickled lower. "The core! We need to put in the master control rod! What do you think, Comrade Technician Popovics?"

Juli got the upper hand by tickling Mihaly's ribs. He rolled off the bed with a thud.

"Too late!" said Mihaly from the floor. "It's a meltdown. In America they call it the China Syndrome."

Juli looked over the edge of the bed. "Where would it melt down to from here? What's on the other side of the world from us?"

"The South Pacific," said Mihaly, folding his hands behind his head.

"How do you know?"

Mihaly lay on the floor, staring up at the ceiling. "I checked a globe for the hell of it."

"So sad," said Juli. "You're thinking about our future again. It's Wednesday evening. Soon you'll be leaving, and it's time to get depressed."

"I was thinking of what I told my brother about Chernobyl."

"Didn't you explain when he visited last week?"

"I told Laz everything was in tip-top shape at the plant. I gave him a rosy picture because of his persistence about something else . . ."

Mihaly got up and sat on the edge of the bed, his back to her. "I've been thinking of divorcing Nina."

Juli pictured Nina in a flowered cotton dress. She'd met Nina and Mihaly's two daughters at the fall picnic. A beautiful wife, two beautiful daughters.

Juli reached out and touched Mihaly's shoulder. "Leave it be, Mihaly. We can see one another on Wednesdays."

"You wouldn't marry me?"

"If you were single, if we lived in one of your parallel worlds . . ."

Mihaly turned, smiled. "How about the South Pacific? How about an island where nobody knows us?"

Instead of answering, Juli put her hand on Mihaly's shoulder.

"It's an idiotic situation," said Mihaly.

"And we're the idiots," said Juli.

Mihaly stood and went to the chair where his clothes lay. "I'd better go. Your roommate will be home soon."

"It doesn't matter," said Juli. "She knows about us."

"You told her?"

"Marina is like a sister."

Mihaly began dressing, turned to stare at Juli. "And I told my brother."

"Did he scold you?"

"Severely."

"We deserve it."

After dressing, Mihaly helped Juli refold the sofa bed. They did not speak, and Juli thought how sad it was to fold the bed. Like folding a dead person's clothing or closing a coffin. So sad. So final.

Juli put on her coat and stepped out on the balcony to watch Mihaly jog across the courtyard. His apartment was a few blocks away, and he waved before disappearing beyond the building across from hers. The last thing he said before leaving her apartment was that the view from her balcony was better than the view from the balcony on his and Nina's apartment. Their apartment faced the red lights of the Chernobyl towers, he'd said, while hers faced the dark horizon of the Belorussian Republic to the north.

Juli had not put on shoes, and the snow stung her feet. She was about to step back inside when she heard something, snow crunching underfoot. She turned abruptly, looked at her footprints and Mihaly's footprints and the impressions his knees had made in the snow. She heard it again, snow crunching. She moved quietly to the railing, leaned out, looked right and left. On the floor of the balcony to the left, she saw boot prints in the snow. Was there a shadow? Had she seen the toe of a boot disappear behind the privacy wall separating the balconies?

She ran inside, locked the sliding door, closed the curtains, turned out the light, and went to the left wall to place her ear against it. There was a gentle thud, a sliding door closing, perhaps the one next door. She kept listening but heard nothing more. Maybe a worker or the landlord had stepped out onto the balcony earlier in the day and made the boot prints. She wanted to believe this because she knew the apartment next door had been vacant several weeks. At least it had been vacant until now.

When the phone rang, she was so startled she backed away from the wall abruptly, fell backward over the hassock, and landed on her hip. She rubbed her hip, cursed the hassock, crawled to the end table, and picked up the phone.

"Hello."

No answer, but someone there.

"Hello," she said again somewhat louder, imagining whoever was in the apartment next door might be calling.

"Hello, I said!"

"Hello," a woman's voice. "This is Nina Horvath. Is my husband there?"

Cold night air seemed to have come into the apartment. She turned to look at the balcony door, but it was closed. The night again, the winter night threatening to swallow her.

"Nina Horvath?" Juli finally said.

"Yes. I asked if my husband was there."

"Why would he be here?"

"Oh," said Nina Horvath. "Then he's not there?"

"No."

"Very well. I presume you completed your business and I can expect him any time. Yes. I believe I hear him now. Good night."

Earlier this evening, while waiting for the bus, she had justified her relationship with Mihaly by telling herself life was too short to worry about the future. Now the future was upon her like a thief in the night. This evening she had played the seductress. Now she felt nothing but emptiness.

Juli wrapped her coat tightly about her, curled up on the sofa, and prayed Marina would come home soon.

CHAPTER 7

April 1986

Pavel and Nikolai sat at their long table in the back room of the Pripyat post office opening-reading-resealing the ten percent of the morning's mail shoveled through the slot in the wall. Last winter the steamer had been welcome. On a warm April day, however, the steamer was an enemy. An exhaust fan clattering on the wall failed to remove the heat and moisture. Their foreheads glistened with perspiration.

"I'm reminded of a steam bath in Moscow," said Pavel, resealing a letter and adding it to the growing pile on his left.

"The steam baths in Kiev are better," said Nikolai.

"In what way?"

"The women."

"I don't believe you," said Pavel. "Not even in these so-called times of change. You play with your nuts underwater, and you see tits on boys."

"That reminds me," said Nikolai. "Soon it will be May."

"What does May have to do with women in the Kiev baths?"

Nikolai resealed a letter he had been reading and tossed it onto the pile. "In May chestnuts and lilacs are in bloom. While we sit in our Pripyat sweatbox, workers prepare for May Day parades. Last year, naked women were in the Kiev parade."

"The recent crackdown on drinking should apply especially to you," said Pavel. "Or perhaps, like the Chernobyl workers, you've taken up hashish."

"Don't be a farmer," said Nikolai, retrieving another letter.

"I'm not a farmer," said Pavel.

"You smell like one."

Pavel tossed a letter onto the pile and gave Nikolai a dismissive wave. "No wonder it stinks in here. With all this idiotic talk and all this heat . . ."

"Captain Putna should issue deodorant," said Nikolai.

They were quiet for a time, reading letters, frowning, and adding letters to the finished pile. Finally, Pavel spoke.

"The postmaster has an oscillating fan in his office. Tomorrow it will be in here."

Nikolai fanned himself with a letter he had just opened. "If we had a window like the postmaster, we'd have a view and be able to smell the spring air instead of reading about it. I'm sick of reading about it." Nikolai read from the letter. "'Spring is pleasant here also. Snows of February and March have nourished the winter wheat. Father has planted our vegetable crop and all is well.' I'm sick of hearing how all is well." Nikolai opened a new letter, examined it. "Here's another to Juli Popovics, the Chernobyl technician babe."

"She's under observation," said Pavel. "Who's it from?"

"I know she's under observation," said Nikolai, somewhat annoyed. "It's in Ukrainian from Aunt Magda in Kiev. She has prepared a room so Juli Popovics can visit for several months while the medical matter is addressed."

"Sounds like she's a *Mommychka*-to-be," said Pavel.

"There must be much activity at Chernobyl," said Nikolai.

"Aside from radioactivity."

Nikolai put the letter to Juli Popovics in the tray for copying and began opening another.

"Still no mail for the engineer stud?" asked Nikolai, glancing at a list on the table headed by the words OFFICIAL OBSERVATION.

"Nothing for Mihaly Horvath since February," said Pavel. "First his American cousin bugs him, then a batch of letters from his brother asking about some matter, then nothing."

"The letters we copied may have had an effect," said Nikolai. "Like other Chernobyl workers before him, he's gone mad and had to be taken away. Perhaps we'll go mad. It's spring and I feel like a caged animal. Can you imagine the heat in this room come summer?"

"I doubt if Mihaly Horvath has gone mad," said Pavel. "As for us, the post office should supply chilled mineral water. Did you hear Gorbachev is now mineral secretary since he replaced vodka at official functions?"

"You already told me," said Nikolai, wiping his brow with his sleeve.

"Don't worry about the heat," said Pavel. "Tomorrow we'll have a fan to cool us, courtesy of our ersatz supervisor, the noble comrade postmaster."

Because it had been stored in the underground garage, the inside of the Volga was cool and comfortable. Major Komarov tried to relax as Captain Azef drove slowly through Kiev's noon-hour traffic. On the far side of Kirov Street, beyond Petrovsky Promenade, office workers lunched on benches beneath chestnut trees and on the green April lawn of Pervomaisky Park. Beyond the park, the river sparkled in the sun. Out in the river, the beach on Trukhanov

Island glowed like a hot ember.

While he drove, Azef talked about automobiles. "Although the Zil is still used by high officials and has certain prestige, I still prefer the Volga. Even modified Chaikas with yellow fog lights are no match for the well-equipped Volga. Look at all those pieces of shit everyone else drives. Even the militia drives shit-box Zhigulis."

Azef glanced to Komarov. "Sorry, Major. I'm speaking too much again."

"Sometimes, Captain, it's not how much you speak. It's the nature of your conversation. Perhaps it would be better to concentrate on our visit to militia headquarters."

Azef stopped the Volga behind a line of traffic waiting for pedestrians crossing to the park. "Will you tell Chief Investigator Chkalov about the investigation into shoddy parts from Yugoslavia?"

"Shoddy parts relates to new construction," said Komarov. "Detective Horvath's brother works in unit four, which is fully operational."

"What about the woman?" asked Azef. "Will you tell Chkalov about her?"

"Detective Horvath's brother managing to impregnate a coworker is of no concern to the Kiev militia. Our purpose today is simply to determine whether the letters Detective Horvath sent his brother earlier in the year might have some relation to Chernobyl."

"Chkalov is a brutish fellow," said Azef.

Komarov glanced at Azef and had to restrain a smile. Azef of the KGB and Chkalov of the militia, what a pair of plump brutes they both were.

When they got out of the Volga at militia headquarters, Komarov had a quick cigarette before entering the building. Azef seemed about to mention the cigarette until Komarov glared at him. Then Azef simply waited for Komarov to finish his smoke.

Chief Investigator Chkalov's office did not look like the office of a man who worked for a living. Except for a brass pen set, an intercom, and telephone, the desk was clear. Behind Chkalov on either side of an ornately curtained window stood flags of the Soviet Union, the Ukraine, the city of Kiev, and the Kiev militia. The walls contained photographs of appropriate officials surrounding a larger rendering of Lenin looking skyward. There were no maps of the city with stickpins, no scheduling boards, no piles of reports. A room meant for giving proclamations rather than the office of the chief of Kiev's detectives, who sat behind the desk picking remnants of his lunch from his teeth with his fingernails.

Captain Azef sat to Komarov's left, slouching in one of the plush guest chairs. Komarov had turned his chair at an angle so he could view both brutes at once. Because there was no ashtray, he did not smoke.

"So," said Chkalov, "the KGB wishes to inquire about Detective Horvath."

Komarov was about to speak when Azef broke in. "Yes, Comrade Chief Investigator. We would like to know something about him."

Komarov glared at Azef. "If you don't mind, Captain."

Azef gripped the arms of his chair as if to pull himself from its depths. "Certainly, Major."

"Thank you," said Komarov, turning to Chkalov, who seemed amused at this pettiness. "Chief Investigator Chkalov, as you know, it is often in the state's interest to gather information about certain citizens. This is not to imply these individuals have broken laws; it is simply part of the overall fact-gathering responsibility of the KGB."

Komarov knew he was stating the obvious. He often used this technique when interrogating officials. A few minutes of this, and Chkalov would relax his defenses. Komarov went on, stating in general terms the need for militia and KGB cooperation. During the speech, Komarov noticed Chkalov sit back, fold his hands on his desk, and smile. When he felt Chkalov was sufficiently relaxed, Komarov began the questioning.

"Chief Investigator Chkalov, is Detective Horvath a convinced or an unconvinced Communist?"

Chkalov's smile changed to a frown. "These are questions of conscience. My men do their duty."

Komarov sat forward, stared at Chkalov. "Surely you know your men. Especially a man like Detective Horvath who has been with you for many years. Is he convinced or unconvinced?"

"He's not a Party member."

"Party membership has nothing to do with it. I want to know if Detective Horvath, who originates from a frontier area and is of Hungarian descent, does his job simply to maintain his position, or if he does it for the good of the system."

"He's a hard worker," said Chkalov, sounding defensive. "Detective Horvath is a bachelor and often makes use of his own time to solve a case."

"Are you aware he has relatives in America?"

Chkalov smiled. "Many Ukrainians and Russians have relatives in America, so it would not surprise me if Detective Horvath has an American relative or two. Perhaps you should have visited the American consulate instead of coming here."

Komarov ignored the smile. "A second cousin visited Detective Horvath here in the Ukraine while he was on holiday."

"I know," said Chkalov. "He told me about it."

"Did you also know Detective Horvath associates with members of the artistic intelligentsia in Kiev?"

"He's a lover of the arts," said Chkalov. "Especially music."

"Hungarians do love their music," said Komarov. "Gypsy music. Contrived emotion so they can alternately dance and weep."

"What does this have to do with anything?" asked Chkalov.

Komarov glanced to Azef.

"Background data," said Azef, obviously glad to join in. "Major Komarov is simply establishing Horvath's character."

"I suppose next we'll go into his preferences in women," said Chkalov.

"Perhaps," said Azef.

Komarov nodded to Azef, a signal to continue.

"For instance," said Azef, taking his notebook from his pocket. "Were you aware Detective Horvath has been seeing a Miss Tamara Petrov, who is editor of a literary review known to publish the works of anti-Soviets?"

"A detective's personal life is none of my business," said Chkalov.

"A moment ago it was," said Azef. "A moment ago you said Detective Horvath has much free time because he is a bachelor, and he uses this time to put in extra duty."

"He doesn't give up all his free time," said Chkalov, obviously annoyed. "I simply meant he is often available on call."

"He should be," said Komarov. "He has a car at his disposal, which he is also permitted to use for personal trips."

"It is valuable to have our detectives in their own cars, Major. This is a large city, and a detective can be called to duty at a moment's notice."

"Do you also permit out-of-town trips?"

"Occasionally."

"A hundred kilometers away?"

Chkalov sat forward, fists clenched on his desk. "I see no point to this questioning. If militia policy is in question, perhaps you would be candid enough to say it."

"On the contrary," said Komarov. "I don't question militia policy. I simply want to inquire about several trips Detective Horvath made to Pripyat."

Chkalov smiled. "Detective Horvath was visiting his brother. Even so, there is a militia office in Pripyat, and it is not uncommon for our detectives to communicate with one another."

"I've visited the Pripyat militia office myself," said Komarov. "I must say, the captain there is also a person of interest. But we're getting off track. I'm here to reveal information regarding Detective Horvath."

"Please do!" said Chkalov abrasively.

"Detective Horvath's brother holds a key position at the Chernobyl Nuclear Facility operated by the Ministry of Energy. The KGB is assigned to protect the facility. Recently, Detective Horvath's brother has had personal problems and has been involved in gossip with co-workers, some of which involves the questioning of authority. In letters from Detective Horvath to his brother, Mihaly Horvath, Chernobyl matters were alluded to. Detective Horvath has subsequently inquired whether these matters were resolved. Now, instead of writing, Detective Horvath has made several trips to Pripyat. Our concern, Chief Investigator Chkalov, is not with an individual's personal life unless his personal life is dedicated to wrongdoing."

Chkalov stood, walked to his window with his hands clasped behind him, then turned. "Detective Horvath is one of my best men. He would not be involved in wrongdoing."

"I didn't say he was," said Komarov.

"Then what the hell are you getting at?"

"His brother," said Komarov. "We're concerned about his brother, and we'd like you to let us know if you hear anything. A compromised Chernobyl engineer is my concern."

"Such methods you use," said Chkalov, shaking his head. "In the militia, when we want to know an answer, we simply ask the question. But I suppose KGB procedures are different."

"They have to be," said Komarov. "In counterintelligence, there are times when we do not know the questions. We simply know a situation exists in which questions should be asked. In the KGB we do not wait for a crime to occur before we do something."

When he and Azef walked through the anteroom after leaving Chkalov's office, Komarov heard what sounded like the violent slamming of a desk drawer behind him. He turned to see Azef smiling gleefully like a fat-faced child.

Although the North Atlantic was over a thousand kilometers away beyond all of Europe, the distant ocean affected Kiev's weather. In winter, northwesterly winds blew across Scandinavia, causing snow squalls, which sometimes paralyzed the city. But now, in late April, the winds had reversed their course, bringing warmth from the Black Sea.

It was evening, and Major Komarov was on the back porch of his small home on the outskirts of Darnitsa, a suburb of Kiev. This afternoon, Komarov had succeeded in intimidating Chief Investigator Chkalov of the Kiev militia. As he sat in the dark on his porch sipping vodka on ice with a lemon peel, he could still see Chkalov's angry round face and Captain Azef's smiling round face. Contemptible brutes, both of them.

The porch faced a grove of trees bordering a creek at the southern edge of the yard. The south wind was fragrant with greenery, momentarily overpowering the smell of vodka and the acrid aroma of the cigarette he had just put out.

Dinner was finished, and Komarov could hear the muted babble of the television inside the house. His wife remained captivated by television, while Komarov, weather permitting, spent evenings on his beloved porch. On the small wooden table beside his chair were cigarettes, a lighter, an ashtray, a bowl of ice, a peeled lemon, his glass, and his bottle.

When he sipped vodka, Komarov's elbow brushed against his side where he felt the weight of the knife in the inside pocket of his jacket. Keeping the knife with him rather than locked away in his desk coincided with his introduction last summer to the suspicious actions of three Hungarians. Although he had not met them, the three had been under operational observation for many months, and Komarov felt he knew them well.

Two of the Hungarians, Mihaly Horvath and Juli Popovics, worked at the Chernobyl facility. If the need arose, the actions of these two would be of interest to the Ministry of Energy, to the power-plant Party secretary, or even to KGB headquarters in Moscow. Somehow Komarov felt this need would arise. He had been requested confidentially to watch for incidents in which Chernobyl personnel questioned safety at the plant. Although he did not know the reason, he felt a Moscow crackdown might come. If it did, he would be ready. He would have his three suspects: a Chernobyl engineer, a technician, and a detective in Kiev.

Three suspects with the blood of Gypsies running through their veins. Three Gypsies whose photographs, especially the Horvath brothers, reminded him of photographs of Bela Bartok, the so-called composer who collected simpleminded folk tunes and pawned them off as art, the so-called composer who went to America to die with his old-fashioned music.

Komarov took a sip of vodka and again felt the weight of the knife against his chest. He reached into his inside pocket and held the knife. If only he had owned the knife earlier in his career and used it. Perhaps on Barbara, the dark-haired Gypsy who humiliated him. If only he had started his climb on the ladder sooner, perhaps in the army before joining the KGB. If only he had been old enough to use the knife to avenge the death of his father, a lover of music, especially Prokofiev.

Komarov gripped the knife tightly and thought again about the night he met the man who would kill his parents. It was some years after the end of the Great Patriotic War. Komarov paused to drink to the victory of the Great War, then regripped his knife and thought back.

It was in Moscow during the time of rebuilding. Although he was only a few years old, the scene was vivid. He and his father had left his mother in the one-room apartment and gone to the opera house to see *Love for Three Oranges*. His father loved Prokofiev's music. "The music of the future," his father said. "Did you know Prokofiev traveled to America, dear Grigor? Of course, Americans did not understand his music. Prokofiev's music of the future belongs here in the motherland." Unfortunately the motherland's future was something his father would never see, because after the opera, the Gypsy landlord killed his parents. In the street outside the apartment building, the landlord, his sinister foul face hidden in the shadow of a brimmed hat, argued with his father about the rent, equated the rent with the cost of opera tickets.

A week later, they were forced to move in with Uncle Ivan in the village north of Moscow. A month later, his father put Uncle Ivan's pistol to his head in the barn. A year later, his mother died of pneumonia in the cold corner of Uncle Ivan's farmhouse, and little Grigor was sent to the orphanage, making the army barracks, years later, seem luxurious.

In the army Komarov learned the old Russian saying and reversed it. Where he should have licked, he did lick; where he should have barked, he did bark. He kept his opinions to himself, praising officials even when he thought they were fools, as when Khrushchev knuckled under to Kennedy during the Cuban missile fiasco. The army gave Komarov comfort and discipline. The army gave him the chance his father never had. While gripping the knife tightly, he wished he'd had its power the night of the opera.

As a boy he would have wanted to be a Brezhnev rather than a Gorbachev, not allowing himself to be duped the way the current administration allowed themselves to be duped. But perhaps, like all things in this modern world, the current situation was a charade, the talk of perestroika a ruse by Gorbachev to lure the movie actor Reagan into his clutches.

Komarov had seen much during his years in the KGB. Orthodox Church leaders working for the KGB after being compromised by Romeo agents. Spy planes collecting air samples routinely doctored by those being spied on. A Brezhnev rather than a Gorbachev. How could he possibly accomplish it today? Perhaps Gypsies were the answer. Gypsies, after all, were much like the Muslims in Afghanistan—male-centered, out of touch with modern culture, using superstitious religion to undo the world. Gypsies allowed their children to smoke. He'd seen them in the slums of Moscow, eight- and nine-year-old boys smoking. Not girls. Boys. The boys in the culture growing up to overthrow governments. The boys of deviant societies bent on destruction while he went into the army and then into the KGB to serve Mother Russia.

Muslims and Gypsies. He'd known of a Hungarian CIA station chief code named Gypsy Moth. Perhaps the code name could be used again. Perhaps the cousin visiting the Horvath brothers had objectives beyond a familial visit. Western secret services actively recruited spies and provocateurs. Perhaps uncovering a network of spies and provocateurs was the key, someone hired by American intelligence to compromise a Chernobyl engineer.

"A Brezhnev rather than a Gorbachev," he mumbled.

Komarov was not certain how long he had been on the porch,

perhaps an hour, perhaps two. But he did know he had refilled his glass several times. He was now in the most comfortable state of his day, a euphoric state in which the cares of the past and present fade and the vodka has not yet completely taken over. It was difficult to maintain this feeling for long. But while it lasted, each evening, he felt it would last forever. Unfortunately, the bottle required one to become drunk and uncomfortable in order to pass through this state. He thought about this for a moment, tried to analyze the logic of it, then took another drink.

A noise in the bushes to his left. Komarov sat forward, put down his glass. A figure moved swiftly along the side, then the front of the porch. Komarov took the knife from his pocket. For an instant he thought of Chkalov, of militia vengeance. He recalled one of his agents, Allika, who had been mysteriously killed last year. He was out of his chair and had begun to open the knife when he recognized his son coming up the stairs.

"Dmitry!"

"What's new, Pop?"

He slipped the knife back into his pocket, allowing it to close within its handle. "You frightened me."

"What else is new?"

"Why don't you use the front door?"

"Why do you sit out here every night?"

"Why do you always ask questions in response to mine?"

"Why do you always ask questions?"

It was no use. Komarov sat back in his chair, took a drink of vodka, lit a cigarette.

Instead of going into the house, Dmitry sat on the steps facing the yard. Komarov stared at the dark outline of his son. So thin he seemed unhealthy. His hair, cropped on the sides and long on top, sticking straight up. His damnable earring catching the light from the house.

"I got a job today," said Dmitry.

"A job?" No. He must not sound overly excited. "What kind of job?"

"At the art museum in Kiev."

"Which one? There are several art museums."

"Not the Museum of Russian Art. This one's a few doors away."

"What matters is you're employed, Dmitry."

"So now you don't have to say your son was kicked out of the university and he's a parasite. Am I right? Is this why you're so impressed?"

"No," said Komarov. "I'm interested. Which museum is it?"

"Oriental and Western Art. I'll work in the gift shop. Fyodor got me the job."

Fyodor, the one Dmitry brought to dinner last month, the one who put his arm around Dmitry as they walked down the street. Komarov took another drink, then another. His own son, the son of a major in the KGB, a homosexual. And now his . . . his what? Mate? Bed partner? Lover? And now his son's lover had gotten Dmitry a job.

"So, what do you think, Pop?"

"I think it's good to have a job." Komarov wanted to be alone with his vodka but knew he must go on, he must try despite the fact he had left the state of euphoria and was descending into the depths of drunkenness. "I also think relationships should be with the right people."

"Like who?"

The wind blew across Komarov's face, but he could not smell the air. All he could smell was the vodka.

"A long time ago," said Komarov, "when I was stationed in East Berlin, there was a woman named Gretchen. Golden blond hair, eyes like fine crystal, skin soft and fair . . ."

Dmitry stood and walked to the back door.

"Where are you going? I was speaking!"

"I've heard this story before, Pop."

"No. You . . . you couldn't have."

"I have. And so has Mom. You always talk about Gretchen when you're drunk. You always tell us how she was murdered and what a hero you were to have avenged her death. You're drunk like this every night. Go ahead. Try to stand up. See? You can't. You don't know what you're talking about. There are no Gretchens here. I have my own friends. Telling me about the old days in Berlin when you used your whore, Gretchen, to lure poor bastards to be tortured doesn't mean anything here. Maybe you killed the bastards she brought to you. Why don't you get your gun and kill me? You can't even get out of your chair!"

Komarov reached into his pocket and pulled out the knife. Before he could open it, Dmitry snatched it away.

"Ha! A knife! You pull a knife on your own son?"

Dmitry opened the knife, held the blade up to the light coming from the window. "Such a big knife for such a little man." Then Dmitry stabbed the knife into the door frame and went into the house, leaving the back door to slam shut like the shot from a pistol.

Komarov held the arms of his chair and twisted to stare at the knife sticking out of the door frame, the knife he'd used so he could be where he was today. But where was he? Was this hell? Was there really a vengeful God? If so, why didn't God kill the Gypsy landlord so he could live a different life? A life along the other path instead of this one with its marriage producing a homosexual son who, despite his appearance, had become stronger than him. What was a man? Were the brutes Chkalov and Azef men? Was he a man?

Komarov picked up the vodka bottle, felt the weight of it, the heft of poison, of slow death. He would fight it. He would regain his manhood. Perhaps he would uncover a conspiracy at Chernobyl, a conspiracy involving the Horvath brothers. Gypsies, whose relatives dress and dance like women while others pick pockets. Gypsies, who converse in languages others cannot understand. Gypsies, who wear earrings. A world of symbols. A world in which a spy from American intelligence can, if he wants, squirm in the bushes like a snake and mount a surprise attack on a KGB official simply trying to get through another evening at his own home.

Komarov stood up from his chair, holding onto the side of the house for balance. He studied the vodka bottle. Although the label was unreadable in the dark, lights from the house reflected in the glass. He tried to feel the reflected light with his thumb, and when he could not, he held the bottle high over his head and threw it against the porch railing. It shattered across the floor of the porch, and eventually he heard vodka dripping through the floorboards to the earth below. He stood swaying in the dark, listening, waiting, and planning his next move.

CHAPTER 8

Spring rains had moistened the Ukraine soil, preparing its rich farm-land for the job of feeding the USSR. In the far northern Ukraine, waterfowl had returned to the Pripyat marshes. East of the marshes along the Uzh and Pripyat Rivers, gulls followed tractors, feasting on unearthed insects. Farther east, where the Uzh and Pripyat emp-tied into the Dnieper for the journey to the Black Sea, waterfowl congregated at a large pond. The pond bordered the Pripyat River but was separated from the river by a man-made dike. Water in the pond was warmer than the water in the river or in any other ponds in the area because it was used to cool superheated steam emerging from several turbines.

From the far side of the pond, the sound from the Chernobyl Nuclear Generating Facility operated by the Ministry of Energy was a steady drone. To some, it was a sound of unlimited power. To others, trained in engineering and physics, it was not one sound, but many sounds. Pumps, turbines, generators, and transformers formed an orchestra. The failure of one instrument would dimin-ish the score.

Early in the morning on Friday, April 25, 1986, a technician in an off-white uniform walked near a turbine and generator of Chernobyl's unit four. The combined structure was over fifty meters long. On the generator side, thick copper bus bars in protective pipe went through the wall of the building to the transformers outside. On the turbine side, large pipes brought steam from the reactor to drive the turbine, and more pipes carried steam off to be cooled. The concrete floor to which the structure was mounted vibrated. The noise was deafening and there was the smell of oil and hot metal and graphite in the air.

One wall of the huge room was a mass of piping, wiring, gauges, solenoids, and valves. The technician paused in this area, watching solenoids and valves doing their work. But to stay long enough to watch every solenoid-valve combination go through a cycle would have taken hours, and the technician had further rounds to make. The operators had already begun the hours-long process of reducing power leading to the tests to be performed during shutdown. The technician mounted a metal stairway, pausing to watch a particular valve, painted red, being actuated. Then he continued his climb. He met another technician at the top of the stairs, and the two shouted to be heard above the roar of the turbine hall.

"How do the emergency cooling switches look?"

"They look . . . content!"

"They'd better be content because the idiots in the control room are insane!"

"Everyone working here is insane! Especially the bosses!"

"They were smart enough to build the bunker below their offices!"

"Who put Pavlov in charge of programming the computer? The dog doesn't know what the hell he's doing!"

"His name fits the situation! I hope we get this bitch shut down for May Day!"

"The parade banners kids make in school have construction

superior to anything here!"

"Antiquated technology is our business!"

The two technicians laughed, slapped one another on the back, and went on their way.

In another wing of the building, in the relative quiet of the main control room, several technicians dressed in similar off-white uniforms sat at a semicircular console. At one end of the console, a two-by-six-centimeter rectangular panel lit bright red for two seconds, then went out. The technician nearest the panel was speaking on the telephone. After the red light went out, the technician looked in the general direction of the panel for several seconds, his hand over the mouthpiece of the phone. Finally he shrugged his shoulders and resumed his conversation.

In a large room above the reactor core, one of the technicians making his rounds walked a catwalk. He paused a moment and stared down at the ends of graphite columns. It looked like a giant circular checkerboard. He reached into the vest pocket of his uniform, took out a dosimeter, held it up to the light, and looked into it. Then he hurried along the catwalk, went out a side door, and descended an outdoor stairway.

Outside the building, the technician paused to speak with the operator of a large diesel front loader carrying gravel. The technician stepped up on the side platform and shouted at the man in the cab. Amid the throbbing of the diesel engine, he pointed to a small high-tension tower a few meters behind the front loader. After the technician dismounted, he stood with his hands on his hips and watched as the front loader left the area.

The technician walked back to the far end of the building and climbed a flight of stairs. Before entering the building, he paused to watch a pair of ducks fly over the yard and out above the cooling pond. He lifted his head and inhaled deeply of the spring air before going inside through a set of double doors to rejoin his comrades in the control room and fill out the morning inspection report.

The morning chatter of birds through the open window awakened her. The previous evening she'd gone for a walk alone. Pripyat's linden trees had thickened, and she'd stood watching skylarks building nests. She went into the bathroom and stared into the mirror, trying to see if she had changed, if her complexion was rosier, her cheeks puffier, her eyes calmer. The only change was a slight thickening of her abdomen. To see it she had to stand on a stool and study her profile. Six weeks, and the baby was beginning to show. She'd noticed the change this week, and now she was certain she could see the bulge beneath her slip.

"It's still too early to see," said Marina, standing in the bathroom doorway watching her.

Marina was like a sister, someone she could confide in. They had spent many nights discussing what she should do, and she had decided to request a medical leave to have the baby. She would stay with Aunt Magda in the town of Visenka during the last months of pregnancy. Finally, the most difficult decision, she would arrange for the baby's adoption.

Juli stepped off the stool and began combing her hair. She glanced to Marina. "I'm going to tell my supervisor today, assuming she doesn't already know."

"No one knows," said Marina. "Nobody was in the apartment next door last winter. The footprints on the balcony were made during the day. The following week, our new neighbors moved in, so there's nothing to worry about. Another pair of powerless women like us."

"Are you going to lecture me again, Marina?"

"Not a lecture, Juli. I simply wondered when you would tell your secret to someone besides me and the doctor and your aunt."

"I'll tell my supervisor late in the day so I'll have the weekend to prepare for the gossip."

"And Mihaly?"

"We've been through this, Marina. I'm not trying to protect him! A fool protecting a fool! His wife finds out about us, and we continue seeing one another! It's an insane situation! Nothing good can come of it!"

"The baby is good," said Marina.

"I know. I didn't mean to yell. I'll . . . tell Mihaly today. After work. After I tell my supervisor and get the hell out of there."

"You still won't consider an abortion?"

"No. Don't ask why. Maybe because my father is dead and I was his only child."

Juli looked in the mirror, saw her own face sneering back at her. "I should have gone to medical school like my father wanted instead of working at a damned nuclear plant. I'd be a doctor in Moscow sitting behind my desk, and on the other side of the desk is an unmarried girl come to get the results of her test. I should have stayed in Moscow after school or gone to some other job away from here so I would never have met Mihaly."

"Do you love him?"

"I don't know. I'm a coward, Marina. If I do love him, I don't have courage to say it."

Marina came behind her, took the brush from the sink, and began brushing Juli's hair. "You're very brave. No matter what I've said the last few days, I want you to know I don't think I would have handled the situation as well."

"I should have handled the birth control so none of this would have happened."

Marina paused a moment, then resumed brushing Juli's hair. "Here we go again. It's the men in power who cause the problems. Always the men who put us into situations we'd rather not be in. Keep reminding yourself you're going through this for a couple who can't have a baby of their own. When you tell Mihaly, remember to also tell him about the couple. They're waiting for their baby. Their baby."

"Last night I lay awake thinking about how Mihaly will react."

"How?" asked Marina.

"Silent, brooding. Then he'll smile, put his arm around me, and ask what he can do."

"Do me one favor," said Marina.

"What?"

"If he thinks only of himself, kick him in the nuts."

Juli turned, and when she saw Marina smiling she couldn't help laughing. They hugged and Juli felt her eyes fill with tears. "I haven't even thought of contacting my mother. She'll never know about it."

"It's all right," whispered Marina into her ear. "You'll be all right."

Marina took Juli's hand and led her out of the bathroom. "Come with me. You need breakfast to feed our couple's baby. Plus, I don't want you to be late. No running for the bus."

In Kiev a man wearing a ski mask despite the warm spring weather had, during the past month, beaten and raped three women in three separate metro stations. Kiev's detectives were put on extra duty. Female militia officers were placed in each metro station as decoys.

But the rapist had not been lured into the trap.

Because he was single, Detective Lazlo Horvath worked several sixteen-hour shifts in a row. His reward was the requisite congratulatory speech by Chief Investigator Chkalov and a weekend off. Chkalov had seemed angry, the speech terse, the weekend off given reluctantly after an odd complaint saying Lazlo should have visited the militia station in Pripyat while visiting his brother. A rumor among detectives linked Chkalov's foul mood to KGB inquiries.

But on this Friday morning, with one normal day shift to go before his weekend off, Lazlo was not concerned with Chkalov's relationship with the KGB. What occupied Lazlo's thoughts this Friday was the plan for Tamara Petrov to spend the weekend at his apartment. This morning, before going on duty, he had cleaned the apartment, a procedure consisting of cramming the accumulation of clutter either into the garbage or into the closet. His bed linen and an assortment of soiled towels and clothing were in the back seat of the Zhiguli to be dropped off at the laundry. The inside of the Zhiguli smelled ripe as he drove along in the morning sun.

Lazlo stopped for breakfast at a pastry vendor on Khreshchatik Boulevard. The last time he'd been there the tea had been weak, so he ordered coffee. He sat on a bench in the plaza near the stairway to the metro. While he ate pastry and sipped the strong coffee from a paper cup, morning commuters disappeared into a metro stairwell like ants heading into a wine cellar. The main post office across the street reminded him of the last letter from his brother. Mihaly said Nina knew about the "other woman," and he and Nina had reconciled. Mihaly would stop seeing the woman and work hard to salvage his marriage.

As he sat in the sun enjoying the warm southerly breeze, Lazlo wondered what this "other woman" of Mihaly's was like. Perhaps Juli was a Gypsy, at least in appearance, like Tamara. If so, if he were in his brother's position, could he be tempted away from Nina and the girls? Of course he could. Being in a profession of trying to make things right did not mean he was better than anyone else. Perfection was for others, perhaps those without ties who could cross the frontier and live in so-called freedom.

A young woman walked past, the breeze making her cotton dress cling to her hips. Like Nina, thought Lazlo, Nina on last summer's holiday. So young and beautiful, but not for him. Tamara was no less beautiful. Not young, his age, but still beautiful.

At the metro stairwell, a young man emerged carrying a guitar case. The man, most likely a student, was perhaps nineteen. His hair was dark. The young man glanced at Lazlo. Dark eyes. Gypsy eyes. The young man striking in his resemblance to the one he had killed. "Boys killing boys," an officer at camp had said. "The strings of his violin silenced in youth," said another. A quarter century had passed, yet he could not get the boy out of his mind. He had killed a maker of music. All those songs left unplayed. All the joy of his music unfulfilled. All because of Lazlo, the Gypsy. Tamara was the only person he'd told of the incident. Soon he would tell Mihaly. Perhaps having two people in his life know about the Gypsy would help.

After the young man carrying the guitar case was gone, Lazlo did his best to return to the present. Horns sounded, and a loud motor scooter roared past. Tonight, after a relatively peaceful day of asking questions around the metro, filling out reports at headquarters, and doing his laundry, he would be with Tamara. Tamara, who often said his constant brooding and moroseness were unhealthy, even for the Gypsy. He disposed of his garbage, went to the Zhiguli, and drove across town to a wine shop that sold a fine Hungarian vintage.

As Juli stood at the bus stop in front of the low-level laboratory building, she felt as if those waiting behind were trying to detect signs of pregnancy. Though her supervisor had promised confidentiality, Juli assumed the entire laboratory knew. She wished she could leave immediately to be with her Aunt Magda near Kiev. The bus wheezed to a stop, giving off a loud groan. Insane. Even the machines of the world seemed to know.

Mihaly sat at the back in his usual seat. Juli could see he looked worried and wondered if he already knew about the baby. But Mihaly was not looking at her. Instead he stared out the window and did not turn to her until she sat down.

"Friday at last," she said.

"But tonight I must return to the station," said Mihaly. "I'll only have time to eat and take a short nap." He looked at his watch. "I'm due back at midnight. Sorry, Juli, if my mind is elsewhere. They've already begun reducing power on unit four. Everyone knows she's unstable at low power, yet they invite visitors from other ministries. The elite in Moscow will have their experiment completed for May Day. Idiots."

Juli thought for a moment, and said, "If something goes wrong, isn't it simply a matter of reinserting control rods?"

"Not necessarily," said Mihaly. "The RBMK, she's got tentacles like an octopus. She can go into power surges. We went to the chief engineer last Wednesday, but he still insists on the shutdown. We're doing a goddamned experiment dreamed up in Moscow. Experiment without analysis—it's how we do things at Chernobyl."

Power, machines, industry. What did her unborn baby mean to them?

"What kind of experiment, Mihaly?" When she spoke, her

voice sounded foreign, overly calm, like a mother speaking to a ranting child.

"They want to see how long the turbines can generate emergency power after a shutdown," said Mihaly. "They've picked us to be the guinea pig for the entire system. Moscow engineers wouldn't want to lose any sleep when we can do their experiment. As if we haven't got enough problems."

"What problems?" Again her voice sounded distant.

"There's been a mysterious warning light."

Juli imagined they were discussing how she could have gotten pregnant instead of discussing the reactor. "Mysterious?"

Mihaly turned with a serious look, a technician anxious to solve technical problems. "It's happened twice in the last week. Two separate operators catching a glimpse of a panel light in their peripheral vision. But they were on the other side of the room, and the light was momentary. Today we took turns watching the board constantly because emergency backups were off so they could be worked on. Tomorrow morning, after we shut down, electricians will install lock-on circuits, so once a light comes on, it won't go off until we shut it off. The lock-ons should have been installed in the first place, but parts weren't available when construction was finishing up."

"Awards handed out for completing projects on time." Juli felt as though she had no control over what she said, speaking as if she were one of the machines.

Mihaly went on. "There are things we can fix only when the unit is shut down. Like clogged pipes. And listen to this one. A few weeks ago, an idiot driving a front loader ran into one of the towers carrying power lines into the control building. Luckily he only buckled one of the legs. If he had knocked the tower down and we lost power, we would've been in real trouble. This morning we caught the same driver taking a shortcut through the yard outside the control room. After we shut down, they'll fix the tower, and we've convinced the chief engineer to fence in the area. Mistakes are piling up, and we've got to fix them before they lead to something else."

The guard on the bus interrupted to check their passes. The sign for Pripyat went by on the right, and Juli knew they would be at her stop soon. If only she could see Mihaly on the weekend, tell him then about the baby. In the past, she could have suggested a rendezvous. Mihaly would have met her, because in the past, the meeting would have had another purpose. It was over. The last time they had been together was weeks ago, before she found out she was pregnant.

Mihaly was looking out the window again. The bus passed a field of wildflowers blooming gold and yellow. Juli decided not to tell Mihaly about the baby tonight. Monday would be soon enough. Monday, her supervisor would confirm her medical leave, and then she would tell Mihaly about the baby.

"Will you work all weekend, Mihaly?"

"Yes."

"And you'll still be on the early bus Monday?"

"Yes. Why?"

"Because," said Juli, "I have to arrive early on Monday, too. I'll see you on the early bus. We have to talk . . ."

Mihaly turned to her, gripped her hand. "I don't like being torn apart by my love for you and my obligation to my family. Why can't we simply keep our secret?"

"Big secret," said Juli. "You tell your militiaman brother, and he tells your wife!"

"Laz didn't tell Nina."

"And you believe him?"

Mihaly stared straight ahead, sat silent as if he were a man of great patience waiting for the vixen's tirade to subside. Finally he spoke quietly, calmly.

"The night I returned home from your apartment, I should have guessed Nina knew." He continued staring straight ahead. "But sometimes, even when we know something, we pretend not to know. We should have both known it was over. We shouldn't have seen one another again because it's made this moment harder for both of us."

They sat silent during the remainder of the ride. Before her stop, Juli asked, "Will I still see you on the early bus Monday? It will give us a chance to think over the weekend."

"Yes, I'll be there."

The bus stopped. Mihaly touched her hand lightly. She stared into his eyes, felt an overwhelming urge to kiss him. But she stood, said good night, which seemed inappropriate because the sun was still high in the sky, and left the bus.

Juli looked back as the bus pulled away and saw several passengers watching her. But Mihaly looked straight ahead, his pointed nose and small chin accelerating his movement away from her. The bus resembled the wall of a gallery devoted to portraits of melancholy. Sad faces, brooding faces. And this on a Friday evening before a spring weekend.

Juli turned and walked to her apartment, wondering about a world in which machines took over the lives of the workers. But most of all, she wondered if Pripyat, a town populated to service the Chernobyl reactor, a town neither rural nor urban, was a place in which a child could be raised properly by a single mother.

CHAPTER 9

Friday night in Ukraine was a night of celebration. Even farmers, merchants, and teachers who worked Saturday used Friday night as an excuse to consume large quantities of vodka and wine. Another week of toil was officially over, and one deserved to overindulge. The result of overindulgence was often a deep, satisfying sleep. For many, Saturday began with snores and dreams and, sometimes, nightmares.

Of course, not everyone drank on Friday evening. Major Grigor Komarov of the KGB, for example, had attended a concert featuring the works of Prokofiev at the Philharmonia with his wife. He had consumed not one drop of vodka, not even at dinner beforehand. Now, after midnight, he lay awake in bed, listening to the gentle breathing of his wife. Although he knew exactly where a full bottle of vodka was located, could visualize its sparkle in the rear corner of the cupboard, he was determined to get through the night without a drink. Even if he could not sleep, he would not drink.

Instead of drinking, and instead of sleeping, Komarov lay awake thinking. He thought about recognition. He imagined elaborate schemes and stratagems to bring the name Major Grigor Komarov to the attention of the KGB's chairman in Moscow. He thought about awards and promotions. But even with these thoughts, the bottle in the cupboard tormented him and kept him from dreaming these dreams in the fantasy world of sleep.

Tonight he and his wife sat in the balcony at the concert. He recalled looking down upon the heads on the main floor and imagining himself dancing about on those heads to Prokofiev's music. He imagined using his knife to create a crime he would eventually solve. While the music played, he reached into his pocket and held the knife. He must have smiled because at one point his wife touched his knee. After the concert on their way home, his wife commented on his change of mood the last few weeks, and they engaged in the playful banter they had practiced when they were younger.

"You seem happier, Grigor. I couldn't help but notice. And I'm certain your superiors will notice."

"You're referring to my drinking, of course."

"I thought it might be bad luck to bring it up."

"It's not bad luck, dearest. I'm a new man, free from the bottle. My energy has returned, and I've taken more interest in my job."

"Ferreting out the enemies of Communism?"

"Perhaps, my dear, pointing out the dangers of capitalism."

"Are you referring to my spending habits, Grigor?"

"Your fur wrap might not be needed on such a warm April evening."

"For one who espouses rigid principles, one would think you are an Islamist, Grigor."

"Not me. Religious fanatics keep to themselves and hate civilized communist society. Look at all the problems in Afghanistan from these so-called cultures."

"I thought you hated Gypsies, Grigor. Now your hatred extends to Islamists?"

"Gypsies, Islamists, they're one and the same. Insane, male-dominated societies. Did I tell you about my boyhood in the slums of Moscow among Gypsies? They allow their children to smoke. Eight- and nine-year-old Gypsy boys smoking while the men create swindles and the women read palms. As for Islamists, the men treat their women like animals, making them cover themselves from head to toe in horse blankets. Religion, fundamentalism, and superstition will cause the end of the world if we're not careful."

"You're quite the philosopher tonight, Grigor."

"Abandoning the bottle has awakened my intellect."

"I'm happy for you, Grigor."

Tonight, for the first time in over a year, Komarov and his wife made love. But in the darkness of the room, Komarov thought only of Gretchen. While his wife moaned beneath him, he played back the scene again, this time to the music of Prokofiev. He closed his eyes and saw Gretchen staring at him in those moments before the knife went in.

After his wife was asleep and the night continued its journey, Komarov lay awake, alternately thinking of the vodka bottle in the cupboard, the look on Gretchen's face as she died, the Gypsy witch from the past named Barbara, and of schemes, yet unrealized, as perfect as the Sherbitsky affair.

In central Kiev, Detective Lazlo Horvath of the Kiev militia was also not asleep. Sleep, he hoped, would come much later, perhaps near dawn. The reason he did not want to sleep was because Tamara was in his bed.

It was dark in the room. Lazlo rested his head on Tamara's breast. He could hear her heartbeat. When he spoke, his upper lip brushed against her nipple.

"Can we stay like this forever, Tamara?"

"In this position, or at this age?"

"Both. Especially this age. The position . . ." He touched her thigh and gently spread her legs. "The position I would like to alter quite soon."

Tamara laughed. "I know you would. That's why I'm staying awake."

"You're a spring flower."

Tamara laughed and pulled at his ear. "Spring flower? You've had too much wine."

"I had to drink it before the campaign against alcoholism began."

"Last year it had the reverse effect," said Tamara. "When does this campaign begin?"

"May Day," said Lazlo. "We have only a few days to consume all the Hungarian wine in Kiev. The local wine and the vodka we'll leave to others."

"When Kiev runs out of alcohol and everyone becomes sober and ethical, what will the Kiev militia do?"

"With no criminals, we'll most likely be ordered to crack down on literary journalists."

"Even members of the Ukrainian Writers' Union?"

"Especially members of the Ukrainian Writers' Union. You are the provocateurs who exposed lapses in construction quality at the Chernobyl reactors."

Tamara giggled. "We are spies."

"Better not to say it."

"Why?" asked Tamara.

"Because there really are spies everywhere. My boss wanted me to do a little espionage the other day."

"No."

"When I asked for permission to drive to Pripyat to visit my brother, Chkalov tells me to visit the militia station and check on the captain there. And now, if you are finished questioning me, I'm hungry."

Lazlo lifted his head and moved atop Tamara, who opened beneath him like a vast warm valley. Her tongue filled his mouth and made him feel as though he would never have to eat or drink again. In the distance, as their breathing quickened, the bell of Saint Andrew's Church tolled the one o'clock hour.

Most others in metropolitan Kiev were asleep. Captain Azef of the KGB slept alone, his apartment filled with the sounds of his snoring. Chief Investigator Chkalov of the Kiev militia snored in harmony with his wife, the combined symphony shaking the bed frame.

Farther north along the Dnieper River, farmers and some of their wives also snored. Except for an occasional rendezvous of young lovers in a barn, it seemed the entire world was asleep. In Pripyat, Nikolai dreamed an avalanche of unopened letters buried him, while Pavel dreamed a dream that would have angered his jealous wife. On the other side of town, Juli had just fallen asleep after another long talk with Marina.

In sleep, the joys and fears and desires of life were diminished, making the world calm and peaceful. At dawn the population would begin to scurry about, many of them queuing up at Saturday markets. But for now, speaking in relative terms, all was silent.

At the Chernobyl Nuclear Facility, it was never completely dark or quiet. The security lighting along the fences shimmered in the cooling pond, and the hum of power continued unceasingly. In the yard outside the main control room, extra lighting had been erected, and a crew of workers in hard hats stood about a high-tension tower. Some drank coffee or tea from thermos cups; a few smoked. Two workers held a measuring tape along a slightly bent lower section of the tower.

Inside the main control room, one could not tell whether it was day or night because the room was wrapped in light from the fluorescent fixtures and the glow of the control console. At the sides of the console, which was over fifteen meters long, more light illuminated the room. A crew of electricians had lit up the back of the console in preparation for their work.

The chairs in front of the console had been pushed into the center of the room. No one sat at the chairs. A dozen or so technicians of various grades, from operator first class to engineer third class, stood at the console, concentrating on the lighted panels before them. All of the technicians were dressed identically in off-white uniforms and caps. Several observers, who stood back from the console area, also wore off-white uniforms. Two of the observers were women, but this was only apparent when they were viewed in profile.

The technicians muttered among themselves, careful not to speak loud enough for the observers to hear. They spoke of the weariness of operating what they quietly called "the bitch" under manual control for so many hours. They spoke about the absence of the chief engineer on this special shutdown duty. Several wondered if "bitch number four" would be shut down soon so they could go home. Others joked about the chief engineer referring to each of the units not as bitches, but as toys.

"The chief engineer home asleep while we play with his toy," whispered one operator.

"I'd like to be there," whispered another.

"Playing with his toy?"

"No, in bed with his wife."

Several laughed quietly.

"You wouldn't know what to do."

"I've got experiments to perform."

"You'd have to do them on yourself. Like our experiment here, seeing how long we can keep the power in our system up after the orgasm is shut down."

Several laughed again.

"Keep talking this way," said one of the assistant engineers, "and the director will have you sent to a place where you'll have plenty of time to play with yourselves."

There were a few chuckles, but not the comfortable laughter of earlier.

The supervisor of the electricians walked out from behind the console and stood with his thumbs hooked into his tool belt. "I don't understand. First it's supposed to be down this afternoon, then this evening, now it's already after one in the morning. Up-down. On-off. Nobody knows what they're doing around here."

Mihaly Horvath, the senior engineer in charge, looked from the console to the supervisor of electricians. "Can't you be a little patient? What's all the noise back there?"

"We're removing access panels," said the supervisor. "How much longer before you shut down? Now? Or do we have to wait until Sunday?"

"Not long," said Mihaly. "What's the big hurry?"

"You should know," said the supervisor. "You're the ones who made us come in for this shift. My boss wants us finished with the lock-ons by the end of the shift, but we can't start until you shut this damn thing down."

Mihaly did not answer the supervisor. Instead he gave orders to the other technicians and told them to watch the panel indicators.

The shutdown process had been in progress twenty-four hours. There were signs of boredom, technicians looking at the clock and yawning, something they would not have done if the chief engineer had been on duty.

During the slow process of lowering the control rods while maintaining steam and water flow, various valves and pumps in the system went through many cycles. It was an excellent time to watch for malfunctions. And, theoretically, it should be a safer time because if anything should go wrong, the reactor was already in the process of being shut down.

The effect of bringing down the power of unit four could be heard in the large room containing the turbine and generator. The sound was similar to a jetliner very slowly shutting down its engines, or to a long, drawn-out sigh of relief. But power was not supposed to drop this fast, and a signal was sent to a panel in the main control room.

"I've got a light!" said one of the technicians in a loud whisper.

Others tried to whisper back, but the whispering got louder and louder and eventually changed to shouting.

"What is it?"

"The power is dropping too fast!"

"Why?"

"How the hell do I know?"

"Pavlov, you dog! Where the hell is Pavlov?"

"Stop calling me a dog, idiot! Especially with visitors here!"

"Did you program the computer?"

"For what?"

"To prevent the bitch from dropping below the minimum!"

"I . . . I don't know."

"You don't know? Mother of God! We already hit the minimum, and look how it's falling! Do something! What happened to the alarms? How come there are no alarms?"

"I . . . We shut them off."

"Tasha! Begin the manual procedure for reinserting the control rods!"

"Reinserting?"

"Yes! Now, before it's too late! Someone run and get the computer printouts! You! Is your foot still in your mother? Run and get them!"

Several minutes went by, during which the technicians who were not at the console went to the console. Everyone was visibly shaken as they watched the semicircle of lights and gauges. Their expressions conveyed confusion, annoyance, fear, and everything in between.

"I don't know what's happening!" said one technician. "First the pressure is down, then it's up!"

"Same with the temperature!" said another technician. "It's the highest I've seen! Wait! It's not going down! There's something wrong with the cooling system! Core temperature up two hundred!"

"All right!" shouted Mihaly, stepping back from the console. "Bring her under control with the backups! Open the primary cooling backup valve slowly! Sergei, call out the temperature changes!"

"But this afternoon . . ." said one of the technicians.

"What about it?"

"The chief had us turn off the backups so we could work on those first."

"They're still off?"

"Yes."

"Sergei!"

"Up another fifty! It's out of control! The fucking rods won't go in! Do something!"

During this exchange, the supervisor of the electricians looked to the ceiling and shook his head. Then he went behind the console and could be heard cursing.

Amid the cursing and confusion at the console, more and more lights came on. Technicians began retreating from the console as a group, resembling children being told to line up in a hallway. Eventually, they gathered beneath the recessed ceiling lights above a conference table in the center of the room. The conference table was often used for meetings and discussions. Their automatic movement to the conference table was an indication that problem solving was needed, and in a hurry. As they gathered beneath the bright overhead lights, many began shouting at one another. No one sat at the chairs around the table. The few who did not shout stood about waiting for orders. Several demanded a solution from Mihaly, and he broke from the group to survey the entire console. When he turned back to the others, the determined look on his face silenced them.

"Everyone get back to their stations!" shouted Mihaly.

While the men returned to the console, Mihaly grabbed one of the technicians by the arm, and headed for the door at the side of the room.

While running, Mihaly shouted, "We'll have to open the lines manually! I'll get the intake valve! You take care of the steam valve! The rest of you stay at the console!"

When Mihaly and the other technician were gone, the remaining technicians glanced alternately to one another, then to the lights flashing on the console. The supervisor of electricians came out from behind the console, followed by two electricians.

"What's going on?" demanded the supervisor of electricians. "Why have the visitors gone away?"

"We were too busy to notice!" shouted one of the technicians. "You tell us why they left! You probably fucked something up back there!"

The supervisor of electricians ran at the technician with his fist raised. "All we did was remove a couple of panels! We didn't touch a damn thing!"

The accusing technician backed away. "How did I know? I thought you might have started working on the circuits!"

The supervisor of electricians glanced at the lights flashing on the console, then shook his fist in the accuser's face. "You'd better not try to blame us for this!" He turned to the others. "None of you!"

The other technicians ignored the supervisor of electricians. Instead they stood at the console, staring wide-eyed at the flashing lights at their stations the way children stare wide-eyed when trapped in an impossible situation. The lights from the console surrounding the technicians gave their off-white uniforms a pinkish hue. When an alarm bell began ringing, everyone froze, standing perfectly still and silent.

A few seconds later, there was an explosion that shook the control room. Dust fell from the ceiling, and the plastic shields from several overhead lights clattered to the floor.

"The core!" shouted someone.

"No! Idiot! A steam line!"

"Get out!"

"We can't! We have to go in there!"

The control console was even brighter now. Hundreds of red lights were glowing in the room like a fire from hell.

After double-checking his gauges, one of the more knowledgeable technicians backed quickly from the console, slamming into the conference table and falling on his back. He wriggled on the table for a moment like an upturned turtle. A few smiled back at him, but stopped smiling when they saw the look on his face. When the technician got off the table, he shouted. "I'm reading more than a thousand rems in the turbine room! If we don't get the fuck out of here, we'll all be dead!"

Everyone in the control room remained frozen for another moment until first one, then another, then all of the men began running for the exit at the rear of the control room. None of them went to the door at the side of the room that lead to the turbine room and the reactors, the door through which Mihaly and another technician had disappeared shortly before the explosion.

In the turbine room of unit four, the sound of the turbine slowing down had reached a low pitch, almost a moan. Off to the side, there was another moan, the feeble moan of the technician who had run from the control room with Mihaly. The technician lay trapped beneath a massive section of steam line blown from the side of the turbine by the explosion.

Nearer the turbine, superheated steam from the reactor gushed upward, blowing out skylights, knocking down sections of catwalk. The room became engulfed in a hot fog. Mihaly crawled on the floor to the man trapped beneath the steam line and began pulling on the man's arms. Nearby electrical fires and sparks lit up the fog in alternate hues of orange and blue.

Across the cooling pond on the narrow strip of land separating the pond from the Pripyat River, waterfowl settled back down after being startled by the steam explosion. Back at the plant, ghost-like figures ran across the yard of the lighted complex. One of the ghostlike figures jumped onto the rear bumper of a utility truck speeding away. Shouts of panic could be heard across the pond as faint whimpers in the night.

Soon after the running figures disappeared beyond the bright lights of the main reactor complex, the core of unit four exploded. From across the pond it appeared as if the roof of the building had been severed and lifted slowly and quietly by a cauldron of flame. Then the sound and the shock wave hit, and all the creatures of the pond were startled from their sleep.

The roof broke into several pieces, turning end over end. Flames shot into the air, lifting fragments that glowed and arced in the sky like fireworks. Flames emerging from the shell of the building lit up the sky and made the thick, black smoke from unit four into a monster dancing in the gentle spring breeze.

It was 1:23 a.m. on Saturday, April 26, and something was very wrong at Chernobyl.

CHAPTER 10

Juli sat up, threw back the blanket, and turned on the lamp, expecting to see Marina's bed empty beside hers, expecting Marina to be in the bathroom or the kitchenette because it would account for the sound. But Marina was in bed, her hair fanned out on the pillow. The clock on the lamp table showed it was after one in the morning.

"Marina. Are you asleep?"

Marina stirred, turned her face away from the light. "Hmm?"

"Marina?"

"Time to get up already?"

"No. It's only 1:30."

"Good. I need my beauty sleep."

"You didn't hear anything?"

Marina turned to Juli, shaded her eyes with her hand. "Was it the neighbors again?"

"It sounded like an explosion," said Juli. "I was asleep, and it woke me."

"Maybe the baby kicked."

Juli held her stomach with both hands. "So soon?"

"I'm joking," said Marina. "It's probably Mihaly tossing stones at the window. Wants to know what was bothering you after work today . . . I mean yesterday. Go to sleep. It's the middle of the night and I have to work at the store early. They're probably already in line to complain to me, as if I can do anything about the idiotic sizes the supplier ships."

Marina turned away from the light, wrapped the pillow about her head. All was silent except . . . except what? Juli stopped breathing and listened. The balcony. There was someone on the balcony! She could hear voices through the glass door and curtains.

"Marina. Listen."

Marina sat up with her eyes closed, opened her eyes, stared at the closed curtains. "Who could be out there this time of night?" Marina got out of bed and walked to the window. "Shut off the light so I can look out."

After Juli turned out the light, Marina parted the curtains. "People are down in the courtyard."

"Who?"

"From ground-floor apartments, I guess. They've got coats on over their bedclothes."

"What are they doing?"

"Looking at the sky. Looking at something orange in the sky."

Outside, a steady breeze blew out of the south. Neighbors in the courtyard resembled plump birds standing about nodding to one another. Everyone wore coats. Showing below the coats were pajamas, nightshirts, nightgowns, and, in some cases, bare legs and bony white ankles. The neighbors stood looking south between Juli's building and the next building.

"It's the atomic plant," said one man. "My brother works there.

Thank God he's not there now."

"Maybe it's a grass fire," said another.

"They're burning palms for Palm Sunday," slurred a man who was obviously drunk.

"It's something for May Day," said yet another man, this one not drunk. "They're clearing a field for the parade."

"Idiots!" said a woman. "They don't burn palms until later, for the next Ash Wednesday. Who would purposely start a fire in the middle of the night?"

"Today is the Saturday of Lazarus," said a woman in a soft voice. "At our church they ran short of palms and they'll use pussy willows this Sunday. A man who lives on Lesya Ukrainka Street was running home when I came out. He said the fir and pine forests are on fire."

"Not a forest fire," said a heavy woman in furry slippers, an overcoat, and a babushka. "Didn't you hear the explosion? It knocked me out of bed."

Two teenaged boys behind the woman laughed, and she turned about to scowl at them. The boys' faces were lit orange by the glow from the sky.

"Look," said one of the men. "Sparks flying. And smoke."

"It's poisonous," said the heavy woman. "It probably has atoms in it."

Another man who had been standing silently to the side said, "Of course it has atoms in it. Everything is made of atoms."

Juli stood with Marina, watching the sky.

"Is it dangerous?" whispered Marina.

The glow in the sky became more sinister as a column of black smoke leaned to the north and merged with the clouds.

Marina held Juli's arm. "You said Mihaly was working tonight. Can't you call him and find out about this? I'm sure he's all right."

"Hey," said one of the men. "You work at the plant. What do you think this is?"

"Juli, he's talking to you. They want to know if you know anything." Marina turned to the group of people gathering slowly like penguins. "She doesn't know anything. We heard you out here and came to see what was going on."

"But she works there in a laboratory. A technician should know what's happening."

"Juli," whispered Marina, "say something."

"I don't know anything," said Juli. "Some of you must also work at the plant."

"Even so, you are a technician," said one of the men. "Therefore, you must have special knowledge of what's going on. You must know if there's danger for us."

"Why us?" said the large woman.

"Radiation," said the man. "If a reactor explodes, it releases radioactive fallout like a bomb."

Several heads turned to look at the glow in the sky. At the far end of the courtyard, a woman sobbed loudly as she ran outside.

"The phone!" screamed the woman. "My husband! He's there tonight, and the phone is dead! Something terrible has happened!"

The man who had mentioned radioactive fallout turned back to Juli. "I know you work in the radiation measurement laboratory. If one of the reactors exploded and there is radiation leaking out, tell us what we should do."

The man walked directly in front of Juli. Marina stepped up to the man. "She doesn't know anything. Because she works there doesn't mean she had anything to do with this."

"I didn't mean it was her doing," said the man. "I simply want to know if there's anything we can do to protect ourselves."

"Yes," said Juli.

"Speak up!" shouted the heavy woman. "We can't hear you!"

"Yes! If there was an explosion and if the explosion involved one of the reactors, the initial radiation will be airborne." She looked to the sky, the dark column of smoke crawling upward. "The best thing to do is go to your apartments. Stay inside and close all the windows. Keep the outside air from coming in as much as possible."

"Then what?" asked the man.

Juli looked from one shadowed face to another. "If there is radiation, the authorities will tell us what to do. But it could be smoke from any fire. It could be nothing."

The sound of a car traveling at high speed came from the main road at the front of the apartment complex. Tires squealed as the car drove through the curve in the road beyond the apartments. After the car passed, a truck came, its lights flashing in the trees. When the truck appeared for a moment between buildings, Juli saw figures in off-white uniforms hanging onto the back.

An hour later, Juli sat on the edge of the bed, looking at the curtains closed over the balcony door. Even if the curtains had been open, she wouldn't have been able to see anything because the balcony faced north. After coming up the stairs, they had run to look out the south-facing window at the far end of the hallway. The fire was definitely at the Chernobyl plant. Flames leapt into the sky at the base of its towers, and Juli knew the glow in the sky meant death.

Marina sat cross-legged behind Juli on the bed, massaging Juli's shoulders as she spoke. "There's nothing you can do," said Marina. "Worrying about it won't help. Even if it was the number four reactor, Mihaly would have been one of the first out of there because he would have known if something was going wrong. He's home right now, sealed in his apartment."

"Mihaly wouldn't have left, Marina. There's no answer at the plant switchboard. They were going to do a shutdown. And now there's no answer . . ."

"How bad could it be?" asked Marina. "My Vasily lives closer to the plant than we do. I wish he had a phone so I could call him. What about the dosimeter you put out on the balcony? Will the do-simeter tell us if it's safe?"

Juli stood, walked to the balcony door, and opened the curtains. She slid the door open a few centimeters, reached quickly outside, pulled the dosimeter inside, and slammed the door.

"You should have asked me to get it," said Marina.

"Why? You said it's probably nothing."

Juli took the dosimeter into the bathroom, turned on the bright overhead light, and held the small lens to her eye. At first she thought she saw the hairline resting at zero. But it was only the zero marker line. Then she thought there was no hairline, and she had trouble keeping the markings in the dosimeter in focus. Her hand shook, so she held the dosimeter with both hands, steadying her knuckles against her forehead.

The hairline was where she had never seen it during her years at the laboratory. If turned in to the rack on Monday morning, it would bring a crew of safety technicians down into the sub-basement to re-move her from the vicinity of the sensitive counting equipment.

Marina spoke from behind Juli. "What does it say?"

Juli turned and did her best to remain calm. "Thirty millirems."

"Is that a lot?" asked Marina.

"Some workers are exposed to as much as a thousand millirems a year. Anything above five thousand a year is considered dangerous."

"Then it's okay, Juli. See? It's fine. Everyone will be fine. Mihaly and Vasily . . . everyone."

"How long did I leave it on the balcony?"

"I don't know," said Marina. "Maybe half an hour."

Juli worked out the figures in her head. It was no use remaining calm. "At this rate, in a day outside on the balcony, the exposure would have been over a thousand. In five days it would have been beyond the danger level. We're three kilometers from the explosion, and the worst of the radioactivity might not even be here yet!"

Juli turned, placed the dosimeter on the edge of the sink, and began washing her hands and arms vigorously, especially her right because it had reached out into the blackness to retrieve the dosimeter.

"But if something's happened, where's the militia?" asked Marina, looking worried.

The ceiling began shaking with a pounding vibration, rattling the balcony door. "What's that?" screamed Marina.

Juli looked up as the pounding became louder before suddenly fading. "A helicopter heading to the plant."

"Should we go out and see?"

Juli went to Marina and held her shoulders. She spoke in a voice that did not seem her own. "We'll stay here. Technically I should go to the plant because I'm a dosimetrist, and in the event of a spill, I should be monitoring the area. But this is no spill. This is a disaster."

Not everyone in Pripyat was frightened. Many slept as moist air swept through open windows. Others, even though they knew of the explosion, did not believe radiation could be allowed to be let loose. Dawn would bring action. Weren't there plenty of sirens now? Weren't firemen being called to extra duty? Obviously the explosion, and the resulting fire, was something entirely controllable? To some, even the metallic taste and smell in the air was a good sign. "Nothing but an ordinary industrial fire," they said.

Lectures from Juli's classes years earlier in Moscow haunted her. Strontium, krypton-85, cesium-137, and the concerns of her co-worker Aleksandra Yasinsky—all of these things from her years of training and working with radiation took on new meaning. Not because of concern for herself, but because of the vulnerability of the baby growing inside her.

And what about Mihaly? One second she imagined Mihaly and his co-workers safe inside the bunker beneath the administration building. The next second she imagined him at home with his wife, both of them looking out their balcony window facing the plant. Yes, Mihaly either at home or in the bunker. In the bunker briefing the power plant Party secretary on the explosion and what could be done. Both of them tying up the phone lines calling in more helicopters. Mihaly and the Party secretary filling in KGB operatives on duty. Mihaly in charge to make sure no one was killed or injured, especially the young, especially the unborn, especially his child growing this very moment inside her.

While Juli watched Marina use the last of the cellophane tape on the side of the sliding door, reality returned. The world she had known was ended. Perhaps the world everyone had known was ended. The great environmental disaster had come, not slowly as Aleksandra had been predicted, but with great speed.

Juli and Marina stuffed rolled-up wet towels at the bottoms of the doors, taped the windows, even taped a plastic bag over the exhaust vent above the stove. There was nothing to do but seal themselves inside and wait. Sealed inside like babes in a womb.

With a shaking hand, Juli held the dosimeter up to the light again.

"What does it say now?" asked Marina.

"Still at thirty."

"And it doesn't mean it's thirty now?"

"No. It's a cumulative measure. Since it was recharged at the lab, it's accumulated thirty millirems. As long as it doesn't keep going up, we're fine. Even if it goes up a little, we'll be okay. At least in here."

"How long will the radioactive dust or smoke or whatever it is stay in the air?"

"Until it blows away. But if the reactor keeps sending out more . . ."

Marina crossed the room, turned on the radio again, switched between the three stations they could receive. Beethoven on one, Prokofiev on another, some jazz on the third. Next she tried the television. Still too early, only snow.

"Why don't they say anything?" asked Marina. "And Vasily lives so close to the plant. I hope he was out somewhere. At one of those men's clubs in Pripyat, drinking himself silly. He's such a joker. He's . . ."

Juli and Marina looked to the ceiling as more helicopters flew over. They hugged until the helicopters passed.

"Why can't Vasily go somewhere where there's a phone and call me? Why is his mother so cheap she can't have a phone?"

Juli looked to the balcony, where Mihaly had held her and kissed her last winter. Everything seemed so long ago. She picked up the phone, dialed the number at the plant, and, again, received a busy signal after a wait of several minutes.

A little past six in the morning, the electricity went out, and Marina brought out her portable radio. At six thirty, the curtains over the balcony door looked the way they did any other morning before work. The glow of day bringing life to the world. But there was not the yellow glow of sunrise on the edges of the curtains. The morning was overcast.

At seven o'clock, Juli tried the plant again, received a busy signal. Without knowing what she would say, she dialed Mihaly's home number.

As the phone rang, Juli imagined Mihaly answering, pretending he was talking with someone else, telling her everything was fine. A small explosion, some release of radiation, and he was fine. But the phone kept ringing.

On the far side of the room, Marina picked up a glass egg she had transferred from a shelf to her bed when the helicopters began flying over. She held the egg in both hands. "No one answers," she whispered. "In the legend, Easter eggs must be decorated every year, or the world will end. No one will answer because they are decorating eggs."

When Juli hung up the phone, Marina came to her, and they hugged.

Meanwhile, several residents with apartments facing the street held curtains apart and watched as a tanker truck came from the center of town, rinsing the street. The water draining into the sewers was dark with a metallic luster.

CHAPTER 11

Although it was Saturday and Nikolai knew he and Pavel were not due back in their stuffy PK room at the Pripyat post office until Monday, here was Pavel at his door. Pavel wore jeans, his hair was messed up, he needed a shave, and he kept glancing up and down the hallway.

"What do you want?" asked Nikolai.

"Let me in. I don't want to speak out here."

Once the door was closed, Nikolai pulled his robe more tightly about his waist and went to the bedroom adjoining the small living area. "I have a business matter to discuss with an associate," he said into the bedroom before closing the door.

Nikolai and Pavel sat at the small table in the kitchenette.

Nikolai nodded to the bedroom. "Without company, it would be a lonely weekend."

"I keep forgetting you are not blessed with a wife."

"Sarcasm?" asked Nikolai.

"Perhaps," said Pavel. "But more importantly, Captain Putna called early this morning. We're getting a new assignment."

"Not at the post office?"

"There's been an explosion at the Chernobyl plant, and Captain Putna has put the PK on special duty."

"What kind of duty? What happened at the plant? Is it sabotage?"

Pavel glanced to the bedroom door, which remained closed. He leaned forward over the table and spoke softly. "I'm surprised you didn't hear it. One of the reactors exploded. Early this morning there was a crimson glow in the sky. Now there's smoke spreading north. Captain Putna says it's not an ordinary fire. Radiation may have been released, but we're not supposed to talk about it. Some technicians working at the plant have been seen fleeing the area. On the way here, I saw people out on their balconies. Even though they've been told to remain indoors, they get a great view from the upper floors."

"Who told them to remain indoors?" asked Nikolai. "No one told me."

"You and your friend have remained indoors, haven't you?"

"What's an accident at the plant got to do with us? What about those ministries? Medium Machine Building or Energy and Electrification. Aren't they in charge?"

Pavel took a notebook from his inside jacket pocket, opened it to a page, and put it on the table. He spoke softly, glancing occasionally to the closed bedroom door. "Captain Putna says he's not sure if it involves sabotage, but we need to investigate the possibility."

"Is it the Gypsy Moth theory we heard about?" asked Nikolai.

"What Gypsy Moth theory?"

"Don't you remember? We were watching for mention of the code name in correspondence. We put it in our report to Captain Putna."

"Pure speculation," said Pavel. He pointed to the open page of his notebook. "Here are the facts. We've been given a list of Chernobyl employees and their addresses. Some have been ordered to the plant to assist emergency personnel but have refused to go. Some were under observation before this happened."

Nikolai took Pavel's notebook, studied the list. "A familiar name or two. Especially Juli Popovics and Mihaly Horvath, the lovebirds. I thought Juli Popovics was pregnant and went to visit her aunt in Visenka."

"If you remember our last report, she's to go there next month," said Pavel.

"Does Captain Putna think a pregnant woman is involved in sabotage?"

"I don't know what Captain Putna thinks," said Pavel. "I know only of this list of people we've been ordered to report on. Captain Putna said Major Komarov is angrier than shit and wants to know the cause of the explosion. Komarov is heading up the investigation himself."

"This radiation," said Nikolai, "do you think it's dangerous?"

"They're hosing down streets on the south side of town." Pavel stood and pulled the chain on the overhead light, but the light did not come on. "The electricity is out at my place, too."

"I hadn't noticed. We didn't need lights." Nikolai smiled, then became serious. "What about your wife?"

Pavel walked to the window, looked up at the mix of smoke and clouds in the overcast sky. "I put her on the early bus to Kiev."

"Were there others on the bus?" asked Nikolai.

"The bus was full," said Pavel.

From inside a helicopter flying at a thousand meters, the fire looked like a kerosene smudge pot used to mark road construction. But as the helicopter flew closer, vibrating violently because of the heavy load of sand swinging below, the fire grew in size.

The helicopter pilot steered south, staying out of the cloud of bluish smoke. He dropped to five hundred meters and saw the spray from several fire hoses below. At one hundred meters, individual firemen were visible. Masks with cylindrical snouts covered the firemen's faces. In their masks and coats and hats, the firemen looked like multicolored beetles.

"It's a graphite fire!" shouted the pilot.

"Graphite's supposed to stop the neutrons!" screamed the co-pilot. "Drop the load and go!"

Inside the low-level counting laboratory, two technicians in off-white caps who had just climbed the stairs from the basement watched the helicopter drop its load of sand and disappear beyond the trees to the west. The man and woman stayed inside the double doors of the building. On the road out front, an ambulance headed for the fire. From where they stood, the man and woman could not see the fire, but they saw the thick smoke rising to the north.

"The graphite is burning," said the woman. "What should we do?"

"The explosion must have cracked the concrete shell," said the man. "We have no choice but to stay inside."

"We've been here for hours with no word," said the woman, heading for a rack on the wall near the door. She took several dosimeters from the rack and began looking into them, aiming one after another at the dull light coming through the glass doors. "They're all at two hundred already. I thought the building was sealed."

The man behind her walked slowly backward away from the doors. "If we've already picked up two hundred millirems up here . . ."

The woman turned. "Where are you going?"

"Back to the basement. If there's still water, I'm going to shower. Then I'm staying down there until this is over. Are you coming?"

The woman dropped the dosimeters to the tile floor and followed the man, removing her off-white cap and throwing it aside as she ran.

Outside the building, farther along the road to Pripyat, a crowd had gathered at the crossroads beyond the main gate. Several vehicles were parked about, some militia and fire vehicles and a few private cars. The crowd consisted mostly of uniformed firemen, militiamen, and plant guards. But there was also a group of civilians who had been stopped at the crossroads, several men and women and even a few children. Many stared at the column of smoke in the distance.

An argument began between civilians and militiamen. A few men among the civilians began pushing and shoving, causing some women to scream. One young woman, slender, wearing a jacket over a cotton dress, held a little girl in one arm while holding the hand of another girl some years older. When a fireman wearing a filter mask approached and swept the slender probe of a Geiger counter in front of the woman and the two little girls, the woman backed away, and the little girls stared wide-eyed.

An ambulance sped to the gate from the plant. Instead of driving through, it skidded to a stop, the rear doors flew open, and at least a dozen firemen with blackened coats piled out. All of the firemen wore filter masks.

The fireman with the Geiger counter waved the probe frantically over the returned firemen and shouted obscenities through his filter mask. A bus drove up, and militiamen, firemen, and guards herded the civilians onto the bus like cattle. One fireman asked the woman with the two little girls the name of the youngest.

"Ilonka!" cried the woman. "Ilonka Horvath! She wants to know what's become of her father, Mihaly Horvath!"

"I don't know," said the fireman, taking the little girl into his arms. "No one is allowed inside the facility except emergency workers. Come, Ilonka! Come, Mother! Hurry! The bus will take us to safety!" The fireman ran onto the bus ahead of the mother and the other little girl.

"Everyone get on the bus!" shouted a militiaman.

"But my car . . ." said one of the men.

"To hell with your car!" screamed the militiaman.

After the bus sped off, two militiamen wearing handkerchiefs over their noses and mouths stood together, looking at a man who had just driven up.

"KGB guard from the Belarussian border."

"How can you tell?"

"He's driving a Zhiguli instead of a Volga, and when he opened the window, I saw his green uniform."

"He didn't leave the window open long."

"Not with this smell in the air. It's like eating coins."

Militiamen and plant guards moved aside as several buses rolled through the crossroads and headed down the road to Pripyat.

"I wonder how many buses are coming," said one militiaman after the buses drove off. "Those came all the way from Kiev."

"Yes, I saw the markings."

"I wish I was in Kiev."

The militiamen went silent, glancing at the KGB border guard in his green uniform who had gotten out of the Zhiguli and begun questioning plant guards.

The dashboard of the car was covered with a wet towel, and wet rags were stuffed into the side vents. From the back seat, Juli could see the road between Marina and her boyfriend, Vasily. Vasily's hair was dark, like Mihaly's. Despite black smoke obscuring the horizon, everything looked normal outside. A couple walking a dog, and a man on a bicycle, a school in session, brightly-lit inside with students raising their hands to a teacher at the front of the classroom.

"It's an upside-down world," said Vasily. "In some places, people are in a panic. Like at the hydrofoil dock on the river when they found out the run to Kiev was cancelled. But in other places, people go about their daily business."

Vasily had come to the apartment to get Marina. He was aware of an explosion at Chernobyl, but because of the news blackout, did not know any details. Vasily was driving them the few blocks to Mihaly's apartment to find out if Mihaly was home, to find out if Nina was there, to find out anything they could. To convince Vasily to take them, Juli had voiced her concern for Mihaly's little girls, children who would be most susceptible to radiation.

So long as they sealed the car and stayed inside, they would be as safe as in the apartment. Juli held the dosimeter up to the light. Forty millirems, another ten while they ran to the car, or inside the car because of Vasily's drive from the village on the other side of the Chernobyl plant. Juli would check the dosimeter every few minutes. If there were increases, she would tell Vasily to hurry back to the apartment.

A militia car rushed past in the opposite direction, ignoring Vasily's high speed.

"I saw plenty of them while driving here," said Vasily. "The militia speeding around like maniacs. City workers washing streets. No wonder some people assume everything is normal."

"What was it like nearer the plant?" asked Juli.

"Never mind how it is near the plant," said Vasily, briefly turning to Juli in the back seat. "You can't go there!"

"I know," said Juli. "I simply wondered."

"Some private cars, all heading for Kiev. I saw people walking south. They carried suitcases. One farmer leading his livestock looked like Noah going to the ark. There were buses lined up on the side of the road outside Pripyat, but there didn't seem to be a plan. When I saw firemen with masks, I kept everything shut up and even tied on the handkerchief. Momma and my sister are doing what you did. All sealed up inside the house."

"But you live closer to the plant," said Juli.

"I know," said Vasily.

At Mihaly's apartment building, all three ran in as fast as they could, went up the stairs, and down the hall. Juli knocked on the door. Knocked again more loudly. A woman with a cane came out of the apartment next door.

"They went somewhere," said the woman.

"All of them?" asked Juli.

"The mother and her little girls. I told her I'd watch them, but she insisted. She drove with a neighbor to the plant. They both have husbands there. She left the door open, so I closed it." The woman glanced at Vasily. "I'm watching the apartment."

"Did Mihaly Horvath come home this morning?" asked Juli.

"No, I told you. He's at the plant with Yuri Skabichevsky. Their wives went to see about them. I can see flames from my window. You want to come in and look?"

"We're in a hurry," said Vasily, leading Juli and Marina back to the stairs.

The woman followed. "Only eight days until Easter, and something like this. Thank God my husband works at the radio factory. Some children went to school, so everything is fine. The firemen are in control. Irina Kiseleva's husband is a fireman. She is very proud. She told me many technicians are from Russia or Hungary. She criticizes their aloofness at times, but I always disagree with her . . . because of my neighbors, the Horvaths. Are you sure you don't want to look at the fire from my window?"

On their way back to the apartment, Vasily drove through a downtown marketplace to see if there was any news posted. But the board at the entrance to the market street contained nothing about the explosion or the danger of radiation.

"I wonder how the radiation will affect the food," said Marina.

"Because of the wind, Belarussia will get it worse," said Juli, looking up at the sky.

"What can be done for the children?" asked Marina.

"They'll give them potassium iodide."

"Will it prevent illness?"

"It will help," said Juli.

Vasily turned the corner at Selskom Market, the largest food store in Pripyat. Instead of an orderly line on the sidewalk, today's line was thick and spilled into the street. The line undulated and wagged its tail as those farther back moved side to side, looking to the front.

Vasily stopped the car across the street from Selskom Market. "This is insanity. No children on the streets and not even many women means trouble."

"Mostly men in line," said Marina. "Angry men."

As she said this, a man squeezing out the doorway with a package under his arm was shoved to the ground. The man got up and hurried away, turning to curse at the others. When Vasily put the car in gear, a plump young woman squeezed through the crowd and walked quickly, ignoring the angry stares and calls of those in line. The woman carried two fishnet bags so full they dragged on the ground. A plump woman . . .

"I know her," said Juli. "Her name is Natalya. She works in my building. She might be able to tell us something."

"Should we give her a ride?" asked Vasily.

"Look!" said Marina. "One of the men from the line is chasing her."

Vasily drove to the other side of the street and pulled to the curb.

Juli opened the back door. "Get in, Natalya!"

Natalya hesitated a moment, looked behind at the approaching man, then squeezed into the back of the car with her load of groceries. The man shouted, "Jewess!" as they drove away.

"What's going on?" asked Juli.

"Everyone wants . . . food," said Natalya, catching her breath. "It's best to get food . . . now before it becomes contaminated. Canned foods . . ."

Juli interrupted. "I meant, what's going on at the plant?"

"Oh," said Natalya, gathering her bags about her. "There's a fire in one of the reactors. I talked to a man who was there. He said it exploded, and it's still burning. He said to stay indoors, seal yourself up. But I needed food. My apartment's to the left up here."

"Did this man say anything about injuries?"

"He thinks several may have been injured. The explosion blew the roof off."

"Did he tell you names of victims?"

"No names. But he said there were many ambulances. People walking around in some streets like nothing's happened, and at the market there were all these rumors. One man said they were evacuating Kopachi. Another said since Kopachi is the closest village to the plant, there might not be anyone to evacuate. Someone said they saw the Pripyat Party boss driving out of town in his white Volga. Another said a man who was fishing at the river returned home with his face turned beet red. Slavs . . . we are of the same mind. We believe in death."

Natalya looked out the window and shouted. "Stop here!"

Before she got out of the car, Natalya placed two cans of beans on the back seat. "Thanks for the ride."

Juli looked out the back window at Natalya scurrying up the walk to her building. Then she looked into the dosimeter.

"What does it say now?" asked Marina.

"Almost sixty," said Juli.

No matter what Juli or Marina said, there was no way to stop Vasily from leaving the apartment and driving closer to the burning reactor in order to retrieve his mother and sister.

"Won't they be safer in the house?" asked Marina.

"The house leaks like a sieve," said Vasily. "I should have brought them with me earlier."

Vasily tied a scarf about his head, another over his mouth and nose. "Do I look like an old babushka?"

"Be careful," said Marina.

"I will," said Vasily. "When I get back, I'll rip out the seat covers before I come inside. Find some clothes for my sister and Mama. Have a full tub of water in case there's no pressure. Gather up food for the trip. We'll head for Kiev as soon as I get back."

Vasily paused before opening the door. "Don't worry, we'll all go to Kiev for Thursday's May Day parade and be back here the following week after things have cooled down."

Marina sat next to Juli on her bed. "It's the only thing we can do, Juli. You said yourself we must leave. Especially your little passenger."

"But I wish I knew what's become of Mihaly," said Juli. "And his wife going there, taking her little girls and going there . . ."

"The old woman said they left when it was dark. Nobody knew about the radiation yet. Maybe Mihaly called and they went to meet him. They could be in Kiev by now."

Juli and Marina hugged, and Juli stared at the curtains over the balcony door through which she had first heard the explosion, then voices, early in the morning. Not even a full day had gone by, yet it seemed like weeks. When Vasily returned and they left for Kiev, more time would have gone by, and Juli wondered if, somehow, she might be able to forget Mihaly. But even as she thought this, she knew it would be impossible, especially because of the baby. Her baby.

CHAPTER 12

Tamara Petrov spent all of Saturday at Lazlo's apartment. They made love, ate, danced to Hungarian records, made love again. They went to a nearby market, bought ingredients for *paprikas* chicken, went back to the apartment, and prepared the meal together. They did not watch television or listen to the radio. The phone rang once during the afternoon, but when Lazlo answered, there was simply a hum, the phones broken again.

After they finished dinner, Tamara got up and put on one of Lazlo's Lakatos Gypsy Orchestra records. The melancholy violin seemed especially sad this night, and Lazlo wondered why. The evening was only beginning, Tamara was wearing nothing but a silk robe, and already the Gypsy was foreseeing its end. Tamara came back to the table, poured more wine. Her eyes were aglow from the candle between them on the table.

"I can't tell if you're melancholy from the music or simply relaxed," said Tamara.

"Relaxed," said Lazlo.

"The last time we were together you acted this way. Initially you measure our time together with a stopwatch. This morning I expected Olympic judges to rush in and tell us we were late for the gold-medal ceremony."

"It's my bachelor life," said Lazlo. "Our first time together after so long makes me act like a boy on his first encounter."

Tamara touched her chest above her breasts. "Some boy. Last night you seemed a dozen boys making up for lost time."

"How do you put up with me?"

"I know you," said Tamara. "I enjoy our seasonal visits. But you should see other women, Lazlo. Life is too short to wait for what you want."

"What do I want?"

Tamara laughed. "Like me, you don't know what you want. We are urban Gypsies, you and I. Instead of traveling from one place to another, we stay in one place. But we still have the need to roam. So we let our desires roam. What do you think, Laz? Is it a good theory?"

"The best I've heard."

"Did you ever come close to marriage?"

The candle on the table reminded Lazlo of church, of candlelight glowing on perspiring faces, of the wedding of Mihaly and Nina. "The closest I ever came to marriage was when I was best man for my brother's wedding."

Tamara laughed. "You are a strange man. You fill your life with melancholy. Militia work is like many of our ministries. Gloomy places. The gloominess overflows even into the streets and parks where babushkas sweep sidewalks and watch for unjustified laughter. But here in your home, you are supposed to shed your gloominess."

"There must be times when I'm cheerful. I simply don't show it."

"Are there times you are able to forget the boy on the Romanian border?"

Lazlo stared into Tamara's dark eyes. "When I'm with you, of course."

"I'm serious. Think about it. When are you truly happy?"

He stared into Tamara's eyes and thought about it.

"Listen to Lakatos on the violin. The way each note stretches to its limit as if he's reluctant to let go and face silence. Call it melancholy, or blame the incident on the Romanian border. But it's more complicated. Tonight, for some reason, the silence at the end of the song seems closer."

Tamara's eyes glistened in the light of the candle as she stared at him. They stayed this way for several minutes, holding hands and staring as if they could read one another's thoughts.

Then Tamara blew out the candle and led Lazlo past the phonograph where the violin of Lakatos cried in the darkness. They danced, swayed in one another's arms until the record was over. They went into the bedroom where the breeze from the south made the sheets cool and moist and fragrant.

After dark, with windows and even the space beneath the door sealed with damp towels, it was impossible to tell what the weather was like outside. The apartment was warm and stuffy. From her bed Juli saw Marina outlined against the faint glow of night light from the patio door.

"Are candles still lit in windows?" asked Juli.

"Yes," said Marina. "It reminds me of Christmas."

"Can you see smoke?"

"No. The sky is too dark."

"I wonder if it's still burning."

"If so, it can't be as bad as this morning when we could see the glow of flames." Marina let the parted curtains close and sat on the edge of Juli's bed. "It's so quiet. Everyone who has a car has probably left. Do you think it's still dangerous to be outside?"

Juli touched the dosimeter on the night table. "I looked a few minutes ago. It's going up about a millirem every hour. Outside it must be higher."

"Should we shower again?"

"No. Save the water in the tub." Juli sat up, put her arm about Marina's shoulder. "Save it for Vasily and his mother and sister because the water pressure is dropping. They'll be here, Marina. Vasily knows how to take care."

There was a rapid hammering above, which grew louder and louder.

"Another helicopter," said Marina.

"They're dumping something onto the fire," said Juli. "At least something is being done."

Suddenly there was a pounding at the door. Marina lit a candle. "It must be Vasily."

But it was not Vasily. It was one of the women from the courtyard. The woman who had assured tenants the church would not burn palms before Palm Sunday. Instead of wearing nightclothes, the woman wore slacks, boots, a coat, and a head scarf.

She looked past Marina to Juli. "My name is Svetlana Alexievich. I have children . . . I wanted to know if you knew anything more."

Juli got out of bed and went to the door. "Are the children in your apartment?"

"Now they are. I did as you said last night. I closed the windows and sealed beneath the door. But later in the morning other children were going to school. One of the teachers is in the apartment next door. She said school was open, so everything must be fine. I let the children go, and now I'm worried. They gave the children pills. My other neighbor says there are buses lining up outside the city. She says we'll all have to leave. She saw the militia station captain driving out of town and said the plant might have been sabotaged. Why would they have school if it were dangerous? My boy says his friends rode their bicycles to the plant to look at the fire. I don't understand why some say everything is fine, while others . . ."

"Please listen," said Juli. "Keep your children inside. If buses come to take us, it's best to go. It would be temporary, I'm sure. But children, especially, should not be exposed unnecessarily. Did the school give them extra pills?"

"Yes," said Svetlana. "They take them every three hours. We have enough for two days."

"Good," said Juli.

Svetlana stared at the candle Marina was holding and licked her lips. "The air . . . it smells like my husband's clothes from the machine works." She paused, looked about. "My neighbor says some residents are burying money and valuables in case we have to take the buses in a hurry. Why do we have school on Saturday? Simply to be different from America? Always to be different, always to surpass the Americans. So, if the buses come, we should leave?"

Juli stepped closer to Svetlana. "Even if the officials are overreacting, it would be best."

Svetlana held both Juli's hands for a moment, then disappeared down the hall.

After closing the door, Juli replaced the wet towel at the opening beneath it, went to the night table, picked up the dosimeter, and held it up to Marina's candle. When she went into the bathroom and began vigorously washing her hands in the water they had saved in the sink, Marina watched in horror. And when the sound of another helicopter vibrated the glass of the windows, Marina began to cry.

The buses, having waited outside Pripyat, lined up one after another on Lenin Street in the center of town and shut off their engines. A driver with a handkerchief tied over his mouth and nose got out of his bus, ran to the bus ahead, and boarded. This driver also had a handkerchief over his mouth and nose.

"What did he have to say?" asked the driver from the bus behind.

"Who?"

"The soldier with the Kalashnikov who just got off your bus. You're first in line, so I thought he might have told you something."

"He said it's the end of the world."

"You are always the comedian, Yuri."

"He was trying to find out if I knew anything. He said earlier today he caught a bunch of kids who had gone to the station to watch the fire. They were outside the fence. Crazy kids. I asked when we would load up and get the hell out of here. He said he hadn't gotten the order yet and didn't know whether it would be tomorrow or the next day. He said we have to wait."

"Why the hell did we speed up here if they're going to wait until Sunday or Monday?"

"What kind of food did you bring?"

"Sausage and bread."

"I snuck in a bottle under my seat. If you would like to bring your sausage to my bus . . ."

"I'll be right back."

At the crossroads where the roads from the towns of Chernobyl and Pripyat joined, more buses were waved through. Militiamen, who had not covered their faces earlier, did so now. A few even had masks with filters.

The militiamen stopped the flow of buses momentarily to allow through several fire trucks heading for the plant.

"Did you see the insignia on the last fire truck?" said a militiaman wearing a scarf over his mouth and nose.

"Where was it from?" asked a militiaman wearing one of the filter masks.

"It said Borzna. That's on the other side of the river."

"They're coming from all over," said the filter mask. "I wonder if the KGB guards over there in their car know something."

"They always do," said the militiaman, tightening the scarf across his face.

Viewed from the far side of the cooling pond, a flicker of flame could be seen through thick smoke coming from the skeletal remains of Chernobyl's unit four. A helicopter with lights shining through the smoke dropped a load of sand and sped away. On the ground near the fire, floodlights illuminated several figures in iridescent silver body suits manning hoses trained on the fire and on surrounding buildings. In the distance, the lights of more helicopters appeared. They looked like airliners lined up for landing at an airport.

It was after midnight, Sunday, April 26, almost a full twenty-four hours since unit four exploded. Waterfowl had settled in for a night in the shallows of the cooling pond. Some waterfowl seemed perfectly healthy, while others appeared disoriented.

CHAPTER 13

Because it was early Sunday morning, the absence of Kiev's buses went unnoticed. Spouses or partners did not think it unusual for a driver to be called in for special duty. It happened sometimes.

A spring shower had cleansed Kiev's streets during the night, the sun filtered through thin wisps of cloud, and smells of rainwater and greenery and breakfast were in the air. Russian Orthodox Palm Sunday had brought out several pedestrians who managed to find a service. They carried palms as they headed back to their apartments.

Lazlo and Tamara walked to a combination café and bakery a few blocks from his apartment. They sat at a small table sipping strong coffee and munching on an assortment of strudel while patrons purchased crackling white bags of sweets at the counter. The proprietress behind the counter was a short, plump woman with skin as white as the powdered sugar abundantly sprinkled on the pastries in the windowed case. Every few minutes the baker, who was the woman's husband, came through a swinging door to replenish the supply in the case. He was skinny, his baker's cap making him look as if it might tip him over on his head.

Tamara had pinned her hair atop her head and wore a sweater

and short skirt, which attracted glances from the men who came into the bakery. Her earrings, with gold stars dangling from chains, swung from side to side as she chewed.

"I like the cheese filling best. Which is your favorite, Laz?"

"Poppy seed."

"I don't usually eat breakfast. Nothing but coffee when I get to the office. Most of the poets who contribute to the journal are skinny as hell. I should bring them here, fatten them up."

"They'd write poems about pastry instead of politics," said Lazlo.

Tamara licked cheese from her fingertip. "Ode to a strudel. Much healthier than politics. Poets are a lot like you, constantly brooding. Sometimes I think they'd all like to go to a labor camp to die the way Vasyl Stus died."

"How did he die?"

"He was typical of many poets who search for connections between the specifics of politics and the universals of life instead of simply enjoying the here and now."

"I'm enjoying myself now."

"And last night?" asked Tamara.

"Metaphorically, last night was like eating a thousand strudels."

The number of carryout patrons increased, and the baker made more trips to keep the case full. The cheeks of the proprietress reddened despite her doughy complexion. A middle-aged man at the counter placed his order in Ukrainian instead of the usual Russian.

"Will your family be able to eat all this?" asked the proprietress.

"My family has doubled," said the man. "My brother-in-law and his family came unexpectedly in the middle of the night. Woke me up saying they had to abandon their home."

"What happened?"

"Some kind of accident at the nuclear plant where he works. He said many have abandoned the area because the air and water may be poisoned."

"The air and water?" said the proprietress. "Where is this?"

"At Chernobyl, to the north. My brother-in-law lives in Pripyat. He said there's no problem here because of the distance. But up there he says people are panicking."

Lazlo felt cold, as if he had been thrust back into the wine cellar with Mihaly last summer on the farm, Mihaly warning of danger at Chernobyl.

Lazlo left the table, stood behind the man at the counter.

The man continued with the proprietress. "My tiny apartment is like a metro station. My brother-in-law has two teenaged daughters. They have already taken over the bathroom."

"Has there been anything on the news about this?" asked the proprietress.

"Nothing. We watched the early news and listened to the radio. I was beginning to think my brother-in-law's moving in with us was part of some clever scheme. But this morning a neighbor heard of another family on the next block whose relatives also arrived last night."

The man picked up his packages. "I'll probably see you again tomorrow. These relatives will eat me out of house and home."

The man tried to leave, but Lazlo stepped sideways, blocking his path. He spoke in Ukrainian. "Excuse me, comrade. I couldn't help overhearing you."

"What do you want?" said the man, eyeing Lazlo suspiciously.

"My brother lives in Pripyat. Please tell me, did your brother-in-law give any details about the accident?"

"Nothing more. You overheard everything I know."

"What about your brother-in-law? I'd like to speak with him."

"I . . . I don't know. It will surely be on the news. Watch the news."

The man tried to step past, but Lazlo blocked him. "Please."

"I must go," said the man.

Lazlo stood his ground, sighed, took his wallet from his pocket, and showed the man his militia identification.

"I've done nothing wrong!" screeched the man.

"Please, my brother and his family live in Pripyat. My brother works at the Chernobyl plant. Perhaps your brother-in-law can tell me something. Perhaps he even knows my brother."

Lazlo and Tamara and the man left the bakery, walked less than a block to an apartment building. Inside the apartment, two women eyed Tamara.

The brother-in-law and his wife were about the same age as Mihaly and Nina, but the daughters were older than Anna and Ilonka. A little boy and a baby, apparently the resident children, were also in the room. It was so crowded the children sat on the floor.

The brother-in-law's name was Yuri Tupolev. Despite Lazlo's assurances, Tupolev worried he would get in trouble.

"I had days off coming. Maybe they need help, but nobody told me to stay. I wanted to turn back, but my family . . ."

"I understand," said Lazlo. "Believe me, I'm also here because of family concern. You say you know Mihaly Horvath?"

"Not personally. I only know he's an engineer. I'm on a maintenance crew. We travel from building to building. I know his name because he once directed work we were doing."

"Were you at the plant when this accident occurred?"

"No. I was at home."

"Tell me what you saw and heard. Start from the time of the accident."

"It was some time after midnight Saturday . . . yesterday. One loses track of time after being awake so long. I was up late and couldn't sleep. When I went outside, I saw smoke and what looked like fire in the sky. A while later, trucks sped past, one pulled up, and my neighbor jumped off the back end. He said one of the reactors exploded. He was there, at the station, and said radiation was released. We tried calling around to see what was up but couldn't get through to anyone. By dawn there were all kinds of rumors. My neighbor had his dosimeter on. He got a small dose while escaping. Later in the morning, he comes over and says the exposure is going up. Right there in his apartment he's getting exposed. So we brought our families to Kiev. He has a little shitbox of a car. We all packed into it, it kept running, and here we are."

"When did you arrive?" asked Lazlo.

"About midnight."

"When did you leave?"

"It was two or three in the afternoon by the time we got everyone together."

"It took nine hours to drive the hundred kilometers from Pripyat to Kiev?"

"By the time we got going, the dosimeter was really going up. We didn't want to take the main road because it went back east past the plant before turning south. We drove southwest, away from the plant and the direction of the wind. The back roads were terrible, and we had to stop for directions several times. We finally followed the Uzh River all the way to Korosten and then took the highway back to Kiev."

"Were there many others trying to escape?"

"No. We thought it odd, but there were only a few cars. It's probably because there was no news."

"Nothing on the local radio and television stations?"

"Nothing but music," said Tupolev. "They even skipped the regular news broadcasts."

"Is there anything else you can tell me?" asked Lazlo.

Tupolev looked down at his hands. "One more thing. Your

brother might have been on duty during the accident. My neighbor said they were doing an experiment and several engineers were there. They were supposed to shut the reactor down. I guess something went wrong."

"Could my brother have been on one of the trucks you saw?"

"I'm afraid I don't know," said Tupolev.

"Your neighbor, the one who came to Kiev with you . . . would he know?"

"I'll write down his name and the address of his parents."

Lazlo quickly supplied pen and paper. While Tupolev wrote the information, Lazlo looked at the faces of the others in the apartment. They looked like visitors to a wake who must now face the next of kin. During the conversation, Tamara came to his side and put her arm about him, holding him gently.

Yuri Tupolev's neighbor said the engineers and technicians at the plant ran from the control room after an initial explosion. He knew nothing more. As for Mihaly, he might have escaped because several cars and trucks were seen speeding from the plant.

After questioning Yuri Tupolev's neighbor, Lazlo stopped at a phone and tried to call Pripyat. Again, the call could not go through and the operator was unable to give a reason. Lazlo called militia headquarters and spoke to the sergeant on duty. The sergeant knew nothing about an accident at Chernobyl, and neither did anyone else at headquarters. However, Deputy Chief Investigator Lysenko, Chkalov's right-hand man, was at the city's boundary on the road leading north and had called for additional uniformed men for some kind of roadblock. Chkalov was not in, and the sergeant could give no further information.

Before driving to the so-called roadblock on the north end of the city, Lazlo dropped Tamara off at her apartment.

"Thank you for being so understanding, Tamara."

"How could I not be understanding? He's your brother."

"I mean about going with me."

"I only wanted to ride in your speedy Zhiguli and listen to the two-way radio." Tamara placed her hand on his knee. "Promise me something, Laz. If you decide to drive to Pripyat, take the long way around."

Tamara put her arm around him, pulled him close, kissed him. As she walked up the steps to her building, Lazlo paused a moment. Seeing Tamara walk away after the weekend they had spent together, and speculating about the trouble ahead, made him feel the elusiveness of life and its pleasures. He put the Zhiguli in gear and sped up the street.

There was no mention of a nuclear incident on the Zhiguli's radio, not even when he managed to tune to Voice of America. He tried the Radio Free Europe frequency, but there was no morning programming. For a moment he began to wonder if it was all a mistake. But the roadblock at the outskirts of the city where the extension of Boulevard Shevchenko curved north was no mistake. Two marked militia cars blocked the road, and uniformed officers turned traffic back to Kiev. Amid the officers, dressed in his Sunday suit, was Deputy Chief Investigator Lysenko, who always wore what looked like a Sunday suit, the uniform of one who seeks promotion. Lazlo pulled to the right of the waiting vehicles and walked to where Lysenko stood in the morning sun, staring at the barren road to the north.

Lysenko turned. "Good morning, Detective Horvath. Are you

here to help?"

Rather than take time to explain, Lazlo used a direct approach. "The chief sent me. He said you should fill me in."

"It's the nuclear plant at Chernobyl."

"I've already heard rumors," said Lazlo, wanting to get on with it. "Do you know if anyone was killed or injured?"

"All I was told is no one should try to drive there," said Lysenko. "The republic militia has blocked the road farther north. Apparently there's some radiation, but the chief said civilians are to be told nothing except the road is closed. It's already caused arguments. These people with their Sunday plans."

Lysenko looked up the road. "Something is puzzling about this. I thought there would be heavy traffic from the north. So far we've only had a few cars come through. I'm beginning to wonder if there really was an accident at the plant."

"Did you question the people coming south?"

"My orders were simply to let no one go north."

Lysenko's profile, with his pointy chin and upturned nose, suddenly looked foolish. Lazlo wanted to call him what he looked like, but instead he said, "You didn't question anyone or take names?"

"No. My orders were simply to let no one go north."

"If you're still wondering, my fine deputy chief, why there are so few cars, perhaps a bit of logic is in order."

Lysenko turned and frowned at Lazlo. "What do you mean?"

"One look at a map would tell you the two largest towns up there, Chernobyl and Pripyat, are very near the nuclear facility bordering this road. If there is radioactivity in the area, citizens might be directed away from this road. If you wish to see accident refugees, I suggest you put men on the road from Korosten!"

Lysenko stared at Lazlo in obvious anger, saying nothing.

After Lazlo sped off, Lysenko turned and trotted to the front of the roadblock.

"What did he want?" asked one of the uniformed men.

"He probably wanted to drive the two hours to the nuclear plant so he could make himself into a hero," said Lysenko.

"But his brother works there. Didn't you tell him about all the fire trucks and buses sent from Kiev?"

"Why should I tell him anything?"

The uniformed man shook his head, muttering as he walked to one of the green and white militia Zhigulis.

Tamara was correct when she said ministries were gloomy places. The contrast between fresh outside air and the smell of floor cleaner and polish was apparent. As Lazlo walked quickly down a long hallway, a washerwoman standing on a ladder cleaning portraits turned to stare at him as if humans mattered less than the portraits of the bastards lining the walls. Bastards like Ryzhkov and Chebrikov and even Gorbachev. All bastards who followed the Party line so workers got lost in the woodwork of buildings like this.

The only person available at the Kiev office of the Ministry of Energy was a deputy minister named Mishin who wore thick glasses and spoke with a northern accent.

"You say everything is fine at the plant?" said Lazlo.

"Yes," said Mishin. "Everything is under control."

"If everything is under control, why are you here on Sunday?"

"The minister ordered it."

"What exactly happened at Chernobyl?"

"I must repeat, everything is under control."

"What about radiation and injuries?"

"We know of none."

Lazlo felt like asking Mishin to remove his thick glasses so he could flatten his face.

"Pardon me if I seem outspoken, Comrade Deputy Minister, but I have relatives in the region, and I'm trying to determine if they are safe."

"I know of no injuries or danger to the population. Because of the possibility of gossip developing, I've been ordered to quell false rumors. There was a minor incident at one of the reactors at the Chernobyl facility. Everything is under control, and no one is in danger."

"Who is your minister?"

"His name is on the plaque at the entrance."

"When will he be here?"

"Tomorrow morning with the rest of the staff. Perhaps by then there will be more news."

In the lobby Lazlo took out his notebook and copied down the name of the minister of electric power, Viktor Asimov. At first all Lazlo could think of was his friend Viktor from the army. But then he considered the last name and wondered if the Chernobyl stories he was being told were science fiction. The washerwoman on the ladder turned to watch him leave.

Because he had visited Chief Investigator Chkalov's house for May Day picnics in the past, Lazlo found it without knowing the address. Chkalov wore a purple satin robe over dress trousers and invited Lazlo into a book-lined study. Chkalov had the housekeeper bring tea, and they sat across from one another in deep leather chairs.

"I understand your concern for your brother and his family, Detective Horvath. I wish I knew more about the situation up there."

"I spoke with Deputy Chief Investigator Lysenko at a roadblock to the north. He said your orders were to stop northbound traffic."

Chkalov stirred his tea with a plump finger. "Deputy Chief Investigator Lysenko phoned and said you were at the roadblock. He said you were upset names had not been taken down."

"Communication to the area is cut off, and no one seems to know what's happened. The Ministry of Energy insists everything is fine, but I heard a different story while sitting in a restaurant earlier this morning."

"One rumor leads to another, Detective Horvath. People become upset, perhaps for no reason."

"I don't pretend to know the facts," said Lazlo. "All I'm asking is that names be taken at the roadblocks."

Chkalov rose and walked about the room with his tea. "Very well, Detective Horvath. I'll order names be taken down. In the meantime, I need you at one of the roadblocks. Report immediately to the road from Korosten, and check with me tomorrow for further instructions. If the number of people coming south from the Chernobyl area increases, arrangements have been made at the Selskaya collective farm. Two hundred people can be housed there should the need arise."

While Lazlo sat in the center of the room with his boss circling him like a fat, purple planet, he wondered what else Chkalov knew but refused to reveal.

"Your prime duty at the roadblock will be to make sure your officers do not add to the spread of rumors. For example, one of the men reports the hydrofoil to Pripyat is not running, yet we have no confirmation of this."

"I must tell you, Chief Investigator, I've been to the Ministry of Energy."

"And?" said Chkalov with a frown.

"I was told everything is under control."

"Detective Horvath, the overall responsibility for Chernobyl is with the Ministry of Medium Machine Building. Since their office is in Moscow, perhaps things are being controlled from there. Is your brother a senior engineer?"

"Yes."

"I'm sure he knows enough to take care of himself. For now, we must maintain calm in our city by avoiding rumors. Go to headquarters and gather officers for your roadblock at Korosten. Above all, avoid rumors."

Lazlo would follow his orders. But Chkalov knew more than he was saying, and had acted the way he'd seen Chkalov act when officers were in trouble. When he stopped at his apartment to pick up his pistol on the way to headquarters, Lazlo found a wineglass from the night before set upright on the table. He was certain the glass had been on its side when he and Tamara had left for breakfast. He remembered Tamara wiping at a droplet of wine from the overturned glass with her finger. Someone had been in the apartment since he and Tamara left this morning. At the roadblock, after picking up his officers, there were other things adding to Lazlo's concern.

First, the number of cars coming from the Chernobyl area was on the rise, and occupants spoke of radiation and asked about the location of Kiev's hospitals. Second, a black Volga was parked off to the side near the roadblock, the two occupants obviously KGB. Normally this would not bother Lazlo, but with his apartment being broken into and with Chkalov saying less than he knew, Lazlo knew the KGB might be there to watch who came from the north to escape the radiation, or they might be there to watch him.

It was after noon on a Sunday, and Kievians out for their drives in the country were angry. While Lazlo watched his men arguing with drivers, he remembered the question he had saved for the wine cellar last summer. The question he had not wanted Nina or the children or the other relatives to hear.

What's wrong at Chernobyl?

Several buses came through the checkpoint as the afternoon wore on. Rather than being from the towns of Pripyat or Chernobyl, the buses had picked up people in outlying areas south of the plant. Some said they were out for a Sunday walk when the bus came by. Others said they were on their way to spend a Sunday in Kiev anyway and welcomed the free ride.

But on one bus there were people from nearer the plant who knew about the accident. This bus overflowed with speculation. They said Soviet army troops controlled traffic farther to the north. A woman doctor on the bus, when asked what might be happening, said, "The children will get iodine prophylaxis, and then everything will be fine as long as the children are protected against any radiation. If there is radiation."

One man on the bus from nearer the plant said the radiation would go north into the Belarussian Republic because of the southerly winds. Another man claimed parents trying to send children away would eventually besiege the railway stations. This same man insisted he saw a long line of buses heading north before he was picked up. A homeless woman wearing rags became hysterical, saying Gorbachev was a devil with a birthmark. A teenaged boy said he was a Young Pioneer and was certain the Pioneers would become involved in any rescue effort.

Lazlo recalled his last visit to Pripyat, when Mihaly wondered if Cousin Zukor could be a spy. If any one of the rumors he heard in a single hour was true, anything could be true.

The day continued with more cars at the checkpoint, more people wanting to go north, but also other cars. Green and white militia Zhigulis, two men in a black Volga watching, a Chaika with yellow fog lights parked up the hill, and a newer Zil, the kind used by high officials.

Do not spread rumors, Chkalov had said. Do not panic. The one thing he wanted to do was jump in his Zhiguli and drive north. But he knew, from years of experience in the militia, it was too late. As rumors spread, so do people. He was certain Mihaly and Nina and the girls were by now away from Pripyat. He only hoped they would be here in Kiev before the day was out.

CHAPTER 14

"Everyone is leaving," said Nikolai.

"Not everyone," said Pavel. "There are still people on the streets. What about the crowd at the Catholic church?"

"It closed years ago. They use it only for marriage ceremonies and meetings."

"So, the people are meeting there trying to get information."

"Or praying because it is their only escape."

"Why pray when there are buses lined up to take them away?"

"They're praying they don't get a drunken bus driver," said Nikolai. "But seriously, the best thing to do about radioactivity is to get far away. Exactly what we should be doing."

Pavel and Nikolai sat in the car assigned them by Captain Putna. Not a Volga like other KGB agents, but a two-year-old Moskvich with an engine clicking like a windup clock as it sat idling off the road across from Juli Popovics' apartment.

"How long do we stay here?" asked Nikolai. "We know she's in there because we saw her at the window. We should simply question her, write up a report, and get the hell out of here."

Anger showed on Pavel's face as he rocked the steering wheel back and forth with his finger. "If we write up a report on Juli Popovics, we'll have no further orders to follow. It would mean reporting back to Captain Putna, who might tell us to start questioning every fuckhead citizen in town! Don't you remember what he said about Major Komarov?"

"I don't know what you're getting at," said Nikolai.

"If Juli Popovics leaves the area, which I'm sure she will, we'll be obliged to follow. To put it more plainly for your pea-sized brain, we'll be able to get out of here without deserting our post, and we'll be fulfilling our duty. The investigation of this so-called accident."

"But what if she doesn't run away?" asked Nikolai.

"She will. Every few minutes either Juli Popovics or her roommate leans close to the window and looks up the road. Someone is coming to pick them up."

"Maybe they're looking at the helicopters."

"They're watching the road," said Pavel. "It has nothing to do with helicopters."

Nikolai leaned forward, looked up through the windshield. "There goes another."

While Pavel and Nikolai sat at the side of the road across from Juli Popovics' apartment building, an occasional car or truck sped past, heading west on the road from Chernobyl to Pripyat. The cars and trucks were packed with people and did not slow down.

"We always seem to be cooped up together in cramped quarters," said Pavel. "I guess it's best we keep the windows closed."

"We'd be safer in a Volga," said Nikolai. "This thing leaks like a sieve. Did you see the last car fly past? Everyone was wearing handkerchiefs over their noses and mouths like bandits."

"I saw," said Pavel, looking at his wristwatch.

"Here comes another tanker truck washing down the street," said Nikolai. "What the hell are they spraying? It doesn't look like water."

When the truck came out of a side street and turned the corner away from them, white foam trailed behind. Immediately following the tanker was a dump truck. The dump truck stopped, and a man wearing a face mask and covered from head to toe in a jumpsuit got out, carrying a shovel. The man ran to the side of the road, lifted what looked like a black rock with the shovel, heaved the rock into the back of the dump truck, and ran back to the cab. The two trucks continued on their way, away from Nikolai and Pavel, who sat staring ahead.

"What the hell was that?" asked Pavel.

"I think it might have something to do with the shitty smell in the air," said Nikolai. "I've read a little bit about our reactors. They use graphite around the core. The explosion was at night when no one would have seen a piece of graphite flying through the air. This could be worse than we've been told."

"But Captain Putna said . . ."

"What does Captain Putna know about reactors and radiation?"

Farther up the street, the dump truck stopped again, the man covered from head to toe running as he lobbed another black rock into the back of the truck.

"It's Vasily!" screamed Marina from the window.

Everything happened quickly. Marina shouting orders, Vasily and his mother and sister undressing and bathing, Juli putting out fresh clothing.

"We wore scarves over our mouths!" shouted Vasily. "You should have seen the crowd at hospital! The airport road was blocked, nobody allowed in except ambulances and buses driven by militiamen."

"Why didn't you come back yesterday?" asked Marina.

"No gas," said Vasily. "But we have a full tank now. I drained it from a truck. Buses are lined up on Lenin Street, but we shouldn't wait. Army troops on the main road carrying Kalashnikovs are stopping people and delaying the buses. The main roads are clogged with convoys of army trucks, and I saw a bus near the power plant in a ditch. I took a shortcut here, and no one is being stopped on back roads to the west."

Vasily continued while Marina had him strip and wiped him down with a wet towel. "Yesterday, before I got gas, a man said soldiers went floor to floor in apartment buildings on the other side of the bridge. They told people to leave but didn't say where to go. Today I saw a farmer herding livestock down the road. Everywhere people are looking out their windows, waiting to be told what to do."

"We can't wait," said Juli.

Vasily, stuffed into a pair of Marina's stretch slacks and a baggy sweatshirt, was first out the door. He carried a box of canned goods Juli packed as a precaution. He wore one of Marina's colorful print scarves over his nose and mouth, and over his head and shoulders were sheets and blankets from the bed to cover the car seats.

Vasily's mother and sister, both shivering from the cold bath, carried extra clothing from the closet in case their clothes became contaminated. Juli and Marina moistened the last of the towels to use for sealing the vents of the car.

Juli wrote a note saying they were leaving, heading southwest and eventually to Kiev. Although the note was not addressed to him, she prayed Mihaly would, on his way out of Pripyat, come to the apartment and read it. Even better, she prayed he and Nina and his little girls had already escaped. She left the note on the floor inside the door and once again looked through the lens of the dosimeter. Eighty millirems. Although there was no exact cutoff, she knew they would soon surpass a year's worth of normal exposure if they did not get out of Pripyat. When they ran to the car, another helicopter passed overhead, chopping the air into miniature explosions.

Not far from the building, four men wearing winter coats and ski masks blocked the road, wanting Vasily to stop. Vasily revved the engine, threatening to run them down. Marina screamed when one man was nicked by the car and thrown into a ditch. But the man was soon up shaking his fist with the others.

Vasily drove very fast away from Pripyat. The road west was bumpy and they all hung on. With the windows closed, it was hot in the car. Juli glanced out the rear window and saw several other cars heading west. Beyond the cars she saw the tops of apartment buildings—hers, Mihaly's, and everyone else's—disappearing behind them. South of the buildings, smoke from Chernobyl's unit four rose into the bright spring sky. When the road dove into a wooded area, Pripyat disappeared. In the front seat, Marina held onto Vasily's arm. In the back seat, Juli and Vasily's mother and sister looked to one another with tears in their eyes. The road became narrower, the woods closed in, and the spring day grew dark.

Although he stayed back from the car carrying Juli Popovics, Pavel sped up when he saw the men standing in the road. The men parted as they passed, but one managed to smash a rear side window with a brick.

"Everyone's gone crazy!" shouted Nikolai.

"They'd better keep their shitbox going," said Pavel. "Look at the smoky exhaust."

"What kind of car is it?"

"An old Zaporozhets painted about fifty times. But they didn't get a window smashed."

"I wish we had guns," said Nikolai.

"We're lucky Captain Putna assigned us a car."

"You and I recruited to follow Juli Popovics makes me think," said Nikolai. "What if there is something to the Gypsy Moth connection and the Horvath brothers?"

"Conspiracy and sabotage," said Pavel. "You're beginning to think like Major Komarov."

"I'm not kidding," said Nikolai. "I wonder how things are at the post office."

"Do you wish you were back there?" asked Pavel.

Nikolai tied his handkerchief over his mouth and nose. "The PK wasn't such a bad life."

As Pavel drove, Nikolai helped out by tying Pavel's handkerchief. Then the two PK agents raised their coat collars against the wind from the broken back window and followed the Zaporozhets into the countryside.

Late Sunday afternoon, two convoys of army trucks and buses converged on the area around the Chernobyl plant. One convoy concentrated on villages and the town of Chernobyl south of the plant. The second convoy led a group of buses to reinforce those already sent to Pripyat, the population center nearest the plant. On the way to Pripyat, several buses detoured to Kopachi, the closest village to the plant. The people of Kopachi were in a state of panic, and when the buses left, each with an armed soldier onboard, dogs belonging to people from the village chased the buses speeding away.

After pausing at Kopachi, the rest of the convoy headed to Pripyat on back roads in order to avoid driving too close to the plant. The Sunday evening sun was low in the sky. It would be the second sunset since the Chernobyl Power Station explosion.

Several kilometers from the entrance to the plant, lights powered by a generator illuminated tents being set up in a ditch along the back road by soldiers assigned to assist firefighters and rescue personnel. When the convoy passed the makeshift emergency headquarters, wind from the vehicles shook the tents, almost knocking them down as they were being set up.

Colonel Gennady Zamyatin of the army's Ukrainian border force was a veteran of the Great Patriotic War long past traditional retirement. He held on to the center post of the headquarters tent as the convoy roared past. Radio equipment had already been brought into the tent. The radio dials were lit up, and a member of the technical unit was wiring the equipment to a makeshift antenna on the raised bank alongside the ditch. Colonel Zamyatin smiled as the convoy passed. The sound reminded him of the Great War, and despite what he knew about the tragedy at the Chernobyl plant, he felt happy for the first time in years.

A truck from the rear of the convoy veered off the roadway and came to a skidding stop at the side of the road near Colonel Zamyatin's tent. Soviet Army Captain Ivan Pisarenko jumped from the truck and ran down the embankment to the headquarters tent. Inside the tent Colonel Zamyatin and Captain Pisarenko quickly introduced themselves, grasping hands and staring into one another's eyes. Both knew the seriousness of the Chernobyl explosion. Both had been briefed by superiors who counted on them to take charge.

Although Zamyatin showed his age, he was a sturdy, red-cheeked man with bright eyes and an upturned nose. Captain Pisarenko was taller, more muscular, and much younger.

"My convoy will be in Pripyat tonight," said Pisarenko. "I've got ten trucks, fifty men, and seventy-three buses from Kiev. Do you have any news?"

"Pripyat is close to the plant, and radiation is bad there," said Zamyatin. "They've been rinsing streets and even some of the buildings because of radioactive dust from the explosion. I've been told they had to chase people away who walked to the plant. The first buses took many away along with injured firefighters. Have your men cover their faces as much as possible. Try not to breathe in smoke from the fire or dust in the air."

"What's happening at the power plant?"

"The core exploded, setting the graphite on fire, so it's best to avoid the area as much as possible. That's why we're setting up here. Water on the fire is ineffective. Many of the early firefighters and workers from the plant were exposed to extreme radiation. I saw men vomiting blood. The serious cases were flown out, headed to the radiation hospital in Moscow. Yesterday helicopters dropped tons of sand on the core. Although somewhat diminished, the fire continues. Today they dropped boric acid and lead along with sand on it. With people living so close to the plant, it's a terrible situation. It reminds me of the Great War when the Nazis rounded up Jews and Gypsies. I don't know what's going to happen to all these people."

"Moscow is ordering collectives to make room," said Captain Pisarenko. "They're also recruiting the komsomols to help. For now, the health ministry gave me boxes of iodine pills to be handed out as people board the buses. We'll tell residents they'll be gone a few days at most. One of my men suggested we have parents tell their children they are going on holiday, or to the circus. Anything to move them along. And only one suitcase per person."

Colonel Zamyatin shook his head sadly. "I was preparing for my retirement on a farm near here when they called me. I sent my wife to Kiev as soon as I heard what had happened. Nothing of this scale lasts only a few days."

"I agree," said Pisarenko. "The people of the village of Kopachi know how serious this is. We got them out of their houses at gunpoint. Some of them were puking as they boarded the buses." Pisarenko paused, wiped his forehead with his sleeve. "When the buses turned around to head south, neighborhood dogs chased them."

Both were silent a moment.

Captain Pisarenko shook Colonel Zamyatin's hand. "I hope we meet again."

One of the radios on a table squealed to life as the technician adjusted the knobs. A loud voice boomed out question after question.

"Who the hell is that?" asked Pisarenko.

"Who else?" said Zamyatin. "The KGB. It's their office in Kiev interfering with the emergency frequencies, wanting to know every fucking detail while they sit on their asses!"

"I'll go now, Colonel."

"Good luck, Captain."

Captain Pisarenko ran up the embankment to his truck, ordering the driver to go before he landed in the seat. The truck sped off after the rest of the convoy and caught up as the line of trucks and buses drove past signs welcoming visitors to Pripyat. Although the sun had set and it was rapidly growing dark, the messages could still be seen. Among the messages were, "The Ideas of Lenin Are Immortal" and "The Proletariat Will Triumph."

Back at the roadside emergency headquarters, another convoy of trucks and buses roared past, heading north, their headlights flashing on the sides of the tents.

The traffic heading southwest increased. To stay on the main route, Vasily simply followed the lights of the car ahead. Likewise, the car behind stayed close, and Juli used this light to look into her dosimeter.

Vasily's fifteen-year-old sister was named Lena. While Vasily's mother slept at the other end of the back seat, Lena, who sat between her mother and Juli, asked questions as they drove through the night.

"What does it say now?" asked Lena.

"About a hundred," said Juli.

"I learned in school radiation is more dangerous for younger people."

"Don't worry, Lena. They'll have doctors in Kiev to check everyone. People get a hundred millirems in a year from natural radiation. My dosimeter goes all the way up to three hundred, and we turn it in every day."

"Aren't you worried for your baby? A baby shouldn't get any."

"Juli's been taking precautions," said Marina from the front seat.

"Like what?" asked Lena.

"Quit being so depressing," said Vasily. "We're out of there, and we can do nothing about what's already happened."

"I was simply asking, Vas. Anyway, you pay attention to driving."

"I will," said Vasily. "But when we get where we're going, I might have to pop you."

Lena laughed, changed the subject, and began talking about her friends at school. No one complained about Lena's talking. There was nothing but somber music on the radio, and the talk of a teenaged girl made the darkness outside less frightening.

"Look," said Lena. "There's a bus parked at the side of the road."

Someone waved a flashlight around as two women squatted behind sparse bushes.

"The men are farther ahead at another bush," said Vasily. "See them standing in the dark? The bus driver picked this place for a toilet break because only plowed fields are ahead."

"It's depressing," said Marina.

"People going to the toilet depresses you?" said Vasily.

"The entire situation," said Marina. "All these people, their lives changed forever." Marina spoke more quietly. "Especially the children. They'll be frightened of rain and snow."

"What will be left for us?" asked Lena.

Although Juli, too, felt discouraged, she tried to be positive. "Nothing is irreversible. What mankind has done can be undone. I think of the radiation as simply another form of pollution. Science will provide answers . . . it must provide answers."

Vasily braked hard as the cars ahead came to a stop. An army truck blocked the lane heading south, with soldiers outside waving the cars around it. Each car was stopped, a soldier leaning into the driver's window.

"What is it?" asked Vasily, when his turn came.

"How many in the car, and where are you from?" demanded the soldier.

"There are five of us," said Vasily. "We came from Pripyat."

The soldier counted out slips of paper from a stack in his hand. "Here are five temporary travel passes. Keep them with you at all times."

"Do you have any information?" asked Vasily.

"Nothing. Drive to Kiev. You'll be told where to go from there." The soldier waved for them to go and stepped back to the next car in line.

Vasily closed his window and drove on.

"Maybe it's a good sign he didn't have his mouth covered," said Juli.

"We'll probably be able to enjoy the May Day parade in Kiev," said Marina.

"Enjoying the parade will be impossible," said Lena. "How can all these people even fit into Kiev? What about the people already there? Look at the cars coming from the side road. Even more people. How will anyone be able to tell all of us where to go and what to do?"

No one in the car answered Lena's questions. But everyone, even Vasily's mother, who was now awake, stared across farm fields at a line of cars and buses from the northeast waiting to get on the main road south. Ahead, at the crossroads, flares were lit, and soldiers directed traffic.

When the line of traffic passed through the town of Korosten, soldiers on both sides with flashlights waved everyone through, making them turn southeast. Near midnight, at a sign saying Kiev was ten kilometers away, traffic slowed to a crawl.

"I told you," said Vasily's mother. "We should have gone to my older brother's farm."

"We've already discussed it!" shouted Vasily. "His farm is too close to Chernobyl. Juli needs to get to her aunt's house in Visenka, the most direct way there is through Kiev, and we'll all be better off in Kiev."

"All right, Vasily. I put my trust in you, and in God. My younger brother is on a collective south of Kiev. If they have room, maybe we'll end up there."

After Korosten, the road widened. Very little traffic headed northwest, mostly army vehicles and empty buses. They were in the lane nearest the side of the road. Occasionally, when a car or bus with open windows came alongside, Vasily lowered his window to see if he could get some news. Others were also trying to get news, and it seemed no one knew much. The Chernobyl plant had exploded, radiation had been released, and the area was being evacuated. But no one knew when they would be allowed to go back to their homes.

Eventually traffic stopped completely, and Vasily turned off the engine to conserve gas. With engines off, they could hear conversation in the bus next to them. The bus windows were open, people inside saying it was hot with so many people onboard. A few men on the bus smoked cigarettes, blowing smoke out the windows. Others stepped outside to smoke, and also to share a swig from a bottle hidden beneath a coat. The talk among women concerned the children. Several mentioned the iodine pills handed out at school the day before, and Juli wondered if they had some on the bus, a spare pill or two for her baby. Two men came to the window and told Vasily the outskirts of the city and the checkpoint were only a few kilometers away. The men said they were going to walk ahead to see what they could find out.

Juli was going to the town of Visenka, beyond Kiev. Vasily's mother had relatives on farms around Kiev. It would be a waste of time for them to drive all the way to Visenka simply to drop her off at her aunt's.

"Marina, I've made up my mind."

"About what?" asked Marina.

"I'm going to walk," said Juli, pulling her small bag from the floor.

"You can't walk."

"Why not? I'll stay over at a hotel and tomorrow take a taxi or the metro to Aunt Magda's. This way you can decide on your destination without worrying about me. I've got a place to stay. I can take care of myself. You need to take care of yourselves. Don't argue with me, Marina. Lots of people are walking."

"But, Juli."

"She's right," said Vasily. "If we go through Kiev and try to get back in from the other side, we might get stuck."

Juli opened her door and got out. "At the checkpoint my having a different destination would only complicate things."

"Are you sure you'll be all right?" asked Marina.

"My aunt's expecting me," said Juli. "I've been watching the dosimeter, and it's fine now. It's time to go."

Marina got out of the car, ran around to the other side, and hugged Juli.

"You're like a sister to me," said Juli.

"You are my sister," said Marina.

After Marina got back in the car, Juli began walking, and soon others came from cars and buses to join her, heading for the flashing lights of militia vehicles in the distance. The sounds of engines and voices and shuffling feet, along with the smell of dust in the night air, reminded her of a night long ago in Moscow when her father took her to the circus. Back then, people lined up to get in to see performers and animals. Here, people were the animals as they bumped against one another like livestock.

"Now what?" said Nikolai.

Pavel shut off the engine. "I'll go on foot. I'm tired of driving anyhow. We have to follow through on this, or we'll have no reason for having left Pripyat without orders. Stay in line. You'll get through eventually. I'll meet you at the KGB branch office tomorrow. If I can't get away, I'll call and leave a message for you at Major Komarov's office so you can pick me up."

Pavel got out of the car, and Nikolai slid behind the wheel.

"You want me to go to Komarov's office?" asked Nikolai.

"Of course. Without Captain Putna around, we'll need further direction. Komarov's orders put Juli Popovics under observation. Think big, Nikolai. This could be our opportunity for promotion. Perhaps the Gypsy Moth information for Major Komarov will bear fruit."

"What information? All we have from Captain Putna is a hint about someone called Gypsy Moth trying to destabilize the country."

"Komarov is pushing for information. We're his contacts directly from the Chernobyl area. If we don't find anything by following Juli Popovics, we'll think of something."

It was a kaleidoscope of conversation as Juli walked between cars and buses.

Some pondered apocalypse—the Soviet Union was falling apart. Environmental advocates had been right all along. It was the end of the world. Christ would come down the following Easter Sunday and take the faithful with him. Because birds fly to heaven in winter, and few had been seen in the area, the birds knew not to return.

Others pondered rumor and myth—alcohol flushed radiation out of one's system. Operators at the plant smoked hashish. The iodine at most pharmacies was gone. Some evacuees were seen burying their valuables because looters were already waiting in the woods like wolves. Party bosses knew about the accident before it happened. How else would they have been prepared to speed out of town in their Volgas?

Because most cars and buses had turned off their engines and lights, the walk between the two lines of traffic was dark. The only light came from flashlights or lanterns aboard buses, the glow of cigarettes, and the bright lights of the checkpoint shining through the dust and haze in the distance. As Juli neared the checkpoint, more and more people joined her, sometimes bumping into her or stepping on her heels. Beyond the lights of the checkpoint, she saw the change in landscape, the downslope of the river valley, and finally, the lights of Kiev.

There was chaos at the roadblock. The few people who wanted to leave Kiev were turned back by Lazlo's men, and the hundreds arriving from the north were being allowed into the city only if they had a specific destination. Those without a destination were directed to the Selskaya collective farm thirty kilometers west of the city. Lazlo's men had already sent several hundred to the Selskaya farm, and now he awaited further orders.

Some local Kievians trying to exit the city to outlying areas complained the so-called accident at Chernobyl was nothing but an excuse for evacuees to head south for holiday. Others claimed officials in Kiev must have known about the accident earlier than everyone else because they kept their children out of school Saturday and started their weekend early, going to their dachas. One man said he'd seen scores of fire trucks head north Saturday. When Lazlo heard this, he recalled his meeting with Lysenko earlier in the day and wondered if there was a reason Lysenko had not given him more details of the enormity of the accident.

Lazlo showed photographs of Mihaly, Nina, and the girls to his men, but no one had seen them. But with the chaos, anyone could slip through unnoticed. When a group of Young Pioneers arrived to help, Lazlo showed them the photographs while instructing them to direct traffic and make sure no one got out of line and blocked the lanes out of the city. Whereas few vehicles were allowed out of the city earlier in the evening, now trucks and emergency vehicles whose drivers had been given passes headed north.

The crowd of people who had left cars and buses grew to an alarming size. Eventually, because there were no fences or other boundaries on the sides of the road, the crowds from both sides merged, making it impossible for the militia to stop those on foot from crossing in either direction. Lazlo tried in vain to help his men maintain order. During this confusion, he was unaware of his brother's lover crossing into Kiev followed by a KGB agent a few meters behind her beyond the lights of the roadblock.

Other KGB agents at the scene were also unaware of the crossing. Two of them, recruited to Kiev from their Romanian border-guard posts, sat in the dark in a black Chaika with yellow fog lights a half kilometer from the roadblock watching Chernobyl refugees pass by on their way into Kiev. Both agents wore their green border-guard uniforms.

One of the agents lit a cigarette. "I don't understand about Komarov."

"What about him?" asked the other.

"There's an accident at Chernobyl, and instead of going to the scene, he stays in Kiev and searches for suspects."

"Bigger fish have already volunteered for the medals they'll get at Chernobyl. Komarov is from the old KGB. He's already got interrogators working on the poor souls they flew to Moscow, and he's got us watching his suspects here."

"So you think Detective Horvath is a suspect?"

"He must be. Otherwise why would we be assigned to watch him?"

Pavel followed Juli Popovics through the mass of angry people. Voices were raised in protest and dismay at what had happened at Chernobyl. As in any crowd where one achieves momentary anonymity, many spoke out against the authorities and against their insistence the population be left in the dark. At one point, a shoving match broke out, and Pavel was actually pushed into Juli Popovics, knocking her down. He helped her up, excused himself, dropped back into the crowd, and continued following her.

Farther away from the roadblock, Pavel kept his distance. Because she was carrying an overnight bag, it was easy to follow her. The only time he had difficulty was when she descended the stairs to the Kiev metro. He had to run in order to catch the train.

She exited the metro in central Kiev at Khreshchatik Station. From there he followed her to the Hotel Dnieper. It was one in the morning. Pavel watched from a corner in the lobby. Juli Popovics apparently tried to register for a room, but was refused. The lobby was crowded with people unable to get a room. So, along with dozens of others, Juli Popovics and Pavel of the PK waited for someone to vacate a comfortable chair or sofa so they could settle in for the night.

Juli Popovics was first to find a chair. Pavel lingered near an open stairway to the second floor. He went halfway up to the landing and sat on a stair at a spot where he could keep an eye on Juli Popovics through an opening in the ornate railing. Glancing behind him, he saw a statue of Vladimir Ilich Lenin in the corner of the landing. Lenin held his hand up as if pointing the way up the next flight of stairs. Pavel wondered if following Juli Popovics here had been the right thing to do. Was there any chance he and Nikolai would even meet Major Komarov? Pavel whispered to himself, "What now, Uncle? Climb the stairs to promotion?" Pavel chuckled, then turned back to watch Juli Popovics, who had closed her eyes.

From conversations overheard during the night, it was obvious even here, in Kiev, with all its newspapers and radio and television stations, no one knew exactly what had happened at Chernobyl. With a news blackout of such magnitude, it was not difficult to surmise a disaster had occurred. For, as any Soviet citizen knows, the less the news, the greater the story.

CHAPTER 15

On Monday, April 28, over forty-eight hours after the explosion of Chernobyl's unit four, news of the disaster finally made it to the outside world. Workers at a Swedish nuclear plant began setting off radiation alarms as they entered the facility. This resulted in quantitative measurements of the atmosphere. Radiation levels fifteen times the normal level were present in the air being blown from the Soviet Union.

Lacking seismic data to indicate a nuclear test, Western scientists concluded an accidental release of radiation, perhaps from a nuclear reactor, had occurred somewhere in the western Soviet Union. When news services got hold of the radioactive-cloud story, ripples of news flowed back across the frontier by way of Radio Free Europe and Voice of America.

After obtaining the Zhiguli as his personal militia vehicle three years earlier, Lazlo installed inside the glove box a used Blaupunkt radio, which received shortwave frequencies along with local frequencies.

The radio provided welcome distraction during many nights on stakeout. Without his secret radio, he would have been forced to listen only to militia two-way broadcasts instead of the strings of Lakatos and other Hungarian Gypsy music broadcast each evening from Radio Budapest.

On his way to the Ministry of Energy Monday morning, Lazlo heard about the radiation cloud over Sweden on Radio Free Europe. The station was easy enough to find, but it was difficult to offset the frequency enough to eliminate the whirring buzz saw of the Soviet jammer. After hearing the report of radioactivity originating in the western Soviet Union, Lazlo switched to Radio Moscow's local frequency. No mention of the radioactive cloud or of the disaster at the Chernobyl plant, no mention of the hordes of people who had come from the north throughout the night.

While the man and woman commentators on Radio Moscow droned on about the agricultural and economic outlook, Lazlo wondered if he'd been assigned overnight at the roadblock to keep him out of the way. Hundreds had entered Kiev, giving names of relatives who would be expecting them. Thousands had been sent to the Selskaya collective farm, which was equipped to handle two hundred.

Lazlo arrived at the Ministry of Energy at seven thirty. He'd spent most of Sunday afternoon and the entire night at the roadblock. He was hoarse from shouting at his men and at Chernobyl refugees. A cleaning woman in the building lobby waited until Lazlo cleared his throat before telling him no one arrived until nine.

Lazlo drove to his apartment. He tried calling Pripyat again without luck. He washed his face, changed clothes, and made himself two boiled eggs and coffee. Tamara's black nightgown still lay across his bed from the night before. He sat on the edge of the bed and lifted the gown. The gown retained Tamara's fragrance, and Lazlo closed his eyes, caressing the gown to his face as if it were the silk edge of a child's blanket.

Twenty-four hours earlier he had been in bed with Tamara, but now their night together and breakfast at the bakery seemed weeks ago. As he sat on the bed fondling Tamara's nightgown, thoughts of Tamara were swept aside by intervening events: the interviews with two Chernobyl workers unable to give specifics about Mihaly, the inept deputy minister at the Ministry of Energy who said everything was under control, and, finally, the long night trying to communicate with terrified refugees. Twenty-four hours since he learned an accident had occurred at Chernobyl and still he knew nothing of Mihaly and Nina and the girls. Was it planned? Chkalov and Lysenko teaming up to keep him in the dark? Sending him to one particular roadblock so he would be unaware of the numerous firemen and militia sent north? Perhaps they'd been worried the Gypsy might have pulled out his old Makarov 9mm and . . .

Suddenly something tore at his face. He opened his eyes with a start, realizing he had begun to doze off. His bristly beard was snagged in Tamara's gown. He placed the gown gently on the bed, got a cup of strong coffee from the stove, and went into the bathroom to shave.

The office of the minister of electric power looked like any other Party official office with the union flag and the requisite portrait of Lenin commanding the center of attention. There was also a portrait of Nikolai Ryzhkov, the Soviet prime minister, but none of Gorbachev, and Lazlo wondered about this.

Viktor Asimov's head was thinner on top than on the bottom because of massive cheeks and jowls. He had an aloof look, reminding Lazlo of Brezhnev. If the smile was as false as it looked, perhaps he would soon wish Asimov was also dead and buried in the Kremlin.

Lazlo politely refused Asimov's offer of coffee or tea and sat in one of the chairs facing the desk. The guest chair was lower than the one behind the desk.

"So," said Asimov, "Deputy Minister Mishin informs me you were here yesterday. Is this an official visit from the Kiev militia?"

"No," said Lazlo. "I want information about my relatives who live in Pripyat, and especially about my brother, an engineer at Chernobyl. After being at a roadblock all night and seeing the panic of thousands, I'm not prepared for the sort of dialogue I had with your deputy."

"What sort of dialogue?" asked Asimov.

"Saying everything is under control," said Lazlo. "Please fill me in as quickly as possible about what you know, Comrade Minister, because I am tired and impatient."

Asimov stood and turned to the window. "Very well, Detective Horvath. I was simply trying to be civil. I'm afraid I have bad news." Asimov paused, continued standing with his back to Lazlo. "Your brother, Mihaly Horvath, senior reactor control engineer, was one of two engineers injured in an explosion at the Chernobyl Nuclear Facility early in the morning on Saturday, April 26. Both injured men worked in the control area of the disabled RBMK-1000 reactor and were airlifted to Moscow for treatment. I am saddened to inform you your brother died from his injuries Sunday, April 27."

The morning sunlight through the window beyond Asimov lay across the floor on bloodred carpet. On the wall, Lenin gazed skyward while Ryzhkov scowled. Lazlo sensed he was in the office, then felt for a moment he was not in the office. An overwhelming sense of guilt assailed him. The image of the dying Gypsy became Mihaly, and he became his brother's murderer. History and time meant nothing. Was he a detective in the Kiev militia? Was he a nineteen-year-old soldier? Or was he a farmer? Mihaly with him, neither of them ever having attended the university in Kiev, neither of them ever having left the farm to be here in hell where machines steal a man's mind and body. Mihaly!

If only closing his eyes could take him to the wine cellar. If only he could see Mihaly dance the *czardas* in his red canvas sneakers made in Czechoslovakia. If only this were a drunken dream caused by too much wine. Mihaly!

"I'm sorry," said Asimov, returning to his chair and staring down at his desk. "It must be terrible, one's own brother, and a younger brother. I asked associates at Medium Machine Building and The Kurchatov Institute if they had further information, but they do not."

"What about Mihaly's wife and children?"

"When I found out about your brother, I personally contacted officials in the area. It was difficult getting information because of the unnecessary panic."

"What's happened to them?"

"They were flown out of the area and are being treated in a Moscow hospital. I've been unable, so far, to determine their condition. If you check back later today, I might have more news."

"How was he killed?"

"I repeat, Detective Horvath, there was an explosion. Two engineers were severely injured, one of them your brother."

"But you must know more."

Asimov forced a look of sincerity. "It will all come out in the investigation, Detective Horvath. Your brother was the engineer in charge at the time, so if there was trouble, I presume he would have been close to it."

"In charge? He wasn't a chief engineer."

"Nevertheless, he was the senior technical person present at the time."

"I see," said Lazlo. "And in this so-called investigation, will you be investigating your inadequate safety precautions and shoddy construction practices? Or will you be examining the character of my brother?"

Asimov pulled a stack of papers from the corner of his desk and began shuffling them. "I'm sorry about your brother, Detective Horvath. The sympathy of the ministry goes out to you and your family. As for investigations, I cannot speak of what has not yet taken place."

The wine cellar. Mihaly describing systematic deprivation of safety procedures and dangerous experiments. Mihaly saying the situation was "fucked." Down in the wine cellar, laughing at the fucked world, and now Mihaly was fucked. Without thinking about it, Lazlo stood and walked around the desk. He stood over Asimov and put his hand on his shoulder. "I'll come back this afternoon. When I do, I want to speak to someone who knows about safety at Chernobyl. Someone technical."

Asimov stared silently up at Lazlo, his jowls visibly shaking.

"Who will I be speaking with this afternoon, Comrade Minister?"

"Who?"

"Yes. Who is your resident technical expert?"

"Vatchenko, the deputy chairman of the engineering council. He knows about safety."

"And he'll be here?"

Asimov nodded his head. "Yes, Detective Horvath. But please listen. There's something Moscow has instructed me to say."

"What's that?"

"They said no news is to leak out except through official channels. They said we are to report to them and to no one else."

The room blurred, and Lazlo took out his handkerchief to dry his eyes.

Asimov pushed his chair back and stood up. "Please believe I'm sorry, Detective Horvath. At times like this, there is nothing one can say or do to set things right."

"Yes, there is."

"What?"

"Find out about my brother's family and have Vatchenko here this afternoon."

The shade of a chestnut tree across the street from the Ministry of Energy made the inside of the Volga comfortable. A few minutes earlier, unable to stand it any longer, Komarov had lit a cigarette. Captain Azef rolled his window partway down and said, because of the nuclear accident, air drawn through a cigarette filter might be better than the air outside.

Komarov knew about the death of Detective Horvath's brother, Mihaly Horvath, the engineer in charge at the time of the so-called accident. These facts, plus the work his KGB branch office had done concerning the Horvath brothers, their American cousin, and Juli Popovics, prompted Deputy Chairman Dumenko to place Komarov in charge of an aggressive investigation in spite of the Chernobyl accident. Already, an agent digging into Soviet army records had uncovered a questionable shooting incident involving Detective Horvath.

The detective was his to watch and, perhaps, catch, like a fish out of water in this scheme, whatever the scheme might turn out to be. And now two of Captain Putna's men had followed Juli Popovics from Pripyat. She was in Kiev, and the PK agent named Nikolai was to meet Komarov at his office later in the day. On the phone this morning, Nikolai sounded gratified to be out of the back room of the rural post office. The same PK agents who first revealed the possible Gypsy Moth connection were here in Kiev. Was it coincidence that, prior to visiting his cousins last summer, Andrew Zukor had stopped at the CIA station in Budapest? Perhaps Zukor wanted to obtain information about the plant from Mihaly Horvath in order to discredit the Soviet nuclear program, or perhaps he was digging deeper, searching for plutonium production numbers the way the Americans had always done.

As they waited across from the Ministry of Energy for Detective Horvath to emerge, Komarov wondered why Juli Popovics had come to Kiev instead of going directly to her aunt's house in Visenka. She might contact Detective Horvath, her lover's brother; such a contact would definitely suggest conspiracy. Yes, everything was falling into place. Even Juli Popovics' pregnancy with Mihaly Horvath's child added to the growing evidence.

Komarov found the business of childbirth and pregnancy distasteful. When he saw duck-shaped women waddling down sidewalks, he was reminded of the birth of his son. At the time, he reacted as anyone would expect. Grigor Komarov, proud father of a son who would grow into a man, follow in his father's footsteps, and carry on his name. But Dmitry had betrayed him. Instead of normal courtship, instead of sewing the customary wild oats, Dmitry was a lover of men, forcing into his father's mind the image of another man's penis in his son's anus or even his mouth. A son who had been held up for him to see while moisture from the womb was wiped from him. These private thoughts of Dmitry made Komarov think of Gretchen, made him recall the feel of the knife entering her womb . . . It was as if he had tried to kill the womb.

Komarov's wife, in her ignorance, welcomed Dmitry's friends into their house. Several nights ago, he watched her kiss Dmitry's current "lover," Fyodor, on the lips. Normally it would have been an innocent greeting, but he could not forget it. Last Saturday night, after intercourse, his wife asked why he no longer kissed her. What was he to say? He could not kiss her because her lips had kissed lips that sucked her own son's penis? He might as well tell his wife her body had, in his imagination, become Gretchen. Gretchen beneath him in the bedroom of the "safe" house. Gretchen musklike following her union with Pudkov, who lay dead in the hall. Gretchen moaning as he touches her with one gloved hand, while in the other hand . . .

"Insane," said Azef, interrupting Komarov's thoughts.

"What are you talking about?"

"The entire situation," said Azef. "An accident occurs, and Kiev's public prosecutor opens an investigation. It does nothing except take our men away from us."

"Only a few men," said Komarov. "Not our best men."

"I agree," said Azef. "We save our best men for genuine investigation. While the Regional Party Committee tells Moscow what it wants to hear, we seek the truth."

"This is why I've assigned men to Chernobyl," said Komarov. "Even though rescue and evacuation take precedence, those in charge must be questioned. Unfortunately, it leaves us shorthanded in Kiev."

"Rather than going to the accident site, you and I must take care of matters here." Azef paused. "But I wondered what you thought about the possibility of another explosion?"

"Nonsense," said Komarov. "I spoke personally with Colonel Zamyatin this morning. He's in touch with scientists from the Energy Ministry at the site. Soon all will be under control at the reactor."

"Some who might know what caused the accident are in Moscow," said Azef.

"I'm aware of that," said Komarov, somewhat annoyed. "The Moscow office assured me they will handle interviews in Hospital Number Six. In case you forgot, Captain Azef, I was fully briefed before you arrived this morning. The evacuation of Pripyat is under way, directors of surrounding collectives will find space for evacuees, Black Sea hotels and campgrounds have been reserved, and komsomols will provide food. During my conversation with Moscow, we estimated as many as one hundred thousand people will need to be evacuated from around the power station. Therefore, Captain, since recovery operations are being handled, we are responsible for determining whether the explosion was an accident or sabotage!"

Komarov realized he had raised his voice. "We are all under pressure, Captain. Because we are not at the disaster scene, you and I must follow through in Kiev before suspects vanish."

"I still wonder whether more resources should be committed to evacuation."

Komarov lowered his window, threw his cigarette out, and stared at Azef in silence.

"I'm sorry, Major. I simply wondered about the justification for Moscow assigning security troops to Kiev instead of assigning them to the Chernobyl region."

"Captain, we have been assigned by the directorate. If you wish to help with evacuation, perhaps I should reconsider your assignment!"

"I wish to continue my current assignment, Major. I was simply considering the magnitude of the situation. The pledge of secrecy issued this morning does not allow me to discuss these things with anyone else."

They sat in silence for several minutes before Azef spoke again.

"There's Detective Horvath. He's coming out of the building."

"Do you notice a difference in his composure?" asked Komarov.

"Possibly," said Azef. "He's looking down as he walks. It's difficult to say if he received news of his brother. He looks like any other person walking down the street with nothing particular on his mind."

Azef started the Volga and followed the Zhiguli, which sent out a puff of smoke at each shift of the gears. Detective Horvath turned onto Volodimirski Street and drove slowly, sometimes stopping and waving pedestrians across. Several times, because they drove so slowly, Azef pulled into a parking space and waited before proceeding.

"Do you think he sees us?" asked Azef.

"I don't know," said Komarov.

Detective Horvath parked the Zhiguli across from the Cathedral of Saint Sophia, crossed the street, and entered the portico of the cathedral with a group of people being led by a uniformed tour guide.

"Do you think he came to pray?" asked Azef.

"I don't see why. The cathedral hasn't had services since the state made it into a museum. Go see what he's up to."

While Azef was gone, Komarov watched the cathedral grounds to make certain Horvath would not escape, perhaps finding a back way out. For a moment, Komarov found himself lapsing into his earlier thoughts of Dmitry, his wife, Gretchen, and the knife. But he forced this out of his mind and concentrated on the cathedral.

The upper domes of the cathedral glittered in sunlight turned off and on by clouds blowing across the sky. Scaffolding was set up on one side, with workmen refurbishing a lower greenish dome. All this expense to appease peasants. Someday a work crew would refurbish the office of Deputy Chairman Grigor Komarov. Perhaps someday soon.

Komarov lit a cigarette and waited.

Azef returned out of breath. "I . . . I had to run to stay ahead. Here he comes."

"What was he doing in there?"

"It was strange. He was praying."

"In what way was it strange?"

"He joined a tour, and I followed. We were in the central nave when it happened."

"What happened?" asked Komarov impatiently.

"He knelt on the floor. Right there in the middle of all those people, he knelt and started weeping aloud. He raised his hands like an icon. It was incredible. People backed away and made a circle around him. He looked to the ceiling, tears streaming down his cheeks." Azef pointed out the window. "See those women? They're still weeping. Everyone was weeping. It was contagious. Even I felt tears in my eyes."

"He doesn't look upset now," said Komarov.

"But it's true," said Azef.

They followed Detective Horvath's Zhiguli the few blocks to militia headquarters. Once Horvath parked and went inside, Komarov radioed for a nearby car to take over and told Azef to drive back to the branch office.

Komarov studied Azef, his eyes red because he had wept with the women in the cathedral. Komarov wondered if his cunning and intelligence instilled as much fear in his enemies as did this fear of the unknown, this irrational fear of a so-called God common among brutes and peasants. Christians, Muslims, Jews, and Gypsies. All the same.

CHAPTER 16

On Monday, April 28, the rumor and speculation the government had tried to avoid spread across the Ukraine. Because of its nearness to the disaster site, an explosion of misinformation hit metropolitan Kiev. First came the evacuees who, without official news, brought stories out of proportion like snowballs rolling down hills. These accounts ranged from the entire Chernobyl complex exploding and the town of Pripyat on fire, to citizens collapsing in the streets like insects sprayed with insecticide.

Adding to the speculation was an announcement on Radio Free Europe about high levels of radiation coming from the Soviet Union. Harsh news would require time for the Soviet News Agency to digest and adjust. Continued silence could mean the situation was so far out of control no one knew what to say. Technicians wielding Geiger counters at checkpoints terrified evacuees, as well as citizens of Kiev living on the outskirts near the roadblocks.

But Kievians were used to rumors, and in south and central Kiev life seemed normal. At lunchtime, office workers purchased lunches from vendors along Khreshchatik and, despite the threat of rain, picnicked in the parks along the river. Only a few Kievians hearing the news harbored thoughts of the world's end, crawling into basements or spending the day on benches in metro air-raid shelters. The usual old women went to church to pray.

The few churches in Pripyat were empty. Residents not yet evacuated were told to seal themselves inside their apartments. Most left on buses Sunday afternoon, some of the evacuees chiding the soldiers forcing them to leave. Soldiers going floor to floor each time a contingent of buses lined up knew little and could only follow orders. The soldiers estimated Pripyat would be all but abandoned the next day.

The sounds in Pripyat came from helicopters passing overhead, army trucks traveling at high speeds, buses lining up, and soldiers shouting through gauze masks, telling residents they had two hours to gather what they could and assemble outside their buildings. Occasionally, when there were no helicopters overhead or trucks or buses on the roads, the soldiers could hear birds and dogs. Birds sang spring songs heralding the cycle of life, not knowing the nests they built here would most likely be doomed. Dogs barked in yards because of the soldiers and because masters had failed to feed them or take them for walks.

Some residents of Pripyat refused to leave. Many were invalids who lived alone. Among them was Mihaly and Nina Horvath's neighbor, the old woman with a cane who had greeted Juli and Marina and Vasily at the Horvath apartment. The old woman stayed in her apartment, fearing looters would take her belongings. On Sunday the woman put her pet canary in its cage out on the balcony. On Monday morning, finding the canary dead in the cage, the old woman made a flag saying, "Help!" out of a bedsheet and hung it out the window. The canary might have been affected by the radiation or, having been an indoor bird all of its life, might have simply succumbed to the overnight chill. Whatever the reason, the old woman stood leaning on her cane at her window, waiting for soldiers to see her sign from the road and come get her.

In farming villages surrounding Pripyat, people waiting to be evacuated wondered what to do with their livestock. Some piled fodder in barnyards. Others released livestock into fields so they could fend for themselves. Inside farm cottages, kitchen tables were set with plates and cutlery for the number of people living in the cottage. This was for good luck to assure all the residents of the cottage would safely return.

If there had been a window in his small corner cubicle, Lazlo would have seen what appeared to be a typical noontime crowd in the street below. But the cubicle had no window. Lazlo never spent much time here. The only reason he came now was to try again to call the Moscow hospital treating Nina and the girls. But each time he called, the line was busy.

Deputy Chief Investigator Lysenko, passing by and looking surprised to see him, leaned into the cubicle.

"I didn't know you were here, Detective Horvath. I have a message for you. It came upstairs earlier this morning and . . ."

Lazlo grabbed the message. It said a woman was waiting at the downstairs desk. It said the woman chose to wait even when told Lazlo might not be in the office today. While Lazlo read the note, Lysenko stood before him, smiling like a fool. The note said the woman was young and attractive, and her name was Juli Popovics.

At first the Hungarian name made Lazlo think of the village of Kisbor, the farm where he and Mihaly grew up. But then he recalled the afternoon last winter when Mihaly confessed to him about his lover named Juli.

Citizens of Pripyat fleeing south to Kiev. It had to be. Mihaly's lover here, to see him. Mihaly dead, Nina and the girls taken to Moscow, and Mihaly's lover comes to him. Lazlo put the note down on his desk, and when he looked up, Lysenko was still there smiling.

"What do you want, Lysenko?"

"I thought I should fill you in. The trouble has begun. We've been told to watch for looters smuggling goods south in hay bales. In villages farther from the power station, children were moved out ahead of adults, so we'll have to watch for them at the roadblocks."

"Anything else?"

"Since you ask," said Lysenko, "I need to tell you Chief Investigator Chkalov questions why you did not visit the militia station when you were in Pripyat. Apparently he wonders if you might have something to add to the current Pripyat situation."

Lazlo raised his voice. "Anything else?"

"Nothing else, Detective Horvath."

"Then why do you stand there like a baggage handler waiting for a tip?"

Lysenko frowned, shook his head. "I thought we would be able to share a professional conversation, Detective Horvath. I thought this woman might relate to a case you're involved in." Lysenko straightened his tie. "Since I am Chief Investigator Chkalov's assistant, it seemed reasonable to take an interest, just as you took an interest in the roadblocks, so much of an interest that you went to the chief investigator's home last night."

Lazlo wanted to grab Lysenko by his tie. But as he stepped closer, he controlled the urge. "Is my brother being killed a good enough reason?"

Before Lysenko could react, Lazlo moved past him and hurried down to the front desk.

Like a true refugee, Juli Popovics carried a small overnight bag and wore a scarf and a coat too heavy for the season. The scarf was not on her head, but tied loosely about her neck. Her hair was dark brown, brushed out straight. Her face had a look of innocence, perhaps because she wore no makeup or perhaps because her eyes, large and greenish-gray and unblinking, were full of questions.

"Detective Horvath, my name is Juli Popovics. I know your brother, Mihaly. I came from Pripyat, where there has been trouble."

"I know." Lazlo led her to the stairs. "I recognize the Hungarian accent in your Russian." When she nodded, he switched to Hungarian. "Come, let me take your bag."

As he climbed the stairs ahead of her, he replayed what she'd said in his head. "I know your brother, Mihaly." He wondered if her use of present tense was similar to the talk of relatives at a funeral, speaking of the deceased in present tense. How could she be in Pripyat and not know Mihaly was killed?

Lazlo put her bag on his desk, pulled his chair out, and sat before her, feeling vulnerable to her penetrating eyes. In the moments of silence before speaking, he stared at her. She did not know about Mihaly.

"Forgive me, Miss Popovics, my name is Lazlo."

"Mine is Juli. We traveled all day yesterday and most of the night. Friends dropped me north of the city and went to stay with relatives. I waited at the Hotel Dnieper until morning."

"Is it bad in Pripyat?"

"People are leaving. No physical damage. The explosion and fire was several kilometers away. But the radiation ... everyone who knows about radiation has gone by now, most coming south because the wind has been blowing north. On our way here, we saw buses and army trucks going north." Juli stared at him, her eyes open wide. "You know something about Mihaly." She forced a smile. "He's come here. Mihaly and his family are here!"

Lazlo stared into her eyes as he spoke. "Until this morning, I knew only about an accident at the Chernobyl plant. I was at the roadblock on the road from Korosten all night waiting for Mihaly and Nina and the girls to come. Anna and Ilonka would run to their uncle, and he would lift them up in the air. I would have driven them to my apartment. I'd still be there if this were true. I'd be celebrating with my brother and his family. But they did not come."

Juli's eyes moistened, her lips held tightly together, trembling. Suddenly he felt very close to her. A link to his brother, as though he were about to tell Nina her husband had died. Where was his anger at this woman who might have torn Mihaly away from Nina?

Tears began to flow down the cheeks of this woman named Juli, tears like his at the cathedral where he'd protested the injustice of Mihaly's death, as if there were such a thing as justice in this world.

Despite her tears, Juli continued staring at him. "It's Mihaly."

"He's dead." Lazlo had to swallow to continue. "I found out this morning."

He expected her to break down. But she simply blinked her eyes and said, "What about Mihaly's wife and little girls? I went to the apartment. A neighbor said they'd gone to the plant to see about him."

"They've been taken to Moscow. I don't know any other details except they are at a hospital there."

A noisy pair of officers passed, and Juli glanced their way. She continued staring at the doorway as if the news were not true, as if Mihaly would appear there. For some time she sat this way, her youthful profile stained as tears began to flow. Her cheeks were smooth, her nose rounded, her chin jutting ever so slightly. Although he had fought the feeling, she reminded him of Nina.

Lazlo stood, went to her, and put his hand on her shoulder. She looked up, leaned her head, and raised her shoulder, pressing his hand against her cheek, squeezing his hand hard between her cheek and shoulder. Finally, she trembled and wept openly.

"Nikolai Nikolskaia?" shouted Komarov. "Who the hell is that?"

Captain Azef shrugged his shoulders. "He said he spoke with you by phone this morning. He was reluctant to give information to anyone but you. I had to show him my identification before he would reveal he is a PK agent from Pripyat. He said Captain Putna ordered him and his partner to locate Chernobyl workers. They followed a worker to Kiev last night. I would have questioned their motive for following a single worker until he told me the worker they followed is Juli Popovics."

"Yes," said Komarov. "I did speak with him this morning."

"Before we followed Horvath to the cathedral?" said Azef, looking puzzled.

"I had my reasons for not telling you. Where is Nikolskaia's partner?"

"The other PK agent followed Juli Popovics to militia headquarters where she inquired about Detective Horvath. Shall I bring Nikolskaia in?"

"Yes, Captain. I'll speak with him alone."

Azef looked disappointed. "Does this have to do with the Horvath's American cousin?"

"Send Nikolskaia in on your way out, Captain. I've gained his trust, and I'll fill you in later. Have my secretary bring tea."

Komarov stood at his window while he waited for Nikolskaia. He remained at the window as his secretary put the tea tray on his desk. Because his secretary was almost deaf, he did not turn to thank her and knew she did not expect to be thanked. Over the years, the old Slav had become good at coming and going unnoticed.

Even though he could not see it, Komarov stared out his window in the direction of Chernobyl. With Juli Popovics in Kiev contacting Detective Horvath, Mihaly Horvath dead, Azef confused, and Deputy Chairman Dumenko backing him, an impression of conspiracy was created. For Komarov, the more killed and injured, the better. Grigor Komarov, the diligent Soviet citizen who helped the union save face in the wake of nuclear catastrophe.

Nikolai Nikolskaia wore a soiled imitation leather jacket, wrinkled shirt, and no tie. He was a young man with soft features reminding Komarov of his son, Dmitry. Nikolskaia watched warily as Komarov adjusted his uniform lapels and tie after sitting at his desk.

"Please sit down," said Komarov in a tone he usually reserved for higher officials.

Nikolskaia sat nervously, staring at the tea tray. "Thank you, Major Komarov."

"I understand you followed Juli Popovics here to Kiev."

"Captain Putna instructed us to observe her. We felt badly about having to leave the area. We would have liked to stay and help."

"I'm sure you would have," said Komarov. "Just as I wish I could be there to help. But critical counterespionage work needs to be done here in Kiev."

"If there is anything I . . . we can do, Major . . ."

"Tell me, Nikolskaia, did it seem to you Juli Popovics was running away from something other than radiation danger?"

"We thought of this . . . it could be."

Komarov poured tea for himself and pushed the tray to Nikolskaia. "From the beginning, give me details of your observation."

After a few sips of tea, Nikolskaia began with letters intercepted at the post office, including those between the Horvath brothers, and from the cousin, Andrew Zukor. Regarding letters from Juli Popovics, Nikolskaia concluded she was pregnant, as indicated in recent correspondence to her aunt. Next he told about their observation of the apartment and the arrival of "others" who drove Juli Popovics and her roommate quickly out of town.

"And then," said Nikolskaia, "as we waited in line at the roadblock, she left the car and went on foot, passing through the roadblock without being stopped. She took the metro and stayed in the Hotel Dnieper lobby until going to militia headquarters this morning."

Komarov swiveled his chair, facing away from Nikolskaia. "Perhaps I should provide some background. During the past year, KGB analysts, at my direction, have researched the Horvath family. The cousin, Andrew Zukor, was given the name Gypsy Moth because, as a moth flies to and from a bright light, Zukor has flown in and out of the Ukraine many times. We've had men watching him. Although he is a U.S. citizen, he bases his operations in Hungary. We believe he is part of a deep-cover operation collecting technological intelligence. Therefore, communicating with Mihaly Horvath, a senior reactor control engineer at the Chernobyl Power Station, has been a concern. To put it bluntly, I am now certain CIA operatives, perhaps answering directly to the movie actor President Reagan, have been working to discredit the Soviet nuclear program. And what better way to do this than to cause an accident at the plant?"

Komarov felt pleased with the scenario he had concocted. A CIA operative attempting to influence a Chernobyl engineer should get Nikolskaia's blood boiling. He swiveled his chair back to Nikolskaia, waited a moment, and when Nikolskaia did not answer, continued. "It's unfortunate we do not have this Zukor fellow here in our country where the court system could deal with him. With existing evidence, it would be a matter of charges, verdict, and prison term. Swift justice and, if necessary, perhaps some telephone justice for good measure."

Komarov could see his conversation was having the desired effect. Nikolskaia looked confused and uncomfortable at having been told too much.

"I'm sorry," continued Komarov. "I assumed you knew in cases of espionage, verdicts are often determined by a Party official's phone call to a judge."

Komarov stood and walked to his window. He turned around to face Nikolskaia, knowing he presented a dark figure against the bright western sky, as he continued a speech he felt would put Nikolskaia in the palm of his hand.

"We know Zukor visited the Horvath brothers at their ancestral farm last summer. We know funds were passed to Zukor from CIA operatives. Therefore, it is obvious the Gypsy Moth seeks to destabilize the union just as his namesake destabilized vegetation in his country. Zukor is a Gypsy, like his cousins. Have you noticed Gypsies have olive-colored skin? These races have a tendency to worship false gods, generate extremists, and do their best to disrupt civilized Soviet society. Haven't we learned our lesson in Afghanistan?

"I'm concerned about our union, Comrade Nikolskaia. At first glance, openness and restructuring seem constructive. But if leaders in their embrace of restructuring fall into a trap, what will they find at the bottom of the pit? Not extremists. They will be at the edge of the pit, looking down. To climb the walls of the pit one must overcome religion, capitalism, homosexuality, and all extremism!"

Nikolskaia sat upright, expanding his chest and staring wide-eyed. Komarov's rant had taken hold. He returned to his desk and sat down, picked up his teacup, and had a sip. Nikolskaia did the same, but his eyes were wide with anticipation. Komarov allowed a minute to pass, saying nothing before continuing in a calmer voice. He commended Nikolskaia on his actions before he began preparing Nikolskaia for what would become a more elaborate version of Juli Popovics' trip to Kiev.

First, because of the speed of the escape, it was obvious Juli Popovics was running from fear of capture. The men who tried to stop the car, Nikolskaia admitted, might have been other agents; indeed, they probably were, since his being a PK agent did not give him familiarity with all KGB operations in Pripyat. Next, instead of merely following others on back roads to avoid the reactor site, the car in which Juli Popovics rode purposely evaded pursuers. Finally, Komarov got Nikolskaia to agree Juli Popovics surreptitiously entered Kiev, leaving the car in which she had escaped Pripyat and going on foot, using methods to avoid authorized KGB observation.

"Juli Popovics knew she was being followed by the KGB," said Komarov. "She has something to hide and has gone out of her way to lose herself in Kiev. Is that correct?"

"Yes," said Nikolskaia, obviously afraid to say no.

By the end of the session, Nikolskaia was more than willing to complete and sign a preliminary report in Komarov's office, with Captain Azef called in as witness. Nikolskaia and his partner would make a full report later in the day. Komarov ordered two men to replace Nikolskaia's partner watching Juli Popovics, and the two PK agents from Pripyat would return to Komarov's office for further orders.

After Nikolskaia and Azef were gone, Komarov lit a cigarette and returned to his window. Down on the street, he saw Nikolskaia enter a battered Moskvich, which smoked as it started. He would keep the PK agents on the case, dress them up in new suits, and give them a Volga to drive. In their new positions as KGB investigators, they would, if there was ever an inquiry, collaborate the evidence of the conspiracy uncovered by Major Grigor Komarov.

Komarov left his window and returned to his desk. He placed a call to Major Dmitry Struyev, the only member of Directorate T in the Kiev office. Struyev was a trusted comrade, a so-called hard-liner. He was rarely in his office, but today he answered his phone.

"I am calling about a matter I brought up some time ago," said Komarov.

"Proceed," said Struyev, a man of few words.

"The American visiting Hungary has become a problem."

"Gypsy Moth?"

"Yes," said Komarov. "He has information critical to our nuclear program and is about to pass the information along. I need to be certain he does not."

"I understand," said Struyev. "Is there anything else?"

"No."

They hung up without further comment. Komarov went back to his window and looked west. Somewhere beyond the Carpathians, Andrew Zukor would soon meet a man sent by Struyev. Whatever knowledge Zukor had would be gone, and the Chernobyl conspiracy would strengthen. As he stood at his window, Komarov felt the irony of his son, Dmitry, having the same name as the man he had just called.

Although Juli took precautions to limit her radiation exposure, she felt there was more she could have done. Instead of waiting to use the ladies' room at the Hotel Dnieper to wash and change clothes, she should have used the ladies' room earlier in the metro station. Back in Pripyat, instead of going to see about Mihaly's family, she should have stayed in the apartment.

As if he knew about the baby, Mihaly's brother seemed anxious, taking time to call a hospital and arrange tests, driving her himself, and waiting for her. When the tests were completed, Lazlo came to her with a look of compassion.

"What did they say?" asked Lazlo.

"The counters showed nothing above normal. They took a blood sample. I'm supposed to call about the results tomorrow."

"Did they give you anything?"

"Potassium iodide. It limits the amount of radioactive iodine in my system, especially my thyroid."

She didn't tell Lazlo the doctor who treated her gave her an extra dose of potassium iodide for the baby and recommended she consider an abortion.

Lazlo asked when she had eaten last. When she said twenty-four hours earlier, he took her to a nearby restaurant, where they ate thick borscht and pork sandwiches.

Lazlo wanted to know about her trip, about her plans. She gave details about the explosion Saturday morning, the precautions she and Marina had taken, the visit to Mihaly's apartment, and the long wait before Vasily came for them on Sunday. She told him about Aunt Magda in Visenka. Lazlo said it was only a half-hour drive to the south, and he would take her.

"We fled south like war refugees," said Juli. "Chernobyl workers and farmers alike. I heard people speaking Russian, Ukrainian, Slavic, and Hungarian. The voices seemed to come from another world."

While Juli spoke, Lazlo stared at her. His eyes were dark and sincere, conveying a feeling of experience, knowledge, and gentleness. A mature Mihaly, a man devoted to duty. His hair was graying but thick, and seemed windblown despite being inside the restaurant.

"We are in another world," said Lazlo. "Mihaly once told me others at the plant considered Hungarians aloof. I remember when I was a boy having to learn Russian. I remember helping teach Russian to Mihaly. When it was time to move to Kiev, we had to learn Ukrainian. But we never lost touch with our first language. We spoke it whenever we were together."

"I also remember learning languages," said Juli. "My father taught me Hungarian while my mother taught me Russian. They fought over which language I should use. When I was a little girl, I used the two languages to pit my parents against one another, to get my way. It was only later, in Pripyat, when I began learning Ukrainian."

"When was the last time you saw Mihaly?" asked Lazlo.

"Friday after work on the bus. He said he would be working on the shutdown."

"What did he talk about?"

"The shutdown, the reasons for it."

"Did he seem nervous?"

"Yes. He said it was dangerous doing the shutdown because of things recently going wrong. He spoke often of inadequate safety at the plant. It was a low-power experiment he didn't think necessary . . . I didn't expect this to happen . . . his wife and girls going to the plant . . . I feel responsible. I could have done something to prevent this. I failed. I . . ."

Lazlo touched her hand. "You can't blame yourself for what fate brings."

"I blame myself because Friday, when I spoke with Mihaly, I felt very selfish. I was the only person in the world who couldn't have what she wanted. Mihaly was going back to his wife, and I was going back to loneliness. So now where is Mihaly? And where is his family?" Juli wiped her eyes with her table napkin. "Forgive me. I'm good at only weeping and messing with lives where I don't belong."

"Would you like to leave for your aunt's now?"

"Yes."

On the way out of the restaurant, several patrons looked at her sadly like those on the buses waiting to get into Kiev, but also like the faces on the bus taking Mihaly away Friday afternoon so long ago.

Before driving Juli to her aunt's, Lazlo called headquarters. Deputy Chief Investigator Lysenko told him that personnel from the Ministry of Energy had joined the militia at the roadblocks and people were being measured with Geiger counters. Technicians sprayed those contaminated with a solution from tanker trucks.

"Who ordered this?" asked Lazlo.

"The Health Ministry," said Lysenko. "In any case, you're due back at the roadblock from Korosten tonight at midnight. The army is evacuating everyone from the area around Chernobyl, and Chief Investigator Chkalov has ordered double shifts."

While driving out of Kiev, Lazlo turned on the radio for local news. Radio Moscow's report was short, the commentator saying an accident had occurred at the Chernobyl nuclear facility north of Kiev, but everything possible was being done.

"Everything possible is being done," commented Juli. "Which is absolutely nothing for all the people who sat in their homes not knowing about the radiation. I should have warned people. I should have gone from apartment to apartment."

When he stopped at a traffic signal, Lazlo looked at Juli. She stared at him, and for an instant he felt a floating sensation, an insane moment when reality slips away to a parallel world created by a slight turn of events. In this parallel world, he marries Nina, and she sits beside him in coat and scarf. It was easy to imagine because Juli's soft features and the green of her eyes reminded him of Nina, or of what Nina had secretly meant to him.

Juli continued staring at him. "I was selfish," she said. "But perhaps I have reason. Last Friday night I was going to tell Mihaly . . . not to make him responsible . . . I was going to tell him . . . I was going away for several months . . . to have our baby."

A car horn sounded from behind, and Lazlo drove on, feeling as though the entire universe had slipped a notch.

The Dnieper River bridge south of Trukhanov Island was sometimes referred to by citizens of Kiev as a bridge between two worlds. On one side was Kiev, with its Monument of the Motherland and its hills and trees and architecture from earlier centuries when a structure was more than mere shelter. On the other side of the bridge was Darnitsa, set back beyond the river foliage on flatlands, its rectangular buildings like so many dominoes.

South out of Darnitsa along the eastern shore of the Dnieper, the hills across the river rose steeply. The river was wide, capturing the shadows of the hills. A passenger steamer heading south to the Black Sea added perspective to the picture postcard. As she watched the view out the car window, Juli imagined she was with the father of her future child on a holiday trip to Odessa and there was no such thing as radiation, or even atoms. Everything was solid and stable and would last forever.

"Last summer," said Lazlo, "at the farm near the Czech frontier, Mihaly told me his concerns about safety at Chernobyl. Later in the year, when I visited Pripyat, he told me about you. I should have followed up about the plant."

"Mihaly was not the only one worried about safety," said Juli. "If you worked at Chernobyl, you got used to constant talk of safety, or lack of safety. The jokes higher officials called gossipmongering caused memos to be sent to supervisors. The chief engineer jokes the plant is nothing more than a steam bath, nothing but hot water. But death is no joke. No one laughs now. As for Mihaly telling you about me, I have my own feelings."

"What do you mean?" asked Lazlo.

"Mihaly and I didn't mean to upset his family life. Our relationship was ending when his wife found out. All three of us were hurt deeply."

"You think I told Nina about you? Mihaly asked if I did. I was angry with him. I felt I was being blamed for what you and he had done. I understand passion. Nothing is black and white. But to tell Nina, to hurt her . . ."

"Mihaly said you wouldn't do it. I didn't believe him. Now I do."

"Why?"

"Because I can see you. It's easy to mistrust someone until you meet him face to face. Mihaly was not like other men, and you are not like other men. Men in power are responsible for accidents like Chernobyl. In their quest for power, they ignore the future and the environment. It is the only thing we have to give our children. And now men . . . always men . . . have destroyed what little we have. But you and Mihaly . . ."

Lazlo looked straight ahead as he drove. His side window was open slightly, causing his hair to blow about. His profile, small chin and sloping forehead, was similar to Mihaly's. A handsome man, but serious, as the situation deserved. A man determined to set things straight.

"Are you worried about your baby?" asked Lazlo.

"Of course. But I don't want to think about an abortion. I'll wait for the blood test results."

"And if the results are not clear-cut?"

"I don't know what to do. I was going to give the baby up for adoption. But now . . . I don't know."

The house was on the edge of the town of Visenka at the end of a road, which continued as a rutted trail into farm fields. The house was small, a cottage, and along the foundation in earth kept warm by the house, spring flowers bloomed. A small arbor covered with budding vines arched over the walk. When Lazlo followed Juli through the arbor, an old woman appeared at the door. She was short and plump and wiped her hands on an apron embroidered with flowers. When she opened the door, Lazlo could smell bread baking. The small size of the house, the farm fields in the distance, the appearance of this woman at the door . . . all of it reminded him of his boyhood in Kisbor. When the old woman hugged Juli and they spoke in Hungarian, the spell was complete.

"Detective Horvath is from Kiev," said Juli. "He was kind enough to drive me here. This is Aunt Magda, my father's sister."

Aunt Magda's hand was wrinkled and tough, a farm woman. She looked at him suspiciously. "I've never met a Hungarian militiaman. Were you born in Ukraine?"

"Near the Czech border."

"What do you know about this reactor business? What can I tell my neighbors?"

"I'll let your niece explain. She knows more than me. I must leave now because I've been promised a meeting this afternoon at the Ministry of Energy office in Kiev."

"Call me," said Juli. "I hope you find out more about your brother's family."

"You have relatives near Chernobyl?" asked Aunt Magda.

"My brother's wife and little girls. My brother worked at the plant . . . he was killed."

"My God," said Aunt Magda, holding Lazlo's hand and looking up to him. "I'm very sorry for you. It's not right these things happen. People killed, and the news says nothing. My God. Killed."

She squeezed his hand. "Is there anything I can do?"

"No." He looked to Juli, who stood behind her aunt, her cheeks wet with tears. "But I'll let you know about his wife and two little girls."

"Please do. I'll pray for your brother and for them. I'll keep candles burning."

Juli turned away, wiping her cheeks with the back of her hand. "Please write down your telephone number for Detective Horvath, Aunt Magda."

When Aunt Magda began searching through a cabinet, Juli stepped close to Lazlo, kissed him quickly on the cheek, and said, "I lived in Moscow when I was a girl. They have the finest hospitals."

When Lazlo left the house and stepped beneath the arbor, he saw a momentary flash of red up the road. He held several thick vine branches apart with his fingers and saw the car parked on the opposite side of the road about fifty meters away, facing the opposite direction. It was a faded red Zhiguli, partially hidden by an old truck. The left taillight was out, but he knew it had been lit a moment earlier.

Lazlo got into his car, turned around, and drove up the road. After passing the old truck, he saw two men in the red car. At the main street in Visenka, he turned north and drove slowly. Soon the faded red Zhiguli was on the main street behind him, and stayed with him as he made several turns to the highway. The Zhiguli followed him all the way back to Kiev. He knew it had to be KGB, KGB driving a faded Zhiguli instead of their usual black Volga.

When the KGB followed someone, they did it one of two ways. The more obvious way was men in dark overcoats driving a black Volga. This method was meant as a warning to the person being followed. The other way was undercover, changing vehicles, using even a cheap red car like so many others on the crowded streets of Kiev. The men in the red Zhiguli followed cautiously, and it was obvious he was not supposed to know.

A light rain began in Kiev, the droplets plummeting down through the upper atmosphere where the wind was changing direction.

CHAPTER 17

Monday afternoon, thirty-six hours without sleep, and Lazlo was back at the Ministry of Energy. The news of Mihaly's death and the hours spent with Juli Popovics seemed transcendental, having happened to another Lazlo Horvath. Had he reached his physical limit, or was something else taking place inside him?

Vatchenko, deputy chairman of the Engineering Council, met Lazlo in a conference room. Minister of Electric Power Asimov left the room after introducing Vatchenko, and Lazlo sat at the conference table, watching Vatchenko draw diagrams of reactor operating principles on a chalkboard. Vatchenko was a thin, intense young man with short, light-colored hair. What had at first glance seemed an overlarge upper lip was actually a mustache of flesh-colored hair. Although he was dead tired, Lazlo listened intently.

The explosion took place shortly after one in the morning on Saturday, April 26. A steam explosion was first, followed by another explosion caused by hydrogen gas. The second explosion disrupted the reactor core and ignited the graphite. Helicopters dropped sand onto the exposed core, followed by boron and lead. Because of the radiation released, a ring of approximately twenty to thirty kilometers was being evacuated.

Vatchenko sat across from Lazlo at the conference table, glancing back to admire his diagrams on the chalkboard. "I can understand your concern, Detective Horvath. It's unfortunate it sometimes takes incidents like this to make higher officials take an interest in technology. Has any of this made sense?"

"The first few diagrams were clear," said Lazlo. "I understand the backup systems, and your lecture on hardware would be fine if I wanted to become a nuclear engineer. What I'm really curious about is quality control, the inspections of all these pumps and valves and sensors. Who does it? When is it done? And mostly, have there recently been changes in procedures?"

Vatchenko smiled. "To understand procedure, one must understand the total system."

"I'm talking about simple inspections," said Lazlo. "I'm talking about changes in the past six months. If plant hardware has not changed since it was put into service, wouldn't reductions in safety procedures during critical testing make things less safe at the plant?"

"This talk of so-called reductions in safety procedures is puzzling, Detective Horvath. I assure you a technical investigation will be conducted by those most qualified."

"Those qualified to place the blame wherever they want?" asked Lazlo.

Vatchenko leaned back in his chair, folded his hands on his chest, and twirled his thumbs. "Detective Horvath, since concern for your brother's role in the incident is obvious, I must tell you that as senior engineer on duty, his actions, or lack thereof, will be scrutinized. I'm truly sorry he has become a victim, but I must be honest with you."

"What about the chief engineer?"

"The chief engineer was not on duty."

"Did he order tests he knew would be dangerous?"

Vatchenko stopped twirling his thumbs. "For someone who knows little about nuclear plants, you imply a great deal, Detective Horvath. You use militia credentials to demand answers. Yet it is too soon for answers. I'm sorry about your brother and for the other victim."

"Only two victims? I've seen the faces of evacuees. They are homeless, frightened, and confused. Perhaps it is better to keep everyone confused. Perhaps for your holy Ministry of Energy it is more important to save face than to care for the people who put their safety in your hands. I can read between the lines of official news from *Pravda*, Comrade Deputy Chairman. I know two deaths announced reluctantly means many more were killed or will soon die!"

Vatchenko smoothed down his flesh-colored mustache with his fingertips and stared at Lazlo for several seconds before speaking. "I am neither a journalist nor a politician, Detective Horvath. But I do understand the need to avoid throwing gasoline into the flames. I assure you everything possible is being done for the people in the area."

"How do you know? You're not there. Is groundwork already being laid for the possibility of a scapegoat being needed? Don't be afraid to talk to me, Comrade Deputy Chairman. I understand how these self-perpetuating ministries work!"

Vatchenko's face reddened, making the fine hairs of his mustache clearly visible. "You act as if the world is in environmental crisis."

Lazlo stood, aware of the bump of his holstered Makarov against his ribs. "Perhaps the world is in crisis! A crisis of shoddy engineering and safety precautions! A crisis created by men in power who want more power and don't care how they get it!"

"I believe our conversation is at an end," said Vatchenko as he stood and left the room.

A minute later, Asimov, the minister of electric power who had arranged for Lazlo to meet with Vatchenko, entered the room, asked Lazlo to return to his seat, and sat across from him.

"Deputy Chairman Vatchenko tells me he was unable to satisfy your thirst for knowledge. During your meeting, I made inquiries of our Moscow representative. Your sister-in-law and nieces are being well cared for at Municipal Hospital Number Six, and their situation is not critical. I'm sorry I have no more details. Let us not lose hope, Detective Horvath. Your brother would certainly have wanted you to remain hopeful."

Hopeful was a word Lazlo had heard misused throughout his life. When his mother was dying, his aunts had said to remain hopeful. When victims of crime were hospitalized, relatives were told to remain hopeful. When he was taken back to the farm village to investigate the shooting of the deserter, his captain said he was hopeful the parents and sister would understand the circumstances. *Boys killing boys. The strings of his violin silenced in youth.*

A person might pray, but remain hopeful? It was an impossible request. A person faced with tragedy must not trust hope. A person faced with tragedy must visualize the future realistically in order to prepare for the inevitable.

Before Lazlo left the Ministry of Energy, Asimov gave him the address and phone number of Municipal Hospital Number Six and said he could inquire daily about any information relayed from Moscow. Asimov smiled and said good-bye, and Lazlo thought, *All of the ministries in the union are populated with puppets attached to Moscow's long strings.*

Outside the ministry, the faded red Zhiguli was parked a half block away on the far side of the street. When Lazlo pulled out into the late-afternoon traffic, the Zhiguli followed. But what did it matter now? He was of no help to Nina and the girls. He was of no help to Juli Popovics. He could barely help himself as he drove wearily to his apartment.

When he parked in front of his building, he didn't even bother to look for the red Zhiguli. Tonight at midnight when he went on duty, they would most likely have switched cars. With several hours of sleep behind him, he would spot them. But for now, as he climbed the stairs to his apartment, a deathlike sleep beckoned him to join his brother, and he tried to forget about the Ministry of Energy, the KGB, and the frightened faces at the roadblock.

Major Grigor Komarov of the KGB stood at the desk and switched off the intercom. He had overheard Asimov's attempts to reassure Detective Horvath. Instead of sitting back down in the guest chair, Komarov walked around Asimov's desk, sat in the larger chair, rested his elbows on the desktop, and waited. When Asimov returned to his office, he narrowed his eyes at Komarov, walked to the window, and looked out. Komarov knew he was expected to vacate the chair because its owner had returned. But he stayed where he was, and Asimov, circling the room like a vulture, finally settled in one of the guest chairs as if it were carrion.

"I assume you continued listening while I spoke to the detective?" said Asimov.

"I listened, Comrade Minister. And I'd like your opinion of what should be done."

Asimov adjusted his position in the chair. "My ministry will keep Detective Horvath informed of the health of his brother's family as we receive information from Moscow."

"What about his provocative antigovernment statements?"

"His brother has died. What can I do? Paint rosy pictures and upset him even more? The Chernobyl situation is serious. The new openness of the general secretary dictates . . ."

Komarov interrupted. "You and your people assume the KGB's goal is concealment, when in fact the opposite it true! For example, your representative never told Detective Horvath what kind of material is being released."

Asimov sat forward in the chair. "What does it matter to you? You are not there."

Komarov glared at Asimov, then continued in a calmer voice. "Comrade, I ask a question, and this is the kind of answer I get?"

Asimov waved his hand in the air. "Many things have been released by the explosion. Iodine, cesium, cadmium, hundreds of radionuclides . . . the same kind of material as in an atmospheric test or at Hiroshima. For this reason alone, the KGB should understand at a time like this, when one's own family . . ."

Komarov interrupted again, but lowered his voice. "The KGB, Comrade Minister, understands many things. Do you think we make a habit of tormenting grieving relatives? Don't you realize we have valid reasons for inquiry? The KGB head in Pripyat met with Party committee personnel immediately after the accident, and I've yet to hear from him. No matter what you think, the KGB will do its part. Disaster suggests violence and terror, and I've come here for information to help deal with those possibilities. Can you guarantee at this early stage what happened at Chernobyl was an accident?"

Asimov stood, walked behind the desk, forcing Komarov to swivel around in the large desk chair. Asimov stared down at Komarov, contempt obvious on his face.

"Major Komarov, what is it you want from me?"

"You must file an official request to the KGB for an investigation of Detective Horvath."

"On what grounds?"

"Comrade Minister, you and I both listened to Detective Horvath's attempts to intimidate your engineer. He asked detailed questions, and in my opinion, your engineer told him too much. We both heard his tirades. He was upset about his brother. But there is something beneath the surface, something I have seen in others who try to hide their true concerns."

"What if I choose not to file such a report?"

"Because I am here on official business, it is mandatory I fill out a report. In my report I will have to say the minister of electric power was reluctant to document a situation critical to the investigation of circumstances surrounding the incident at Chernobyl."

Komarov stood, invited Asimov to sit in his own chair behind his own desk. Before he left the office, Komarov gave Asimov the address of Deputy Chairman Dumenko's Moscow office to which the request for investigation should be sent. He told Asimov to have the request ready by nine the following morning so a KGB courier could pick it up.

When Komarov left the building, he lit a cigarette and walked slowly to the Volga, where Captain Azef waited. He continued smoking the cigarette after entering the car.

"What did I miss?" asked Azef. "Detective Horvath left some time ago. Our men radioed to say he went to his apartment."

"The energy minister and an engineer fresh out of university with fur on his lip empathize with Detective Horvath and in doing so have forgotten their duties."

"Where do we go now?" asked Azef.

"To militia headquarters to see our old friend Chkalov."

"Ah," said Azef. "The next victim."

Komarov puffed on his cigarette and glared at Azef, who faced forward and began driving. Azef was wrong. These were not victims.

More like stepping-stones on his journey to his chairmanship. As Azef drove past late-afternoon homebound workers exiting a metro station, Komarov visualized a circus performer walking upon the bobbing heads of the crowd.

Chief Investigator Chkalov was arrogant until Komarov informed him of the death of Detective Horvath's brother, and of the meeting with his brother's lover in Kiev.

"On orders from Moscow," continued Komarov, "the Chernobyl incident will be subject to an in-depth investigation leaving no stone unturned. I'm here to inform you of anti-Soviet statements made by your detective."

"What anti-Soviet statements?"

"Today at the Ministry of Energy, Detective Horvath made accusations concerning the operation of the Chernobyl plant. He used his authority as a militia detective to gain access to officials. He used a method the Germans refer to as *schrecklichkeit*. Show your badge and intimidate relentlessly until the victim gives in."

"Detective Horvath is not that kind of man," said Chkalov. "It sounds more like something the KGB would do. Or better yet, since you bring up methods used in the last war, the old Cheka!"

Komarov leaned forward, placed one fist gently on the desk. "I should have brought my assistant with me to witness your lack of cooperation, Chief Investigator Chkalov."

"Who says I'm not cooperating? I simply don't understand this vendetta you have against Detective Horvath. His brother is dead, yet he continues his duties."

"He didn't know about his brother until this morning."

Chkalov shrugged. "But he went on duty, knowing his brother

222

was in the area of danger."

"He went on duty at the roadblock so he could watch for his brother. Perhaps he was to meet Juli Popovics *and* his brother at the roadblock. I must consider the possibility of sabotage at the plant. I must consider the possibility of Mihaly Horvath and Juli Popovics working together and Detective Horvath providing an escape route!"

"Impossible!" shouted Chkalov.

"Nothing is impossible," said Komarov in a calmer voice. "There has been a Hungarian connection under KGB observation for some time. A relative of the Horvaths has met with CIA agents in Budapest. The Horvaths and Juli Popovics share Hungarian lineage. Imagine the consequences, Comrade Chief Investigator, if a conspiracy exists and if you, despite your knowledge of the situation, allow Detective Horvath to remain in his position."

"You want me to suspend him?"

"Not yet. I want you to observe him. He may lead us to others."

"And if I don't cooperate?"

"I'll be forced to report that the Kiev militia refuses to cooperate in a KGB investigation ordered by Deputy Chairman Dumenko in Moscow."

"What do you expect me to do?"

"When the time comes, suspension will put Detective Horvath on notice. He will know the investigation is closing in."

"And if he's innocent?" asked Chkalov.

"I doubt it," said Komarov, standing to leave. "We've already had a foreign relative under observation. If Horvath is innocent, the price of a few days' lost pay is a sacrifice any citizen would gladly bear to wipe the slate clean. Please remember, Chief Investigator, it is most important to my investigation you do not suspend Detective Horvath until it is time."

Before he turned to leave, Komarov noticed Chkalov's fists

clenched tightly on his desk.

Outside militia headquarters it was dusk, the streets emptied of homebound workers, and a light rain fell. Captain Azef started the Volga as Komarov got in.

"No cigarette?" asked Azef, turning on the windshield wipers.

"I have other things on my mind besides smoking. Drive to the office."

"Yes," said Azef. "There are inquiries from Moscow to answer."

"You will answer them by repeating the situation at Chernobyl is under control and the evacuation is almost complete."

"Surely we'll want to provide more information . . ."

Komarov interrupted. "We must follow through on the Horvath investigation. I want those two PK agents from Pripyat back on duty."

"What are they going to do?"

"Tomorrow they'll resume their observation of Juli Popovics."

"Shouldn't trained men be used for such an observation?" asked Azef.

"Not necessarily, Captain. A noisy observation serves a purpose. It brings others out of their holes. On the other hand, I want our best men watching Detective Horvath."

When Captain Azef turned onto Volodimirska Street, Komarov looked back to his left where he could see the lighted cable-car railway climbing the steep dark hill to the northeast. The lights of the ascending and descending funicular cable cars glistened in the droplets of rain on the window like medals pinned to the breast of a uniform. Atop the hill, holding his crucifix, was the statue of Saint Vladimir. The statue was outlined black against the darkening sky, a fearsome outline of someone entirely in control.

Komarov felt the weight of the knife in his coat pocket as he reached for a cigarette. He lit the cigarette and blew the smoke in Azef's direction, causing him to cough as he drove.

CHAPTER 18

Men, women, and children who arrived day and night at the road-block were like war refugees, wide-eyed as if opening their eyes wider would make room for them in Kiev. Hotels and inns were full. And even though many Kievians had fled south, this simply resulted in locked and empty apartments. There was not enough room in Kiev for Chernobyl refugees. Therefore, collectives were put to work. Day and night, Lazlo and his men sent refugees on their way to collective farms to the west and south. Day and night, militiamen shrugged their shoulders when asked obvious questions. "When will we be able to return?" "Where will we live in the mean-time?" "Will it be safe where we are going?"

When Lazlo and his men asked about the situation at and around Chernobyl and Pripyat, the answer was always the same. Except for being told to evacuate, except for knowing a nuclear plant had exploded, these poor souls knew only rumors. Do not drink milk because it stores radiation. Stop eating leafy vegetables. Drink vodka and wine to purge radiation.

When a vehicle or its passengers caused a technician's Geiger counter to chatter, a tanker-truck team gave them a shower. Day or night, the scene at the roadblock was surreal. The refugees in line reminded Lazlo of wide-eyed schoolchildren on inoculation day, imagining an enormous needle in the hands of an unpracticed nurse plunging into their bones.

Because of sixteen-hour shifts at the roadblock, Lazlo lost track of time. Tuesday or Wednesday night—he wasn't sure which—he went to his car and rolled up the windows so he could think, so he could assure himself he had done everything in his power for Nina and the girls. What more could he do? Asimov said they had already been examined at Hospital Number Six and taken to temporary housing. They were, according to Asimov, in perfect health. Lazlo would have felt better if he could have spoken to Nina, but the overtaxed phone lines made it impossible.

During his last break, Lazlo went to the Ministry of Energy again, and, having received no further news on exactly how Mihaly died, he drove to see Juli Popovics at her aunt's house. Lazlo felt uneasy because of Juli's connection to Mihaly. It was a strange unease, similar to déjà vu, like returning to his boyhood home. Both Juli and Aunt Magda spoke Hungarian, Aunt Magda's cooking reminded him of his mother's cooking, and Juli reminded him of Nina.

After telling him the Kiev hospital had called to say Juli's blood test showed radiation levels "within the range of acceptability," Juli and Aunt Magda inquired about Nina and the girls. Not the way someone asks who is simply being kind. They wanted details—the color of hair and eyes, the height of the little girls in relation to him. When he spoke of Nina and Anna and little Ilonka, he saw motherly love in Juli's eyes. More than once she referred to future generations and how children needed to be protected from this disaster.

Back at the roadblock, whenever Lazlo saw a woman holding a child, he thought of Nina. But he also thought of Juli. He had to admit this to himself. He thought of Juli many times during the long night as he recalled her tender kiss on his cheek when he saw her last. Amid cars and buses and green and white militia vehicles and crowds at the roadblock, he felt his deep-seated urge to make things right, and linked with the urge, he kept seeing images of Juli Popovics in the faces of the refugees.

Early in the morning before dawn, as his holstered Makarov rubbed against his side, and as more refugees assailed him with questions, he heard a new term. The refugees had a name for themselves. They called one another Chernobylites.

Tuesday, April 29, 1986, three days after Chernobyl's unit four exploded and two days before May Day, transportation out of Kiev was difficult. Buses were almost nonexistent because so many had been sent north. Trains and planes to other major Soviet cities were full, with long lines at stations and terminals. But there was always priority. There were always people of status or authority able to bypass lines.

The Aeroflot jet was supposed to take off from Kiev at dusk. But it was late, and a few minutes into the flight, Komarov could see nothing but blackness out his window. Every seat had been occupied when he arrived, forcing Komarov to use his credentials to have a window-seat passenger removed.

The chain of events beginning with the Chernobyl explosion had led to this. Major Grigor Komarov of the Kiev KGB flying to Moscow on official business, but also invited to join Deputy Chairman Dumenko and other high officials as they celebrated the revolution. He would mix business with pleasure and, if all went well, begin his climb to chairmanship. He would deliver the letter he carried with him, and he would attend May Day festivities.

Deputy Chairman Dumenko had asked if Komarov wished to bring his wife along. Although Komarov's wife enjoyed the prestige and advantage of his position, she did not like traveling to Moscow. Getting iodine delivered to their home shortly after the Chernobyl accident was one thing, she had said, but traveling to Moscow was quite another. "There will be turmoil in Moscow, Grigor. Dmitry and I will stay here where it is safe."

"What do you think of all this reactor business?"

The woman in the seat next to Komarov had spoken. He could see her reflection in the window as she leaned forward to get his attention. A fat, middle-aged woman who had, until now, been content with her *Pravda*.

"I beg your pardon?" said Komarov, turning to look at her.

The woman held the paper open to an inside page with a story about Chernobyl. "This reactor business at Chernobyl, what do you think of it?"

"It must be of little consequence," said Komarov. "It's not on the front page."

The woman stared at him, her jowls expanding, her eyes becoming narrow slits. "You're joking. The news has been coming from everywhere. The only reason it's not on page one is because they don't know what to say."

"What do you think?" asked Komarov.

The woman hesitated, inspected his suit, perhaps looking for a lapel pin sometimes worn by officials. "I've seen people arriving in Kiev. I've seen crowds and heard foreign broadcasts. As a mother, I'm frightened for the children. There are rumors about avoiding milk and eating only canned food. Do you have children, comrade?"

"I have a son."

"How old is he?"

"Twenty."

"How nice. Is he in the army?"

Komarov imagined Dmitry in a crisp army uniform instead of the tight-fitting slacks he always wore. "Yes, he is in the army."

"One of my sons is in the army," said the woman. "He's a guard on the western frontier. Where is your son stationed?"

Komarov imagined how life might have gone. "He's in a military hospital. He was wounded in Afghanistan."

"How terribly sorry I am. Your wife must be distressed."

"She is."

"And here I am, worrying whether they'll recruit my son's unit for some kind of evacuation or cleanup at Chernobyl. While waiting at the airport, I spoke to a woman who said a freight train was sent back from Moscow because it was contaminated with radiation. She said there was meat on the train from the Ukraine and it would have to be buried."

"Perhaps," said Komarov, "it will need to be buried because it will have spoiled by the time it leaves the train."

"With so much going on, it's difficult to think of everything," said the woman. "First we have war in Afghanistan, now this."

"Foreign cultures and foreign workers make life difficult for all of us."

The woman opened her eyes wider so they were no longer slits. "Do you think foreign workers are to blame for the disaster?"

"Anything is possible when openness is allowed for its own sake."

The woman stared at Komarov for a moment, then proceeded to tell him about all her children. Komarov turned and stared out the window as she continued speaking. He leaned against the window, looking forward ahead of the wing, watching the horizon for the lights of Moscow. He wanted a cigarette badly but had left his cigarettes in his luggage.

Nina Horvath wore a white cotton dress like one of the nurses he'd seen walking between the hospital complex and the surrounding apartments. Her face was thin, and she wore no makeup. Komarov assumed she would appear vulnerable, but there was something in her eyes as she stared at him. Despite the situation, she seemed confident, as if she were in control, as if she had an agenda. Her hair was brown and disheveled.

"What does the KGB want from me?" said Nina Horvath, standing to face him.

"Information to set the record straight. I need details of events surrounding the disaster. I realize your husband is dead, Mrs. Horvath. However, duty does not permit a delay of my report. Information has a way of slipping through one's fingers unless it is gathered promptly."

"My husband . . . what's left of my husband . . ." She paused for a moment. "He's being buried this afternoon in a lead-lined coffin."

"I know," said Komarov.

He could see hatred and mistrust in her eyes. She was the victim, and he was in control. He returned her stare, waiting a moment to see if she might make a counterrevolutionary statement he could use later. Finally, he began his questioning.

"You have two children. What are their names?"

"Ilonka and Anna."

"Are they here with you?"

"They're with the woman in the next apartment."

"How did you get here from Pripyat?"

"By plane."

"Why didn't you leave with the others?"

"What others?"

"Those evacuated by bus."

"I went with my neighbor to the plant after we heard about the explosion. We were put on a bus, taken to the local hospital, then to the airport. It all happened very quickly."

The questioning was also going too quickly. In order to find out more about Mrs. Horvath and her husband, and especially to find out if there was anything he could develop concerning the dead husband's activities, Komarov decided to proceed more slowly.

"Did your daughters receive their pills?"

"What?"

"Iodine pills. It is especially important for children."

"Yes, they gave us iodine in Pripyat and again here."

"You also had iodine?"

"Yes."

"I wanted to be sure before we continued. I'll try to keep my questions to a minimum."

Komarov asked Nina Horvath about her marriage to Mihaly Horvath, about their move to Pripyat, and the exact ages of her two girls. When Nina Horvath rushed ahead to cut off the interview, Komarov traced backward with detailed questions about family and everyday life. The purpose was to look for keys to the way he would ask his ultimate question. The purpose was to uncover a negative in her relationship with her husband and connect it with suspicions about her husband's possible role in sabotage.

Unfortunately, Komarov could not get Nina Horvath to say anything negative about her husband. He even dwelled upon the recent past, the time during which he knew Mihaly Horvath had been seeing Juli Popovics. But still there was nothing, not even a visual reaction as Nina Horvath stared at him with obvious hatred.

Komarov backtracked in time, getting Nina Horvath to talk of pleasant topics. The girls and how well they were doing in school.

The home and the neighborhood. Friends. A future filled with possibilities. When Nina Horvath's eyes began to water, Komarov dropped his bomb.

"Mrs. Horvath, are you aware of your husband's role in sabotage at the Chernobyl plant?"

Nina Horvath's expression remained unchanged, as it had during the entire interview. "I know of no such thing."

Komarov asked the question from several angles with the same result. When he left Nina Horvath, he'd made only one entry of importance in his notebook. "Mrs. Horvath did not seem surprised I had asked such a question about her husband."

But even as he walked out of the apartment house and crossed the street, joining the nurses and doctors and ambulance drivers scurrying outside Hospital Number Six, Komarov knew Nina Horvath had expected the question as soon as she saw his KGB identification. Therefore, not acting surprised meant nothing, unless he made something of it in his report. And, of course, he would.

The only other time Komarov visited KGB headquarters on Lubyanka Square in central Moscow was years earlier, after his promotion to captaincy following the Sherbitsky affair. At the time, the Fifth Directorate considered him for an assignment tracking down dissidents. Unfortunately, Vladimir Kryuchkov gave him a short interview, dismissing him quickly. Later he discovered Sherbitsky and Kryuchkov had trained together as KGB recruits.

The building was yellow brick, several stories tall, and shaped like a coffin. As Komarov walked across the square to the entrance, he recalled stories about the building being the tallest in Moscow even though it definitely was not. The joke went: Even from its basement—the location of the prison cells—one can easily see Siberia.

Inside the main entrance, Komarov's heels clicked on familiar parquet floors. From his visit years earlier, he vividly recalled the sound and smell of the place. The main hall echoed, cavern-like, and smelled like boot polish and cigarette smoke even though, as he looked about, he saw no uniforms or boots or lit cigarettes. KGB officers visiting the Lubyanka for business dressed as businessmen. Komarov was aware of his knife tucked inside his jacket with the letter he would deliver. While he waited for the elevator he saw a single half-smoked cigarette smoldering in an ornate Neo-Renaissance ashtray mounted to the wall. The smoke from the ashtray smelled like burning hair. During the elevator ride, Komarov transferred the letter from his inside pocket to an outside pocket.

Deputy Chairman Dumenko's office on the third floor was the largest Komarov had ever seen. Although the ceiling was low, recessed lighting and an expanse of pale green walls and maroon carpeting gave the office and its adjoining conference room a spacious feeling. Wood and leather furniture was dwarfed by the space. Ironically, a small portrait of Vladimir Kryuchkov shared the wall behind the desk with one of KGB Chairman Chebrikov and, of course, a larger portrait of Lenin. Komarov felt he should speak softly lest his voice escape into the hall. But echoes from the hall subsided when the assistant who brought him to the office closed the door. As a courtesy to his superior, Komarov did not smoke.

Dumenko wore half glasses as he opened and read the letter from Kiev's minister of electric power. Dumenko's bald head reflected the overhead light while he finished the letter, took off his half glasses, placed them on his desk, and stared at Komarov.

"Have you read this letter, Major?"

"It was addressed to you," said Komarov.

"But you know the nature of it."

"I know it has to do with inquiries made by Detective Lazlo Horvath to Minister Asimov."

"It's a request for an investigation of Detective Horvath regarding a possible connection to the Chernobyl incident. Have you been pursuing the KGB's investigation as we discussed?"

"I am, sir. This morning I spoke with Mihaly Horvath's widow. Although she denies corrupt activities on the part of her husband, she may simply want to bury all of this when she buries her husband today. I tried to have her husband questioned after the Chernobyl event, but it was too late."

"I understand he died quickly," said Dumenko. "Two deaths. I spoke with the television and radio chairman today. He hopes there will be no more bodies. I spoke with the health minister. He says there will definitely be more bodies. The agriculture minister is concerned about hundreds of thousands of square kilometers of our richest farmland. Did you know, Major, they have started herding livestock away from the area?"

"I didn't know, sir."

"Some livestock will have to be destroyed. Entire towns and villages evacuated, and it is feared many more will die. Did you know the resources of hospitals are already strained?"

"Yes, sir. I visited Hospital Number Six this morning."

"What prompted your visit?"

"After my interview with Mrs. Horvath near Hospital Number Six, I felt I should see some of the injured firsthand in order to acquaint myself with the extent of the emergency. I saw firemen who had been brought in. They had no hair and . . ."

Komarov saw Dumenko raise his eyebrows and touch the top of his shiny head.

"I'm sorry, sir. I didn't mean to imply any connection with your . . ."

"Never mind, Major. Mine was not burned off by radiation. What else about these firemen?"

"Some had peeling skin and were inside plastic tents. The doctors said radiation destroys bone marrow. As a result, white blood cells cannot be produced and the firemen's lives can be threatened by any infection."

Dumenko stood from his desk and paced back and forth beneath the portrait of Lenin hung above the other portraits. "Tell me, Major, what should be done about all this?"

"We must find the cause of the disaster. If we find the cause, everyone will rest easier and life can go on."

"I was looking for something more specific, Major. Most experts assume it was an accident. The general secretary wants the KGB to forward all information about Chernobyl to his office. Having told you this, what shall we do about your investigation of these Hungarians?"

"My men are gathering and forwarding all Chernobyl information as ordered, sir. However, on the chance it was not an accident, I believe I should pursue the possibility of sabotage. Mihaly Horvath's lover has already contacted Detective Horvath, and I have my best men watching them. She worked at Chernobyl's Department of Industrial Safety and had access to significant information. Some time ago, if you recall, a colleague named Aleksandra Yasinsky was detained. I have a feeling Detective Horvath and Juli Popovics continue to be in contact with Western intelligence."

"Who is their contact?"

"The Horvath family cousin from America named Andrew Zukor. He visited the Horvath brothers last summer, if you recall my report."

"I recall," said Dumenko, turning to look up at Lenin's portrait. "I believe our agency has given him the code name Gypsy Moth."

Dumenko turned back to Komarov. "Am I correct?"

"Your memory is impressive, sir. I've been concerned for some time about the Horvaths and this Gypsy Moth. At first, I thought the name *Gypsy* applied to Horvath because our research has shown his father was of Gypsy origin. A fact the family kept quiet during the war years for obvious reasons. But the name actually came later. Detective Horvath has a history in the army of having served near the Soviet frontier and was involved in the death of a fellow soldier. The fellow soldier killed by Horvath was nicknamed Gypsy, and Horvath's comrades, in typical gallows humor, gave him the name. But back to the cousin, Andrew Zukor, the American Gypsy Moth. He provides the connection to Western intelligence. And with this established connection to the United States, there exists the possibility of sabotage, leading to destabilization, leading to . . ."

"Go on, Major."

"A coup d'état."

"You're saying a detective in the Kiev militia and a Chernobyl worker planned this so-called accident as a first step in a coup d'état?"

"Not alone, Comrade Deputy Chairman. I'm simply indicating a portion of the puzzle available to me. There are many pieces of evidence. Not only Juli Popovics and her lover at Chernobyl, but also the fact Detective Horvath has leaned to the West and is friends with anti-Soviets, literary review editors, and the like."

Dumenko rubbed his bald head. "Since you speak of puzzles, Major, what do you think Detective Horvath and Juli Popovics will do next? If they try to escape capture, we can't be expected to guard the entire frontier at a time like this."

"I've arranged to have Mihaly Horvath's wife and children sent to Kisbor, near the Czech border, where the rest of the Horvath family lives. I will assign men to the area on the chance Detective

Horvath goes there."

"Is Juli Popovics from the area?"

"No. Her mother lives in Moscow, but I don't think she'll come here. Her mother doesn't know she's pregnant."

"I suppose you would like to assign more men to the case."

"Yes, Comrade Deputy Chairman."

Dumenko smiled. "Because you've had a fine record in the KGB, especially during your time in East Berlin, I must take these matters seriously. Perhaps we in Moscow have been too busy with Afghanistan to watch under our own noses. Perhaps we've been overburdened with the possibility of change at high levels . . . talk of the union's future and individuals looking out for themselves. Officials at the highest level will suffer because of Chernobyl. A chairman I cannot name suggested the event might be a test to determine how nuclear war would affect government. Events like this bring out the rats below the Kremlin."

Dumenko sat back at his desk, opened a drawer, took out an envelope, and handed it to Komarov. "Very well, Major. I authorize you to use the resources necessary to investigate this situation to its swift conclusion. In order to help, I'm assigning another man to your office. Captain Brovko's orders are in the envelope. He was previously assigned to East Berlin. My reason for his assignment is because he's had training in nuclear engineering. If this case continues, his technical expertise will be useful. I'm told he's also good at interrogation."

"Thank you, sir."

"Major, you realize, of course, if there has been a conspiracy to commit sabotage, the national and international implications will be extensive."

"I know," said Komarov.

"By the way, Major. Did you and your wife and son receive

iodine, should the radiation reach Kiev?"

"We have."

Dumenko shook his head sadly. "It's a terrible situation. I'm told Black Sea campgrounds, hotels, and sanitoriums are filling up. An old comrade of mine, Colonel Zamyatin from the Ukrainian border force, has come out of retirement to take charge of the evacuation."

"Zamyatin is a hero, sir."

Dumenko smiled and rubbed his hands together. "Enough tragedy, Major. Will you stay for tomorrow's May Day celebration?"

"It would be an honor, Comrade Deputy Chairman."

"You can join me in the reviewing stand. Gorbachev will be above and to our left. Tomorrow night you'll join my wife and myself for dinner. Was there anything else you wanted to attend to in Moscow besides the obligatory visit to Lenin's Tomb?"

"I'd like to go to an opera. When I was a boy living outside Moscow, my father used to take me to the opera."

Dumenko came around the desk and clapped Komarov on the shoulder. "Stay for a visit to the Bolshoi. And when you go back to Kiev, Captain Brovko will be waiting for you."

Komarov thanked Dumenko and left the building.

Rather than taking a taxi, he decided to walk from Lubyanka Square to Lenin's Tomb. It wasn't far, and if it rained, he'd seek shelter at the Bolshoi or the Central Lenin Museum.

While he walked, Komarov thought back to his visit to the Lubyanka years earlier. The streets in Moscow formed a bull's-eye, and he had been in the center of it once before. If only things had gone differently back then. If only he had been assigned to operations in the United States in his younger days. How different was it now? Was the fellow who took the job he could have gotten from Kryuchkov involved in escalating the Iran-Contra problems of Reagan these days?

In front of the National Hotel, a man hurrying out the main doors bumped into him, almost knocking him down. The man grasped Komarov's shoulders to steady him.

"I am sorry, comrade. I should not have been so clumsy."

The man wore a hat and coat too warm for spring. He had a thin face and wore thick glasses. "I was in a hurry coming out the door," continued the man. "It is my fault. I called a taxi. Can I offer you a ride?"

The man looked familiar. Was it someone from his past? Someone from a previous Moscow visit? The man's breath smelled of onions.

Komarov pulled back. "I prefer walking."

The man stepped forward and touched Komarov's sleeve. "Are you sure? The taxi will be here soon. We can ride together and have a pleasant conversation. I'd like to talk to someone about this Chernobyl business?" The man let go of Komarov's sleeve, took off his thick glasses, and stared at Komarov, smiling as if Komarov should recognize him.

Komarov began walking away. "I'm not interested in your conversation."

He expected the man to follow, to continue harassing him. And when the man did not, Komarov glanced back to see a taxi pull to the curb and the man get in. When the taxi sped past, the man stared straight ahead.

Perhaps he was being followed. The man could have been from the Seventh Directorate, simple surveillance, or even from Directorate T. Perhaps the man had some connection to Major Struyev in the Kiev office. He had asked Struyev to attend to the Gypsy Moth in Hungary, and in the process Directorate T followed him. No matter. One could always expect to be followed in Moscow. But why should he recognize the fellow? A thin-faced man wearing glasses, about his age. What if the man was foreign intelligence? What if there really was a planned coup d'état linked to Chernobyl? No matter. He had his own work to do, his own ladder to climb. What happened in Moscow might make a difference or, as was often true these days, might make no difference at all.

It was beginning to darken and a light mist fell. In Red Square, final preparations were being made for the May Day parade. Komarov walked along the Kremlin Wall to the Senate Tower. Beneath the tower, the queue of people in front of the Lenin mausoleum was short, probably because of the rain.

CHAPTER 19

On May 1, 1986, the cities of Moscow and Kiev both held parades. While Moscow's parade was surrounded by Kremlin walls and paved squares wet with rain, spring greenery and lilacs blooming along paths down to the river surrounded Kiev's parade. The morning was sunny, but by midday the wind changed, and an ominous cloud descended.

Kiev's parade went along Khreshchatik past the university with its red facade, past the post office, past the Hotel Dnieper, and onto Lenkomsomol Square. Speeches were typically patriotic, with no mention of the Chernobyl incident. The assembled crowd was quiet, so much so, traffic in the underpass below the square could be heard. The absence of the usual food vendors was obvious. News of roadblocks and technicians with Geiger counters had spread throughout the city. Although in subdued voices, rumors made the rounds.

"Did you hear? Ration coupons may be issued, along with compensation for evacuees."

"Collectives are full, and they're sending Chernobylites to vacation on the Black Sea."

"Whatever you do, don't eat leafy vegetables or drink milk."

"Be careful on the phone. If you even mention Chernobyl, the line goes dead."

"Perhaps we should put our shortwave radios back in the attic for the time being."

The mood on the square during the speeches was somber. Even the sound of traffic, which could be heard through storm drains in the floor of Lenkomsomol Square, became ominous. Heavy traffic meant many citizens were leaving Kiev and perhaps the danger was greater than anyone imagined. Some in the crowd referred to the radiation as "the silent killer."

Two days after the parade, Major Grigor Komarov was back in Kiev, standing at his office window smoking a cigarette. He looked down to where he would have seen the parade had he been in Kiev on May Day. From his office, the people would have looked like multicolored beetles, the vehicles like toys, the banners like miniature flags used in cemeteries.

Even though it had drizzled, attending the Moscow parade was a high point in his career. The parade, with thousands of more participants than any Kiev parade, was impressive. And by simply glancing over his left shoulder, he could see Gorbachev and other members of the Presidium. Perhaps some of them, even Gorbachev himself, wondered who stood with Deputy Chairman Dumenko. Someday soon, they would know.

Were some in Moscow already speaking of Komarov? Had gossip remained behind? During the dinner party at Deputy Chairman Dumenko's residence, he reassured Mrs. Dumenko and several other guests. He spoke of the orderly movement of evacuees, the generous aid provided, and the cooperation of Kiev's citizens and surrounding collectives. Later, after most guests were gone, Dumenko took him aside and commended him for his tact.

Because many were leaving Kiev rather than going to Kiev, Komarov had spent the peaceful trip back with an empty seat beside him. He'd thought about puzzles and chess games and how easily even intelligent men could be manipulated. He drew a diagram in his notebook in which Detective Horvath was represented by a circle surrounded by women—Juli Popovics, Nina Horvath, Tamara Petrov—all of them with power over this man, each a string connected to the superstitious puppet. And if Komarov could manipulate the strings . . .

On the plane, Komarov had imagined himself as clever as Dostoevski's Porfiry in *Crime and Punishment*. Detective Horvath a brooding Raskolnikov. But in this case he would have to be more clever than Porfiry. The potential existed others would step in to take credit or, worse, discover some bit of evidence to set the Gypsy anarchists free. The line between revolutionaries, anarchists, and terrorists was a fine one.

Komarov went to his desk and called Captain Azef. He told Azef to send Captain Brovko, the new man assigned by Moscow, up to his office.

"Deputy Chairman Dumenko and Captain Azef filled me in on the case, Major."

"So now you are an expert?"

"Definitely not. I wish to gain more knowledge from you."

Captain Brovko was thirty-five, unmarried, formerly stationed in East Berlin as a counterintelligence interrogator. His training in nuclear engineering was from the army. He was tall and muscular, his hair the color of sand, his eyes blue. He spoke fluent German and, in the GDR, was probably mistaken for the grandson of an SS officer. All of this had been in Brovko's file, which Komarov studied earlier.

"I understand you have skills as an interviewer," said Komarov.

"Interrogation was my specialty in KGB training," said Brovko.

"We are from the same mold, Captain. I also trained as an interrogator. Of course, the mold might have changed somewhat since then."

Brovko laughed politely.

"As for your nuclear training. Can you tell me exactly what happened at Chernobyl?"

"Not without more facts."

"Deputy Chairman Dumenko said you would look into the situation. I assumed you had."

"I've looked into a Pandora's box, Major. Chaos and confusion make it impossible to come to a conclusion at this time."

"I need your best guess as to what happened, and what will happen. Please be concise."

Captain Brovko leaned both elbows on Komarov's desk. "Very well. The Chernobyl RBMK reactors are pressure tube devices with graphite blocks to slow neutrons. Apparently the plan was to test reactor number four at low power during maintenance shutdown. Normally this would be a routine test, except for two factors. The RBMKs are notoriously unstable at low power, and several safety systems were disabled too early in the test. A power surge could not be handled by control rod insertion, the temperature rose quickly, a steam explosion cracked the concrete shell, steam came in contact with hot graphite, and there was a second explosion exposing the core and igniting the graphite. The first firefighters were fatally exposed to radiation and will die. The fire still burns, and there is talk of tunneling beneath the reactor to keep the molten core away from the water table to avoid another, more serious, explosion. Radioactive dust blown into the air required evacuation of an area of thirty kilometers around the reactor. I spoke with Colonel Zamyatin, who is in charge of the evacuation. He said on May Day, Pripyat was a ghost town in which one could hear only the barking of dogs abandoned by their owners. He ordered his men to shoot dogs and cats because they carry radioactive contamination on their fur. And during my briefing here from Captain Azef, I was told trains have been readied on the chance there is a second explosion and Kiev must be evacuated."

Komarov lit a cigarette and blew the smoke over Brovko's head. "You have done your research, Captain. However, evacuation of Kiev is fantasy. There will be no second explosion. As for the first explosion, correct me if I'm wrong, but unless one were actually there at the time, unless one could reconstruct the reactor as it was before the explosion . . ."

"Correct," said Brovko. "Even with a thorough investigation, close approximation is the best we can expect."

"It's too bad, with all the facts at hand, we can do nothing to limit idiotic rumors. People claiming milk and vegetables and even Kiev's water are contaminated. Have you come across rumors during your investigation before coming here, Captain?"

"I heard many from agents and soldiers in the zone. Fish with two heads, alien space vessels, a military plot. One old man on a train heading north claimed the explosion was manufactured in order to move the Ukrainian population to Siberia, where the Stalinist work camps were already rebuilt."

"Our battle against disinformation has begun," said Komarov. "The West will provide more rumors. Imagine our general secretary wanting us to put more trust in the West. Sometimes I think we here in Kiev have become more Soviet than those in Moscow."

Brovko did not react, but simply stared at Komarov.

"So," said Komarov, "you were stationed in the GDR. I don't suppose you've heard of the Sherbitsky affair. I can't imagine anyone in East Berlin these days knowing of it."

"On the contrary, Major. You're the man who caught Sherbitsky."

"I didn't mean to boast, Captain. I simply wondered, since so many years have passed . . ."

"It's still spoken of in the region. In fact, the 'safe' house is still there. The room where the murders were committed is called the Sherbitsky room."

"Quite a grisly affair," said Komarov, putting out his cigarette. "Walking into the room and seeing the bodies is an image I cannot forget. And when I discovered the knife belonging to a man I admired . . . Enough, we're here to do a job."

"What can I do?" asked Brovko, sitting more erect.

"For almost a year prior to the so-called accident at Chernobyl, our office has had several individuals under operational observation. I assume Deputy Chairman Dumenko briefed you about the Chernobyl employees, the Kiev militia detective, and the Horvaths' American cousin?"

Brovko took a notepad from his pocket and referred to it. "One Andrew Zukor, who may also be called Gypsy Moth by the CIA."

"You are aware we have reason to believe Zukor visited the CIA station in Budapest prior to visiting his cousins last summer?"

"I am." Brovko looked at the ashtray where Komarov's cigarette still smoldered. "Of course, Deputy Chairman Dumenko reminded me you were his only source for this information."

Komarov stood and walked to his window, staring up to the sky where thick clouds obscured the sun. "Perhaps you have misunderstood your assignment, Captain."

"I beg your pardon?"

Komarov turned to face Brovko and raised his voice. "I am in the midst of a serious investigation, which could very well involve sabotage, Captain! The Gypsy Moth may be a spy simply trying to uncover information about Chernobyl, or he could have been actively recruiting his cousins! In either case, I would very much appreciate your help!"

Captain Brovko stood halfway up, then sat back down. "My role as an interrogator is sometimes spontaneous, Major. I'll do what I can to carry your investigation to its conclusion."

Komarov returned his desk. "Thank you, Captain. I'm sorry. Sometimes one's involvement in these cases is personal. You say Azef filled you in on Detective Horvath?"

"He did."

"Then you know about the women in his life. I want you to interrogate one of them. I want you to bring her here Monday and find out what she knows."

Komarov walked to the window again. He stood with his back to Brovko and lit another cigarette. His decision not to trust Brovko with his inner feelings had been the correct decision. Perhaps there was even a chance Dumenko had assigned Brovko to observe him.

No matter. He would put his plan in motion in spite of what others thought. Part of the plan was being played now as he waited to see how long Brovko waited before asking which woman to pick up Monday, the day after Russian Orthodox Easter, the day of resurrection.

After a quick dinner of borscht and buttered bread, Lazlo drove to militia headquarters before returning for the overnight portion of his fifth sixteen-hour shift. He didn't bother looking for the KGB tail. They had followed him all week. Monday it was the faded red Zhiguli when he took Juli to Aunt Magda's. Tuesday through Thursday a different car or sometimes a van would stay far back, and he would have to turn several corners before detecting them. This morning, Saturday, they had switched to a Chaika.

In his office he called Tamara.

"You haven't called in days, Laz. I was worried."

"I've been on sixteen-hour shifts. Evacuees are angry, and I can't blame them. We've been told to watch for looters. The people escape, and their belongings follow them to Kiev. We caught one looter on a hay wagon with radios and televisions stuffed into the bales of hay."

"Did you learn anything more at the Ministry of Energy?"

"Only what I've told you. I'm still trying to contact Mihaly's wife in Moscow. I'll try again after I hang up. I've met a woman who knew Mihaly. Her name is Juli Popovics . . ."

"I assume from your hesitation, she was involved in some way with Mihaly?"

"Yes. Involved. She spoke with Mihaly the night before it happened. I'm going to talk with her again tomorrow. Her aunt invited me for Easter dinner."

"Good," said Tamara after a pause. "You'll get something nourishing to eat. Perhaps soon things will be back to normal. Perhaps I'll acquire a taste for chicken paprikas."

"It will be better next time. The last chicken was too skinny."

Tamara laughed. "But I didn't have to hug a skinny chicken in bed."

He said good-bye to Tamara and asked the operator to put him through to Municipal Hospital Number Six in Moscow.

He was transferred from one operator to another. When he did get through, the operator said she didn't have a list of arrivals from

Chernobyl. But this time the operator mentioned transferring him to someone in temporary housing. Suddenly, before he could think of what to say, a woman came on the line and said she would get Nina Horvath, who was down the hall.

"This is Nina Horvath." Nina's voice was soft, like a child anticipating punishment.

"Nina. It's Lazlo."

"Lazlo. Laz . . ." She began crying. A few seconds later she spoke again. "I'm sorry, Laz. I'm so sorry . . ."

"You don't have to say anything. There's nothing we can do now."

"I . . . they buried him today. I went to the service."

"I wish I had been there, Nina."

"The girls ask for you, Laz. First they ask about Mihaly. But now they know, and they ask for Uncle Laz."

"Do you want me to come get you? I'll bring you back here to my apartment . . ."

"Don't come to Moscow, Laz. They're sending us to Kisbor."

"Kisbor? Why would they send you there?"

"Because our relatives live there. Because we can't go back to Pripyat."

"I'm your relative. Why can't you come here?"

There was static on the line, followed by silence.

"Nina?"

"I'm still here, Laz. I wanted to come to Kiev, but they insisted we can't because of refugees already there. They said for the children it's best to go farther away. In Kisbor the girls will be with people they know. Bela and Mariska and their baby . . ."

Nina sobbed for a moment before continuing. "I'm sorry. I need to tell you something. The KGB questioned me about Mihaly's work at Chernobyl. They're trying to implicate Mihaly, and I know they're wrong. But there's a woman . . . a technician named Juli

Popovics. Mihaly . . . was involved with her."

"Nina . . ."

"Don't talk. I know Mihaly told you about her. I knew months ago. Mihaly promised they would stop seeing one another. I was so angry. I remember thinking at the time I wanted to make them suffer. Mihaly slept on the floor, and I slept in bed, alone with my anger. And now . . . now I'm simply alone. When I heard about the explosion, when my neighbor said she was driving to the plant, I took the girls, thinking it would help. I thought we could get Mihaly. He'd come out and we'd all go away together, and this other thing, this relationship with Juli Popovics, would be finished. He'd see us there, his family come to get him . . ."

When Nina finished weeping, Lazlo knew he would have to question her. But what could he say? Speaking of Juli and her pregnancy was out of the question. He also needed to avoid mentioning Cousin Andrew Zukor because of the possibility the phone was bugged.

"Nina, it's not the right time, I know, but I must ask several questions. I have reason to believe the authorities might try to blame Mihaly for the accident."

"But . . ."

"Listen. I've talked to the Ministry of Energy and . . . I've talked to Juli Popovics."

"She's there?"

"She came to Kiev with thousands of others. I think because of her relationship with Mihaly, they may try to use her in some way. Tell me, if you can remember, what kind of questions the KGB asked you."

Nina told Lazlo about the interview, how the interrogator asked general questions about their family, about life in Pripyat, and finally said he knew of Mihaly's affair with Juli Popovics. She told about the blatant suggestion that Mihaly was involved in sabotage. When Nina gave the name of the KGB officer who interviewed her, Lazlo asked her to repeat it.

"Komarov, first initial G. A major. Do you know him?"

"He's head of the branch office in Kiev."

"And now he's here in Moscow . . . trying to put blame on Mihaly."

"We can't know for certain, Nina. Most important now is you and the girls. Did doctors examine you thoroughly?"

"They say Anna and Ilonka weren't overexposed. They've gotten plenty of iodine. But I've talked to others. I know it could affect the girls in the future."

"What about you?"

"It's the same for me, but worse for children. Radiation is especially dangerous for growing cells. All I can do is pray. We ask God for help, and he gives us this. We'll go to Easter mass here tomorrow, they'll fly us to Lvov, and we'll go to Kisbor. Come visit us there as soon as you can. And, Laz?"

"Yes."

"Is Juli Popovics safe? Did she make it to Kiev without getting hurt?"

"Yes, she did."

"Good. I have to go. Others are waiting to use the phone."

"Kiss the girls for me, Nina."

"I will."

Easter dinner with Juli and Aunt Magda reminded Lazlo of boyhood Easters. Sausage, veal loaf, cheese, bread, and hard-boiled eggs, all prepared on Good Friday, put into the Easter basket, and taken to church to be blessed on Holy Saturday. The smell of the food evoked images from boyhood. His parents healthy and strong, his kid brother, Mihaly, running to keep up as they walked uphill from the village of Kisbor with the blessed food.

The Easter meal is served cold on a large platter. After prayer, a single blessed egg is peeled and divided equally among those present as a reminder of who shared the Easter feast. According to tradition, if you experience misfortune during the coming year, you will remember those with whom you shared the egg, and this will give you strength.

Aunt Magda's Easter tradition was the same. She said decorated eggs dated back to before Christ. According to legend, as long as someone in the world decorated Easter eggs, the world would continue. While he ate his portion of the blessed egg, Lazlo wondered if Mihaly had a chance to think of tradition before the reactor exploded.

After the shared egg was eaten, Lazlo uncorked the Hungarian wine he brought. He, Juli, and Aunt Magda gave a toast to safety and peace of mind for all Chernobyl victims and refugees. Aunt Magda said because she had no children, she had celebrated Easter alone since her husband died several years earlier. This year she was grateful to have guests. During their toast, Lazlo noticed that, although she held up her glass, Juli had only a sip of wine.

As they ate, the conversation naturally turned to questions about Chernobyl. Radio Moscow's latest report was two deaths and a hundred or so injured. Lazlo described the roadblocks, the refugees sent to collective farms. Juli said years of illness and an increased probability of cancer could be expected among refugees and emergency workers.

"We may all die of this someday," she said, putting down her fork and looking out the window. "Not suddenly, but gradually. Chernobyl children will be frightened of rain and snow. Even those receiving potassium iodide have no guarantees."

"No iodine for me," said Aunt Magda. "I'd rather the children have it. Neighbors have asked about Chernobyl because they know Juli worked there. I don't know what to say. Yesterday while I weeded the garden, Mariya Grinkevich said men are watching the house."

Juli nodded and turned to Lazlo. "I've seen a car on the road with two men inside."

"Don't worry," said Lazlo. "If you see them, it means they want you to know you're being watched. It's simply a warning."

"Do they watch everyone who worked at Chernobyl?" asked Aunt Magda.

"I'm not sure," said Lazlo.

"I think they would like to," said Juli. "Mihaly said the KGB was constantly around, waiting for something to happen so they could cover it up."

After dinner Aunt Magda stayed in the kitchen while Juli and Lazlo went into the living room. Lazlo sat on the sofa, watching as Juli walked to the front window. Her cotton dress hung loosely about her waist. The sun through the window enveloped her. Although Juli's child did not show, the loose dress reminded him of Nina several summers earlier, pregnant with Ilonka.

"I can't see the car now," said Juli. "You said if I can't see them I should worry."

"I saw them on my way here," said Lazlo. "They're parked up the street near the corner."

When Juli left the window and sat beside him on the sofa, Lazlo stared at her profile, wondering why she reminded him of Nina. True, they both had brown hair, both were slender and about the same height. But Nina's eyes were brown, whereas Juli's were greenish-gray. She moved slightly closer and turned to face him. The sun from the window shadowing her face brought forth an image from youth. The visage of a fictitious young woman from boyhood dreams. A young woman not only beautiful, but someone to save from danger. The age-old boyhood fantasy, becoming a hero. However, boyhood was long gone, stolen away by the world of guns and reactors and the KGB.

Juli put her hand on his hand. "I'm sorry, Lazlo. I've done nothing but add sadness to your life." Tears came to her eyes. "Your brother is gone, and I'm . . ."

"You haven't created sadness, Juli. It's always there, a part of life. Please go on. We need to talk about Mihaly."

Juli took out a handkerchief and wiped her eyes. "So much of Mihaly is gone. He was always joking. It was part of him. He joked when he didn't want to talk about something. He joked when I brought up his family. It was because the effect of our relationship on his family overwhelmed him."

"How would he have reacted to the baby?"

Juli looked down. "I've imagined it a thousand different ways, selfish ways with Mihaly deserting me, or blaming me."

"Do you think he would have blamed you?"

"No. I imagined it because I thought it would be easier to say good-bye. I was going to tell him about the baby Friday on the bus. But he was worried about the reactor. Instead of telling him, I kept it from him and . . . we argued. The same argument. One of us saying we must end it. The other softening. Back and forth . . ."

Juli folded her hands in her lap and looked up at him. "Technology rules our lives. We act like the machines. All this damned logic when nothing is really logical. Bringing children into the world, keeping them healthy, giving them moments of happiness along the way. And after they've grown up, happiness disappears."

When Aunt Magda brought plum brandy, Juli went into the kitchen for water instead. Back on the sofa, when Juli looked at him above her water glass, Lazlo saw the emotions of a woman. He was reminded of Nina sipping wine at dinner last winter in Pripyat. He was reminded of Tamara's eyes glowing in candlelight at Club Ukrainka. He saw in Juli's eyes a sadness he had seen in his mother's eyes when she was alive.

"I wonder," said Juli, "if the KGB knows what Mihaly told me."

"You mean the test on the reactor?"

"Yes. What if the chief engineer was knowingly doing something dangerous? Mihaly said the plant might be a guinea pig. The chief engineer wasn't there. Why wouldn't he be there when the experiment was his idea?"

Lazlo did not answer. An experiment; Mihaly, the scapegoat. Would they blame it on error or laziness? Would they accuse Juli of seducing Mihaly, causing emotional upset in his life? And what about Cousin Zukor last summer at the farm? Lazlo mistrusted Zukor and had the feeling his questioning of Mihaly about Chernobyl might turn up again.

Juli's eyes, reflecting light from the front window, did not blink. Lazlo wondered if *he* was performing an experiment. Staring into this woman's eyes to see how it would affect her, or him. His chest felt suddenly smaller in size, breathless, his thoughts veering away from the logical path of investigation.

Before considering the consequences, Lazlo leaned forward and kissed her. And she kissed him. They did not embrace. They did not close their eyes. When he withdrew, he expected a reaction, a comment. Instead, Juli sipped her water and began speaking again as if nothing had happened.

"When I was a girl, my father took me skating in Gorky Park. His friends were there, and he'd tell them about my schoolwork. I remember being embarrassed. When I was older, he wanted me to go to medical school. 'A career based on compassion, perfect for a woman,' he said. I should have followed his advice. If I'd become a doctor, none of this would have happened. I would have been in Moscow. And at Chernobyl, Mihaly's boss, compassionate and aware of Mihaly's family, would not have put him in charge during the experiment."

When Aunt Magda returned with brandy to refill Lazlo's glass, he declined because soon he was due back at the roadblock. Juli had turned, her knees pressing against his leg. The house was warm. The brandy made him even warmer. And now this woman carrying his brother's child immersed him in womblike warmth. He wanted to kiss her again. He wanted to hold her. He wanted the rest of the world to go away for at least this brief time before the devil named duty called him back to the cold world.

Although Lazlo reminded her of Mihaly, he was not Mihaly. Lazlo was a man of his own making, sensitive and honorable, but with a mysterious past. A man filled with melancholy. She felt it deep inside when he kissed her. A man so alone, so wanting to encompass her life. How could he do this? How could he fall in love with her now? And why did she want so much to embrace him? Insane! Mihaly dead, and now his brother sits so close, so close.

Juli recalled the photograph she'd seen in Mihaly's apartment. Lazlo in the wedding party, smiling with pride. Lazlo looking so much like Mihaly, but also looking like her father. A man brought to her by fate, speaking about a wine cellar on the farm where he and Mihaly grew up.

"We spent a lot of time in the wine cellar last summer. Down there we could go back in time. If we stuck our heads up out of the hole, we'd see our mother in the yard hanging laundry. When the wine began to flow, we confessed our sins. Because we were brothers, because we trusted one another, the confessions were more revealing than those to a priest."

Lazlo turned to the window, the resemblance of his profile to Mihaly's profile making her shudder. He turned back to her. "What Mihaly told me in the wine cellar might account for both of us being followed. He said there were serious problems at Chernobyl. He worked in the control room. He was around the reactor all the time. He saw what went on."

"So did others," said Juli. "The so-called 'disregard for safety' at the plant generated jokes. It was a way of coping. Officials disciplined anyone who spoke openly. Some were sent away to psychiatric hospitals."

"Initially Mihaly said he would resign because of the probability of an accident. Later he said he'd mentioned problems at Chernobyl to avoid telling me about you."

"But he did tell you about me."

"He told me. I hadn't even met you and I hated you."

"Do you hate me now?"

Lazlo put his hand on her knee, leaned close, and whispered, "How could I?"

The KGB had more aggressive methods than monitoring correspondence and telephone conversations when it came to keeping track of suspected anti-Soviets. Most common was direct observation, noting movements and contacts.

Pavel and Nikolai discussed the ramifications of KGB methods as they sat in a shiny black Volga parked up the street from Aunt Magda's house.

"So," said Nikolai, "you're saying there's no point placing

microphones or even reading the mail because guilty people won't say anything to begin with?"

"Right," said Pavel. "Our work in the Pripyat post office was a waste of time."

"Then there's no point to any of this." Nikolai motioned with his hand at the dashboard of the Volga and at his new suit of clothes. "What we're doing here is as useless as reading those idiot peasants' letters."

"Would you rather be back in the post office?" asked Pavel. "Or worse yet, getting a fatal dose of radiation hunting down idiots stupid enough to stay in Pripyat?"

"No," said Nikolai. "I'm simply bored. And I'm really hungry. I think the iodine we took increases appetite. Do you smell food? Someone's cooking somewhere."

"My sister-in-law's probably cooking an elaborate dinner for my wife right now," said Pavel.

"How far away is your sister-in-law's place?" asked Nikolai. "If we get a break, we could go for a bite, and you and your wife . . ."

Pavel waved dismissively. "Not a chance. Anyway, I don't smell food. All I smell is the newness of the car and perhaps your foul breath."

"Careful," said Nikolai. "We carry pistols now. In the post office all we did was throw crumpled letters at one another."

"I wonder if anyone will ever be allowed back in Pripyat," said Pavel.

"A tragedy," said Nikolai. "Banners for May Day prepared, and no one to use them. Maybe the whole thing was a conspiracy planned in Moscow. A big distillery hidden among the reactors at Chernobyl to keep employees happy, and Moscow destroyed it as part of their campaign against alcoholism."

Pavel shook his head, smiled, and resumed staring at the house.

"I wonder how long we'll have to sit here. This so-called subversive Juli Popovics hasn't made a move. You'd think she'd at least give us an opportunity to drive about occasionally."

"We'd have the opportunity if we were following Detective Horvath. Of course, we wouldn't be able to use a Volga." Nikolai looked out the back window. "Where do you think his tail is today?"

"Could be the van down the block," said Pavel.

"Such strange methods, not identifying the agents assigned to Detective Horvath. What if something happens and we start shooting one another? And Horvath's a strange one. Did you see the way his mouth moved when he was walking into the house earlier? My mother always said men who talk to themselves have a second soul that refuses to die, like a devil."

"You should tell Major Komarov you think Detective Horvath is a devil, Nikolai."

Nikolai shook his head. "He'd put us back in our Moskvich, return our contaminated clothes, and send us to Pripyat. I'm content to stay here. Besides, your wife is nearby."

"Don't keep reminding me," said Pavel.

Nikolai laughed. "At least you have someone. I wonder what became of my date from last weekend in Pripyat. I hope she got out all right. Young and firm, not yet fattened up."

Pavel frowned at Nikolai, then sneered.

"Sorry, Pavel. By the way, what does your wife think of all this?"

"She thinks something's wrong. She says it's strange we should be rewarded for running away from Pripyat. Everyone else working for Komarov knows more than we do. It might be more dangerous than we've been led to believe."

"Look," said Nikolai. "Detective Horvath is leaving. Too bad Juli Popovics isn't going with him."

Detective Horvath drove past them and turned north to the

main highway.

"He didn't even look at us," said Nikolai.

"He doesn't have to," said Pavel. "He knows we're here. It's the others he's watching for."

While Nikolai and Pavel watched, the van down the street followed Detective Horvath's Zhiguli at a careful distance. Now they were alone, two PK agents in their shiny Volga, wearing business suits and carrying brand new Makarov 9mm pistols in leather shoulder holsters still aromatic from the tanning mill.

CHAPTER 20

Monday, May 5. May Day and Orthodox Easter were over, and more than a week had passed since Chernobyl's unit four exploded. Even though technicians were seen waving Geiger counters above vegetables at local markets and canned goods were running out, television broadcasts showed films of people swimming in the Pripyat River. Another film showed a woman milking a cow with a soldier checking the milk with a dosimeter and the camera zooming in to show the low radiation count. Everything was fine. Or was it? For example, why had Kiev Party officials, having taken their children out of school early the previous week, not yet returned from southern regions?

Northwest of Kiev on the road from Korosten, a busload of Chernobylites had spent two days on their journey because of various complications. When they piled out of the bus and saw bread, sausage, and tea being served by young men and women from a Kiev komsomol, one old man, unable to control himself, stuffed food into his coat pockets until he resembled a circus bear. The old man had a thin face, reminding Lazlo of his father. When the man finished stuffing his pockets and retreated to the dark side of the bus to eat, Lazlo recalled stories his father had told him and Mihaly about Stalin's 1932 famine. His father going on about the devil Stalin, his mother stopping his father when he began recounting the tale of the little boy who failed to show up to school one day. The boy, it was later discovered, had died and been pickled in a jar by his parents.

As Lazlo stood near his car, his hands deep in his pockets to ward off the evening chill, he wondered if Juli would have been better off going with the people who brought her from Pripyat. She could have disappeared and become an anonymous victim forced to leave home. But she was in Visenka with the KGB watching her in an obvious way, while they watched him in a not-so-obvious way.

Several hundred meters down the road, a van sat at the side of a gasoline station closed for the night. The van's side door was out of his view, and he was certain peepholes were most likely drilled in the side of the van to coincide with the stenciled markings of a construction collective. Obviously the KGB either suspected Mihaly of sabotage, or because he was dead they assumed he would make a convenient scapegoat.

Stash, one of Lazlo's militiamen, ran up. "A car just arrived from the north with a pregnant woman! They say she needs medical attention! She's gotten out of the car and . . ."

"Give them directions to hospital and let them through," said Lazlo.

After Stash ran back to the car, Lazlo could see the woman was quite far along and had to be helped back into the car by a concerned-looking young man. If only Juli Popovics had a husband. Instead of being watched by the KGB, she would be simply another woman passing through the roadblock. But she had no husband.

Except for her aunt who provided a temporary home, she had no one. She was beautiful, attractive, alone, and constantly on his mind.

It was different with Tamara. Although Tamara was a friend and lover, she had her literary magazine and her literary friends. He admired Tamara, enjoyed being with her. But so did other men. Everything was different when it came to Juli Popovics. Crazy. He was going crazy. First he thinks Tamara is different; next he thinks Juli is different. What was going on?

Last week he drove Juli to Visenka. Last week he visited to inquire about her hospital tests. Yesterday he spent the afternoon with her. Yesterday he kissed her, and in accepting his kiss, she drew him to her like one of the howling dogs left behind by the Chernobylites. He was hers. Even now, forty kilometers away, he was hers. Had he, after the explosion at Chernobyl, purposely sought out Mihaly's lover? If he could not have Nina, could he at least have Juli?

Insane brooding fool. Instead of accepting what life offers he plays mind games. Lazlo took his hands from his pockets, rubbed them together, and went to join his men at the roadblock.

Stories told by refugees, taken one at a time, might or might not be true. But when stories repeated themselves, they became believable. Livestock being herded south shot by soldiers. Dogs running after buses. A radius ranging from twenty to fifty kilometers contaminated. Fire still burning at the reactor, and radiation still being released. Another Chernobyl accident in 1982 covered up. Speculation about whether Pripyat residents would ever be allowed to return.

Speculation made people do strange things. In one car, all but the driver were drunk. Even a boy of eight or nine was drunk, having been urged to drink red wine and vodka because of the rumor this would protect him from radiation.

Lazlo and his men had interviewed refugees for several days. At first, his men shook their heads and even smiled in reaction to the stories. Then they became tired of hearing the same things over and over. Tonight, Lazlo noticed his men looked worried. Would there be a shift in the wind? If the fire was still burning and there was a shift in the wind . . .

A little before midnight, Stash summoned Lazlo to a car stopped in the northbound lane. "It's a time warp," said Stash. "An old Zil limousine from the Khrushchev days."

The huge old Zil rumbled loudly through a bad muffler. When he approached the car, Lazlo noticed the grill and front bumper missing and recalled seeing the car before, recalled parking near it somewhere in Kiev, somewhere at night.

There were no passengers, only a driver. The man had a black beard and mustache, and his hair was thinning. He looked Middle Eastern and had a familiar face. The man switched off the ignition, and the Zil's engine coughed and sputtered to a stop.

"Where are you going?" asked Lazlo.

"One goes where one must in the dark of night when a friend beckons."

"What?"

The bearded man continued. "Friends, bodies separate but joined at the head, brain juices mingling. Borscht."

Then Lazlo recalled where he'd seen the man. Club Ukrainka. One of Tamara's poet friends. He leaned close to the Zil's window.

"An admirer of the poet Vasyl Stus sent me," said the bearded man. "Vasyl Stus from the labor camp I am not, but if I dare . . ."

"No poems now. Tell me what you came to say."

"It's Tamara," whispered the man. "She's at the club. She wants you there."

"Is she all right?"

"I don't know. She appears normal, although Tamara is by no means a normal person. She said to find you and bring you to her."

"I have my own car. I'll drive. You can follow if you like."

After he directed Stash to take charge at the roadblock, Lazlo sped off in the Zhiguli. Behind him, the Zil tried to keep up. And behind the Zil, its headlights illuminating the Zil's smoky exhaust, was the van from the closed gasoline station.

Club Ukrainka was quiet. Tamara sat at her usual table in the corner, alone, the candle on the table unlit. She wore no makeup and did not stand to cheerfully call Lazlo to her table. A glass of red wine stood before her. He ordered the same and sat across from her, moving the unlit bottled candle aside. She looked tired as she sipped her wine. She pulled the shawl she wore tightly about her.

"Something is wrong," said Lazlo.

When the bartender brought his wine, Lazlo noticed even he sensed Tamara's anxiety.

Tamara waited for the bartender to leave before speaking. "The KGB picked me up this morning. They questioned me all day and let me go only two hours ago."

"What did they want? Did they hurt you?"

Tamara took a gulp of wine, put the glass down, brushed her hair from her forehead. "I thought it would be about the writers' union Chernobyl articles again, but it wasn't. They wanted to know about you, Laz. How often you come here, what we talk about. They wanted to know what we talked about last weekend when we were together. I said it was none of their business. They said by the end of the day, I would not only tell them what we talked about, I would tell them what we did."

Tamara wiped at her eyes. "And I told them, Laz. I told them what we did. I told them about the dinner you made. I told them we danced. I told them everything, because we did nothing wrong. They said if I didn't cooperate, we'd both be in trouble. The main interrogator was kind at first. A handsome young man simply doing his job. I was wrong to cooperate, Laz. They hinted about my sanity being in question. They had copies of the literary review and pointed out articles they insisted were anti-Soviet. I didn't want to go to the psychiatric hospital, Laz. I didn't want to be made into a crazy woman . . ."

"Tamara, if you're trying to apologize, it's not necessary. You did the right thing. With these fools it's best, if you have nothing to hide, to simply tell everything."

"But they wanted me to say things about you."

"Like what?"

"The young man kept referring to what you did when you weren't with me. He wanted me to agree you and your brother and his lover . . ."

"Juli Popovics?" asked Lazlo.

Tamara tried to smile. "It was funny in a way. His name was Brovko, Captain Brovko. At the same time he's implying conspiracy at Chernobyl, he's trying to make me jealous. I said you told me about Juli Popovics yourself and I didn't think it at all unusual for a friend of your brother to come to Kiev and . . ."

"And they didn't hurt you during the questioning?"

"Except for helping me into the car, they didn't touch me. In the end they simply wanted me to agree your trips to the Chernobyl region were mysterious. I told them because your brother lived there, it was obvious they were trying to create crimes where none existed. Brother visits brother, and the KGB breaks wind."

"They don't like being made to look foolish, Tamara."

"What should I have done, Laz?"

"Told them the truth and not volunteered your own opinions. Said whatever you had to in order to protect yourself. Describe this Captain Brovko."

"Tall, well-built, in his thirties. Spoke a refined Russian and looked almost German. Light hair and blue eyes."

Lazlo looked about the room. The same few people were at other tables. The only new arrival was the bearded poet from the Zil, who sat alone at a table reading a book. The KGB men in the van, if they had kept up, were probably parked outside.

"What should I do now, Laz?"

"Nothing. And it would be best if we didn't see one another for a while."

Tamara reached across the table and touched his hand. "How long?"

He squeezed Tamara's hand. "I don't know where this will lead, but I have bad feelings about it. If I need your help at some point . . ."

"Simply tell me, Laz. What the hell, I can take it."

Even though the club was closing up, Lazlo felt it would be best not to drive Tamara home. When he pulled away from the curb, he saw Tamara pause to look his way before getting into the ancient Zil with the bearded poet.

When Lazlo opened his apartment door, there was an envelope on the floor. Inside, a typed message on Chief Investigator Chkalov's stationery said he was to meet Chkalov promptly at eight in the morning. Although he was dead tired, he knew it would be a sleepless night—the men in the Volga watching Juli, the van following him from Club Ukrainka to his apartment, the KGB questioning Tamara, and now this message from Chkalov.

In bed he thought about the KGB outside. He imagined them taking him away to KGB headquarters on Boulevard Shevchenko, first to the room where they interrogated Tamara, then to one of the basement rooms . . .

In the nightmare he is on a blanket beneath the chestnut tree in the yard of the old farm. Uncle Sandor sits on the blanket beside him, coughing up asthmatic sputum, spitting it into a scaly palm, and showing it to him. In the yard he sees Mihaly climb down into the wine cellar. A woman screams, the scream muffled as if she is in the house . . . or down in the cellar. Suddenly, the wine cellar erupts with a red liquid explosion, and he awakens. On the clock at his bedside, only ten minutes have passed.

He lay awake recalling the wine cellar, the things Mihaly said about Chernobyl the previous summer. Mihaly referring to the Chernobyl reactors as female. Was this the scream he heard in the nightmare? He pieced together what Mihaly and Juli had said about safety problems, experiments, and backup systems being shut off. None of the information came from his visit to the Ministry of Energy. It came from Mihaly and Juli. And now Mihaly was dead and Juli was being watched and might at any time be picked up for questioning by the KGB.

He looked at the clock again. After three. In less than five hours, he was due in Chkalov's office. He got up, shaved, dressed, and went out into the night. He drove as fast as he could to militia headquarters, all the while glancing in the mirror in hopes the van speeding several blocks behind would crash and kill its occupants.

For the remainder of the night, Lazlo maintained a vigil at his small desk at militia headquarters. First he called Juli at Aunt Magda's and told her he would be calling periodically. Juli said she was glad, not only because she was frightened of the men watching the house, but because she wanted to talk to him.

"If I can't see you, at least I'll hear your voice. I'll sleep on the sofa. The phone is under the cushion so it won't wake Aunt Magda."

After his first call to Juli, Lazlo called militia headquarters in Visenka. He pretended to be a neighbor of Aunt Magda's reporting a prowler. Two hours later, after talking twice to Juli, he called Visenka headquarters again, disguising his voice and again reporting a prowler.

The hours before dawn alternated with a strange feeling of peace during his brief conversations with Juli, and intense feelings of anger as he waited to see Chkalov. By sunrise he decided he would tell Chkalov the KGB was harassing him. And Chkalov, who had no love for the KGB, would agree with him, at least in principle.

But at eight o'clock when he walked into Chkalov's office, he could not complain about the KGB because the KGB's Kiev chief, Major Grigor Komarov, was there, sitting in Chkalov's chair behind the desk.

Komarov smiled, saying nothing as Chkalov closed the door. Komarov's head was lowered, his eyes partially hidden by his thick eyebrows and high forehead. The skin on Komarov's cheeks was mottled, the red lines of a drinker. Lazlo smelled stale tobacco smoke. Even though he had never met Komarov, he hated him.

Chkalov circled the desk while introducing Komarov. Obviously Chkalov expected Komarov to give up the chair behind the desk. Finally, when Komarov did not relinquish the larger desk chair, Chkalov sat in the guest chair beside Lazlo.

"Major Komarov would like to ask a few questions," said Chkalov.

Komarov glanced to Chkalov. "Only a few, Comrade Chief Investigator? I didn't know there was a limit."

Chkalov stared back at Komarov with a look of contempt.

Komarov looked to Lazlo. "Chief Investigator Chkalov tells me you left your post last night, Detective Horvath."

"I had important personal business."

"Personal business." Komarov nodded to Chkalov. "Personal business."

"I heard," said Chkalov, gripping the arms of the guest chair. "No need to repeat."

"I simply want to be certain Detective Horvath's desertion of his post is a matter of record." Komarov turned back to Lazlo. "Detective Horvath, where exactly did you go when you left your post at eleven thirty-five last night?"

"I drove across town to Club Ukrainka in the theater district."

"Why did you go there?"

"To see a friend."

"What is this friend's name?"

"Tamara."

"Her full name."

"Tamara Petrov."

The questioning went on like this. Komarov asking a simple question, Lazlo giving a minimal answer, which prompted the next question. A game, Komarov obviously trying to make Lazlo angry enough to blurt out something. But Lazlo maintained his composure.

Eventually, through the back-and-forth questioning, he told Komarov he visited Tamara because she was frightened. He told Komarov about Mihaly being killed and how Tamara was with him Sunday morning when he learned about the Chernobyl explosion. He told Komarov about Juli Popovics coming to see him and the unpleasant task of telling Juli about Mihaly's death. He told all of this because he knew Komarov, being head of Kiev's KGB office, either knew these things already, or could easily find them out.

Because he was himself a skilled interrogator, Lazlo knew exactly how much information to give in order not to appear he was holding back. He told Komarov the obvious. The details of events of the past several days amounted to nothing more than his movements about Kiev. He and Tamara at the bakery hearing news about Chernobyl, him at the Ministry of Energy trying to find out about Mihaly, Juli coming to Kiev and finding him, him taking Juli to the hospital, then to Visenka. All obvious to Komarov because of the agents following Lazlo and Juli.

During the interrogation, Lazlo watched Komarov's eyes. Despite apparent outward calm, Lazlo recognized the eyes of a man who asks questions as a device with which to examine the suspect's character. Two interrogators watching one another's eyes. But there was something else in Komarov's eyes. Lazlo had seen it in the eyes of hardened criminals. Komarov was full of deceit, saying what he needed to say in order to twist the facts in a certain direction.

After Lazlo told of Easter dinner with Aunt Magda and Juli, Komarov paused and reached into his jacket pocket. Lazlo's initial reaction was defensive, an awareness of the position of his own pistol in its shoulder holster. A reaction ingrained during years of investigation in Kiev, where a black market Makarov or Stechkin could turn up anywhere. But of course, Komarov did not produce a weapon. Instead he withdrew an aluminum film can. He placed the small can on Chkalov's empty desk, unscrewed the cap, placed the cap beside the can, and waited.

Chkalov coughed and shrugged his shoulders. Lazlo knew Chkalov would like nothing better than to invite Lazlo to draw his pistol so the two of them could blast this idiot to hell. Finally the purpose of the film can was revealed. Komarov took out a pack of cigarettes, lit one, and began smoking, using the film can as an ashtray.

"On my last visit, there was no ashtray," said Komarov.

Komarov drew deeply and often on the cigarette, filling the room with smoke.

Komarov cleared his throat before speaking. "Since there is so much speculation these days, why don't you and I speculate a bit, Detective Horvath? We are both investigators. We know crimes are solved through speculation."

"I've told you everything I know about what's happened the last few days," said Lazlo. "If you want to speculate, fine."

Komarov blew smoke in his direction. "Very well. Assume for a moment the Chernobyl explosion was not an accident. Anything is possible, even sabotage. Not out of the realm of possibility, is it? So, who would do it? Better yet, who could do it? Someone who works at the reactor. Suppose this someone, in the process of committing sabotage, is killed. Who knows why? An explosive device gone off too soon? No. Too obvious. A Chernobyl worker would be smart enough to make it seem an accident. A Chernobyl worker could simply compromise safety systems until a so-called accident becomes inevitable."

Komarov put his cigarette out in the film can and immediately lit another. "Of course, if this was the case, if the saboteur established an environment in which an accident were inevitable, he probably wouldn't want to be there. But what if it could not be avoided? If he suddenly excused himself because of illness, how would it look?

So, he creates an escape plan. He has an accomplice, another person working at the facility ready to help him escape. Better yet, the accomplice works in an area where radiation cannot penetrate. There is such place at Chernobyl. It's the low-level counting laboratory operated by the Department of Industrial Safety. The deepest basement of the building is buried beneath concrete and steel. In fact, two technicians, a man and a woman, were rescued from the basement of the building. Instead of running away from the area, as most did, they made a rational decision. They gathered what food they could find, showered, found fresh clothing, and went down to the deep sub-basement of the building. When rescued, they were found to have received a lower radiation dose than farmers many kilometers away. So you see, if someone worked at Chernobyl, if someone knew how to protect himself from radiation, he could survive."

The interrogation was having its effect. So easy to use Mihaly because he is dead. So easy to use Juli and Mihaly together. But Lazlo knew he must control himself. And, though it went against his nature, he feigned ignorance.

"This man and woman," said Lazlo, "the ones found in the counting laboratory. Do you think they were involved in sabotage?"

Komarov blew out another stinking cloud. "What do you think?"

"Perhaps if you gave me their names, I could ask Juli Popovics about them. She also worked at the Department of Industrial Safety and might be aware of something pertinent to your investigation."

Komarov looked to Chkalov and shook his head. "Your Detective Horvath speculates quite well, doesn't he?"

Chkalov coughed and cleared his throat. "If you say so, Major."

Komarov turned back to Lazlo. "An investigator should understand that no stone can remain unturned."

"I understand quite well, Major."

"Then you'll not be offended when I remind you your brother

was on duty at unit four when the so-called accident occurred. Shall I go on?"

"If you wish," said Lazlo.

Komarov put out his cigarette but did not light another. "It's a matter of logic, Detective Horvath. Unit four was in the process of shutting down and was especially vulnerable. A saboteur, aware of its vulnerability, would have chosen this moment to act."

Komarov stood, walked to the window, split the ornate window curtains with his fingers, and looked out. When he came back to the desk, he lit another cigarette and sat down. "You see, Detective Horvath, the saboteur had everything planned. On Friday afternoon, since there were other experienced technical personnel about, he would have been able to make up an excuse to leave the building and go to another part of the site. He might have gone to the low-level laboratory and joined his accomplice in the sub-basement. She would have hidden him there and stayed with him while everyone else . . ."

Komarov waved his hand dismissively. "I'm not saying any of this has to do with your brother, Detective Horvath. However, his intimacy with both unit four and Juli Popovics—who, as a dosimetrist, was supposed to report for duty in the event of an accident—is of interest. Other names in the mix come to mind. A cousin named Andrew Zukor, and also a close friend of Juli Popovics named Aleksandra Yasinsky, a known counterrevolutionary."

Komarov smashed out his cigarette and stood. He laughed. "Oh well, it's simply speculation. Right, Detective Horvath? Chief Investigator Chkalov?"

"It sounds serious," said Chkalov.

Komarov emptied the film can in Chkalov's wastebasket. "A reactor explosion is serious. We all need to think about the details leading up to it. You'll think about the details, won't you, Detective

Horvath?"

"I will," said Lazlo.

When Komarov walked past to leave the office, Lazlo imagined dragging Komarov to the floor and strangling him. Instead he said, "Good morning, Major," and Komarov was gone.

Chkalov stared at Lazlo for a moment, and finally said, "You're due back on duty at three. Everyone is working sixteen-hour shifts until further notice. You are no exception. This time make sure you stay until six."

On his way out, Lazlo saw Komarov waiting in the reception area outside Chkalov's office. Komarov stood at the window looking out. There was a cloud of smoke about him, and the receptionist was coughing.

Lazlo sat in the Zhiguli in front of militia headquarters. Down the block he saw the construction collective van, which had alternated with a gray Moskvich for the past two days. He needed sleep, but he needed to see Juli more. If Komarov believed what he said, they would pick Juli up for questioning.

He had no other choice but to go to Juli. He would sleep there, perhaps in her arms. But first he would go to his apartment and appear to run errands to cover the only real errand necessary. He would stop at the bank to get out all his money, or however many rubles they would allow. He needed to be free, like a Gypsy, ready for anything.

Komarov waited until Detective Horvath was gone before confronting the chief investigator at his office door.

"Why not speak with me about Detective Horvath?" asked Chkalov in a harsh whisper.

"Because I've already spoken with you," said Komarov. "So, if I may speak with the deputy chief investigator . . . what was his name?"

"Lysenko," growled Chkalov. "I'll show you to his office."

Deputy Chief Investigator Lysenko's office was smaller than Chkalov's, his desk stacked with papers, indicating Lysenko was busier than his boss. Lysenko was trim and dressed in a tailored suit.

"How may I help you, Major?"

"I'll come right to the point," said Komarov. "It's about Detective Horvath. I'm afraid I must inform you he is being investigated by the KGB in regard to events leading up to the incident at Chernobyl."

"Is there anything I can do?"

Lysenko looked serious but not overly surprised. Komarov decided he might be able to use Lysenko later as well as now.

"Yes. If you can observe Detective Horvath when he's here at headquarters, I would appreciate it."

"By all means," said Lysenko.

"And one other thing," said Komarov. "Leaving one's post at such a critical time is a serious matter, is it not?"

"It is, Major."

"I'm afraid I might have to file an official KGB report unless . . ."

"Unless what?"

"If the report came from the militia's own office, it might be much better . . . for the militia. To put it bluntly, Deputy Chief, I think you should file an official report to your chief immediately. Otherwise, like I said, I'd have to file a report from my men who were watching Detective Horvath last night. It wouldn't gain me or the KGB anything, but it would be our duty. You, on the other hand . . . well, I'll let you decide. I understand leaving one's militia post is often disciplined by at least a temporary suspension."

"Certainly," said Lysenko.

"Copy me on your report." Komarov turned to leave. "If I don't hear from you by five this afternoon, I'll file my report."

"I'll file a report immediately and have a copy sent to you by messenger," said Lysenko.

Back in his car, when Captain Azef asked what had gone on in militia headquarters, Komarov answered with an exhale of smoke.

"Drive me back to the office, Captain. I have a meeting with Captain Brovko."

Komarov stood at his office window, smoking a cigarette and looking out at the evening lights of Kiev. It had been a busy day. This morning's visit to militia headquarters had put Horvath firmly in his grasp. Later in the morning, Captain Brovko filled him in on the interrogation of Tamara Petrov. Although there was nothing specific concerning the Chernobyl incident, Brovko's list of incidental factors could be pieced together to discredit Horvath's character. Brovko was an intelligent young officer; someone to be careful of should he try to position himself for promotion at Komarov's expense. Keep Brovko busy. Keep Brovko out of the way while his own plan reaches its climax.

By tomorrow the connection between the Horvath cousin and possible sabotage at Chernobyl would have a life of its own. Especially after tonight's final meeting, the final link in the chain. Komarov went to the outer office where Nikolai Nikolskaia's partner had been waiting to see him for over an hour.

The former PK agent was light-skinned and effeminate, reminding him of Dmitry. After leading him into his office and closing the door, Komarov sat across from the agent, making a show of examining his KGB personnel file.

"Pavel. May I call you Pavel?"

"Of course, Major."

"Good. After speaking with your fellow PK agent, I wanted a chance to meet you. Nikolskaia is an interesting character, unmarried." Komarov flipped through the file. "I see you are married. Was your wife able to leave Pripyat safely?"

"She came to Kiev after the accident. She's staying with her sister."

Komarov put the file down and lit a cigarette. "How would you like to be permanently stationed here?"

"And not return to the PK in Pripyat?"

"Both, Pavel. I wish to permanently assign you as one of my agents here in Kiev."

"I don't know what to say, Major. I'm honored."

"Good. I'll need to provide you with more detailed information concerning the Chernobyl case and Detective Horvath."

"We've watched him visiting Juli Popovics."

"I've admired your thorough reports, Pavel. It is also convenient you learned Hungarian in KGB language school. The reason I've asked you in tonight, besides wanting to meet you, is because I need you to bring Juli Popovics in for questioning tomorrow. It might be routine, or it could be serious. We'll know tomorrow." Komarov leaned back in his chair. "Because you and Nikolskaia were involved in the case from the beginning . . ."

Komarov paused, giving Pavel a chance to volunteer information.

"From the beginning?"

"Yes. While at the PK office in Pripyat, you and Nikolskaia brought the Horvath cousin, one Andrew Zukor, to my attention. He's been given the code name Gypsy Moth. However, this is in question because the Gypsy Moth might be someone else."

"Who?"

"According to information transmitted from the First Chief

Directorate in Moscow, Detective Lazlo Horvath may be the Gypsy Moth. Someone has been passing Chernobyl information to foreign intelligence for years. Efforts to measure Soviet plutonium production using clandestine air sampling have gone on for decades... You look puzzled. You have heard of these programs?"

"Plutonium . . . yes."

"Good, Pavel. Then you should not be surprised to learn Detective Horvath, his brother, and Juli Popovics may have formed a triumvirate. Ukrainians bent on destroying their republic. But perhaps I've revealed too much. I want you to concentrate on the assignment at hand. You will bring Juli Popovics into this office for questioning tomorrow. If necessary, you will use force. Do you understand?"

"Yes, Major. I . . . we understand. Should we do it in the morning?"

"At exactly nine o'clock. And you will return back here at ten. If it is a routine matter, we'll question her briefly, and you can return her to Visenka. If it is not routine . . ."

"You really think it involves the Chernobyl explosion?" asked Pavel.

"I do," said Komarov. "But remember, at this point evidence remains circumstantial. We'll know more tomorrow."

Komarov stood, and this prompted Pavel to stand.

"Oh," said Komarov. "One more thing. If this is conspiracy, the parties involved might become desperate. I spoke with Detective Horvath today, and he seems an aggressive type. If he tries to get in your way, we'll be certain of conspiracy and of his involvement in it. You have weapons. If it becomes necessary, I expect you to use them."

Komarov turned his back to Pavel and looked out the window. He raised his voice. "Make note of this, Pavel. Juli Popovics must be picked up in Visenka at exactly nine tomorrow morning and be in this office at exactly ten. Timing is critical. If you fail, there are other agents who would like to have the luxury of bringing their wives with them to Kiev. You are lucky, Pavel, to have followed a suspect in this case. Otherwise you and your partner would be in serious trouble. Nine o'clock in Visenka, and ten o'clock here. There will be no mistakes! Am I understood?"

"Yes, Major," said Pavel in a feeble voice.

"You may go."

Komarov stayed at the window as his office door closed gently behind him. The lights of the city dazzled. Tuesday was almost over. Tomorrow, Wednesday, a day he had awaited since the Sherbitsky affair, was near. Tomorrow the Chernobyl affair would blossom like a spring flower, and by summer, medals would be pinned on his chest where the knife in his pocket felt like the pressure of a woman's breast.

Outside Komarov's office, Pavel felt dizzy. He paused, hoping the major would call him back to say the final statement had been a joke to keep him alert. The mention of Moscow's First Chief Directorate and plutonium production had upset him because he didn't know what Komarov was talking about. He didn't want to know secrets. All he wanted was a job in Kiev, maybe back in a PK office. And the comment about Nikolai not being married . . .

A bearded, foreign-looking man sitting in a chair outside Komarov's office stared at Pavel. "How, now," said the man.

"What?"

"What, when, where, why," said the man in a singsong voice. "All good questions if they evoke images for the poet's muse."

Pavel walked out the door of the anteroom, taking his confusion with him. Tomorrow at ten, he and Nikolai would be here again with Juli Popovics. If not, they might end up at a committee hearing for abandoning their posts.

CHAPTER 21

Wednesday, May 7, 1986. While driving the streets of Kiev at seven thirty in the morning, Lazlo noticed a subtle change. Instead of the usual straight-ahead or downtrodden look of pedestrians, he saw sideways glances, a few looking his way, perhaps recognizing an unmarked militia Zhiguli. Ten days had passed since the Chernobyl explosion. By now, shortwave receivers were down from closet shelves and attics, with wire antennas strung across living rooms. Literally and figuratively, Chernobyl was in the air in Kiev.

A half hour ago, he had been rudely awakened by a call from Deputy Chief Investigator Lysenko and told to meet with Chief Investigator Chkalov promptly at eight for another morning meeting. He wondered if Major Komarov was back looking for scapegoats.

The usual morning pastry vendors along Khreshchatik were absent, and several people climbing up from the metro wore handkerchiefs over their mouths and noses. It was an insane world. He had been asleep just over an hour when Lysenko called. He'd been within a familiar nightmare, the Gypsy deserter already shot in the face, yet pleading with him not to shoot. He could collapse any moment, run the Zhiguli into the curb. "Look here!" those on the sidewalk would scream. "It's the radiation in the air! We're all going to die!"

Yesterday he had spent several hours in Visenka with Juli. He had been too tired to talk and napped after lunch. In the afternoon, when it was time to go on duty, Juli had awakened him with a kiss. It had not been a dream. Juli was real. Everything around him was actually happening, despite the sensation of floating he felt as he drove through Kiev.

He stopped at a café and gulped two cups of strong tea. Back in the car, he turned several corners and circled back on the van following him. As he passed the van and sped to militia headquarters, he rolled down the window.

"Your foot is still in your mother!" he shouted in Hungarian.

The driver, a round-faced, pudgy young man, simply frowned.

Chkalov was alone in his office and avoided looking directly at him. He was like one of the pedestrians walking down the sidewalk. Even though Komarov was not here, Lazlo smelled a setup. At the last meeting, Komarov had mentioned his cousin, Andrew Zukor. Even he wondered if Zukor's visit last summer had been for the purpose of speaking with Mihaly about Chernobyl.

Chkalov finally looked at Lazlo. "Many of us are going without sleep these days. I'll get to the point, Detective Horvath. It has to do with you deserting your post without notifying the officer in charge."

"I was in charge."

"Regulations specify you were supposed to notify the officer in charge here at the office before you left your post. You could have radioed instead of abandoning your men."

He thought, *Should I have wiped their asses, too?* But he said, "I left an officer in charge."

"Detective Horvath. Leaving an officer in charge without notifying the officer in charge at the office is not the way it's done."

"So, an officer in charge in the field is not necessarily an officer in charge unless the officer in charge at the office is notified?"

Chkalov scowled. "I find it necessary to suspend you, Detective Horvath."

"Did Komarov tell you to suspend me?"

Chkalov's face reddened. "The militia is independent of the KGB!"

"Independent?" shouted Lazlo. "If we're so independent, then why the hell am I being followed day and night? I'll tell you why! Komarov is investigating Juli Popovics and me and my dead brother because he needs scapegoats for Chernobyl blunders!"

Chkalov's fists clenched on the desk. "Impossible! It was an unfortunate accident!"

Lazlo stood up. "How long will I be suspended?"

Chkalov stood, but because he was shorter, he had to look up to Lazlo. "I don't know! Check back weekly with Lysenko!" The flesh at Chkalov's neck shook violently. "Don't stand there looking at me! Get out! Leave your car at the motor pool!"

In the hallway, Lazlo passed Lysenko standing at his office door. "Good morning, Detective Horvath."

Lazlo raised his fist, and Lysenko backed into his office. In Hungarian, Lazlo said, "Your foot is still in your mother."

"What?" whined Lysenko.

"It means the Gypsy is not pleased." Lazlo continued down the hallway.

"Detective Horvath, a message . . ." said Lysenko, calling him back.

"What?"

Lysenko handed him an envelope. "It just came up from the front desk."

Lazlo took the envelope and continued walking. DETECTIVE HORVATH, KIEV MILITIA. The handwriting was unfamiliar. He tore open the envelope and stood in the hallway reading it.

My dear Detective Horvath

The when is now

The who is one plus someone more

The where is east of the river

The what is danger to the one plus someone more

Foreshadowing the fate of Vasyl Stus

The why is a flower with deadly pollen

Flattening the grass to wormwood

A friend of a friend of Shevchenko

Who would be a friend of a dead nineteenth-century poet? A poet? The bearded poet in the Zil who brought the message from Tamara. A friend of a friend could mean the message was from Tamara.

Lazlo read the lines again. East of the river. East of the river in Visenka there was danger for Juli and her baby—the one plus some-one more. Tamara said Vasyl Stus was a poet who died in a labor camp. Danger to Juli because of the deadly pollen of Chernobyl, the Chernobyl grass, the wormwood Mihaly had spoken of. He recalled telling Tamara about the biblical Chernobyl star. She would know. She would refer to the fate of Vasyl Stus.

He ran down the hall to the stairway. He pushed through the front entrance of militia headquarters, almost knocking down a uniformed militiaman coming in. Was the message literal? Was Juli really in danger? If so, how would Tamara know?

The van followed him around the corner. Chkalov had said to return the Zhiguli to the motor pool, so he was simply following orders. He sped into the fenced-in motor-pool yard where marked patrol cars were parked. One of the garage side doors was open, and he skidded inside to a stop amid the shouts of mechanics.

"Imbecile! Who are you trying to kill?"

Too many mechanics around to switch cars. They would question him, demand papers. Although cars were parked in the aisle, he was able to drive through with no more damage than removing a side mirror from another turd-green Zhiguli.

"Madman! Stop!"

The back door of the garage was closed. He jumped out and pushed the door up on its rollers. While running back to the car, a mechanic threatened him with a large wrench. The mechanic dropped the wrench and stepped back when Lazlo drew his pistol. Other mechanics gathered at the back door to watch him drive down the alley.

From the front of the garage, everything would seem ordinary, the KGB men in the van waiting for him to come walking out of the garage. Lazlo drove slowly so he would not attract attention. He turned northwest, went several blocks at traffic speed to make sure the van did not follow. If a car followed, he could not tell because there were too many on the street.

When he turned southeast, back through the heart of the city, he sped up, back to Khreshchatik, past the post office and the café, where he had stopped for tea. Khreshchatik would take him to Lenkomsomol Square. He would go through the underpass, branch south onto Kirov Street. If he took the ramp fast enough, he would be able to see if anyone followed, because they would also have to speed through the underpass. If not, they would lose him in the

MICHAEL BERES

maze of ramps and exits.

Ahead, the gaping mouth of the underpass was busy swallow-ing slower traffic. When he plunged into the underpass, he flashed his headlights at cars ahead, moving them out of the way. He was below Lenkomsomol Square, where he often walked to lunch in hot weather. Would he ever walk here again? Would Kiev, his world, ever be the same again? Would he get out of the underpass without killing himself and perhaps others?

A sputtering Zaporozhets nearly lost control as it fishtailed to avoid being rear-ended. Lazlo had never driven this fast through the underpass. The sunlight coming through drainage grates on Lenkomsomol Square flashed like strobe lights. The Zhiguli's tires squealed, the echo screaming through the tunnel. When he hit a wet spot in the tunnel, the Zhiguli lunged sideways, tipped up on two wheels, dropped back to the pavement, and slid into the wall. The wall straightened the Zhiguli, clawing away metal on the passenger side as he exploded up onto the Kirov Street ramp to daylight.

There had been many turns in the underpass, and he had been too busy to see if anyone followed. But now, as he shifted the Zhiguli into high gear and sped onto Kirov Street, he saw a gray Moskvich driving like mad behind him.

They were after him and would not let go, two men in a gray Moskvich, one of the cars alternating with the van earlier in the week, probably radioing the van right now. If he was going to lose the Moskvich, he had to hurry.

Right on Karl Liebknecht, left on Revolutsii, right on Mech-nikov. His city. His Kiev, the streets he knew. But the KGB agents also knew the city. They stayed behind him, seemingly anticipating each turn. This was not getting him to Juli, east of the river where there was danger. But if he drove to Visenka with the KGB in tow, and if the danger came from the KGB . . .

He turned onto Lesya Ukrainka and headed south. The boulevard was wide and straight, and he could maintain his speed by crossing from lane to lane, passing moving cars as if they were parked haphazardly in the street. He would soon cross over Friendship of Peoples Boulevard, the fastest route to the bridge over the Dnieper, the fastest route to Visenka.

He maintained his speed and stayed in the left lane as he approached the overpass. The ramp down to the boulevard was on the far right. He would cross several lanes of traffic and enter the ramp at the last possible second. He only hoped the Moskvich would miss the turn.

An old woman stepped from the island, and he had to brake and swerve to miss her. A marked militia Zhiguli passed in the opposite direction. In his mirror, he saw its roof light come on as it U-turned to join the chase behind the Moskvich.

The ramp coming up. No choice. Horns and tires screaming as he veered right across lanes of traffic and plunged down onto the ramp. A quick glance in the mirror, and the Moskvich was there, sliding sideways before entering the ramp.

He had to get to Juli! He had to get rid of these men now!

He turned the wheel, braked, spun the Zhiguli around, and sped up the ramp directly at the grinning grill of the Moskvich.

"Bastards!" he screamed.

The Moskvich turned abruptly to avoid him, lost control, and smashed into the guardrail. The militia car taking up the chase behind the Moskvich followed the Moskvich like a dog latched onto a rabbit's tail, the driver thinking this was the only way to avoid the maniac coming up the ramp in the wrong direction. The militia car slammed into the back of the Moskvich, the sound of the impact making Lazlo look back to see if there was an explosion. No explosion. But both cars were disabled.

Lazlo drove north two blocks so that north would be the direction radioed to the KGB and militia headquarters. But once out of sight, he took side streets back to Friendship of Peoples Boulevard and sped onto the bridge across the Dnieper River. As the Zhiguli crested the bridge at high speed, he saw in his rearview mirror, through the haze of the city, flashing lights of multiple militia cars converging at the overpass crossing over Friendship of Peoples Boulevard.

Leaving Kiev, on the east side of the river, traffic became lighter. During the frantic chase, he had shifted in the seat, his jacket twisting sideways, pressing his Makarov uncomfortably against his breastbone. He adjusted himself in the seat, listening to Kiev militia frequencies on the radio. A broadcast repeated a description of his Zhiguli, but the broadcast focused on Kiev west of the river. There were thousands of Zhigulis the same turd-green color as his Zhiguli. He would get to Visenka, he was certain of it. But what would he do about the KGB men watching the house?

The message from Tamara by way of the bearded poet told him Juli was in danger. Had the KGB contacted Tamara again? Or did Tamara have underground contacts? And what about Komarov, who flew all the way to Moscow to question Nina, yet did not bother to question Juli? He knew where she was. His men were watching her.

Speeding to Visenka, Lazlo recalled the last time he visited. There had been a KGB faded red Zhiguli, then a KGB black Volga, first one then the other following him before taking up positions down the street from Aunt Magda's. Aunt Magda's street a dead-end. No way out if they tried to stop him from taking Juli . . .

The farmer's field at the end of the street. He'd seen the twin ruts of its trail leading into the field. The sign for Visenka was ahead, so he turned east onto a gravel road peppered with ruts that shook the Zhiguli violently. The steering wheel was transformed into a frenzied serpent trying to escape his grasp. With any luck he would be able to see Aunt Magda's house, with its spring flowers and its arbor, across the fields.

In spite of the sun shining through colorful curtains, the house was a prison. Like her unborn child, Juli could not escape. This morning she had gone out to look at the flowers. From the front of the house, spying through the arbor, she looked up the street and saw the black car. While she watched, another black car with two men arrived, and the first car drove away.

Aunt Magda was at the stove, putting cut-up vegetables into soup for lunch. Juli wondered if Lazlo would come for lunch again. Falling in love so soon after Mihaly's death tormented her. She tried to tell herself it was fear, her need to latch onto someone strong. Aunt Magda said she was being foolish, that it was natural to desire such a man. Aunt Magda said his knowledge of the baby made their feelings for one another even more powerful.

"These are untainted vegetables," said Aunt Magda, turning from her soup pot. "I went to the market before the Chernobyl explosion. I have enough for another week, and then I'll use the canned vegetables I put up last summer."

Aunt Magda came to the table and sat across from Juli. She put down her paring knife and lowered her head, mimicking Juli. "Don't be sad, Juli."

"There isn't much to be happy about except being with you. People forced from their homes, Marina and Vasily and his mother and sister at a collective somewhere, Pripyat probably abandoned

forever, all the others who were at the plant. There's always someone on duty at the building where I worked. I keep wondering what
happened to them."

Aunt Magda frowned. "Pripyat abandoned forever? Is such a
thing possible?"

Juli reached out and touched her aunt's hand. "Knowing what
I know about radiation, it's more than possible. The levels of radiation causing Mihaly and others to receive lethal doses in so short a
time, the half-life of plutonium. And now, here sits a sad fool because the brother of her dead lover is not here."

Aunt Magda grasped both Juli's hands. "Finding a friend in a
troubled world is not foolish. During the war . . . God forgive me,
I said I'd never tell. Your uncle was my cousin. Why do you think
we had no children?"

Juli stared into her aunt's tear-filled eyes. "You didn't have to
tell me."

Aunt Magda let go of Juli's hands, took out a handkerchief, and
wiped her eyes. "We were cousins, but we loved one another. And
with war, love was the only thing left. Instead of wondering about
those you cannot help, perhaps you can help Lazlo."

"You're right. I should be doing something instead of sitting
here waiting for him to visit." Juli stood. "Mihaly is dead, the
Ukraine is coming apart, and I sit here getting fatter every day with
his brother's child!"

"Please don't shout," scolded Aunt Magda. "You're not getting
fatter. You're not even showing. Besides, a baby growing inside is
not called fat. It's a human being!"

Aunt Magda stood and went to the kitchen sink. "It's your baby.
You're responsible for it. If a man loves you, responsibility is shared."

"Is it love, Aunt Magda? We've known one another only a few
days."

Aunt Magda looked out the window. "If you keep asking about it over and over, it's love. It's love!"

"I hope he's coming today."

"He is."

"What?"

"He's coming."

"How do you know?"

"Because he's in the backyard."

Aunt Magda opened the door, and when Lazlo came into the kitchen, Juli could see by the look on his face something was terribly wrong. It was the same look he had before he told her about Mihaly's death. She ran to Lazlo and hugged him.

"We don't have much time," whispered Lazlo in her ear. "I've got to get you out of here."

Juli let go of him, looked past him into the backyard. "Why do I have to leave?"

"I don't have time to go into details. The KGB and the militia are after me. I was followed, but I lost them. It can't be long before they decide I've come here. The head of the KGB in Kiev has dreamed up a plot involving your connection to Mihaly. We must leave now."

Aunt Magda ran from the kitchen. "I'll get a coat and your bag."

"What about Aunt Magda?" asked Juli. "If they come and I'm not here . . ."

"I know."

Aunt Magda came back with the coat and bag. "I already washed the clothes and repacked them. With a car out there night and day, I felt something would happen."

Lazlo turned to Aunt Magda, held her shoulders. "Listen. This is important. After we leave, I want you to watch the street. If someone comes, I want you to call the local militia immediately and tell them I took Juli away. Tell them you protested but were unable to stop me."

Aunt Magda took out a handkerchief and blew her nose. "No. You're trying to protect me. I won't tell them anything. I'm old. I don't care what they do to me."

Juli touched Lazlo's arm, but Lazlo continued holding Aunt Magda's shoulders and staring at her.

"It's not for you," said Lazlo. "It's to get them off the trail, a diversion. You must call the local militia. If someone comes, call immediately and say we just left. If no one comes, call the militia exactly one hour after we leave. Do you understand?" Lazlo shook Aunt Magda's shoulders gently. "Do you?"

"I understand. Call if I see them coming. But if an hour goes by and no one comes, call anyway. But . . ."

"There's no time to explain. It's for Juli's safety and my safety. A diversion." Lazlo hugged Aunt Magda. "You are a good woman. You remind me of my mother."

Juli put on her coat, kissed Aunt Magda, and clung to her until Lazlo said they had to go.

The Volga's powerful engine idled like a predator. Nikolai sat behind the wheel, waiting for Pavel to tell him when it was time to go. Pavel looked at his watch every few seconds.

"Why are you so nervous?" asked Nikolai.

"Major Komarov makes me nervous," said Pavel. "He's in charge of security at Chernobyl, yet he stays in Kiev."

"He's smart," said Nikolai. "Only a fool would go there now. Maybe he sent the homosexual agents to Chernobyl."

Pavel turned and stared wide-eyed at Nikolai. "What do you

mean by that?"

Nikolai shrugged. "When I met with Komarov, he seemed unusually upset about homosexuality and religion and ethnic groups in general." Nikolai tapped his forehead. "You know what I mean?"

Pavel nodded. "When I met with him, he mentioned you weren't married, if you know what I mean . . ."

Nikolai reached out to Pavel. "Why should I marry when I can hold my partner's hand?"

Pavel shook Nikolai's hand away. "This is no time for jokes!"

"Why not? It's boring as hell sitting here."

"It won't be boring for long," said Pavel. "If the Horvath brothers were involved in a plot with their cousin, and if Juli Popovics is involved . . ."

Nikolai interrupted. "Maybe the Gypsy Moth cousin will show up before nine o'clock."

"That's another thing," said Pavel. "Komarov implies all kinds of things, as if he is purposely trying to upset us. He says perhaps Detective Horvath is the Gypsy Moth. He says things about plutonium and air samples. Everything is ambiguous except to be precise about our timing."

"Why all this exactness with the time?" asked Nikolai.

"How the hell do I know? All I know is, Komarov said to pick Juli Popovics up *exactly* at nine and have her at KGB headquarters *exactly* at ten."

"Relax, Pavel. We can do it."

"It's easy for you to be relaxed," said Pavel. "You weren't personally threatened. My wife, too. All of us back to Pripyat and even up on charges if we don't do this right."

"If Detective Horvath is dangerous and if Komarov wanted to guarantee Juli Popovics be brought in without a hitch, why didn't he simply assign more men?"

"Finally you understand," said Pavel.

"It's a game," said Nikolai. "We're simply not used to Komarov's methods."

Pavel looked at his watch again, touched the bulge of the shiny new Makarov 9mm pistol in its shoulder holster. "All right, enough. It's time to go."

Nikolai touched his own Makarov in its shoulder holster, put the Volga in gear, and drove slowly down the street to the house at the dead-end.

"I hope she doesn't scream or fight," said Pavel.

Nikolai laughed nervously. "Be brave. One woman against two men."

"Don't forget the old woman."

When Pavel got out of the car and began walking through the arbor to the front door, he heard Nikolai call to him from the car.

"Pavel, look!"

"What?"

"Out in the field. I think I see Detective Horvath's car!"

Pavel stepped back to look around the side of the house. "Holy Mother of God! There's someone inside the car!"

For a second, Pavel acted like a man on a high wire, not knowing which direction to go. Finally he ran to the front of the house, trampling the flowers as he peered into the front window. He saw the old woman staring back at him. She was on the phone.

Nikolai had restarted the Volga's engine and was gunning it. "Hurry! She's in the car with Horvath! I saw her!"

The front door opened as Pavel turned back to the Volga. The old woman shouted to him. "Wait! Stop!"

"What is it?" shouted Pavel.

"I have to tell you something!"

Pavel hesitated.

"Come on!" screamed Nikolai. "They're driving away!"

Pavel screamed back to the old woman. "What do you want?"

Aunt Magda waved her hand in disgust. "I'm going back inside. If you want to know what I have to say, I'll be in here."

"What if she's not in the car?" said Pavel. "What if she's in the house?"

"I saw her," said Nikolai. "At least I think I did."

Pavel ran to the house, banged the door open. "Where is Juli Popovics?"

Aunt Magda looked about. "Who?"

Pavel held up a clenched fist. "Your niece! Where is she?"

"I tried to tell you. You don't have to worry because I've already called the militia. He took her away. A man named . . ."

Pavel ran out the door.

"Wait! Don't you want to know his name?"

When Nikolai and Pavel drove into the field, a cloud of dust was all they could see. Back at the house, Aunt Magda stood at the front window, her hands folded and her lips moving rapidly as she prayed to herself.

The car bounced violently, and Juli held on tight. She turned in the seat to look out the rear window, but saw only dust churning behind them. When the bouncing lessened, she realized they had left the field and were now on a gravel road.

"I hope Aunt Magda is all right. Was calling the militia really part of your escape plan?"

"No. If she calls the militia, she won't be in trouble."

"What's your plan for us?"

"I don't have one yet."

Juli looked out the rear window again and saw the black car pursuing them through the finer dust of the gravel road. "I see them! What will we do?"

They slid sideways as Lazlo turned onto another gravel road heading west, the morning sun behind them. The sun kept its distance, but the black car was catching up.

"They've got a faster car!" shouted Lazlo. "If they stop us, I'll go on foot across the field. You tell them I kidnapped you."

"I can't!"

"You have to, Juli! They're going to catch us!"

"But you said there was danger!"

"There is! But if we can't get away . . ."

"Maybe they're simply following us."

"They're too close! In a moment they're going to pass! I'll let them. Stay down. When they get alongside, I'll try to force them over. The ditch is deep here. If I can hang them up . . ."

Nikolai gripped the wheel with both hands, his fists pumping, a boxer holding off an opponent. Dust from the Zhiguli seeped into the Volga and danced on the dash. The Volga rocked back and forth, its powerful engine taking them closer and closer to their prey.

"We're almost up to them!" shouted Nikolai. "Quit looking at your damned watch! The time won't matter after what's happened!"

"If we catch them soon, we can still make it back to Kiev on time!" shouted Pavel.

"What should we do with Detective Horvath?"

Pavel took out his pistol. "We'll take him with us!"

Nikolai glanced at Pavel. "Don't wave your gun around! I'll try to run them off the road!"

Chunks of gravel from the Zhiguli banged against the metal and glass of the Volga as Nikolai drove closer.

"Shit!" shouted Nikolai.

"What?"

"We should have radioed in!"

"Look!" shouted Pavel. "You can pass now!"

Nikolai pressed the accelerator to the floor, and the Volga moved alongside the Zhiguli.

"I'll force them off . . ."

Pavel raised his pistol and pointed it at the Zhiguli.

"No!" screamed Nikolai. "Wait!"

An explosion of glass slammed Pavel sideways onto Nikolai's lap. Nikolai braked, and as the Volga skidded to a stop, he looked down at his friend Pavel. Pavel's eyes were open. Pavel was smiling despite blood gushing from his temple.

When the car stopped, Nikolai let go of the wheel and held Pavel's head in his arms. The gush of blood wet Nikolai's trousers.

"Pavel!"

Pavel did not react. After a few moments, the blood stopped gushing, but Pavel still smiled up at his friend.

"Pavel!"

Finally, recognizing the grin of death, Nikolai hugged his friend to his chest and wept.

After firing the shot, Lazlo drove on for a few seconds, but then slammed on the brakes and turned their car around. Juli saw the grief on Lazlo's face. When they drove up, she saw the driver of the Volga holding the other man.

Lazlo picked up his gun from the seat and opened the door.

"Stay here."

Juli stayed low, watching as Lazlo approached the Volga carefully, his pistol aimed at the driver. After Lazlo opened the door and stared inside for a few moments, he lowered his pistol and bent over. Obviously the driver was not a fighter. Lazlo placed his hand on the driver's shoulder and spoke to him. The driver handed two pistols out of the car butt first, and Lazlo put them into the pockets of his jacket. The driver, visibly upset, got out, and Lazlo helped the driver carry the man who'd been shot to Lazlo's Zhiguli. The man's arms swung limply, and there was a lot of blood. When they came closer, Juli saw the tears streaming down the driver's cheeks.

After Juli got out of the Zhiguli, Lazlo reached inside and yanked the microphone out of the militia two-way radio. He and the driver of the Volga lowered the dead man into the Zhiguli's passenger seat.

The driver stood to the side and looked at Juli. "He wasn't meant for this kind of work. I told him not to point the gun. We worked in a post office. We read peoples' mail and joked all day. We didn't want to hurt anyone."

The man took off his shoulder holster and handed it to Lazlo. Lazlo took the holster and retrieved Juli's bag from the back seat. He motioned to the driver with his pistol.

"Get in my car and drive back to Kiev. Don't stop anywhere. Don't go to a phone. Simply drive to Kiev. I'll be watching, and if you stop anywhere . . . I don't want to be forced to come after you."

The driver shook visibly as he got into Lazlo's Zhiguli.

After the Zhiguli drove slowly away, Lazlo threw Juli's bag and the two shoulder holsters into the back seat of the Volga. He found an overcoat on the back seat and spread it over the bloodied front seat. Juli got in next to him.

"Sit close to me," he said. "There's no window on your side."

He turned the Volga around.

"Are you going to follow him?" asked Juli.

"Only until we get to the main highway."

"Won't he stop and report us?"

"No. They didn't even radio in."

"How do you know?"

"An old Hungarian saying: When a man weeps, he's telling the truth."

"Are they really KGB?"

"A branch of it. Did you hear him mention the post office? They were recruited from the PK. This has been planned. They were supposed to panic, kill or be killed."

"Why?"

Lazlo put his arm around her. "To make us as guilty as Komarov wants us to be."

When they reached the paved highway, the Zhiguli turned north. Lazlo stopped the Volga and turned on its two-way radio. A female voice directed a numbered car to return to headquarters. No frantic calls to cross the river east of Kiev and go to Visenka.

Juli looked up to Lazlo, his profile so serious and sad. "What are you going to do?"

"I don't know yet. I'm thinking."

The morning sun was high and bright in the sky.

CHAPTER 22

Daylight coming into Komarov's window made the smoke from his cigarette into a wriggling, iridescent snake. He looked at his watch, after ten. By now the PK agents should have had Juli Popovics here for questioning. Because they were not here, he should be angry to be kept waiting, but he was content. He knew Detective Horvath would interfere with the pickup.

There were several possible outcomes. The PK agents might have injured or killed or captured Detective Horvath. Or Detective Horvath might have killed or injured them. Perhaps the van tracking Horvath was being used as a hearse. Perhaps Horvath tried to shoot it out with the PK agents and the other men following him. The confrontation might have gone many ways, but somehow Horvath would be his, the evidence pointing to sabotage and conspiracy closer to completion. Horvath would become the Gypsy Moth with ties to the CIA. No one would know he had arranged Horvath's visit to Visenka this morning. Horvath would have destroyed the poet's note so as not to involve Tamara Petrov. As for the poet, his silence was guaranteed.

Earlier this morning on his way in to Kiev from Darnitsa, Komarov met the poet at their usual spot near the Monastery of the Caves. The poet wanted payment, but Komarov felt he could no longer fund the arts. The poet was careless, especially his unannounced visit to KGB headquarters yesterday, and Komarov found it necessary to use the knife.

The knock on Komarov's door was heavy-handed. He expected news from Visenka. Instead, Captain Azef entered slowly and asked if he could speak about a personal matter. Azef, who normally resembled a henchman, sat across the desk, looking like a bald, stuffed bear.

"What is it you want, Captain? I'm busy with my investigation."

"The investigation is the reason I'm here," said Azef, looking down. "I'm concerned my position as your assistant is being taken over by Captain Brovko."

Komarov forced back a smile at this petty jealousy. "What makes you think Captain Brovko is here to replace you?"

Azef looked up, folded his arms defiantly. "He was sent from Moscow, assigned to the Chernobyl case. Him instead of me, Major, even though I was involved from the beginning when we began observing the Horvath brothers. I have handled matters here in Kiev, having the Transportation Ministry prepare trains in the event of a second explosion, keeping Kiev's print and broadcast information under control . . . I have performed as directed, yet Brovko investigates the Horvaths."

Komarov put out his cigarette and stared at Azef. "After years of working together, you suddenly question my judgment?"

"Not your judgment," said Azef. "I simply wish to be more involved in the Chernobyl investigation rather than emergency readiness."

Komarov raised his voice. "Captain Brovko is a nuclear expert assigned by Deputy Chairman Dumenko. Because the Chernobyl matter keeps me occupied, I need you here at headquarters. We have men working in Hungary, researching Horvath's ties to the West. I've heard talk among officials in Moscow looking for ways to feather their nests at the expense of our disaster victims. I need you here at all times to interpret data as it arrives. You are my backup, Captain! Or have you forgotten?"

Azef unfolded his arms. "I'm sorry, Major. Perhaps this was the wrong time to bring it up. With all this new information coming in . . ."

"What new information?"

"The men following Detective Horvath called in to say they lost him. They said the militia following Horvath also lost him."

"When did this happen?"

"About an hour ago."

"An hour ago?" shouted Komarov.

"The men just called in. I reprimanded them for waiting and immediately called militia headquarters to see if I could get further information . . ."

"And?" shouted Komarov.

"A few minutes ago, two of our men arrived here in Kiev."

Komarov gripped the edge of his desk and stood. He felt like leaping over the desk and using his knife on Azef. "Captain!" he screamed. "Don't spoon out the facts! Speak up!"

"The two PK agents assigned to watch Juli Popovics were in Detective Horvath's car. One of them is dead, and the other said Detective Horvath got away in their car. He was last seen driving the Volga in Visenka. The PK agent still alive is Nikolai Nikolskaia. He's being questioned at militia headquarters."

Komarov lifted his phone and rang his secretary. "Have my car brought around to the front immediately! I'll drive myself!"

He slammed the phone down and went to the door, leaving

Azef sitting at the desk. "Captain! If you ever delay important information again, you won't have to worry about Brovko or anyone else because you'll find yourself sitting at a record clerk's desk in the basement!"

Before speaking with Nikolai Nikolskaia, Komarov visited the basement morgue at militia headquarters. While standing in a brightly-lit viewing room, waiting for them to bring the body, Komarov wondered if the body of the poet was also here. Perhaps a passerby, or a tourist gone to see the Monastery of the Caves, had walked closely to the old Zil and seen the poet in the front seat. The poet with his neck sliced ear to ear as if someone had grabbed him by the beard and tried to tear off his head. The poet eliminated the same way he had eliminated Pudkov so long ago in the "safe" house hallway before going in to see Gretchen. The sound of death remained with him, the knife slicing into flesh and muscle, the victim's voice interrupted by an involuntary attempt to inhale and, at the same time, withdraw from the blade.

The Berlin morgue where he had viewed Pudkov and Gretchen smelled the same as this place. Perhaps all morgues throughout the world smelled the same. Men and women reduced to flesh and bone, the dead releasing moisture and gases overcoming the postmortem chemicals.

The former PK agent named Pavel looked the same in death as he did in life. Except now his skin was even lighter than before, making him into an albino. Komarov remembered how Pavel had reminded him of Dmitry, a man, yet in some ways not a man. As he viewed the body, he imagined Dmitry lying on the cart instead of Pavel. His son, Dmitry, sent on a dangerous mission. His son dying honorably instead of killing his father with shame.

After identifying Pavel's body, Komarov took the stairs up three floors in militia headquarters to where Nikolai Nikolskaia was being held for questioning. While slowly climbing the stairs, Komarov recalled the previous night when the poet arrived unexpectedly at his KGB office. Pavel had been there and seen the poet on his way out. But now, with both men in the morgue, the possible flaw in his plan was eliminated. Now it was the duty of both the KGB and the militia to find Detective Horvath and Juli Popovics. If they weren't found immediately, bait was available for the trap—Tamara Petrov, Aunt Magda, and Nina Horvath.

"You didn't know Pavel," said Nikolai, wiping at his reddened eyes with his sleeve. "He was a sensitive person."

"You've spoken of his sensitivity several times," said Komarov. "Do you blame me for his death because I spoke to him of duty and honor and the importance of the case?"

Nikolai folded his hands on the table and blinked to clear his eyes. "No, Major. I simply meant that Pavel and I weren't used to dangerous work. Pavel overreacted and aimed his gun before I had a chance to run their car off the road."

And, thought Komarov, *you should have used your gun instead of weeping like an old woman.* While Nikolai told his account of what happened, Komarov wondered if all men in the world were being feminized. Under normal circumstances, he would have berated Nikolai. Under normal circumstances, he would have assigned him back to Pripyat and let the radiation fry his skin. But these were not normal circumstances.

"I understand your concern," said Komarov. "I was unaware

training for PK agents was so limited in the area of combat. If I had known, I would not have assigned you. But we're short on men, and when you followed Juli Popovics here from Pripyat, I felt you wanted a chance to stay on the case. You gave me reason to believe this when we last met."

"I know," said Nikolai. "It's my fault for being enthusiastic about the case. If I had known this would happen to Pavel, I would have told the truth."

"What is the truth?"

"You had to have been in Pripyat to understand the situation, Major. Staying there would have been suicide. Everyone was leaving. People had masks on their faces. Peace-loving men tried to stop cars with their bodies. The metallic smell in the air was the smell of death!" Tears ran down Nikolai's cheeks. "We were trained as PK agents. We went to language school, not combat school. If we hadn't followed Juli Popovics to Kiev, we might have been dead, or in Moscow where they're taking the injured. I'll probably get cancer because of this."

Komarov stood and walked around the table. He placed his hand on Nikolai's shoulder. "I'm sorry about your comrade. I will see to it his widow receives a commendation. But for now, Nikolai Nikolskaia, life must go on. Our duty is to serve the state, to bring conspirators to justice. Detective Horvath is obviously more dangerous than I thought. Besides being involved in sabotage with his brother, he is a murderer who will, if not stopped, murder again."

Komarov let go of Nikolai's shoulder and paced about the small room. "I'll need your help, Nikolai. The tip of the iceberg is melting away, revealing a serious plot launched from the United States. At this point, I can say to you with all seriousness, we are witnessing a critical time for the future of Communism. If I am to apprehend Detective Horvath and his co-conspirator Juli Popovics, I will need your help. Do I have it?"

Nikolai again wiped his eyes with his sleeve before looking up and nodding.

Back in his office at KGB headquarters, Komarov met with Captain Brovko.

"I was able to speak with Colonel Zamyatin again, this time by radio," said Brovko.

"What did the colonel have to say?"

"Not only are his men shooting dogs and cats on the loose, but local farmers who refuse to leave the area are shooting livestock."

"Imagine," said Komarov, "if such an accident happened in America."

"I beg your pardon?" said Brovko, looking puzzled.

"In America, where guns and vigilantism run rampant, they would be shooting more than dogs and livestock. Here it is different. Here everything is under control. Our veterans give up their arms and take up shovels to bury the radiation."

After a pause, Brovko nodded. "Colonel Zamyatin said a local veterans group has called for volunteers to go to the Chernobyl region. Zamyatin says they may have to cancel the Day of Victory Parade because no veterans will be in Kiev to march. The volunteers already have a name for themselves. They call themselves liquidators."

Komarov stood and walked to his window. "I joined the KGB right after we shot down the American U-2 spy plane. I was told at the time the plane carried more than cameras. American agents have always had an interest in our nuclear programs. Not only to monitor our every move, but also to slow things down. During our first meeting, I told you of my concerns regarding sabotage, Captain.

Those concerns have not gone away. You were sent here to help find out exactly what happened at Chernobyl." Komarov walked back to his desk and leaned on it. "I expect answers, Captain!"

Brovko sat forward, his fists on the desk almost touching Komarov's hands. "Very well, Major. May I speak openly about my findings so far?"

Komarov sat down, taking a moment to compose himself. "Of course, Captain. We all work together in this office."

"Thank you," said Brovko. "I'm not sure how you will react, but I'm afraid I must tell you the people at the Ministry of Energy don't know what's going on."

"Who does know, Captain?"

"Not the technical personnel here in Kiev. The little they know comes from Moscow, and they're getting information from so-called experts who stayed in Pripyat. In Kiev they're doing nothing more than running around with Geiger counters."

"What about the cause of the explosion?" asked Komarov.

"Frankly, Major, they simply don't know how it happened."

"Is there talk of sabotage?"

"Some. Especially the chairman of the engineering council."

"Does he have evidence?"

"I think his professional pride refuses to allow him to even consider system failure. He seems to be considering either sabotage or human error on the part of Mihaly Horvath, the engineer in charge."

"Very good, Captain. During our first meeting, I spoke of an investigation I've been pursuing involving Mihaly Horvath's brother, his girlfriend, and the American cousin."

"Andrew Zukor, the CIA Gypsy Moth."

"Your memory is excellent," said Komarov. "But now recent findings lead me to believe Detective Horvath may be the so-called Gypsy

Moth. He arranged meetings between Zukor and his brother."

"You think Horvath sent his brother on a suicide mission?"

"No, Captain. A stronger possibility exists. Fed by resources supplied through Zukor, the Horvath brothers and Juli Popovics could have been the conspirators. It's possible the escape plan for Mihaly Horvath failed, and now his brother and former lover are on the run."

Komarov saw mild interest in Brovko's eyes, an interrogator observing an interrogator. He filled Brovko in on the basics of the case, including the events at Visenka that morning. Of course, he did not tell Brovko about the inexperience of Nikolai and Pavel, or about his harassment of Horvath leading to suspension, or about the note delivered by the poet.

When Komarov finished, Brovko rubbed his chin and, unlike Azef, looked sincerely interested. "What can I do to help?"

"You'll be in charge of the field agents searching for Detective Horvath and Juli Popovics. You'll also need to observe the aunt in Visenka and Tamara Petrov here in Kiev."

"Will I be interviewing Tamara Petrov again?" asked Brovko.

"For now put two good men on her. And one more place I want watched." Komarov paused. "The Horvath family farm in Kisbor."

"It's over five hundred kilometers from here."

"Horvath's sister-in-law is in transit there, and I want all possibilities covered in case he decides to leave Kiev."

When Brovko left, Komarov thought about the past. Brovko was about the same age as he himself had been during the Sherbitsky affair. If Brovko barked when he was expected to bark, and licked when he was expected to lick, Komarov would certainly allow him a portion of the glory.

Komarov was in the middle of his reverie, imagining himself as deputy chairman, when Captain Azef burst into the office.

"Has knocking gone out of style, Captain?"

"I needed to tell you something right away, Major. Chief Investigator Chkalov is on the phone. It's about Detective Horvath. I told him he should speak with you."

Azef tried to linger in the office after telling the secretary to transfer the call, but Komarov ordered him out.

"What can I do for you, Chief Investigator?"

"You can tell me what's going on," said Chkalov.

"What do you mean?"

"I've been patient with the KGB," said Chkalov. "And I've been more than cooperative. But now I have a murder to investigate. Regardless of the fact the victim is one of your men, I must still do my job."

"Am I stopping you?" asked Komarov.

"Major Komarov, I am a busy man. I have an entire militia to take care of, and this Chernobyl business does not help. If you knew something about Detective Horvath and chose not to tell me, I cannot be responsible for not having suspended him sooner. If, as the evidence seems to indicate, he is guilty of murder, I fear you have withheld information. When this case is over, I will have to report everything."

Komarov paused, waiting in silence while he imagined Chkalov's fat face growing redder and redder. Finally he said, "Are you finished, Chief Investigator Chkalov?"

"No," said Chkalov. "Even though I am busy, I still cooperate in hopes one day I will receive the honor of your cooperation in return!"

"The KGB is involved in classified investigations," said Komarov. "The deputy chairman in Moscow has given me full authority in this case. Cooperation is not a kindness you can hand out like a gift. It is essential to state security!"

Chkalov was silent for a few seconds before speaking in a mono-tone. "I have two items concerning the case. Number one, Juli Popovics' aunt in Visenka called militia headquarters before your men got there and reported that Detective Horvath came and took Juli Popovics away against her will. Number two, the Volga report-ed missing was found a half hour ago at the metro station near the bridge in Darnitsa. There was much blood on the front seat. The car is being towed to militia headquarters. Your men can see it there, where it will remain as evidence."

Neither commented or said good-bye. After he hung up, Koma-rov went to his window. He knew the metro, bisecting the city east to west, passed close to KGB headquarters. On the east, the metro crossed the river to Darnitsa. On the west, the metro stopped at the Central Railroad Station. Detective Horvath and Juli Popovics might be at Central Station or already on a train heading south or west. With the chaos and confusion involved in any travel because of Chernobyl, they might be able to escape.

Detective Horvath was smarter than he thought. Had he really kidnapped Juli Popovics? Or had he simply made it appear a kid-napping in order to clear the aunt of collaboration? Had they really taken the metro, or was this another trick?

The pedestrians and vehicles below Komarov's window made him think of games and puzzles. The entire city of Kiev was a vast game board, the territory of the players. Detective Horvath would stay, hiding somewhere in Kiev because this was his city. To run away now, when the game had only begun, would be unfair.

Komarov removed his jacket. He unlocked his desk and took out his pistol and shoulder holster. After he checked to be certain the pistol was loaded, he slipped on his shoulder holster and his jacket over it. In the inside pocket of his jacket, the knife rested against his heart.

CHAPTER 23

Although films of people swimming in the Pripyat River were finally stopped on Soviet television, commentators insisted the extent of the accident was exaggerated, and undamaged Chernobyl reactor units would soon be back on line. But as any Soviet citizen knows, what remains unsaid is all-important. Already eleven days since the explosion and resulting radiation release, but still no official speech from Gorbachev.

In Moscow, continued lack of news spawned a string of rumors: the military conducting an experiment caused the accident; evacuees being shipped by train to old Stalin camps already under reconstruction vomited blood until they died; the accident was a conspiracy by regional Ukraine officials to send their families and friends to Black Sea resorts for extended holiday. A joke whispered among Kremlin workers went as follows: "To the Soviet government, Chernobyl is the czarina's stallion." "I don't get it." "It fell from its tethers and killed her when she had it suspended above her bed."

In Kiev, the mayor said children should be kept indoors and ordered more potassium iodide be available. Supplies of canned food were running out in the markets. Some Kievians decided it best to avoid the Chernobylites, as they were being called. A joke making the rounds in Kiev came from the Chernobyl plant: "Around here you can eat all you want, but be sure you shit in a lead box." Another joke among locals: "The Chernobylites will march in the Day of Victory Parade. A head count taken at the start and at the end will help researchers calculate future life expectancy."

But despite rumors and warnings, life went on in Kiev. People went to work, babushkas swept sidewalks, and criminals did their business. Early in the morning on May 7, a man was found murdered in an old Zil limousine near the Monastery of the Caves. Later the same day, a KGB agent was killed on a farm road outside the town of Visenka, east of the river. Neither of these deaths, even if they had been publicized, was of consequence to most Kievians. So, what was important to Kievians? Eleven days after the Chernobyl explosion, the incident was being revealed by rumor rather than the Wednesday evening news broadcast.

On Wednesday evening, Juli sat on a bench in a brightly-lit hallway near a double set of glass doors that reminded her of the low-level counting laboratory building entrance. She could see headlights on the street as dusk set in and was reminded of the many evenings she had waited for Mihaly's bus. But those evenings were gone forever. She was not at the low-level counting laboratory. She was in the central Kiev hospital where she'd been tested before going to stay with Aunt Magda. It seemed long ago, yet here she was, sitting in line on a long bench with dozens of others to be checked for radiation contamination. At the rate the line progressed, it was unlikely she'd be checked until morning.

Most in line were women, a few with children. Every hour or so, an orderly with a Geiger counter came out of an examination room and scanned newcomers. The last time he did this, a man set the counter clicking. Without touching him, the orderly commanded the man to move down the hallway. The contaminated man reminded Juli of Marina's Vasily. Even as he was being led away, the man smiled and nodded to those lining both walls. Later the man returned wearing white coveralls. His hair was damp, and on his way back to the end of the line, he nodded and smiled, repeating, "A cold shower for my hot body." Those around him smiled back but did not laugh, and they gave him plenty of room.

Juli overheard snatches of conversation as she waited. One woman said ration coupons and ten rubles' compensation would be handed out. Another rattled on about a story she insisted was in the Bible—a kingdom whose leader had the mark of the devil on his head in the form of a birthmark. She said the kingdom was doomed because its leaders dabbled in science, messing in God's business. Someone mumbled, "Gorbie," and the woman put her finger to her lips.

After potassium iodide pills were passed out to those in line, many spoke of folk remedies for radiation—milk, vodka, and red wine among them. The man in coveralls at the end of the line spoke loudly of government bonuses, which would be handed out when it was time to go back into the area to harvest crops. He laughed loudly, saying vodka made from wheat in the Chernobyl region would provide an extra kick, making the drinker glow like an ember. The joke, and the man's laughter, put a damper on conversations when the orderly with the Geiger counter returned and, keeping his distance, motioned for the man to follow.

While she waited, Juli thought about many things—her final bus ride with Mihaly, their dilemma of wanting to be together but being unable to do so, the trip to Mihaly's abandoned apartment in

Pripyat, the trip to Kiev with Marina, Vasily, his mother and sister, and especially the baby growing within her. She worried about Aunt Magda. But mostly she worried about Lazlo.

She remembered the look on Lazlo's face after he shot the man in the Volga. She remembered the despair she could feel as Lazlo drove the Volga to the metro station and as they rode together on the metro into Kiev.

Although it seemed months ago, it was only this morning that Lazlo had come and the men had chased them. Only a few hours ago, they had entered Kiev as fugitives. Only two hours ago, she had hugged Lazlo, praying it would not be the last time. Lazlo did not tell her his plan. He simply said there was something he must do before they fled Kiev. He said he would be back that night, and they would leave tomorrow. "After the situation has cooled."

When they arrived in Kiev, Lazlo purchased clothing for them at a secondhand shop. They changed in restrooms near the hospital entrance. Lazlo emerged in baggy trousers and a mismatched worn shirt; she in a tired print dress. They looked like farmers. That's what she was supposed to say if they were questioned. Olga Petavari, farm wife from the Opachichi collective, being checked for radiation and separated from her husband during the journey. When Lazlo left, he took with him some of their clothes in a fishnet bag. On her lap, the overnight case she had brought from Pripyat contained more clothing from the secondhand shop. Olga Petavari. She repeated it to herself until the woman to her right began speaking.

The woman's name was also Olga. She had a baby boy of five months who slept over her shoulder, his fists clutching his mother's back like a little boxer. Without getting into specifics, Juli told Olga the made-up name and said she was from the Opachichi collective. This, and her saying her husband was helping at another collective during the evacuation, satisfied Olga.

Olga was about Juli's age. While they spoke, Juli tried to imagine how it would be to have a baby. In her recent past as a single woman with a job and an apartment, it seemed impossible to keep the baby. But now she had changed her mind. Despite being a fugitive, she looked forward to raising the child, feeding it, and loving it. Perhaps she would be able to spend time with Lazlo before the baby began to show, and before he had to strike out on his own. And afterward? Besides becoming a mother, afterward was too far away to consider.

"You should have seen the excitement in my village when they came to evacuate us," said Olga, shifting the baby to her other shoulder. "It was the day before May Day. We thought army trucks were part of the celebration. Were you also evacuated in an army truck?"

"We rode in a neighbor's car," said Juli. "Was the trip uncomfortable for your baby in the army truck?"

"Not him," said Olga. "He slept through it. But for me . . ." Olga reached behind and rubbed her lower back. "The pains of pregnancy returned. I should have left in the morning with my husband instead of waiting. He's a bus driver. He's been taking people out of the area around the power station for days. I don't know how he does it. He left a message for me at the terminal here in Kiev. When I was there, his boss said he was a hero and might even get a medal from the Transportation Ministry."

"You must be very proud."

"I am, but I worry about the radiation. Do you know anything about radiation?"

"No," said Juli, "I don't."

An hour later when it was dark outside, two uniformed militiamen came through the double doors and walked slowly along the hallway, looking at the people waiting to be examined. Lazlo had told her not to look away from officers. She was supposed to be a farm wife, and a uniformed person might offer some hope. Looking away or hiding her face might make an officer remember they were looking for a woman her age, a woman named Juli Popovics last seen with Detective Horvath, who was wanted for murder.

When the militiaman on her side of the hallway approached, Juli began to shake, bouncing lightly up and down on the bench and staring at the officer as he passed. Olga had grown tired of holding her baby and Juli had offered. Juli bounced the baby, feeling his fists tapping her shoulder, while the officer tipped his cap and smiled.

The baby was warm and soft, his hair sweet. As the night wore on, Juli held the baby boy closer, wishing Lazlo would return to hold her tight and close.

Komarov felt like a young man again. Instead of going home to Darnitsa, he stayed the night at the office. Every Kiev district KGB agent carried a copy of the Horvath photograph supplied by the militia. According to Deputy Chief Investigator Lysenko, militia officers on duty also had copies. Lysenko had become Komarov's militia contact and would stay on duty through the night, unlike his boss, Chkalov, who went home to sleep like an overstuffed bear. Although Horvath's photograph was being shown to clerks, waiters, and bus drivers, they did not have a photograph of Juli Popovics. Normally they would have gotten one from the Chernobyl plant, but because of the situation, it was impossible to retrieve records from the Chernobyl plant offices. As for Komarov's oversight of Chernobyl security, he had assigned Azef, who sent regular reports to Moscow saying everything was under control. With other ministries up to their eyebrows in shit, Komarov was free to pursue his own interests.

Komarov needed to create a connection from Detective Horvath to Andrew Zukor to the CIA, and even to the Reagan administration in the United States if necessary. His visit to Deputy Chairman Dumenko in Moscow had set the stage. Because Zukor and his wife were required to report to Intourist in Uzhgorod during their summer visit to the Horvath family farm, evidence of Zukor's contact with Detective Horvath was established. Detective Horvath would become the Gypsy Moth. Detective Horvath, who had used his brother in an attempt to destabilize the Soviet Union by causing an "accident" at Chernobyl, was perfect in his new role. Who could be better than a Kiev militia detective on the run with an army record that included the cover-up of a questionable shooting along the Romanian frontier? A questionable shooting, which actually did earn him the nickname, Gypsy.

Everything in Komarov's final report would support his assertion of Horvath's guilt, even the encounter with the stranger outside the National Hotel in Moscow who inquired about "this Chernobyl business" would be used against Horvath. In the Soviet Union, so-called "intelligence" was easily manipulated, especially with the help of old comrades such as Major Dmitry Struyev in Kiev, an old-school Directorate T professional who could be trusted.

When Komarov called home to say he would spend the night at headquarters, he expected his wife to answer. Instead, Dmitry, his son, who was rarely home, said, "Good evening. May I ask who is calling?"

"I'm surprised to find you home," said Komarov.

"Who is calling, please?" repeated Dmitry in a singsong voice.

"Never mind the jokes. Is your mother there?"

"She's not here. Although you are able to refer to her as my mother, you seem to have forgotten who you are."

"What are you talking about?"

"When I ask who it is, you cannot bring yourself to say you are my father."

"This conversation is meaningless."

"I agree. So, what's up?"

"I won't be home tonight. Tell your mother I'm involved in an important case."

"A man from the Nuclear Institute delivered more iodine tablets. Is the radiation a danger to people in Kiev? Should Mom and I run south and become Chernobyl Gypsies?"

Komarov tried not to shout, but Dmitry had probed a nerve. "Don't taunt me with talk of Gypsies! No one should be running away! The danger to us is created by Western propaganda! They're wallowing in our misfortune!"

Komarov's outburst caused Dmitry to remain silent.

"Tell your mother I'll call tomorrow."

"I will, Father."

After he hung up, Komarov recalled the night he had threatened Dmitry on the back porch. Perhaps the lack of a father to speak with after dinner night after night had been the root cause of Dmitry's problems. No! A son should be stronger, especially his son.

Komarov did not want to think about Dmitry. Instead, he sat at his desk and thought about the Sherbitsky affair. He remembered his early years here in this office when he often stayed overnight because he was young and enthusiastic and strong. Komarov was about to have a cot sent up from the basement when the phone rang. It was the overnight guard at the front entrance.

"What is it?"

"There's a woman here," said the guard. "She wants to speak with someone in charge."

"What's her name?"

There were muffled voices before the guard came back on. "Her name is Tamara Petrov."

Komarov could not believe it. Tamara Petrov questioned by Captain Brovko only two days ago and now she comes here of her own free will? "Bring her to my office. And contact Captain Brovko. Wherever he is, tell him to come and see me at once."

Although he had seen Tamara Petrov's photograph, Komarov was surprised at her appearance. The photograph revealed long black hair and an olive complexion, reminding him of Barbara, the Romeo agent long ago in the GDR. The photograph had not revealed Tamara Petrov's bracelets, long earrings, slender fingers, and loose silken blouse open at the neck. She wore a short skirt, and Komarov sat in a side chair rather than behind his desk so he could have a clear view of her shapely legs.

"I feel uncomfortable coming here," said Tamara Petrov, crossing her legs. "I wouldn't want my friends and associates to know."

"Please be more specific, Miss Petrov."

She leaned forward, her hands agitated, her bracelets jingling on the desk. "I need assurances, Major. I never want to have to repeat any of this at a hearing."

Komarov felt excitement on two levels as he glanced at the shape of her breasts while at the same time wondering about the reason for her visit. "If you mean you want to remain an anonymous informant, Miss Petrov, then you have come to the right place."

She stared into his eyes, trying to see something there. A Gypsy. All she needed was her crystal ball. But no one could see into another's mind, especially his mind. He had proven it during the Sherbitsky hearings. Patience was always better than rushing into things.

"I'm here to help if I can, Miss Petrov. I know your journal published articles about Chernobyl, the shortages during construction, the quality of components, all of it. I realized long ago it was your duty to reveal these things, just as it is my duty to uncover wrongdoing at the power station. We have similar goals."

Suddenly, something happened Komarov never expected. Tamara Petrov, who looked the part of a strong woman, broke down and wept. After a minute of sobbing and sniffling amid reassurances from Komarov, she was finally able to speak.

"He had no right coming to me."

"You are speaking of Detective Horvath?" asked Komarov, careful not to sound anxious.

"Yes."

"Please tell me about it, Miss Petrov."

"I was coming home from the review office. I sometimes walk in the park along the river. He approached me near the footbridge to the island."

"What did he say?"

"He said he needed help. He said . . . he needed a room for himself and a woman. He said I had influence at hotels and could find them a room."

"What did you tell him?"

She wept again, and Komarov was forced to wait.

"I was going to tell him I couldn't help and ask him to leave. But he insisted I was involved. He said I had sent him a message about this woman, Juli Popovics. He said I had saved them from the KGB. I knew something was wrong. I knew he had done something illegal and was dragging me into it so I would feel forced to help. I don't want to do anything illegal. I've never done anything illegal before in my life. I have my literary review and my friends. I have my own life. To get rid of him, I . . . told him I could help him. And now, because I'm not a criminal and I fear Lazlo has done something against the people he's supposed to protect, I'm here to tell you where he is."

"You know where he is?"

Tamara Petrov wiped at her eyes with a billowy sleeve. "He's waiting for me to meet him. I'm to bring clothing and have a taxi waiting." Tamara wept again. "This is very hard for me, Major. This was a man I admired. But I can't become a criminal. I can't!"

"You are very brave, Miss Petrov. Your secret will be kept, even from Detective Horvath. Now please, tell me where he is."

"He . . . they are at the Hotel Dnieper, registered under the name Yuri Antonov . . . Yuri Antonov and his wife."

On his way out, Komarov took Tamara Petrov with him. Captain Brovko met them on the stairs, causing Tamara Petrov to shriek.

"It's all right, Miss Petrov. He's not here for you."

Komarov told Brovko to gather men and come with him. He left Tamara Petrov with the guard and told him to arrange for a car to take her home.

The night air was cool and moist. When he got into the car, Komarov felt adrenaline surging through him. He felt young and was glad to have the company of Captain Brovko instead of Azef. If he had to share the glory of this night with anyone, let it be with a young man recently assigned who would relinquish credit to Major Grigor Komarov for the capture of Detective Horvath and his co-conspirator.

If it was necessary to kill Horvath and the woman, so be it. Evidence gathered in silence was often much more convincing. In less than a block, two other cars joined the Volga, racing along the night-dampened streets to the Hotel Dnieper.

CHAPTER 24

Although the Moskva Hotel on October Revolution Street was newer and the Ukraine Hotel on Shevchenko Boulevard was larger, many tourists preferred the charm and location of the Hotel Dnieper, bordering Lenkomsomol Square. The Hotel Dnieper was centrally located near tourist attractions, including museums and cathedrals. The Philharmonia, the library, and the cinema were directly across from the Dnieper. If your tastes were less cultural, you could stroll down Vladimirsky Spusk to the riverbank for a boat ride or take the path through the park for a walk across the footbridge to the beach on Trukhanov Island.

This night, the beach was empty. And even though it had been warm enough to swim during the day, only a handful had ventured into the Dnieper River because of news coming out of Chernobyl. According to bus drivers from the north, the banks of the Pripyat, which drained into the Dnieper, were being shored up to avoid radioactive contamination to Kiev's water supply. Outspoken bus drivers showed off face masks they'd been given to wear on their drives back and forth, and they spoke of soldiers on the roads, with Chernobylites hiding to avoid being bussed out. There were rumors of looting, buses abandoned, and entire villages bulldozed. However, despite the tragedy to the north, Kiev, the beautiful city, was peaceful, especially when viewed from the seventh floor of the popular Hotel Dnieper.

The window of the room in which Lazlo had registered as Mr. and Mrs. Yuri Antonov faced north. In the distant hills, beyond the quaint lights lining Lenkomsomol Square, he could see the planetarium and the ascending and descending funicular cable cars. Farther west was the lighted bell tower of Saint Sophia's Cathedral. Straight ahead, a hundred kilometers beyond the black northern horizon, was Chernobyl. Lazlo thought of Mihaly telling him several times about the KGB snooping around at Chernobyl, looking for something to happen so they could cover it up. He thought of Mihaly's body covered with radioactive debris from the explosion, Mihaly shipped to Moscow not for treatment, but for burial. He recalled the day over a week ago when he had gone to the cathedral and wept. Almost fifteen years earlier, when Mihaly came to Kiev to attend university, the cathedral was one of the first tourist spots Lazlo took Mihaly. He remembered the look on Mihaly's face, an eighteen-year-old boy looking aloft at the domes and icons, Mihaly viewing the vast possibilities of his future. Last week, Lazlo went to the cathedral to pray for Mihaly. Now, several blocks away, Saint Sophia's bell tower was outlined in the black of night.

Below the window of the room, when he opened it and leaned out far enough, Lazlo saw the window washers' scaffold left hanging outside the sixth-floor windows for the night. That was why he had picked a room on the seventh floor with a northern view. It was part of his plan.

Lazlo took off his jacket and sweater, unbuttoned his shirt. Juli had given him undergarments from her overnight case. These he'd brought with other clothes in a fishnet bag. He rinsed and hung

Juli's undergarments to dry in the bathroom. He turned on the shower and left it running. Soon the room was warm and moist despite the open window. He sprinkled perfume Juli gave him into the tub, giving the room the pleasant scent of a woman.

He looked at his watch. Almost nine thirty. Tamara would have gone to KGB headquarters by now, and soon they would arrive. From his room, the sidewalk in front of the main entrance was visible. When he had asked Tamara to go to Komarov, it was obvious she knew that part of the plan was to put her in the clear, as he had done with Aunt Magda.

He went into the bathroom and turned off the shower. He carried a dripping washcloth out of the bathroom and to the window, allowing water to drip on the floor as he went. At the window, he held the cloth outside and let water drip onto the windowsill and the window washers' scaffold below. When he took the washcloth back to the bathroom, he moistened a towel, dried his hands on it, and threw it with the washcloth onto the floor. He glanced at Juli's brassiere and underpants hung to dry on the shower bar, left the light on, and closed the bathroom door.

In the main room, he pushed the tall-backed heavy sofa in front of the open window, leaving enough room for him to stoop behind it. He lowered the window enough so it would not appear open when viewed from the door, yet would still allow him to squeeze through.

Everything was ready. He sat on the sofa facing the door and waited. Next to the door on the hinged side, so he would be behind the door when it opened, was Vladimir Ilich Lenin holding a Makarov 9mm pistol.

Actually, it was only a statue of Lenin, and he wasn't really holding the pistol. The pistol, one of the shiny new ones taken from the KGB agents in Visenka, was tied to Lenin's outstretched hand with one of Juli's nylon stockings. The other nylon stocking was stretched over Lenin's head, his pointy beard forming an inverted tent over his face. Around Lenin's shoulders, partially concealing the stocking holding the pistol in place, was Lazlo's overcoat. The coat and stocking over the face gave Lenin color. The statue looked like a thief with stone-gray gloves and slacks, who had put a nylon stocking over his face as a disguise.

The statue was from a secluded stairway landing off the lobby. Lazlo gave the elevator operator ten rubles to keep his mouth shut and take him with Lenin to the seventh floor. He told the elevator operator it was for a joke on a friend and the statue would be put back the same evening. The statue was heavy, but he'd been able to tilt it slightly and roll it like a barrel of wine.

Lazlo stood and took out his wallet. He emptied the money out of it, stuffed the money into his pocket, and placed the wallet on the lamp table. He would leave his identification and other papers because he no longer needed them. Leaving his identification would prove he was there as Tamara had said, on the remote possibility the agents coming through the door did not recognize him. He took his old Makarov 9mm pistol from the side pocket of his trousers and inserted it into the back of his waistband where it would be hidden from view. The other shiny new Makarov from the agents was with his shoulder holster, clearly visible on the bed. He turned off the floor lamp next to the sofa, leaving only the lamp on the bed table lit. This lamp cast its brightest light on the pistol and shoulder holster on the white bedspread. When he looked back to the door, he could see Lenin in the shadows, looking almost alive.

Everything seemed in order. He checked once more to make certain the door was locked, returned to the sofa, and waited. From the open window behind him, he could hear the sounds of traffic. Other than this it was quiet.

After a minute or so, the elevator bell clanged in the hallway. He felt his muscles tense, aware of the cool outside air at the back of his neck. There were voices in the hallway, men and women speaking, but he could not tell what they were saying. A woman laughed loudly, like the shriek of a bird. A door slammed, and it was quiet again. But he did not relax on the chance the KGB had gotten off the elevator with the revelers. He wondered if they would take the stairs instead. No, both. Men on the stairs, he hoped above the sixth floor, and men on the elevator. His only problem would be if there were men on the stairs between the second and sixth floor.

On the second floor, he had hidden a waiter's jacket behind a fire extinguisher outside the door to the stairwell. Once on the second floor, he would put on the jacket, go through the restaurant's kitchen and out the back, where there was a metal stairway down to the alley. He would avoid the lobby and front entrance. The plan depended on a clear stairwell between the sixth and second floors. If not, he might have to kill again.

Although it seemed an inappropriate time, Lazlo could not help thinking about the man he killed today. He remembered the man's face when he raised his gun and pointed out the car window. The man's face held a look of panic, of not knowing what to do next. The reason Lazlo had fired first was because in the past he'd seen criminals with the same look on their faces. He'd also seen this look years earlier, when the deserter who'd shot Viktor turned the gun on him slowly, so slowly.

Today, with the partner weeping and even admitting he had not radioed for help, Lazlo theorized that two amateurs had been purposely assigned. This afternoon in the park, his theory of a setup was proven correct when Tamara said she had not sent the message saying Juli was in danger. The only message Tamara had sent through the poet was the one after her interrogation.

Lovely Tamara in the park on a spring afternoon, joining him behind thick bushes along the bank of the river, speaking softly as the water trickled and lapped the shore. Lovely Tamara promising to help, then telling him about a woman who ran a market in the mountain village of Yasinya near the Romanian and Hungarian frontiers. Tamara saying it was a way out. Tamara kissing him before running along the bank so she could resume her walk beyond the concealment of the bushes as if no one had been there. He wondered if he would ever see Tamara again.

The elevator bell clanged in the hallway. He could hear the doors slide open, stay open a few seconds, slide closed again. Enough time to let off very quiet passengers who did not speak or clomp about or push a key loudly into a lock and slam a door. He knew it was them.

Room 702, registered for one night by Mr. and Mrs. Yuri Antonov, was not far from the elevator. Komarov passed the door quietly and took a position with Brovko at the turn in the hall. Two of Brovko's men stood on either side of the door with Stechkin machine pistols ready. When the men released the safeties, Brovko held his hand up for the men to wait. Komarov withdrew his own pistol from his shoulder holster.

Perhaps it would end here for Detective Horvath, thought Komarov as he imagined Stechkins unloading their clips at full automatic, causing the Gypsy Moth to dance his last dance. And what about the woman? Would she have one of the pistols taken from Pavel and Nikolai?

It did not matter to Komarov. In this game, he had all possibilities covered. One of his men had been killed. If Horvath or Popovics survived, he had the authority to become witness to confessions of conspiracy and have the conspirators put away forever. The path to his chairmanship, and to his recognition by the Presidium and the Council of Ministers, were behind the door to room 702.

While waiting with Brovko for the men coming up the stairs, Komarov imagined living in Moscow. He'd have an office in the Lubyanka. He'd salute Lenin's Tomb each day. He'd attend operas at the Bolshoi. His wife would enjoy Moscow. Dmitry would remain in Kiev with his friends. On the other hand, perhaps his wife would not want to go to Moscow, and he would meet other women. He imagined it. An opera at the Bolshoi, dinner at a quiet restaurant, then back to his Moscow apartment. He tried to visualize a woman with him, a woman beneath him in bed while the music from *Prince Igor* or *The Duma* rings in his ears. The woman he pictured beneath him was Tamara Petrov. Komarov reached inside his jacket and touched his knife, felt reassured by the good fortune it had brought him in the past.

The stairwell door at the far end of the hall opened, and two men holding pistols stepped out, one of them shaking his head from side to side. Brovko nodded and turned to one of the men near the door, who raised his Stechkin with one hand and reached out to knock with the other.

Lazlo stood to the side of the door opposite Lenin.

"Who is it?"

Silence. He waited, but not so long they would decide to break in the door.

"Who's there?"

"I'm from housekeeping. Please open the door. Something needs checking in the room."

"Come back later!"

More silence, followed by a very loud knock.

"Detective Horvath! Unlock the door and step five paces straight back into the room with your hands over your head! If you don't do this immediately, we'll begin shooting!"

He heard a door slam, probably someone looking out and seeing the men with guns.

"Detective Horvath!"

"Very well! I'll unlock the door now and step back as you said!"

After unlocking the door, Lazlo stepped back more than five paces. He stood at the side of the sofa with his hands above his head.

The doorknob twisted slowly, then the door was propelled open, banging into Lenin. For a second all he saw was the opposite wall of the hallway. Eventually two machine pistols appeared, followed by two men peeking around the edge of the door frame. Both men stared at him for a moment, and finally one stepped into the room, aiming his machine pistol two-handed at Lazlo. The second man quickly stepped in, glanced at the gun on the bed, stepped around the door, and was confronted by Lenin. When the machine pistol began unloading, the man watching Lazlo dropped to the floor and also turned his pistol on Lenin.

The move behind the sofa and out the window went as quickly as it had when he'd practiced it. What he hadn't practiced was the drop to the scaffold. He fell in a crouched position, experiencing the horrible sensation of the fall in his abdomen. When he hit the scaffold, he lurched sideways but held on with his arms. His legs hung over the edge and his ankle burned with pain, but he managed to clamber up onto the scaffold. He stood up quickly, took out his pistol, held it as high as he could beneath the open window, held his breath, and listened.

When the firing in the room finally ceased, gun smoke billowed out the doorway, a few shells rolled into the hallway, and Komarov ran into the room with Brovko.

Their two men were prone on the floor, their machine pistols aimed at a sofa against a window. Bits of what looked like plaster were scattered about the men's feet. One man on the floor pointed to the sofa, the other pointed back behind the door. The men from the stairwell joined them, crowding into the room. Brovko aimed his pistol behind the door before shaking his head sadly and turning to the sofa.

Behind the door Komarov saw a statue with a pistol fastened to its hand. On the bed was another pistol in a shoulder holster. He aimed his own pistol at the sofa with the others.

"Come out, Horvath!"

When a shot exploded from behind the sofa, Komarov, along with the others, opened fire.

The firing continued at least five seconds. When it stopped, the sofa was smoking, tufts of stuffing floating above it.

Brovko approached the sofa carefully, aiming his pistol. Once behind and to the side of the sofa, he looked back to Komarov. "There's nobody here."

"What?"

"But he jumped back there," said one of the men on the floor.

Brovko shoved the sofa out into the room.

"The window!" screamed Komarov.

"We're on the seventh floor," said one of the men.

Another man was at the bathroom door, pushing it open, aiming.

Komarov already knew there would be no one in the bathroom. He saw water flecks on the tile floor and trailing across the carpet to the window. Both he and Brovko ran to the window and looked out. Below the window a platform swung gently. On the platform, in the light from a window below, Komarov could see more droplets of water. Along with the sulfurous scent of burnt gunpowder, there was a scent of perfume in the air.

"Hurry!" shouted Komarov, running from the room. "They've gone down a floor!"

Brovko screamed into his handheld transceiver, telling the men on the street to circle the building. Komarov did not bother with the elevator. He ran to the stairwell and, when he entered it, heard the echo of a door slamming below.

Lazlo's ankle was on fire as he ran. When he put on the white waiter's jacket, blood smeared the sleeve, and he realized he had cut his wrist on the scaffold. His left side ached where he shoved the pistol into his belt beneath the jacket before running through the hotel kitchen.

Several kitchen workers stared at him. One, a fat man in a chef's hat, stepped to the center of the aisle to block his path. Lazlo pulled up his sleeve, held out his bleeding wrist, and said, "I've cut myself," and the man stepped aside.

He ran down the outside metal stairway and through the alley as fast as he could. He tried to ignore the pain, but it was more intense with each step, as if an animal were inside chewing his anklebone. The alley exited at the side of the building on the street bordering Lenkomsomol Square. He ran across the street. There was a shout behind him.

"Stop!"

He ran onto the sidewalk as fast as he could, but the man behind was faster, and was joined by a second man, the two shouting encouragement to one another in Russian, young men running fast, so fast. The pain, how long could he run with the pain?

When he rounded a corner, a crowd making their way down the street from the Philharmonia confronted him. He dodged one person after another, shouting, "Watch out! Move over!" Behind him he heard the two men doing the same as they rounded the corner. The white jacket was like a flag as he ran among people coming from the concert in dark formal wear.

A restaurant ahead, patrons going in, a crowd. He went through the doorway, pushing a man and a woman aside. The man cursed him in Ukrainian and Russian.

Through the dining room, pushing a dessert cart out of the way. He found the kitchen door at the back just as he heard the commotion at the front entrance. In the kitchen he removed the white jacket, knocked over a man standing on a stool, then ran into a cart full of pots and pans, which spilled over, some of the pans bouncing ahead and underfoot. Near the back door, there was a black overcoat on a hook. He took it and ran out the back door.

The alley was dark and quiet, but through the door he could hear a man shouting, "Hey! Stop! My coat!"

Lazlo tipped a heavy garbage can against the door, put on the overcoat, and took out his pistol. There was a loud racket in the kitchen. He crouched down behind another garbage can and aimed his pistol at the garbage can leaning against the door. When the door pushed outward, he fired two shots. When the door was pushed closed by the garbage can, he ran past the doorway in the opposite direction and found a gangway out to the street, where he joined a crowd of people walking slowly back to the Hotel Dnieper.

The people chatted about the concert, one woman saying Prokofiev was "elevating," a man saying the music was "overly Westernized." Lazlo put up the overcoat collar, which smelled of onions.

He put his hands in the pockets, his right hand still gripping his pistol. He walked as smoothly as he could despite the pain in his ankle. He was rounding the corner back to the hotel when he heard footsteps run up the gangway. Once around the corner, he ran again.

Across the street from the hotel he slowed to a walk. There were at least five KGB men outside the main entrance, looking about in all directions. He had caught up to a group of four people leaving the concert, but they veered to the right and began crossing the street to the hotel. Lazlo walked straight ahead to the end of the block and onto the lighted pathway leading to Lenkomsomol Square. He wished he had gone the other direction to the metro, but there had been no crowds going that way. He could not turn around now because he could hear the men who had chased him through the restaurant back at the corner.

The men at the hotel entrance began spreading out, one coming toward him, but not running. The man paused before crossing the street to allow a speeding taxi by. There was something familiar about the man, something about the shape of his head, his receding hairline. Suddenly the man stopped short and shouted, "Horvath!" and Lazlo knew it was Komarov.

Running. The pain again. Running out onto Lenkomsomol Square. Nowhere else to go. All these men chasing him, and nowhere to hide. All these men led by Komarov a hundred meters behind. Would he be shot through the head like the deserter from the Romanian border? Perhaps he deserved it.

A shot fired, causing a young couple ahead on a bench to dive to the ground. If only he could stop running. If only he could become invisible. But what would happen to Juli? What would happen to Juli if he did not return?

As he ran farther out onto the square, he heard a violin playing in the distance, a violin playing a Hungarian *prima*, the violin crying its song into the night, a song he recognized, a song called, "If Someone's Sad."

Another shot, a piece of stone on the square set free, skittering beneath his feet. The violin stopped playing. Only the pain remained, and Juli waiting for him.

The footsteps behind were like marbles bouncing on the paving stones. The men closer, perhaps seventy-five meters back. Ahead, the few strollers who had been in the distance were gone, crouched down behind planters and statues, waiting for these insane men to disappear.

A sound. He had run past a sound below. A truck shifting gears. The underpass! The road beneath Lenkomsomol Square! The road branching from the traffic-signaled intersection near the square! One summer he had reprimanded boys for dropping stones from the planters through the drainage grates onto the traffic below. The grates lined up over the road here.

He could smell diesel fumes. He turned down a path at the edge of the square and saw the grates lined up beneath the lampposts. He ran past one grate after another and heard a truck starting up, shifting out of first gear, the sound of the truck coming from grates behind him.

Down on his knees, his pistol into the edge of the grate, prying it up. Fingers beneath the grate, the grate pressing into his flesh. Pushing. Pushing the grate over. The truck's yellow cab lights below. A trailer so close. A short drop. But how close? How close to the floor of the square? How close to the ceiling of the tunnel?

No choice. He dropped, spread-eagled like a skydiver. He landed on the truck on his chest and, for a moment, could not breathe. He lay flat, his pistol clenched in his hand. He looked ahead and saw the opening of the tunnel, the road climbing as the truck driver shifted again and the truck lurched forward. And as the truck went faster, the ceiling came closer. Then the ceiling touched him, was at the back of his coat pulling him backward. He would die. He would die.

But suddenly, the echoing sound of the truck's engine opened up about him, and when he looked up, he knew he was outside the tunnel. The truck, with him onboard like an insect clinging to an automobile windshield, headed west on Khreshchatik and would soon pass the metro station.

"He's ducked behind a potted plant!" shouted Brovko.

"I saw him turn up there at those benches!" shouted one of the men with a machine pistol.

"Spread out!" screamed Komarov.

A few seconds later, one of the men shouted, "Over here!"

Komarov ran, saw two men standing with their guns lowered. Could Horvath be dead? Why hadn't he heard the shot? When he ran closer, all he saw was a hole in the ground, a hole the size and shape of a grave. But this was not ground. There was a street below! Komarov stopped at the hole, gasping for breath as he looked down with the others at the traffic passing below, the traffic going west.

Despite his gasping, Komarov ran with the others to the west end of Lenkomsomol Square. At the railing, all he could see was the traffic. There was no one running. No one on a car or truck. Did he expect Horvath to stand on whatever car or truck he must have taken for a ride and wave to him? Mock him? Wasn't it enough he had escaped?

"Back to the hotel!" Komarov gasped for breath. "Find the woman!"

A few meters away, a violinist who had ducked behind a row

of benches because of the commotion stood and started playing a Hungarian song. A Gypsy song!

This was too much. Komarov put his pistol away and walked up to the violinist, a somber, skinny wretch of a man in a tattered brimmed hat playing his idiotic tune. Komarov felt the weight of the knife in his pocket as he walked. He stopped before the old man, pulled out the knife, and opened it.

The old man stopped playing. Komarov held the knife underhanded, not certain if he could stop, not certain if he would.

Then he felt a hand grip his wrist. When he turned, he saw it was Captain Brovko. Behind Brovko, Komarov could see insects hovering below the lights lining the square. Beyond the lights was the sparkle of the Dnieper River to the east. How would he be able to blame the Chernobyl explosion on the Gypsy Moth if he could not catch him?

"Come, Major," said Brovko, staring at the knife. "We might still find the woman."

Brovko watched as Komarov folded the knife and put it away. They joined the other men running back to the Hotel Dnieper.

CHAPTER 25

On May 14, 1986, eighteen days after the Chernobyl explosion, Gorbachev finally addressed the nation. Seven had died, and 290 were hospitalized. After speaking of the seriousness of the disaster and praising rescue workers, Gorbachev criticized exaggerations by the West. But most importantly, he spoke of the lessons the Chernobyl disaster should teach the world, comparing the disaster to the even greater threats that could be unleashed by nuclear weapons.

A few days after Gorbachev's speech, the death toll was said to be thirteen, with many thousands exposed to radiation. The fire was out, and construction workers were building a cement tomb around the reactor. Livestock within a twenty-kilometer radius had been destroyed, and other livestock and fields of winter wheat were being monitored. Outside the Soviet Union, Common Market countries banned the import of Ukraine meat and produce.

On Sunday, May 18, a day one would expect to see crowded streets and parks, almost all of Kiev's children were gone. Perhaps labels appearing on milk containers saying either "For Children" or "For Adults" had been the final Pied Piper leading children away. Many parents went south to be with their children, leaving Kiev with its old and middle-aged.

But the world did not stop. There were quotas to be filled and a few extra rubles to be made for those shrewd enough to take advantage. Kiev morning radio quoted a *Pravda* editorial criticizing Black Sea resort owners who had increased their rates, taking unfair advantage of parents who wanted to be with their children during this difficult time.

Standing at his office window, Komarov watched old men and women wearing dark coats amble out of a church on Boulevard Shevchenko. It reminded him of the night Detective Horvath made fools of his men at the Hotel Dnieper. The Philharmonia had let out, and the crowd gave Horvath the cover he needed. Idiots in the crowd making way instead of stopping him. The same idiots who more than likely applauded Gorbachev's idiotic Chernobyl speech a few days later in which he warned of the global nuclear threat instead of keeping his mouth shut.

Over a week had gone by, and there was still no clue as to where the two Hungarians had gone. Outgoing airlines, trains, and buses were being watched. Members of the KGB and militia carried photographs of Horvath and Juli Popovics, but still there was nothing. The militia also wanted Horvath for questioning regarding the poet's murder because officers had seen the poet talking to Horvath at the roadblock.

Komarov had gone over the scene at the hotel again and again—the time that passed after the knock on the door; the time needed to lower Juli Popovics, still wet from the shower, onto the scaffold; the statue of Lenin holding a pistol; the sofa in front of the window; the gunshot from outside the window; the exit through the hotel kitchen disguised as a waiter; and finally, the escape through the floor of Lenkomsomol Square. But where had Juli Popovics gone? The search of the hotel after Horvath's escape had done nothing but upset patrons and prompt calls from both Chief Investigator Chkalov and Kiev's public prosecutor to Deputy Chairman Dumenko in Moscow. Idiots!

In less than an hour, Dumenko's flight would arrive in Kiev. Komarov needed to blame the incident on someone else while convincing Dumenko the case was still worth pursuing. He sent Captain Brovko to Kisbor, telling him Horvath had to go there because his sister-in-law, Nina Horvath, was the one remaining woman with power over him. Brovko's implication that Komarov had lost control by pulling his knife on the violinist in Lenkomsomol Square made it necessary to get Brovko out of Kiev, and the Horvath farmhouse would be a good place for the captain. Brovko would be in charge of several less skillful agents in Kisbor on the western frontier, including Nikolai Nikolskaia.

The thought of Brovko and Nikolskaia sitting atop a dung heap surrounded by peasants was humorous. But the thought of Dumenko's arrival made laughter impossible.

"I find it difficult to believe your men would be so easily fooled by a statue!" shouted Dumenko. "Perhaps, if their memory is poor, you might place miniature statues of Lenin on the dashboards of their cars!"

"I agree it seems preposterous, Deputy Chairman, but the statue was disguised. He had a jacket about his shoulders and a woman's stocking stretched over his head."

Dumenko raised his eyebrows. "A woman's stocking over

Lenin's face? And a pistol fastened to his hand?"

"Yes, Deputy Chairman."

Dumenko shook his head, the sun from the window reflected off his hairless skull. "It is all quite clear now. Your men defended themselves against what they thought, at first glance, was a live gunman with a stocking over his head." Dumenko raised his voice again. "But please tell me why, if the pistol never fired and the statue never moved, your men found it necessary to put so many holes in Lenin? The hotel manager will now have to replace him!"

"The men who fired at the statue carried Stechkin machine pistols, Deputy Chairman. I'm afraid they were set on full automatic."

"Perhaps we should issue field artillery to the Kiev office! Instead of simply blowing Lenin's crotch away, they could have blown off his head and put the poor man out of his misery!" Dumenko pounded his fist on the desk. "Next time, Major, I expect more control of these situations! Do you realize the extent of damage to the walls and ceiling? Do you realize how many guests were scared shitless? Not to mention the female hotel guest yanked from her bath because she, like Juli Popovics, had dark hair!"

Dumenko shook his head. "KGB agents shooting the balls off a statue, mortally wounding a sofa, and pulling a woman out of her bath. I feel sorry for you, Major. This brain disease of yours is taking its toll. Perhaps your men had a nip of vodka to give them strength. Is that what happened?"

"None of my men drink while on duty, Deputy Chairman."

Komarov knew it was necessary to go through ridicule so that Dumenko would eventually listen to him. At last, after several more sarcastic statements, Dumenko asked about the escape of Detective Horvath and Juli Popovics. In the process of answering these questions, Komarov placed the blame for the incident on Captain Brovko.

"Captain Brovko's training in interrogation and nuclear engineering did not adequately prepare him for an emergency field situation."

"You feel a more experienced man might have performed better?" asked Dumenko.

"I do not wish to blame the captain entirely, Deputy Chairman. I take responsibility for giving him the field assignment."

"I see," said Dumenko. "I suppose I should also take some responsibility for assigning Brovko to you, and even the chairman is responsible for giving me authority to assign men, and so on up the line all the way to the president and general secretary. Is this how you view your responsibilities, Major?"

"No, Comrade Deputy Chairman. Not at all. I take full responsibility. I did not mean to imply you were responsible in any way."

Dumenko waved his hand. "Enough of who is responsible and who is not. Times have changed. These days everything hangs in the open like laundry. So, what are you going to do about the investigation?"

"I will continue to pursue it, Deputy Chairman. One of my men is dead, and Detective Horvath is a suspect in another murder case, a poet who was apparently an informant for Horvath. He's a dangerous man. We have a twenty-four-hour guard on the woman who told us where to find him."

"Tamara Petrov. I read your report." Dumenko raised his eyebrows. "And I've seen photographs of her in the interrogation room. Quite a handsome woman, one worthy of our protection." Dumenko polished the top of his head with his palm and smiled. "Perhaps someday you can introduce me to Tamara Petrov. I find the literary arts fascinating."

Dumenko placed his hands back on the desk. His smile vanished.

"Major Komarov, I must tell you the initial reason for your

343

investigation seems weak in light of new information. Yesterday I spoke with the chairman of the State Atomic Energy Committee. He seems convinced the incident at Chernobyl was an accident."

Komarov stood and paced back and forth behind his desk to emphasize his seriousness.

"Comrade Deputy Chairman, I've been involved in this case long enough to know I am not mistaken. Juli Popovics, hiding her treachery behind outspokenness for the environment, is a key figure. Transcripts from meetings with Mihaly Horvath and his fellow engineers often refer to 'the bitch.' I have evidence to convince me 'the bitch' is none other than Juli Popovics. She was most likely recruited long ago by Aleksandra Yasinsky, currently imprisoned for anti-Soviet activities. Mihaly Horvath is also a key figure, but weaker than Juli Popovics. In correspondence with his brother, Mihaly Horvath spoke often of his greed—purchasing an expensive car, getting a larger apartment, the usual capitalist goals. He indicated he might be able to obtain funds from his American cousin, Andrew Zukor."

Komarov paused dramatically before continuing. "I know I've sent reports saying the situation at Chernobyl is under control. And the explosion and resulting fire remain under control to the best of our ability. However, if I am guilty of anything, it is my naïveté concerning the Horvath brothers, their American cousin, and Juli Popovics. There is conspiracy here." He pointed to his chest. "I can feel it. I've heard the reports of human error at Chernobyl, and I still feel it. Of course, the ministries in charge are saying human error. What else can they say? But later, with all the facts on the table, when the radiation has diminished sufficiently to find clues indicating tampering, the KGB's investigation will pay its dividends, Comrade Deputy Chairman. We'll be ready to stand before any committee of inquiry. And if they are captured, Juli Popovics and Detective Horvath will confess. They have already lost one of their own. On Friday afternoon, when the shutdown was originally scheduled, Mihaly Horvath would have been able to escape. They were tricked by fate, Deputy Chairman. We should not be tricked so easily!"

When Komarov finished his speech, he was breathless. He sat back at his desk, stared at Dumenko, and waited. After a minute of silence, Dumenko spoke.

"You present a strong case, Major. Very well, you may continue the investigation." Dumenko stood and walked to the door, where he turned back and pointed his finger at Komarov. "But remember, Major. I will not tolerate another Hotel Dnieper incident. Is that understood?"

"Yes, Comrade Deputy Chairman."

The last time Komarov spent an evening alone on his back porch was the night after Detective Horvath and Juli Popovics escaped the Hotel Dnieper. The investigation had stalled, and he had relapsed, fallen victim to the bottle's talons. When he awakened the next day, his wife told him she and Dmitry had carried him into the house and, unable to awaken him, almost called the doctor. It had taken his system two days to recover. Having vowed never to drink again, having come to his senses enough to convince Dumenko this afternoon to allow the case to continue, he was out on his porch again, alone and sober.

To the west, three kilometers away, was the metro station where the Volga had been found. Across the river was the Hotel Dnieper and a million other places in which to hide. Detective Horvath would know them all. But were they still in Kiev, or had they moved on?

Komarov lit a cigarette and thought back to his boyhood outside Moscow, where he'd seen groups of Gypsies camped across the river. He remembered hearing violins in the forest late at night while he was trying to fall asleep. He remembered the talk at school about Gypsies being run off by militia because they had been caught stealing livestock from local farmers. It seemed innocent then. Gypsies taking a few chickens to eat, the way he and his friends took a tomato or an onion from the fields when they were hungry. But later, when the Gypsy landlord confronted his father after the opera, he knew Gypsies were not the children of the forest they claimed to be.

Gypsies hid among civilized citizens. The landlord who killed his parents was a Hungarian Gypsy. Barbara, who seduced and humiliated him during his hazing in the GDR, was half-Russian and half-Hungarian. Hungarians, Gypsies, people famous for their supposed contribution to the arts. The musical *Czigany*. The so-called poets and writers. Perhaps Horvath and Popovics were among them, hidden away in a Kiev garret.

Komarov inhaled deeply on his cigarette, thinking of Tamara Petrov. Earrings flashing, bracelets clanging, hair as black as the night, black hair making her olive skin appear lighter than it was as she wept in his office, weeping because she had turned in one of her own.

This afternoon, even Deputy Chairman Dumenko had fallen briefly under Tamara Petrov's spell when looking at photographs of her in the interrogation room. Tamara Petrov grimacing and frowning and even laughing at the hidden camera while Captain Brovko questioned her. More trickery, appearing courageous when she was really a coward. Or was she?

Komarov felt something on his finger and realized his cigarette had burned down to a butt. He put the cigarette out and lit another. He rubbed the surface burn, brought his finger to his nose, and smelled the acrid odor of burned flesh. The odor brought back memories of his years in the GDR at the "safe" house outside East Berlin. An old captain from the Great War named Alexeev used the method often. The captain would lean close to the victim, speaking softly, like a grandfather whispering to his grandchild. Then he would lock the victim in a grip with one arm and press his lit cigarette to the victim's neck. Komarov had smelled this mixture of cigarette smoke and smoldering flesh many times when passing the interrogation room and hearing the screams of victims. It was a smell he had never forgotten.

If Captain Alexeev had come back from the dead to terrorize Tamara Petrov in the interrogation room, would more have been revealed? Perhaps it would be wise to interrogate her again. Perhaps he could do a better job than Captain Brovko, especially if he did it under different circumstances.

Komarov stood and put out his cigarette. He went into the house, where the only light came from the glow of the television in the living room. The television showed a rerun of Gorbachev's spineless Chernobyl speech. On his way out the front door, he told his wife he would be gone at least two hours on business. Her only response was to raise her hand limply.

Komarov parked a block away from Club Ukrainka and walked. He would be able to check on his men. And if his men did not recognize him, there was no need to explain his follow-up questioning of Tamara Petrov. Better to visit Club Ukrainka as a stranger in an overcoat with the collar drawn up about his face. When he passed the Volga, he saw both men inside. A flashlight lit up the seat between them for a moment. They were playing cards. He walked on, purposely giving himself a slight limp, and entered Club Ukrainka.

The place was dark, the air thick with smoke and the smell of Turkish coffee. He sat at a table near the entrance and put out the candle on the table. He ordered coffee and paid for it as soon as it was delivered. He kept his coat on and held the cup in front of his face.

Tamara Petrov was on the far side of the room at a table to one side of the small stage. Onstage, a thin, bearded man made his saxophone sound like an old man who had eaten too many beans. When the man stopped playing, a few people clapped, and the man went to Tamara Petrov's table. The man's cheeks had been puffed up when he played. Now they were sunken, and, in profile, Komarov recognized Jewish features. First the Gypsy, now a Jew who blows farts on his saxophone while she applauds him, smiles at him, invites him to her table, and perhaps to her apartment.

Komarov imagined Tamara Petrov kissing the bearded Jew, using the wiry black beard to clean between her teeth the way prostitutes clean their teeth on pubic hair. Suddenly, he thought of Dmitry with a man, in bed with a man, the taste of salt and the feel of hair inside one's mouth. A wave of nausea came over him, nausea so strong he had to go to the washroom and splash cold water on his face. The water from the spigot smelled metallic. He took deep breaths from the open window in the washroom. When he finally recovered, he returned to his table, held his coffee cup in front of his face, and watched Tamara Petrov.

The saxophonist was back onstage, puffing his cheeks and playing something reminiscent of a Hungarian song played on a violin, a ridiculously romantic elongation of melody, a sound like someone weeping, the sound made by the old man with the violin in Lenkomsomol Square the night Detective Horvath escaped. And there was Tamara Petrov smiling at the Jew. When the Jew switched to a Middle Eastern melody and gyrated his hips, Tamara Petrov stood and applauded.

If only Detective Horvath could be here now. If only he could see his Gypsy lover swooning like a child bride experiencing her first orgasm. Perhaps Horvath would be jealous enough to leave the club in anger, wait for Tamara Petrov in an alleyway, and confront her. A woman who first turns him in, then replaces him with a Jew so she can play his saxophone penis.

Komarov held his cup in one hand, reached inside his coat, gripped his knife, and thought of Pudkov and the poet, their necks like wet muted violin strings as he sliced across them. He thought of Gretchen staring at him with surprise as he pushed the knife in and twisted.

When the saxophonist approached the climax of his disgusting wail, and as Tamara Petrov remained standing, applauding, and gyrating her hips like a belly dancer, Komarov left Club Ukrainka. Outside, he lowered his head into his collar and took up his limp. When he passed the Volga, the men inside paid no attention to him. He walked a half block and hid around the side of a building in a dark alleyway. From this position, he could see the entrance of Club Ukrainka and he could see the heads of the two KGB men who would soon be disciplined severely for allowing Tamara Petrov to be murdered under their very noses.

CHAPTER 26

The village of Kisbor on the Ulyanov collective was on a dry plateau less than twenty-five kilometers from the Czechoslovakian border. Although the Chernobyl accident was a topic of conversation, Kisbor residents felt relatively safe because Kiev was much closer and Kiev television news did not show citizens dropping dead in the streets. Instead of worrying about the reported insignificant amount of radiation in their area, citizens of Kisbor and the Ulyanov collective were more concerned with spring planting.

Nikolai stood in the yard of the Horvath farm, watching the sunrise. The farmhouse was on a slight hill above the village, and only the tallest houses in Kisbor were visible, their peaked roofs like black witches' hats against the orange sky. The morning was cool, and on the distant plain he could see patches of ground fog. According to local legend, these patches of fog were the last breaths of a person who had recently died. Perhaps one of the patches belonged to Pavel, his last breath drifting on the wind all the way from the town of Visenka, outside Kiev, and arriving now, his last breath wandering about until it came upon his friend Nikolai, who cradled him like a babe in his arms as he died.

Nikolai walked around the side of the farmhouse where a rooster strutted back and forth on the tin roof of a lean-to chicken coop. The rooster's claws on the roof sounded like someone scratching from inside a coffin. The rooster stopped strutting, puffed up its chest, and greeted the sunrise with a high-pitched wail.

When he went into the backyard, Nikolai passed a weathered wooden box set in the ground. The box had an old oilskin tablecloth draped over it, and on it were two battered tin plates holding water from the last rain. Tarnished and bent knives and forks rescued by local children completed the make-believe table setting.

Children. At the funeral, Pavel's wife said they were going to have children. She repeated it over and over as he helped carry the coffin to the grave site set aside for Kiev's KGB agents and militiamen. "He was only twenty-seven and no children!" screamed Pavel's wife as the coffin was lowered.

Shortly after Pavel's funeral, Nikolai was sent here. In the farmhouse there were three children—a baby belonging to the Sandors, who lived in the house, and the two daughters of Nina Horvath, who had come from Pripyat by way of a Moscow hospital. Walking beyond the oblong box with its oilcloth, discarded utensils, and border of untrimmed weeds, Nikolai wondered about Detective Horvath's boyhood here with his brother, little boys playing games just as he and Pavel had done when they were boys. Today the games were more serious. The winner's prize was to remain alive. Today's orders were to be alert for the possibility Detective Horvath and Juli Popovics might show up. And tomorrow? Who knew?

Nikolai was not alone. He and the others took twelve-hour shifts alternating between the farmhouse and the small hotel in the village. Originally there had been four men. Now, with the arrival of Captain Brovko and three others, the total was eight. At any given time there were at least three of them at the house.

Nikolai reached the end of the yard where tilled soil began, looked at his watch, and turned back when he heard tires on the gravel road. He had been at the house for his twelve-hour shift and, walking to the side of the house, was glad to see Captain Brovko in one Volga and three replacements climbing out of a second Volga. One of the men stretched and yawned loudly. Nikolai joined the other two who had spent the night at the house, each of them alone, alternating positions every two hours. One man in the house, one in the car, and one walking about the perimeter, all three armed with Stechkin machine pistols.

Nikolai was about to get into the second Volga with his two partners when Captain Brovko called him over and sent the other two ahead to the hotel. As the men drove away, Nikolai wondered what more could possibly happen to him.

"Come," said Captain Brovko. "I'll drive you back."

The inside of the Volga was warm. For the moment, as Captain Brovko drove down the road into the dust of the other Volga, Nikolai felt safe. Here, in a warm Volga with his machine pistol stowed on the floor and his new captain driving, he was assured of not being attacked from behind by Detective Horvath returning to his boyhood home. No matter what Captain Brovko had to say, even if it was a reprimand, he was glad to be away from the house with its dark yard and the women inside who conveyed hatred by simply looking at him. Last evening when he took his turn in the house, Mariska Sandor, the resident farm wife, played a game with the little girls in which she claimed she could tell their fortunes by observing teacup stains. During the game, Mariska Sandor had turned to him and claimed she could tell how long he was going to live. The smile on her face when she said it frightened Nikolai, filling the remainder of the night with visions of Detective Horvath sending him to join Pavel in the grave.

Shortly after the road curved and dropped down the small hill, Captain Brovko pulled over to the side and parked. Ahead, and slightly below, the village greeted the sun, clay tiles on the roofs taking on the color of rouge on a woman's cheeks. The Volga carrying his two partners disappeared into the main street of the village, leaving only the dust settling above the road.

He and Captain Brovko spoke of their pasts. Nikolai described the PK and his and Pavel's assignment in the Pripyat post office. Captain Brovko described working in Moscow and in the GDR. Captain Brovko said he missed Moscow because he had a girlfriend there. Chernobyl had ruined plans to spend a furlough with her. Nikolai mentioned his latest girlfriend in Pripyat, wondering if she had escaped. He told Captain Brovko how Pavel had come to the door the Saturday morning after the explosion and found him in bed with his girlfriend. Captain Brovko laughed with him, and this, combined with the morning sun shining through the windshield, made Nikolai feel more relaxed.

After a pause, during which they stared ahead at the awakening village, Captain Brovko asked about the assignment. "What do you think, Nikolai? Will Detective Horvath and Juli Popovics really come here?"

Nikolai knew it was time to choose his words carefully. "Because we are here, Major Komarov must have reason to believe so."

"What do you think of him?"

"Detective Horvath?"

"No. Major Komarov."

"I . . . I don't think anything. I simply follow orders."

Captain Brovko chuckled. "Don't worry, Nikolai. I'm not trying to trick you. We're in this together, assigned to a farmhouse in the middle of nowhere. Can you tell me why Detective Horvath would come here when he knows we're waiting?"

Captain Brovko turned to stare at him. "I don't blame you for not answering. Especially after being uprooted from your PK assignment and sent on a field mission during which your partner was killed before your eyes."

Nikolai was silent as he stared at Brovko's eyes.

"You and your partner were unprepared for the situation. Afterward you were angry because of the inappropriateness of the assignment. Correct?"

"Yes."

Captain Brovko leaned closer. "Now I'll tell you something, Nikolai. I believe Detective Horvath will come here. He'll be drawn here because his brother's wife and children are here. There are things about this case even I don't know, things Major Komarov, for whatever reason, has chosen to keep to himself."

"The major is a driven man," said Nikolai.

"In what way?" asked Captain Brovko.

"He is willing to do anything to prove Detective Horvath is a saboteur."

"What has he done so far?"

"I can't say more, Captain. I'll get myself in trouble the way Pavel got in trouble because he didn't know the consequences of aiming a pistol at an armed militia detective."

"Tell me," said Captain Brovko, "why do you think, with the men available to him in Kiev, Major Komarov chose to send you and your partner to retrieve Juli Popovics?"

Nikolai looked out at the road, where an ancient battered bus began climbing slowly up the hill. "I don't know, Captain. Pavel and I were both inexperienced. I don't even know what I'm doing here."

The bus lumbered past, lifting dust from the road. In the windows Nikolai saw the faces of wide-eyed farmers staring at the strange sight of two men sitting at the side of the road at dawn in a black Volga.

"The farmers are off to their fields," said Brovko as he started the Volga and began driving down to the hotel in the village.

Five hundred kilometers east, near the town of Korostyshev, another collective bus drove down a dusty road. The bus was full of men and women wearing layers of clothing to keep away the morning chill. Some on the bus commented on the dry weather of the past few days allowing planting to progress. Some talked about family matters. But most conversations eventually turned to a more serious matter. These workers, belonging to the Kopelovo collective, a hundred kilometers southwest of Kiev, were now providing food and shelter for several hundred refugees forced to flee the Opachichi collective near Pripyat.

A man in a leather cap at the front of the bus stood facing the back, firing questions at those sitting near him.

"How do we feed our own families? That's what I'd like to know."

"You're not starving," said a woman in a yellow babushka.

"Not yet," said the man. "But we're the ones working the fields. We need food so we can continue working."

The man sitting next to the woman in the yellow babushka waved his hand. "Nothing makes sense when people are forced from their homes. How would you like to lose everything and be forced to sleep in barns and tents and practically beg for food for your children?"

"At least," said the man in the leather cap, "they could come work in the fields. What else have they got to do?"

"The people in my barn wanted to work," said the woman in the yellow babushka. "But the chairman said no. He said they all have to stay where they are because officials are arriving today from Kiev."

"What for?"

"A census," said the woman. "The chairman says they might relocate some people farther south and west."

"Good," said the man in the leather cap. "Maybe things will get back to normal and I'll have a decent meal. Look how thin I am."

The bus passengers laughed, and even the man in the leather cap smiled as he turned to look out the bus windshield. The only one who didn't laugh or smile was the driver, who was in his own world, the world of the throbbing engine and the shifting of gears and the dodging of holes in the road.

Within the Kopelovo collective village, behind one of the houses lining the road, Lazlo lifted the canvas tent flap and looked outside. The tent opening faced away from the house, with a view of the family's freshly planted private plot. A thin layer of ground fog was being burned away by morning sun. The damp morning air smelled of livestock and smoldering trash fires.

Lazlo heard footsteps in the weeds, leaned out, and saw the man from the next tent over. The farmer from the north lived in a tent with his wife and two children. A goat tethered outside during the day was allowed inside the tent at night. The farmer walked back from the outhouse carrying a rolled-up newspaper in one hand and a tin cup in the other. He hummed a Ukrainian folk song. Although Lazlo did not know the name of the song, he knew it glorified morning. A cheerful song of hope and hard work, a song he sometimes heard the skinny baker at his favorite bakery whistle in the back room before bringing out a fragrant tray of pastry.

The thought of the warm Kiev bakery made Lazlo shiver. He

dropped the tent flap and sat back on his heels. He reached up to touch the warm slope of the tent where the orange of the sun glowed. Although the cut on his wrist was healed, his ankle still ached from the jump to the scaffold at the Hotel Dnieper. He turned and crawled to the back of the tent where Juli slept. He lifted the blankets carefully so as not to let in cold, damp air. Beneath the blankets, he felt Juli's warmth against him and his shivering stopped.

After the narrow escape at Lenkomsomol Square, Lazlo met Juli at the hospital. Dressed as peasants and with Lazlo wearing an eye patch to disguise himself, they'd gone to one of the roadblocks and joined the line of people trying to enter Kiev. Lazlo had worked the roadblocks long enough to know how to use the situation to their advantage. He knew that instead of being allowed in, they would be transported with others to a collective many kilometers away. He also knew they could do this without identification because during the rapid evacuation, many refugees failed to obtain passes. He let Juli do most of the talking, saying they were from Pripyat and had worked in a department store. He kept his face hidden, and none of the militia officers recognized him.

They had been here at the Kopelovo collective a full week, freezing in the tent each night and keeping trim on the daily ration of food provided. Kiev was a hundred kilometers northeast, and he might never see it again. His sprained ankle had healed, and he was ready to move on. The question was where to go and when. The only logical direction was west, to Czechoslovakia or Hungary or even farther. The time would be soon, because yesterday there were rumors of relocation. Paperwork would be completed, names put on file, and representatives of the militia or the KGB milling about.

They were fugitives, both considered criminals—him a murderer and Juli his accomplice. It didn't matter if the agent aimed his pistol at them. To the KGB, one of their own was dead. No matter if the incident was a setup and Tamara's poet friend was a KGB informer.

He recalled Tamara's anger at the poet when he met her at the river, saying she would kill him if she saw him again. Lazlo had insisted she not make trouble for herself. He needed her to follow through on the faked betrayal so she would not be implicated when he and Juli escaped.

Would he ever see Tamara again? Would he tell her about his confusion when he realized he was attracted to Juli? Would he tell her about the past week, during which he and Juli posed as husband and wife living in an army tent on the Kopelovo collective? Would he tell Tamara he was in love?

As he lay beside Juli, Lazlo could feel the heat of her breath on his face. He kissed her cheek and held her close. But at his back the chill of morning touched him, reminding him that Nina, Anna, and little Ilonka were in Kisbor. Komarov would know Lazlo must go there. If he and Juli escaped across the frontier without going to Kisbor, Komarov would take revenge. The thought of going to Kisbor and of what he must do became icy fingers pulling him away from Juli and her unborn child.

Coming awake, Juli thought she felt her baby move. She wondered if time had sped up, if months had passed and she was in a bed in an apartment with Lazlo by her side. But when she opened her eyes, she saw the tent roof. Time had not sped up. They were still at the collective. She was still in her seventh or eighth week of pregnancy and certainly would not have been able to feel the baby move. The momentary thought of being in a bed with Lazlo was a dream. But at least part of it was true. Lazlo was with her, holding her tightly.

"I thought you were my baby."

Lazlo kissed her cheek. "I am your baby."

"When you moved, I thought it was my baby moving. I dreamed we were somewhere safe with no one looking for us. I was big and fat, and you still loved me."

Lazlo smiled. "It's a wonderful dream."

"I hope it comes true."

"It can if we cross the frontier. We'll be able to go to a good hospital and get you and your baby checked. We'll be able to tell someone what you know about Chernobyl. We'll find somewhere to live instead of a moth-eaten tent." Lazlo sat up and looked down at her with a broad grin. "It's nothing but good news from now on."

"I like seeing you smile, Laz."

"I rarely smiled before I met you."

They kissed and made love beneath the rough army blankets.

After a breakfast of canned sardines, bread, and bottled water, Juli reviewed with Lazlo the information about Chernobyl they hoped to get to officials at the International Atomic Energy Agency in Vienna. The information included what Mihaly told Juli before he died—the experiment to see how long the inertia of the turbine could generate emergency power, the emergency backups turned off while the reactor was still running, the absence of the chief engineer who had ordered the experiment, printouts of reactor conditions not available directly to control-room personnel, speculation about Chernobyl being used as a guinea pig for other reactors of the same type throughout the country. Juli had memorized as much as possible and recited the details each day to Lazlo. She also included information she knew from her job, including specific figures she recalled concerning radionuclide sampling around the power station before the explosion.

"It's like being in school again," said Lazlo. "A big tough guy with his Makarov pistol strapped to his chest back in school."

Juli touched Lazlo's chin, realizing how much he resembled Mihaly. "You're not such a tough guy, Laz."

"What am I?"

"A Gypsy, like me. I've always wondered what it would have been like to live somewhere else, to be someone different. We can't help it. It's in our blood. It was in Mihaly's blood."

Lazlo lifted her hand from his chin, kissed her hand, stared at her. "Mihaly wasn't attracted to a desire to try something new. He was attracted to you because you're special."

"How can you say that? I'm the one who initially thought of our affair as a game. I wasn't married so who could get hurt? No, Laz. Don't call me special."

"I'll call you whatever I like," he said in a deep voice.

They both laughed, pulling the heavy blankets over their heads so others would not hear them and wonder who would be insane enough to tell jokes in a situation like this.

Later in the morning, while Juli washed the tattered peasant clothes they managed to pick up along the way, officials arrived. She was behind a nearby house using a washtub set up for refugees. From where she stood, she could see a militia car pull up and three men get out. Two men in suits and a local uniformed militiaman. Juli stayed at the washtub, watching as Lazlo stood in line to speak with the men. Lazlo looked like any of the other farmers, his hands in the pockets of baggy trousers, his ill-fitting cap pulled down tightly on his head.

Because they had agreed not to panic, Juli stayed at the wash-tub. If Lazlo recognized any of the men, he would not have gotten in line.

One of the officials had a clipboard. When a refugee made it to the front of the line, the man would flip through pages on the clipboard and write something down. The procedure took only a minute or so for each. But when Lazlo got to the front of the line, the man with the clipboard kept flipping pages, Lazlo kept shrugging his shoulders, and the militiaman standing to the side stood closer. Finally Lazlo leaned forward, pointing at something on the clipboard and the questioning became more serious. They questioned Lazlo for several agonizing minutes. When he was finally allowed to leave, Juli hurried to the tent to join him.

Lazlo retrieved the sock in which he kept his money and his pistol from the hole dug in the ground through a slit in the tent floor. He took the pistol out, checked the magazine, put the pistol in one pocket and the sock with the money in his other pocket, and turned to Juli.

"We've got to leave."

"Do they know who we are?"

"Not yet. But I couldn't convince them I was on the list. I tried mispronouncing a name to see if I could fake one, but they wanted family details. I guess you saw what happened when I tried to look at the list myself."

"I thought they would arrest you."

"I pushed them close to it. Soon they'll report back about a man and wife named Zimyanin, a name not on the refugee list."

"Where should we go?"

"I don't know yet. There's a bus due early tomorrow morning for those being shipped out. We're supposed to stay here until the officials come back. If we get out of here tonight, or at least before morning, maybe they'll think we got on the bus. We'll spread the word we've been told to leave on the morning bus."

Lazlo took off the hat he had worn, combed his hair, and put on a shirt with fewer holes in it. "I'll be back as soon as I can. Get ready while I'm gone. I like your idea of posing as radiation technicians."

"I'll put things together."

After Lazlo kissed her and left the tent, Juli looked out and watched him go. He walked quickly, one hand deep in the pocket where he had put the sock containing money saved during his years in the Kiev militia, the other hand deep in the other pocket where he had put his pistol.

Juli had gotten the idea to pose as radiation technicians when she saw technicians in lab coats while being bussed out of Kiev. Creating makeshift lab coats out of bedsheets had taken three days. The needles and thread and a pair of scissors were available at the village store. Although they were simply smocks rather than coats, it didn't take much to look official in this region. Especially when she made a fake Geiger counter by taping an old radio tube from the local trash to a length of wire and inserting the other end of the wire into her black overnight case.

Juli removed the fake lab coats from the overnight case and spread them on the floor of the tent to get out the wrinkles. She took out a bottle of pink nail polish she had purchased at the village store and closed the overnight case. The smell of nail polish quickly filled the tent as she pulled out the brush connected to the cap. Juli did not polish her nails. Instead, she pulled the overnight case close and began filling in letters she had earlier outlined on the side of the case. The letters spelled out in Russian the words, DANGER, RADIO-ACTIVE SAMPLES.

CHAPTER 27

The sun was still well below the horizon, the gray dawn barely illuminating his office. It was deathly silent, no voices in the hall, no computer printer clattering outside the door. Komarov lit a cigarette, watching the dance of flame from his lighter. After closing the lighter, he inspected the cigarette's tip. He thought of the shortness of life and the necessity to make the best of it while the glow still existed. Although he could not see the smoke, he saw a slight darkening of the slit of light shining beneath his office door. A shadow was there, and when he waved the smoke away, the shadow remained.

Three quick knocks on the door were soft and tentative. He waited a moment, then said, "Come in!" rather loudly.

Light from the hall swept across the office, and a sizable creature stood in the doorway.

"Are you here, Major Komarov?"

"I am, Captain Azef."

"Why are you sitting in the dark?"

"I'm helping the state in this time of energy shortage, Captain. I was not in need of light at the moment, and one of our major generating plants is incapacitated. You can turn it on now."

Despite the initial glare of the overhead light, Komarov kept his eyes open wide and watched as Azef sat across from him. Azef looked tentative, the initial darkness in the room putting him on the defensive.

Azef glanced at Komarov's pistol and shoulder holster resting atop his desk, then looked to the window. "Still dark outside."

"Never mind how dark it is, Captain. After days of silence, a twig has snapped in the forest. Yesterday a man without papers was interviewed at the Kopelovo collective to the west. Being without papers is not unusual, but he was with a younger woman he claims is his wife. The man said his name was Zimyanin. After interviewing him, officials on the scene questioned others about Zimyanin because the name was not on the refugee list. The questioning revealed Zimyanin is not a peasant but an educated man who speaks Russian, Ukrainian, and Hungarian. The man and his supposed wife fit the description of Detective Horvath and Juli Popovics."

Komarov felt the heat rushing to his face and knew he would no longer be able to contain his anger. He finished in a loud voice after smashing his cigarette out in the ashtray.

"All of this was known to the Interior Ministry yesterday! And when am I told?" He looked at his watch. "A full sixteen hours after the fact! Shcherbina in the Zhitomir branch office learned about it and called me at home. Unfortunately he was not informed by phone. The ministry fools sent a note via the republic militia! The note didn't reach Shcherbina until this morning when he arose for his morning exercise!"

Azef waited an appropriate few seconds to make sure Komarov's tirade was finished. "What are you going to do, Major?"

"I'm going there myself as soon as the idiot driver arrives! If Zimyanin is Horvath, the ministry asses and local militia will most likely let him escape if I'm not there!"

"He most likely moved on after the questioning."

"I know. But if he was staying at the collective with Juli Popovics, there will be evidence remaining, people who saw them or spoke with them. There may even be evidence of contact with outside intelligence. I refuse to trust local idiots to do any more interviewing!"

"I understand, Major. Will you be gone long?"

"However long it takes. If the Zimyanins have left and if I find evidence proving they are Detective Horvath and Juli Popovics, I will have Horvath in my grasp."

"How will you have him in your grasp if he escapes?"

"Put yourself in his place, Captain. Try to think like him, as I have. Why would a clever man with militia connections giving him access to fake papers, perhaps even confiscated passports and visas, not have crossed the frontier by now?"

"I don't know."

"Don't you see, Captain? He can't leave. He needs to wipe the slate clean by eliminating those who know of his involvement in sabotage. Our agent in Visenka was just the beginning. The poet, an associate of Tamara Petrov, was next. And, before leaving Kiev, Horvath obviously murdered Tamara Petrov. A vengeful man becomes desperate, and a desperate man becomes careless. He will be captured if someone doesn't bungle it! I will not let him escape!"

"What about Chkalov, Major? He called twice yesterday wanting to speak with you." Azef smiled slightly. "He told my secretary an underling would not do. When I asked if he considered me an underling, he said the secretary had put words in his mouth."

"Not words," said Komarov. "His foot, or something else if he could reach it over his belly. Don't worry about Chkalov. He won't have any choice but to speak with you because you'll be in command while I'm gone. Chkalov's only concern now is the fact he allowed a saboteur and murderer to remain under his command in the Kiev militia!"

Komarov stood. "Leave me for now, Captain. My driver and the men who will accompany me are waiting . . . I have things to gather before I go."

Azef paused at the door. "Should I use your office while you're gone, Major?"

"By all means, Captain."

After Azef was gone, Komarov put on his shoulder holster, with extra cartridges loaded into the strap holders. He pulled on his jacket, put his overcoat on his arm, and picked up the valise containing two changes of underwear and a dozen packages of cigarettes. At the door he put the valise down and patted his pockets. He had not forgotten. The knife was there, resting against his chest.

A shame about Tamara Petrov. He admired her defiance. Like a true Gypsy, she had spit in his face. But once the knife went in and twisted, she opened her eyes wide and, like the others, glowed for a few moments in the ecstasy of dying.

Komarov picked up his valise and went to join his men.

As Juli walked along a dirt road on the farmland belonging to the Kopelovo collective, her overnight case tugged at her fingers. The sunrise, initially bright, was now cut off by clouds hanging low at the horizon. The land was flat, with plowed fields on both sides of the road. A dog barked in the distance, perhaps at the collective village a kilometer or two behind her. But it wasn't the bark of a dog she listened for. What she wanted to hear was the sound of a car.

Lazlo had left long before dawn to get the car. A white car, he said. He had purchased it yesterday and left it hidden several kilometers away so as not to arouse suspicion. He planned to meet Juli on the dirt road heading straight west out of the village. She was to keep walking along the road until he picked her up.

Yesterday, Lazlo's journey to the town of Korostyshev, the purchase of the car, and the long journey back had taken hours. She'd been alone most of the day and well into the night. It had been cold last night, more so because after sunset Lazlo was not beside her. He returned near midnight and left again early this morning. During the few hours with him, she held him tightly. Now he was gone again, and she shivered with cold as she listened intently for a car on the road.

After a few minutes, she heard tires thumping into ruts in the road behind her along with the struggle of a misfiring engine. When she turned, she saw it was not a white car. As it came closer, she saw it was a battered old bus.

She wondered if she should hide. After spreading the news yesterday, saying she and Lazlo were leaving on the relocation bus early in the morning, could she afford to be seen out here? Obviously the bus coming down the road was not the relocation bus, but the dilapidated bus used to transport collective workers. She looked about and realized the ditch at the side of the road was too shallow to hide her. But why should she hide? If the people on the bus saw a woman walking along the road, what would it matter? She would simply look away when the bus passed.

When the bus approached, she turned the overnight case so the lettering she had applied faced out into the field. It would not do to have passing passengers see a radiation warning sign now. The farmers on the bus might remember her and Lazlo, especially if agents came to the village asking questions.

Instead of going past, the bus pulled to a stop, coughing and sputtering as the front door scissored open. The door was slightly ahead of her. She placed the overnight case on the ground with its message facing the field and watched as a thin man wearing a leather cap leaned out. The idling engine clattered like a thousand mechanical hearts.

"Where are you going?" asked the man in the local Ukrainian dialect.

"I'm waiting for someone."

"Funny place to wait." He pointed up the road to the west. "How come you're walking this way?"

"Because it's the way we'll be going when my friend picks me up."

"This also is funny because after several kilometers the road ends in the middle of fields. Perhaps you're on the wrong road."

"The wrong road? Yes, I must be. I'll return to the village and call my friend from there."

"You're one of the refugees, aren't you?"

A story, something to make this meeting insignificant to the militia or the KGB. "Yes, my mother and sister and I have been living in your village for almost a week. We are very grateful for your hospitality."

The man smiled. "So, why are you leaving?"

"I'm not leaving. I'm simply meeting someone."

The man glanced at the overnight case on the ground. "I see . . ."

"My laundry. I know someone who lives in Korostyshev. She has a washing machine . . ."

"Is she picking you up?"

"Yes, here, on the . . . the east road out of the village."

"Aha!" said the man. "This is the west road."

"Hey!" yelled the driver from inside. "Tell her to get in and I'll drive her to the village on my return trip."

The man jumped down, reached for the overnight case. "Come on."

Juli held onto the case. "No! I . . . I'll walk."

"Come on. It'll only take a few minutes." He snatched the case from her.

A horn sounded, and when she turned, she saw a white car approaching behind the bus.

She grabbed at the case, and the man let go. She held the case in her arms, the lettered side against her.

"My friend is here. She knew I'd take the wrong road."

Juli waved to the car, waved for it to stop if it was Lazlo. The car pulled off to the side and waited. She turned back to the man who had removed his cap and was scratching his head.

"Thank you for everything you've done."

"Me?" said the man. "I didn't do anything."

"Don't let your wife hear you!" shouted the driver. "She might get the wrong idea. Especially with all the Chernobylites at your doorstep."

Juli hurried back to the car, away from the joking voices of the man and the driver cut off by the closing door. When she glanced up, she saw the faces of the farmers staring at her. Men and women were out of their seats, their heads stacked at the bus windows like multiheaded monsters, or like an investigative committee considering the verdict. Some smiled, but many frowned.

"Try to look like a woman. I told them I was waiting for a girlfriend to pick me up."

Lazlo pulled the visor down as Juli got in. Beneath the visor he watched through the dirty and cracked windshield. The bus pulled away, leaving a cloud of smoke.

"It's a good thing you stopped when I waved. I don't think they saw you. We have to turn around because this road doesn't go anywhere."

"I know, but I didn't think about a bus carrying farmers. And the car got stuck in the mud where I'd hidden it."

Lazlo cranked the wheel to turn around. When he reached for the shift lever, he felt Juli's hand on it. He turned to her, and they kissed, holding one another tightly. He held Juli until she stopped shaking. Then he turned the car around and drove back to the main road.

He drove south, heading for the town of Zhitomir. There was little traffic, only an occasional farm truck and other buses carrying workers to fields along the way. After he had driven about fifty kilometers, he glanced at Juli. She leaned against his arm, her eyes closed.

While Juli slept, Lazlo recalled the transaction for the car, the man suspicious about his use of cash and wanting the car immediately rather than waiting for the cracked windshield to be fixed. He'd found the car at a gasoline station and, seeing it had an expired plate, inquired about its sale. In Kiev it would have been easier to buy a car. But out here there were no dealers, no parking lots where locals struck bargains.

The purchase of the five-year-old Skoda from a stranger had depleted his savings, and he wondered if it would have been better to steal a car. Perhaps before this was over, he would have to steal a car. Cars were scarce in the countryside, and stealing one would have attracted the republic militia. Even so, stealing a car would be nothing. He only hoped he would not be forced to kill again. But he knew he would if he had to, especially if someone were foolish enough to aim a gun at him and Juli the way the agent had in Visenka.

Before falling asleep, Juli had related the story she told the man from the bus. If they were to get over the frontier, they would both have to be clever, perhaps tell many more stories. Although there seemed no room for mistakes, he felt he had already made one. Instead of filling the gas tank when he purchased the car, he'd left with a half tank. In an hour or so, he would have to stop for gas. He kept glancing at the Skoda's gas gauge and wondered how accurate it was.

After sleeping less than an hour, Juli awakened. "Where are we? This doesn't look like the main road."

"I'm taking a route around Zhitomir. It's a sizable town with an active militia. We'll stop for gas at Berdichev. After Berdichev we'll take back roads to the Carpathian foothills."

"They'll be watching for a man and woman. I'll lie on the back seat beneath the blankets. If you put on a lab coat and leave the case with its lettering clearly visible, I'm sure the station attendant will want to get rid of you as quickly as possible."

The gas stop in Berdichev went exactly as Juli said. At first the attendant wanted to talk about the Chernobyl accident, saying how terrible it was and asking if Lazlo knew anything. But when the man began cleaning the windshield, it was obvious by the speed with which he finished the windows and completed filling the tank, he had read the Russian words on the case. When Lazlo handed the ruble notes over, the attendant handled them with thumb and fore-finger, as if picking up a baby's diaper.

On their way out of Berdichev, Juli stayed hidden in the back seat while Lazlo stopped at a local market for some sausage and canned vegetables and fruit. Before going inside, he took off the white lab coat and put his own coat back on. He also turned Juli's overnight case so the lettering faced down.

"We'll have a picnic," said Lazlo, driving again.

"I can smell the sausage from here," said Juli from the back seat.

"I'll find a place where the car will be hidden from the road."

"What kind of car is this?"

"A Skoda. It's a Czech piece of shit. We'll see more of them as we head west."

"From back here it sounds like a dog growling."

"The muffler's right below you. I think it has a hole in it. That's why I'm keeping the windows open."

"How much longer do I have to stay back here?"

"Not long. We're almost out of town."

"Do you see our picnic grove yet?"

"No. But don't talk now. There's a militia car behind us."

In his mirror Lazlo saw only one man in the green and white Moskvich. He was certain it was a local militiaman because republic militiamen normally traveled in pairs. The Moskvich followed closely, the driver obviously trying to read the license plate. Although the registration was expired, Lazlo had smeared mud on that portion of the plate. But if the car was stolen, or if the man who sold it to him had reported it stolen instead of sold . . .

Railroad tracks ahead and a station to the left. Lazlo turned in, but the Moskvich followed. He parked near the station's passenger ramp, pretended to yawn so the militiaman would not see his mouth moving.

"Juli. Stay where you are and don't move. We're at a train station. I'll go in and pretend I'm waiting for someone."

"How long?"

"I don't know. Until I get rid of this fellow."

Lazlo rolled up the windows, got out of the car, and locked it. Then he walked up the passenger ramp, trying to look as casual as possible. He found out the next train wasn't due for a half hour. Outside the station, he saw the militiaman had gotten out of his Moskvich. The militiaman walked up to the Skoda and bent to look inside.

Don't move, Juli. Please don't move.

After looking inside the Skoda, the militiaman went to the back of the car, bent down to wipe at the license plate with his finger, stood and glanced to the station, then walked slowly back to his Moskvich. He did not drive away, but waited.

The stationmaster had a side business selling wine and bottled water. Lazlo bought two bottles of water and a bottle of wine and carried these back to the Skoda.

"I'm back," he whispered, pretending to examine the wine bottle label.

"Is the militia car still there?"

"Yes."

"What are you going to do?"

"We'll wait a while. His car is too fast to outrun in this piece of shit, and I don't want to pick a fight with anybody unless it's necessary."

"Why don't we keep driving?"

"He'll stop us before we get out of town."

"How do you know?"

"Because he's watching us. I don't think he's used his radio. It's a dull morning, and he has nothing better to do. An expired license plate is one thing, but being covered with mud . . . He'll stop us unless he gets another call."

"And if he simply sits there?"

"A train is due in half an hour. It's coming from Kiev so the engine and the lead cars will have to stop across the road. We'll get over the crossing before he does."

"Sounds dangerous," said Juli.

But what else could they do? If they tried to outrun the Moskvich, more militiamen would follow. The station was on the south end of town. If they could get out of town, perhaps embarrassing the militiaman in the Moskvich . . .

Lazlo handed the bottles of water and the wine bottle between the seats and had Juli secure them in back so they wouldn't roll around. After waiting in silence for twenty-five minutes, Lazlo heard the distant whistle. He reached out and started the car.

Juli whispered from the back seat. "I'm frightened, Laz."

"So am I. But listen. I'll turn right when we leave the station, away from the tracks. If he follows, I'll make a U-turn and go back before the train crosses the road. It won't be going fast, but we will. You might get bounced around."

When he saw the train appear from behind a warehouse building along the track, Lazlo estimated its speed and its rate of deceleration. He counted to twenty. He put the Skoda in gear and began moving forward, counting again.

One . . . two . . . three . . .

The Moskvich closed in behind him.

Four . . . five . . . six . . .

He turned right, back toward downtown Berdichev, and the Moskvich followed.

Seven . . . eight . . . nine . . .

In the rearview mirror, the locomotive appeared above the station-house roof.

Ten . . . eleven . . . twelve . . .

Five or six seconds to get back to the tracks once he turned.

Thirteen . . . fourteen . . .

Now!

He cranked the wheel left and pressed the accelerator to the floor. The Skoda spun about, its tires squealing, its engine sputtering and missing, but finally roaring like a snarling dog. He didn't bother shifting out of second gear and kept the accelerator pressed to the floor. In the mirror, the Moskvich was still turning around. Ahead, the train engine was beginning to cross the road, faster than he had estimated. Too fast! He wouldn't make it past the gate! Instead he aimed for the gate on the right, a hole to freedom ahead of the massive train engine, which now blasted its whistle.

"We'll make it, Juli!" he shouted.

The gate smashed into pieces and flew over the Skoda. The front of the locomotive to the left was a moving wall. When the Skoda flew over the tracks, Lazlo felt a slight sideways jump of the Skoda's tail like the skittering of a cat.

Behind him the Moskvich flashed its lights. But the flashing disappeared as the locomotive and the first few cars of the train filled the rearview mirror.

He couldn't believe it. They had escaped!

In the side mirror he saw a dent in the rear fender of the Skoda where the locomotive had touched them. A gentle touch for a locomotive, a good-luck kiss.

Lazlo could see the mountains ahead as he shifted the Skoda into high gear and pushed the accelerator to the floor. "You can come out now!" he shouted to Juli in the back seat.

By midday two Volgas sped up to the Kopelovo collective office. Five men got out, three of them spreading out and questioning farmers who had gathered. Another man stayed by the cars and watched the road through the village. The fifth man was Major Grigor Komarov, who went directly to the office of the collective chairman and was told the location of the Zimyanins' tent. When he left the office, Komarov summoned two of his men.

"What do others say about the Zimyanins?" asked Komarov.

"A man and woman claiming to be from the Opachichi collective near Pripyat," said one of the men. "The description matches Horvath and Popovics."

"A woman over there says they took the morning bus going to a collective farther south," said the other man. "She saw Mrs. Zimyanin leave with a small suitcase." The man pointed to the smoky yards behind the houses. "Their tent is the third one in over there."

Komarov sent the men ahead, ducking below a clothesline as he followed. The men drew pistols, and the sight of them entering the tent made Komarov laugh. The flare of the tent reminded him of the massive skirts worn by a Wagnerian Valkyries he'd seen at the opera. His wet-behind-the-ears men entering the tent bent over with pistols drawn were like adolescent boys sneaking a look beneath a woman's skirt. A toothless old man peeked out from another tent nearby. The old man grinned, his gums glistening pink in the morning sun. The entire scene, with campfires, tents, rundown houses, and peasants wandering about, *was* an opera.

Komarov laughed with the toothless old man until his own men came from the tent. Their pistols were put away, and one man shrugged his shoulders as the other spoke.

"They're gone."

"Of course, they're gone," said Komarov. "I expected them to be gone. But at least now we have a trail."

Komarov sent his men to the collective chairman's office, where there were two telephones his men were to use immediately. He ordered the bus heading south be searched by regional KGB personnel when it reached its destination and the passengers be thoroughly questioned. He ordered all militia offices within one hundred kilometers be contacted and given descriptions of Horvath and Popovics. He ordered the refugees and residents of the collective be informed they must tell all they know about the Zimyanins and their whereabouts or face penalties of noncooperation. Finally he ordered more men be sent from Kiev.

While his men used the phones at the collective office, Komarov went to the Zimyanin tent and went inside. An army blanket was spread on the floor of the tent. He kicked the blanket into a corner and found a slit cut into the floor. He reached through the slit and found the hard soil loosened. He poked around in the loosened soil. Nothing was there now, but it had recently been used as a hiding place.

After he searched the floor of the tent and found nothing, Komarov flipped the blanket over to see if anything had clung to it. The smell of damp wool was annoying, like sniffing beneath someone's clothing. He carefully spread the blanket across the floor, lit a cigarette, and sat down. When he examined the blanket more closely, he noticed bits of white thread clinging to the wool. There were long pieces and short pieces, thousands of them, as if a white garment had been reduced to its elements. One piece of thread was attached to a small square of white cloth. He also found several strands of long hair, and holding them up to the light coming through the tent ceiling, guessed they were brown.

If he expected to catch Horvath, he should begin thinking like him. Horvath the fugitive, escaping at Visenka and going back to Kiev, staying at the Hotel Dnieper within blocks of KGB and militia headquarters. Horvath the refugee, remaining for days in one place, living in a tent instead of running. Horvath doing the opposite of what one would expect.

Outside the tent, Komarov could hear children running about, pots banging together. He had been in the tent long enough for life in the camp to return to normal. Family life. He blew cigarette smoke at the ceiling of the tent, imagined he was Detective Horvath with Juli Popovics by his side. If he were Detective Horvath, he would find somewhere to leave Juli Popovics and go to the only place he could go under the circumstances. Komarov threw his lit cigarette out through the narrow opening at the tent flap. Outside, a man began complaining loudly about his precious roll of toilet paper being stolen.

Komarov stood and left the tent. He walked quickly to the collective chairman's office, waited for one of his men to finish a phone call, then called Captain Azef and ordered that extra men—no matter how green they were—be sent immediately to the Horvath family farm on the Ulyanov collective in the village of Kisbor near the Czechoslovakian frontier.

CHAPTER
28

Already four weeks after the Chernobyl accident, yet news from Radio Moscow seemed like the confessions of a naughty boy caught in the devious act. The boy would be silent, acting as if nothing had happened. Then, when someone pointed out the obvious, the boy would confess in a way that would implicate others. The spooning out of information caused anger in cities and lively meetings on collectives. Farmers wanted to help their fellow farmers in need, but they also wanted to be told the truth about the danger and the outlook for the future.

At a collective farm three hundred kilometers southwest of Kiev, an evening meeting was held in the living room of the chairman. The collective was small and far enough from Chernobyl so no Chernobylites had yet been sent there. The meeting had been called to tell collective committee members that the Agriculture Ministry had designated seven families be permanently relocated there. The committee argued about where the people would stay and who would build them houses. They argued about what jobs the new members would perform and whether one of them should be allowed on the committee. They argued about the small size of their school. One man on the committee wondered if the new members could bring radiation with them. A woman on the committee spoke against this, saying whatever harmful radiation the people received was locked in their bodies and would affect only them.

"The Chernobylites might have it in their clothing," said the man.

"These people are checked by technicians," said the woman. "If their clothes are radioactive, they get new ones. And quit calling them Chernobylites."

The man waved his hand at the woman. "If technicians told you the reactor never really blew up, I suppose you'd believe them."

"You're talking nonsense," said the woman.

"Ha! We might not be safe from radiation even here."

"How can you say that? Kiev is much closer. Kievians aren't dying."

"Not dying," said the man. "But they sent all their children to the Black Sea. I spoke with my cousin in Kiev. He said they have special milk only for children, and Kiev is building an aqueduct to bring fresh water into the city. One cannot escape radiation. In a year or two, we'll all be dying of cancer."

It was the woman's turn to wave her hand at the man. "You're a fool. How can you say such a thing? We have no radiation here! And you're a fool for talking about such things to your cousin in Kiev on the telephone!"

The man paused a moment and smiled to everyone on the committee before speaking. "If I'm such a fool, why did I see technicians at the pond today?"

"What pond?"

The man continued to smile. "We have only one pond on the farm, the very same pond where your favorite pigs are taken to drink."

The woman pretended to spit. "I have no favorite pigs, not even you!"

The chairman stood and asked for order. He told the man to tell about the technicians at the pond and to refrain from sarcasm.

"Very well," said the man. "I was on my way past the pond with a can of oil for our tractor, which burns more oil than gas, when I saw a car parked and a man and woman picnicking on a blanket. They looked like doctors, both wearing white coats. I said hello and thought I might get some advice about my arthritis. They said they weren't doctors but technicians checking for radiation. I asked if they found any. They said no."

"I told you," said the woman.

"But wait," said the man. "When I walked past their car, I managed a peek inside and saw a carrying case saying it contained dangerous radioactive samples."

"Ha," said the woman. "A carrying case talks to him."

"It didn't talk. Words were printed on it."

"What words?"

"It said, DANGER, RADIOACTIVE SAMPLES, in Russian. If they were carrying radioactive samples, they must have gotten them from here."

"They probably carry the case around in case they find radioactive samples," said the woman, looking to others for support. "Besides, you know very little Russian."

"So, tell me why they left the car to eat." Now the man looked to the others. "I'll tell you why. Because it's not good to eat around radiation. It gets inside and eats you from the inside out. It turns your cells against you. It's the worst cancer there is. And I know plenty of Russian."

"Describe these technicians," said the chairman.

"They weren't Ukrainian. I could tell by their accents. They could have been Russian or even Czech or Hungarian. Maybe Belarussian."

"Why Belarussian?" asked the chairman.

The man thought for a moment before answering. "Reports said radiation was very high in the Belarussian Republic to the north. Perhaps the technicians camped out here were on their way south to escape with samples from their own area. Technicians would know best about the cancer danger and would want to go south."

The mention of cancer and the description of technicians who might be fleeing Chernobyl radiation silenced the meeting, reinforcing the inevitability of damage already done. Many who would be affected by future disease were already impregnated. Except for having children drink potassium iodide the first few days after the accident, there was nothing anyone could do but pray their own cells would be strong enough to stave off the attack from within.

As far as the Chernobylite refugees were concerned, the committee members began seriously discussing where to house them and what jobs they could do on the farm.

Juli lay back on the pile of straw, aware of the warmth stored in the barn from the day's sun, and of its smells—livestock, leather, straw, and fresh paint. She looked up at the rafters, saw bird droppings on timbers darkened with age. One rafter was worn thinner at its center where a rope must have been tied, or many ropes wearing the wood away over decades. She wondered what the ropes had been for. She wondered if a rope tied to the rafter had ever been used to hang someone. They were in the Carpathian foothills, the Skoda having coughed and sputtered its way. The Czech and Hungarian frontiers were nearer, just across the northern range. They were already within the region of border disputes and turmoil, which took place during the last war. Perhaps the rafter above had been used for hanging dissenters. And now abandoned, with no other task, the barn awaited future hangings.

"Do you think we'll make it?" asked Juli.

Lazlo was in the center of the barn, putting the finishing touches on the car with a brush and a can of oily black paint he had found. "We'll make it. If anyone tries to catch us, they'll stick to our fly-paper."

"Isn't it drying?"

Lazlo dabbed at the roof. "Slowly. The part you did is only sticky now, not wet."

"Our little Skoda with a brand-new skin."

While Lazlo continued painting, Juli shook out the blankets they had taken from the Kopelovo collective and arranged them on the bed of straw near the stone wall at the back of the barn. Last night they had slept in the car. Tonight would be more comfortable. After the blankets were spread out, she stuffed straw beneath the bottom blanket at the end nearest the wall to form a wide pillow. When she finished making their bed, she took off her slacks and blouse and got under the top blankets. Lazlo was stooped behind the car and hadn't seen her undress. The lantern was aimed at the car, and their bed was in the dark corner against the wall.

Although the barn was in good condition, it seemed unused. Lazlo said it might be used to house livestock in the winter. It was some distance from the collective village and was probably left over from a time when one family owned the farm. Near the barn there was an overgrown foundation, which might have been a house before one of the wars.

Because the barn walls were made of stone, they were not worried about anyone seeing light through a crack. Earlier in the evening, after lighting the lantern, Lazlo went outside to make certain. To celebrate their find, they ate some of the food Lazlo had purchased at a local market. While eating, they took turns with the brush changing the Skoda from white to black. If someone questioned the last farmer who saw them today, he would say the technicians eating lunch by the pond had driven a white Skoda.

When Lazlo finished painting, he washed using the bucket of water drawn from the covered well outside. He sat inside the car using the mirror to shave with the razor he'd purchased back at Kopelovo. When he finished, he closed the car door, took off his shirt, dried his face with it, and hung it on a nail on a post. His shoulder holster and pistol also hung there. Finally he blew out the lantern, came to the dark alcove, and climbed into the bed of straw.

"How long have we known one another?" asked Juli.

"A thousand years," said Lazlo.

"Either clocks and calendars are all wrong, or we've gone mad," said Juli. "Which is it?"

"Both."

She pulled Lazlo to her, and they fell quickly into the momentary otherworld of not knowing what had happened or what could happen. She thought only of Lazlo, how she needed him and loved him. When he was inside her, she felt complete. Even if someone told her that in a few moments she would be tortured and hung from the rafter herself, it didn't matter because the momentary otherworld had opened, and she and Lazlo had tumbled into it.

After what seemed only a few moments of sleep, Lazlo awakened. Juli was in his arms, her head on his chest. Even though she had washed her hair several days earlier at Kopelovo, it still smelled sweet. He pushed his face deeper into Juli's hair and inhaled.

"What do you think about when you lie awake?" asked Juli.

"I thought you were asleep."

"And I thought you were. What do you think about?"

"About you. About us. About everything around us."

Juli turned her head on his chest and faced him. "It's a dilemma, isn't it? All these things happening around you, people depending on you even though you're the one in the most danger."

"You know I must go to Kisbor before I can cross the border. If I simply leave, I'm afraid Komarov will hurt Nina and the girls, and even Bela and Mariska."

"He's vindictive, one who can never forget?"

"Yes. It's his game. He knows I'll go to the farm because I know he'll go there. Going there will not guarantee their safety, but I can't leave Nina and the girls alone as long as Komarov is in power. I should have gone after him in Kiev instead of waiting for him to act."

"You sound like Mihaly."

"Perhaps I am Mihaly."

They were silent for a time, the only sounds their breathing and a mouse somewhere in the corner of the barn tunneling beneath straw. Juli broke the spell.

"How long will it take to get to Kisbor?" she asked.

"It's a few hours' drive across the northern range. The Hungarian frontier is only about a hundred kilometers away. Kisbor is another hundred northwest at the edge of the steppes. When we were boys, Mihaly and I sometimes worked in fields near the frontier when other collectives needed help during the harvest. Last June on holiday, I told Mihaly we would have been better off staying on the farm. We were in the wine cellar. The cemetery's not far from the house. The wine cellar's about as deep as a grave, and I can't help wondering if Mihaly had been predicting his death. There we were down in the ground . . . we even spoke about how I used to be frightened that dead people from the cemetery visited for a drink now and then . . ."

Lazlo paused, and when Juli remained silent, he knew it was time to tell her about the deserter he'd killed on the Romanian border when he was a boy soldier. He told of the snowy day, he and Viktor leaving the army truck with their rifles. He told of their officers' anger at Khrushchev's Cuban missile fiasco, taking revenge anywhere they could. He told of the silenced violin in the village, the pistol in the violin case, the boy deserter shooting Viktor, his own rifle aimed, the trigger pulled, the blood exploding from the deserter's face, the mother and sister screaming. He told of the return visit with his captain, the sister's eyes as she stared at him, and finally his baptism with the name Gypsy, the name taken from the deserter he had murdered.

"I was going to tell Mihaly about the deserter, but he is gone. So now I have told you."

Juli hugged Lazlo to her. "You used the word *murderer*. Promise me you will never use it again. I saw what happened in Visenka. I saw the agent aim the pistol at us. You are not a murderer, Lazlo! Never, never use the word again!"

Juli held him tightly for a long time, long enough for him to shed a decade of tears. She wiped the tears away with her hands and with her lips as they kissed. They lay together in silence until Juli spoke.

"My father wanted me to be a doctor. He said lots of women were becoming doctors. He said women were better at healing. When I didn't become a doctor, I felt I had disappointed my father. The past is gone. Even if you had stayed on the farm and I had become a doctor, we might still be running away together."

"We're not in control," said Lazlo. "We feel we're in control from minute to minute or even from day to day, but in the end, destiny rules. My destiny is to guarantee nothing happens to Nina and the girls."

"We're back where we started," said Juli.

"The dilemma."

"Yes."

They lay silent again, listening to the mouse in the corner. During the silence, Lazlo kept visualizing the farmhouse, the yard, the exact placement of trees, the position of the wine cellar in relation to the house, the border of the private plot at the back. Since it was spring, there would be no tall crops to hide among. Then he remembered the lazy afternoons beneath the chestnut tree, Anna and Ilonka and Mariska's baby playing, the cover over the wine cellar a make-believe tabletop. Perhaps they had set their make-believe table again. If they did, if they had placed a tablecloth over the entrance, who would know it was a wine cellar? Even when it wasn't covered, it looked like a discarded box or the cover of an old well. If necessary, it would be a place to hide, or to hide others, Nina and Anna and Ilonka.

"Are you asleep, Juli?"

"No."

"You know I must go to Kisbor right away."

"I'll go with you."

"No. I'll go alone."

"Part of Mihaly is in me. His wife and children are in danger. I'm going. After we're finished, we'll go to Budapest. They have a renowned radiation clinic there."

"You seem to have our plans all in order."

"Will we drive to Kisbor tomorrow?"

Lazlo kissed Juli's neck.

"Laz, you can't stop me from going."

"We'll go tomorrow."

Lazlo lowered his head and kissed Juli's breasts. Again, for a few minutes, they left the world of destiny and dilemma in which they were trapped.

CHAPTER 29

While Nikolai anticipated another long night at the Horvath farm-house, a caravan of three Volgas and a van raced up the hill from the village of Kisbor. The dusk had been peaceful and cool, but now tires on gravel and stones against fender wells sliced the evening apart like an ax. A cloud of dust followed behind the caravan as it skidded to a stop in front of the farmhouse.

A dozen men piled out of the cars and the van. The four from the van carried AKM assault rifles with folding stocks. They were young recruits, wearing determined looks on their faces as they slipped the AKM straps over their shoulders and spread out around the house. The men from the Volgas headed for Nikolai. Except for Major Komarov and Captain Brovko, Nikolai had never seen any of them before. All but Komarov and Brovko were young, like the men from the van.

Nikolai stepped off the stone path to the front door as the group marched past. The only one who looked at him was Captain Brovko, who raised his eyebrows slightly with a puzzled expression. Major Komarov did not acknowledge Nikolai's presence.

Nikolai imagined how crowded it must be in the small farmhouse with the family and eight more men inside. But soon five young recruits marched out, shouldered their AKMs, and took up positions around the house with the other four. The men spread out in all directions, the farthest being a hundred meters away, where he stooped down and disappeared into the weeds.

In a little while, Captain Brovko came out, told Nikolai to maintain his post on the front path and not to stray because of the other men. Then Brovko went back into the house. Nikolai did not stray, afraid to move after dark for fear one of the new men would empty an AKM in him. But finally, tired of standing in the path with no support, Nikolai walked backward slowly to the house. Once there, he leaned against the wall, feeling somewhat relieved. If Detective Horvath came now, there would be many others for him to confront besides Nikolai Nikolskaia.

At ten o'clock, after the muffled sounds of voices had ceased coming from the house, it was quieter than previous nights because the night bugs, disturbed by men in the weeds, were silent. Nikolai leaned against the front wall of the farmhouse, trying to imagine how men out in the weeds must seem to bug-sized brains. To bug brains, life was simpler. One was either alive or dead, either well-fed or on the verge of starvation, either free to move about or about to be eaten. Perhaps the world of men was not much different.

At eleven o'clock, the front door of the house opened. Captain Brovko came out and motioned for Nikolai to follow. They sat in the captain's Volga parked at the front of the other Volgas. The captain's clothing smelled smoky, and Nikolai remembered Komarov was a heavy smoker.

"What do you think of all this?" asked Brovko.

"I was wondering what the local militia thinks," said Nikolai. "I haven't seen a militiaman since we've been here."

"Ordinarily one would assume the local militia would supply manpower for an operation like this. Major Komarov has a special interest in the case, as well as connections in Moscow. It's become embarrassing."

"Embarrassing?"

"Yes, Nikolai. For several hours, I watched Major Komarov question these poor people. The adults have taken it well. They are frightened, but not for themselves. They are frightened for the children. I detest situations like this."

"I thought you were trained as an interrogator."

"I am accustomed to questioning those who have either done something wrong or who are hiding facts about those who have done something wrong."

"Are you saying Detective Horvath did nothing wrong?" asked Nikolai.

"What do you think?"

"I'm sorry, Captain. This is the way our conversation began."

"Very well, Nikolai. I understand your hesitation to speak openly. I'm not asking you to condemn Major Komarov. And I'm not using interrogation techniques to trick you."

Nikolai looked out at the dim light coming through the curtains at the windows of the house. Beyond the house he saw the shadow of one of the men move behind the house. The man had been outlined for a moment against the light from the village of Kisbor. In the hotel in the village was a bed he wished he were in right now. But Captain Brovko was waiting for his reply, seemingly anxious to criticize the actions of Major Komarov.

"One month ago," said Nikolai, "I was a PK officer in the town of Pripyat. My partner, Pavel, and I spent our days in the back room of the Pripyat post office reading incoming and outgoing mail. Mostly it was dull—how the weather was, how crops were doing. Patience was part of our training. Pavel and I were good at our work. He knew Hungarian, and I knew Ukrainian.

"Then the reactor at Chernobyl exploded and everything was in turmoil. Instead of doing what we were trained to do, Pavel and I were told to keep an eye on workers from the Chernobyl plant. It was obvious the smart ones like Juli Popovics were getting the hell out of there. Instead of staying around to keep watch on not-so-smart workers, Pavel and I followed Juli Popovics out of Pripyat. Two birds with one stone, as they say. Follow Juli Popovics, who is under 'official observation,' and get the hell away from the radiation.

"What we did not expect was to be given pistols and a Volga and told to act like agents trained to do something other than read mail. We were not trained for the confrontation with Detective Horvath. If I could live it again, I would have taken the pistol away from Pavel."

"A man should never aim a pistol at another unless he is ready to use it," said Brovko. "Everything would have turned out differently if your partner had pulled the trigger first."

"He would have missed," said Nikolai. "He was a poor shot."

"Did Major Komarov know this?"

"He had our files, our training records. Not only was Pavel a poor shot, anyone who studied his record would have concluded he wasn't the best person to put in a dangerous situation. Pavel was my friend, Captain. I knew him better than anyone except, perhaps, his wife. But there were things even his wife didn't know. There were incidents from KGB school, incidents documented in Pavel's training record . . ."

"Did Komarov tell Pavel Detective Horvath was dangerous?"

"I've thought about this endlessly since Pavel's death. I've come

391

to the conclusion Pavel had been indoctrinated. He was in a state of tension after meeting with Major Komarov. The major did not simply tell Pavel Detective Horvath was dangerous. He wanted something to happen. What he did not want was a clean capture or an escape without incident. Putting Detective Horvath in deeper trouble was the goal. It didn't matter whether Detective Horvath or Pavel died . . . or me."

"I appreciate your honesty with me, Nikolai."

"Will you arrest me for insubordination now?"

Captain Brovko laughed. "No. If I did, you could deny it, or repeat what I said earlier about Major Komarov's interrogation of the family in there. He even quizzed the little girls, repeatedly asking them about Uncle Lazlo. No, Nikolai, your secret is safe with me."

Captain Brovko turned in his seat, spoke more quietly. "I should tell you two of my men located Juli Popovics' roommate and her boyfriend, who drove her to Kiev. From what they said, Juli Popovics does not sound like the type who would be involved in sabotage. And from my discussions with Kiev militia personnel, Detective Horvath does not seem the type who would murder past associates."

"Did Detective Horvath kill someone besides Pavel?"

"A man and woman who had contact with Detective Horvath were recently murdered in Kiev. A female friend of Horvath named Tamara Petrov and a male informant. Major Komarov insists Horvath committed the murders while on the run. Both were killed with a knife, the man's throat slit and the woman stabbed viciously in the abdomen. Does any of this sound familiar, Nikolai?"

"I knew nothing about it. If Detective Horvath murdered these people, everything I said is wrong."

"You change your opinion easily, Nikolai. I didn't say anything about it being proven that Detective Horvath committed the murders."

"I thought you were trying to trick me."

"The only trick here is getting to the truth while carrying out my orders. I'm concerned about all these young men with AKMs and Stechkin machine pistols. I'm concerned that you and I were both sent here when it seemed we had disappointed Major Komarov."

"The men I arrived with say Major Komarov is a powerful man who puts duty above all else," said Nikolai. "They say he gained power many years ago by pursuing and killing a fellow officer wanted for murder. Have you heard of the incident, Captain?"

"It was called the Sherbitsky affair. I researched it before Deputy Chairman Dumenko assigned me to assist Major Komarov. My research into Major Komarov's past is what prompted this conversation."

"What shall we do?" asked Nikolai.

Captain Brovko leaned closer. His voice took on a threatening tone. "Perhaps you do not understand about speculation, Nikolai Nikolskaia. I said nothing about taking action."

"But, Captain, I didn't mean . . ."

Captain Brovko grasped Nikolai's arm. "As KGB officers, we are not in a position to question orders. We will follow Major Komarov's orders until the orders are overridden. And you, Nikolai Nikolskaia, will repeat this conversation to no one until the time comes!"

When Nikolai resumed his position at the front of the house, the damp chill of night invaded the space between his clothing and his perspiring skin. He wondered if, somewhere, a bullet in a magazine already had his name on it. After a little while, Captain Brovko started the Volga and ran the engine to use the heater. The steam from the Volga's exhaust rose and hovered above the road like ground fog, the fog, local legend said, was the last breath of someone who had recently died.

The farmer's name was Bela Sandor, Detective Horvath's cousin, a shorter, more red-faced fellow. The house smelled of cabbage until Komarov smoked a few cigarettes, making the buxom wife, Mariska, sneeze repeatedly. The Sandors were plump and dressed like typical collective farmers, the woman even wearing slacks beneath her dress. In contrast to these two was Nina Horvath, who was slender and wore tight blue jeans and a bulky sweater to keep warm in the drafty old house.

There were two rooms and an inside bathroom. Nina Horvath's daughters and the Sandors' baby were asleep in the smaller bedroom. The larger room was a combination living, dining, and kitchen area. A short while ago, Bela Sandor drew a large curtain resembling an old blanket across the center of the room, leaving Komarov alone in the kitchen area. Komarov sat at the table, staring at the blank television screen just on his side of the curtain. Despite an occasional cough from Bela and sneeze from Mariska, he lit another cigarette and wondered about the sleeping arrangements of the Gypsies on the other side of the curtain.

Komarov stood, walked to a cabinet next to the television, and opened it. The top shelf was filled with unlabeled bottles of wine, the rotgut Bela Sandor used to paint his face red. In the center of the cabinet was a phonograph and a stack of records. Komarov flipped through the records. All were Hungarian, Gypsy music, the album covers with photographs of men and women in ridiculous multicolored attire. One album showed a photograph of a man in a bushy mustache throwing twisted circular bread loaves onto the ground for a woman in a full skirt and boots to dance around. The woman reminded him of Mariska Sandor, who had just released a barrage of sneezes behind the curtain. The man on the album cover had a red and green handkerchief around his neck and reminded him of the Gypsy landlord who had killed his father.

Komarov closed the cabinet and returned to the table. While he sat smoking, he heard what sounded like wheezing coming from behind the curtain. Soon the wheezing changed to a snore. After the questioning this evening, Bela Sandor had taken a half-filled bottle of wine from the table and gone behind the curtain with it. When Komarov could stand the snoring no longer, he put on his coat and went out the front door into the cool night air.

Nikolai Nikolskaia, on guard at the door, stared at him with eyes wide.

"Go inside and keep guard until someone relieves you," said Komarov.

"Yes, Major."

Komarov joined Captain Brovko in his Volga. They sat silently, the Volga's heater blowing warm air over their faces. During this silence, Komarov wondered what Brovko might be thinking, wondered if Brovko knew it was he who had taken the blame for the fiasco at the Hotel Dnieper.

"Because of the necessity to question those in the house, I did not have the opportunity to speak with you earlier, Captain."

"We have the opportunity now, Major."

Komarov lit a cigarette, lowered his window slightly, and blew the smoke outside. "The militia found the crook who sold Horvath a car in Korostyshev. Two days ago, the car was seen in Berdichev. Due to the ineptness of the local militia, Horvath escaped by outrunning a train. Yesterday, a man and woman said to be radiation technicians were seen by farmers in Kolomya. They were seen again later in the day by more farmers. Idiot farmers and idiot local militia who fail to communicate with one another when specific orders were given to apprehend the pair! In any case, the man and woman we must assume as being Horvath and Popovics were seen traveling west on the road to Yasinya in the mountains. Their car had changed from white to black, but the pair fits the description."

"If they crossed the mountains, they might be in Romania or Hungary by now," said Brovko.

"They will come here, Captain. Or at least Horvath will come. Deputy Chairman Dumenko agreed to have Nina Horvath sent here in order to guarantee it. This farm is where the cousin, Andrew Zukor, met with the Horvaths. Therefore, Nina Horvath may be involved. The supposed affair between Mihaly Horvath and Juli Popovics may be part of a larger scheme."

Captain Brovko paused some time before commenting. "What will you do if Detective Horvath doesn't come?"

"That is for me to decide, with Deputy Chairman Dumenko's assistance, of course."

"Of course," said Brovko.

Komarov detected sarcasm in Brovko's voice but felt it would serve no purpose to question him. Instead he asked to borrow a flashlight.

"Be careful of the recruits, Major. They might mistake you for Horvath." More sarcasm?

"I'll keep the flashlight on so they can see me, Captain."

Komarov left the Volga, turned on the flashlight, and circled the house. The lights from the village were cut off by a hill so only the top windows of a few buildings were visible. Perhaps this is where Horvath would make his approach, the hill hiding him until he is within a few hundred meters. Komarov scanned the yard with the flashlight. Near the house beneath a tall tree was a fire pit and a few rusted cooking forks stuck into the ground. Near the fire pit was a tree stump with a rusted ax embedded in it. Upon closer inspection, he saw blood on the stump and realized this was where chickens were beheaded. Farther out in the yard was a wooden box shaped like a small coffin. A tattered tablecloth was over the box, and broken utensils and tin plates were placed neatly. A child's game. The little girls already pretending they are mothers.

It was quiet here. Komarov closed his eyes, breathed the cool night air, and remembered his own yard, his porch, a place in which he was alone with his thoughts of the old days in the GDR and of Gretchen and success. When he thought of Tamara Petrov, especially the way she stared into his eyes after she'd spit in his face, Komarov realized he had an erection. Komarov opened his eyes, turned to the house, and imagined Horvath sneaking up at night like the Gypsy landlord sneaking up on his father after the night at the opera.

As he walked back to the house, Komarov remembered the phonograph and the Gypsy records. How fitting it would be to greet Horvath with the melodies of his ancestors.

Before he went into the house, Komarov turned and saw in the distance the shadow of a man outlined against the lights of the village. The man turned slightly, and the outline of his AKM was visible for an instant. Then the man stooped back down and disappeared.

Komarov lit a cigarette and entered the house.

CHAPTER 30

At dawn, in a field not far from the village of Kisbor, a black Skoda flecked with bits of straw sat in a ravine. From the dirt road bordering the field, the Skoda could not be seen because of the ravine's depth. One would have needed an aircraft to spot the Skoda, and it would have looked like a derelict because of its dull black finish and the dust and dirt and straw covering it.

So he would not have to go out into the morning chill to change, Juli helped Lazlo put on the ragged peasant clothing they had stolen from a clothesline during the night.

"Remember," said Lazlo, "if I'm not back by three o'clock tomorrow morning, you leave for the Czech border."

"I remember. But it wouldn't hurt to wait a little longer. I can stay here for days with the groceries you bought in Yasinya. So there's really no reason for me to hurry off."

Lazlo stopped buttoning his shirt and stared at her. "Three o'clock, Juli."

"I don't want you to have to hurry, Laz. I'll wait a little longer."

Lazlo picked up the trousers he had removed, took the sock out of the pocket, and handed it to Juli. "The rest of the money is in here. Enough rubles to bribe a guard. The road west of here parallels the frontier. Go to the first guard post to the north. Ask the guard for directions to Uzhgorod. Once he gives you directions, ask if he knows where Laborets Castle is. If he launches into a lecture about how Prince Laborets was murdered in the year 903, bring out half the money."

"How do you know all this, Laz?"

"Yesterday in Yasinya I bribed the woman in the market."

"How did you know she was a contact and not an informer?"

"Tamara."

"We owe Tamara a lot. If Nina and the girls are with you when you return tonight, will there be enough bribe money for all of us?"

"I don't know," said Lazlo.

"Why don't you take back some of the money in case you need to use it later?"

"I'm hoping I won't have to bring Nina and the girls with me. If there is no Komarov, there will no longer be danger for Nina."

"You'll kill him."

"If I can."

"What if he's not there?"

"He'll be there. He's put his reputation on the line, even sacrificing his own men to make us into suspects. Now he must protect his interests. And he must do it personally so no one will uncover what he's done."

"You don't think higher officials are involved?"

"If others were involved, news coming out about Chernobyl would be different. They'd be talking sabotage, piling up evidence."

Juli held out the sock containing the money. "Don't make me take all the money, Laz. Take half. We'll meet somewhere on the other side."

Lazlo squeezed her hand around the money. "I can't. I don't

know if it's enough for two. If I don't come back by three in the morning, you've got to go. I'll still meet you on the other side."

Juli felt tears in her eyes. "Why didn't you simply tell me you kept half the money?"

Lazlo held her shoulders and shook her. "Because I can't lie to you. And you can't lie to me, Juli! I've got to leave for the farm knowing at least your freedom is guaranteed! The woman in Yasinya said you can't go to the guard post once it's light out. You must leave here at three!"

When Lazlo left the Skoda, Juli lowered the dew-soaked window and watched him climb the ravine and walk along the rim. In the brimmed hat, loose-fitting trousers, and tattered coat, he looked like one of the farmers at the Kopelovo collective where she wished they could have stayed and lived together in the tent forever.

Before disappearing beyond the edge of the ravine, Lazlo turned once and waved. The sun was beginning to rise in the east. A new day was born. Juli held her abdomen and wept.

Finding the workers of the Ulyanov collective farm was a matter of elimination, a matter of finding unplanted fields and locating the mechanical planters. Because the collective was several kilometers across, it took Lazlo most of the morning to locate the planters. Cousin Bela was a mechanic and was always in the vicinity of equipment that had to be kept running.

From a ditch at the edge of the field, Lazlo watched three planters traverse the field, sometimes abreast, sometimes one or the other pulling ahead. After watching the planters for an hour, they finally passed close enough for him to recognize Bela aboard one of the tractors.

It was eleven o'clock. A truck carrying seed for the planters was at one end of the field. Lazlo had seen workers stop at the truck for water and knew they would eventually go there for lunches they brought with them. On his way to the end of the field, he saw a woman standing on the platform of a planter. She was thin and wore a brightly colored skirt over trousers. She reminded him of the previous week at the Kopelovo collective, how Juli had looked when she dressed this way, her long brown hair coming out from her kerchief and blowing in the wind as she bent to join him in the tent after an afternoon at the washtub with other women. The simplicity of the image made his eyes water as he crawled along the ditch.

Shortly before noon, the tractors turned the three planters around, the engines shut off, and farmers converged on the truck. As Lazlo wondered how he would be able to speak with Bela in private, Bela walked out to one of the tractors and peered into the engine compartment. Lazlo knew he might not have another chance. He stood and walked quickly out to the tractor.

Lazlo lifted his brimmed hat as he approached. "Bela. It's me, Lazlo."

"Lazlo! I didn't recognize you. How did you get here? Have you been to the house?"

"No."

"Don't go there. They're waiting for you."

"Hey!" shouted one of the men near the truck. "Who's the idler out there?"

Bela stood in front of Lazlo and shouted back, "It's Lajos from the Kalinin collective! He needs mechanical advice!"

"Hello, Lajos!" shouted the man.

Lazlo waved but kept his head down.

"Come behind the tractor," said Bela.

They stooped behind the tractor, Bela peering through the open engine compartment until he was satisfied no one was coming.

"They hate Lajos," said Bela. "No one wants to hear his constant complaining. If you shake your fist like this occasionally, you will look the part."

Bela shook his fist. Lazlo repeated the gesture.

"Good," said Bela. "I ask again, how did you get here?"

"By car, back roads to the south, then over the mountains at Yasinya. What's important is that I'm here. Tell me what's going on at the house."

Bela shook his head sadly. "It's the KGB, Lazlo. At least a dozen men spread about the place. During the last few days, there were only a few, but last night a major arrived with all these men armed with automatic rifles."

"Komarov?"

"Yes, Major Komarov, back there at the farm with Mariska and Nina and the girls."

"Has Komarov questioned any of you?"

"All of us. He's a demon from hell, Lazlo. I'm trying to make Mariska and Nina think everything will be fine, but I'm frightened of what he'll do. I wanted to stay home, but he insisted I go to the fields as usual."

"He didn't send a man to watch you?"

Bela peered through the tractor's engine compartment. "Shake your fist at me."

"What?"

"Shake your fist so the others will be satisfied you are Lajos."

Lazlo shook his fist. A slight breeze blew the scent of hot oil from the tractor's engine compartment across his face as he looked to make certain no one was coming.

"Lunch is almost over," said Bela. "What are you going to do?"

"Quickly, Bela, tell me about the other men, the ones who arrived earlier and the ones there now. Komarov is a madman, and I need to know how loyal the men are to him."

Bela watched to be sure no one was coming while he spoke. "The first group arrived a week ago. They didn't question us at all, simply said they'd been assigned to guard duty. We knew they were looking for you because of what Nina told us. Poor Mihaly." Bela grasped Lazlo's arm. "I nearly forgot."

"There's nothing we can do for Mihaly now, Bela. The men. Tell me about them."

"At first there were only three, then three more and a captain. During the week they took turns guarding the house three at a time. One in front, one in back, and one inside. There's still one man inside with us day and night. Except last night it was Komarov with his cigarettes stinking the place up. The men Komarov brought with him are stationed outside, at least a dozen, all of them young and fired up.

"It's hard to say how loyal the men are to Komarov. The first men seemed amateur, friendly enough fellows except they carry these enormous automatic pistols beneath their coats. They wouldn't tell us anything. Then a captain named Brovko arrived. He spoke a lot more. He wanted to know about you and Mihaly. He asked about the farm and your mother and father and even Cousin Zukor's visit last summer. But it was all in a friendly way, not the way Komarov asks questions. In fact, one evening before Komarov arrived, two of the men played cards with me. And while we played . . . you know how you can tell about a fellow when he's playing cards."

"What did you find out?"

"These men don't understand why they were put on guard in and around the house instead of simply watching the road. And something else, something they didn't say but I could tell by their reaction whenever his name came up. They despise Komarov. At least the men who arrived earlier. And Captain Brovko . . . the second in command since Komarov arrived . . . he wonders why Komarov is after you with such vengeance. I watched his eyes. I watched him while Komarov interrogated us. You can tell a lot by watching eyes. Mariska's mother often told us about the old days when she was a fortune-teller. I know this is important, Laz."

Bela peered through the engine compartment and continued. "The men who arrived last night with Komarov haven't been in the house, so I'm not sure about them. But on my way to the bus this morning, I passed one who was stooped down in the weeds along the road. When he saw me he frowned, motioning his back ached. When they arrived with Komarov, they were full of spunk. But this morning, the one I met didn't look happy with the situation. I have a feeling all the men feel this way. They arrive ready to fight, but there is no fight. The only men with enthusiasm are Komarov and Brovko. But their enthusiasm goes in opposite directions. While Komarov is intent on . . . I have to say it, Laz, he wants to kill you, and he wants to discredit you. He hates us for being related to you. While Komarov is this way, Brovko seems intent on finding out about Komarov's motives. I don't think Komarov will simply go away if you don't come. He was hard on Nina last night. When Brovko went outside, Komarov struck her. And when I went at him, he pulled a knife from his pocket and held it to Nina's throat."

Through the engine compartment, Lazlo saw a worker walking out to one of the other tractors. While Bela spoke, Lazlo tried to imagine going to the house after dark, tried to remember a way he and Mihaly might have snuck up on the house when they were boys. But, except for the cover of darkness, he could remember no safe approach to the house because of the way it was situated on the hill.

"We have to hurry, Bela. How many men are out at night, and where?"

"Usually one out front, either by the door or sitting in a car.

Always one in back. From what I saw this morning, the men who arrived last night circle the house at a one-hundred- to two-hundred-meter radius. So it's one man in the house, probably Komarov if he stays the night again, two men immediately outside, and at least seven or eight out in the weeds. The man I saw this morning was on the south edge of the road where the hill starts down to the village."

Bela grabbed Lazlo's arm. "They're coming! What are you going to do?"

The workers began walking out into the field. A man and woman sang a Hungarian folk song. "Geraniums in my window, come to my window."

"Bela, if I kill Komarov, will the other men leave you and Mariska and Nina in peace?"

"I don't know the answer to that, Laz. But we must do something."

"I'll come to the house tonight," said Lazlo, shaking his fist and meaning it. "I'll come at ten o'clock. You'll be in bed if he lets you. Wait! The wine cellar! Do they know about the wine cellar?"

"The wine cellar. No. The children were playing on the cover. It's got a tablecloth on it."

"Listen, Bela. Before ten o'clock, see if you can get the women and children down there."

"How? There's a guard in the back."

"What if they go out the side bedroom window?"

"Yes," said Bela. "They'll go out the side window, and I'll run out the back door to keep the guard busy. Somehow, I'll get to the back door! It's up to us, Laz!" Bela motioned across the field. "Go now. Hurry before someone recognizes you. If I'm unable to get the women out, I'll leave the bedroom window closed. If they get out, I'll leave the window open. You enter the house through the window. Do you have a gun?"

Lazlo opened his coat to reveal his Makarov in the coat pocket.

"I'll shoot Komarov. If I'm successful, guards will converge. Don't try to help me. Tell them you didn't want anyone hurt so you sent the women and children to the cellar. If I'm not successful . . . if Komarov survives, don't say anything about the cellar, no matter what."

"I understand, Laz. Go now."

As Lazlo walked across the field, he shook his fist in the air without turning back. One of the workers yelled out, "Good-bye, Lajos, my friend! It was pleasant speaking with you!"

Lazlo shook his fist once more, then walked south on the dirt road in the direction of the Kalinin collective where Lajos lived. While he walked, Lazlo felt the weight of his pistol bouncing against his chest. Because he had left the shoulder holster behind at the Hotel Dnieper, the pistol hung loosely in the pocket of the musty old coat. Behind him tractor engines started, and the task of spring planting resumed.

To avoid being seen, he bypassed the village, taking a long circular route to the hill on which his boyhood home waited. It was at least a ten-kilometer walk on plowed fields. He stopped frequently to scan the horizon for men or vehicles on the dirt roads bordering the fields. The sky was clear, the sun baking the turned earth creating a fragrance he recalled from boyhood. He took off the coat as he walked and put his pistol into his belt.

If it was clear tonight, it would be cool again, the sky blanketed with stars. He thought of the moon, thought back quickly to the previous night with Juli in the Skoda, remembered trying to see her as they embraced in the dark. There was no moon last night, and there would be no moon tonight. The men out in the weeds would huddle down, trying to keep warm. Unless a storm came, it would be quiet. The weeds, brittle from winter, would sound like dry twigs underfoot.

Lazlo stayed well away from several farmhouses he passed as he worked his way to the family farm. At one point a mongrel dog from one of the farms chased him, making a sound like the Skoda when it had barely outrun the train. Rather than be seen by the woman who came out of the farmhouse to see what the dog was after, Lazlo lay down in the weeds and prepared to defend himself. He found a broken fence board partially buried in the ground and poked at the dog, keeping it at a safe distance. But the dog would not give up and kept howling at him. Finally, after the dog bit into his shoe, he whacked the dog on the head and sent it whining back to the farmhouse, where the woman in the yard scolded it for chasing the neighbor's vicious cats.

It would have been good to be a cat or to be able to change into whatever animal suited the situation. Lazlo the vampire. He was not being foolish. He was doing what he had always done when trying to solve a difficult case in Kiev. In his mind he would consider all possibilities, no matter how impossible they might seem. Burrowing through the dry weeds on all fours, in much the same manner as a cat, he kept his mind open, letting the ideas flow freely without interference from negative thoughts. Now, more than ever, he dare not brood. Now he had to think and plan as if he were a predator on the verge of starvation.

At approximately three hundred meters from the house, Lazlo found a spot from which he could observe the back and sides of the house without being seen. He was in a clump of weeds bordering the back of the neatly plowed private plot. He had followed the border of weeds to this spot and knew he could go no farther without being seen.

Without the aid of binoculars, he had to squint to see the area surrounding the house clearly. For a while he saw only one man standing near the back door. But as he waited and stared and studied the area for movement, he saw another man off to the village side on the downslope of the hill. Then he saw a third man at the other end of the house, near the chicken coop, and a fourth man in back at the far end of the private plot. This man was only about two hundred meters away, and he could see his AKM with its skinny folding stock. The guard looked young. He was smoking, blowing the smoke at the ground to dissipate it. Lazlo recalled Mihaly speaking of the workers at the Chernobyl plant. "Too many cooks in the kitchen," and "Overmanning." Was the same true here?

Lazlo looked at his watch, almost four o'clock. In a few minutes, he had seen four men spaced about the house. In three or four hours, it would be dark and perhaps he could get closer. In less than six hours, Bela would try to get the women into the wine cellar. He could see the cover of the wine cellar, the red and white tablecloth on it, probably the same tattered oilcloth the girls had used last summer.

Lazlo looked at his watch again, exactly four o'clock. In eleven hours, Juli would leave for the west. He tried to imagine succeeding and going with her, but negative thoughts piled up against the dream like water against a dam. Beyond the house, where he could not see, he knew his mother and father were buried in the cemetery. The most negative of thoughts was that soon he, and others, might be there.

Because of the sun's heat and the long wait ahead, Lazlo worked his way back a hundred meters or so to a well he had passed. The well was near where the dog had attacked him, but the dog was apparently being kept inside. After drinking his fill from a battered tin pail dipped into the well using a long rope, he worked his way back to his original position. This time a striped cat crossed his path, raising its back and hissing. Lazlo responded by raising his own back and hissing. The cat reacted by slinking off into the weeds. Yes, now he was an animal.

Back at his position, where he had a clear view of the farmhouse, he lay on his back to wait. A jetliner passed overhead, its vapor trail dividing the sky. The jet headed southwest, to Budapest or Vienna, anywhere but here. He watched the jet until it disappeared beyond the horizon. Then he sat up to watch the house again and saw yet another man with an AKM walk around from front to back. In a little while, he would close his eyes until sunset, not to rest, but to prepare his night vision.

When Juli heard what sounded like a truck up on the road, she left the Skoda, locking it and taking her bag with her. She hid in a crevice at the far end of the ravine. She had been watching a jet pass overhead when the truck approached. Now, as she lay flat in the crevice, she could hear the voices of two men.

At first the men argued about the age of the car, one saying it only looked old because of the terrible paint job. After a few minutes of inspecting the car and arguing about its worth, the men lowered their voices, and Juli could hear only occasional words. One said something about reporting it to the militia. The other apparently wanted to wait. As the two men walked away, they seemed to be discussing whether or not the car might belong to them if no one claimed it. One said he thought he might go back and take the windshield-wiper blades. The other said no, they might as well wait a few days when they could strip anything they wanted off the car because it was obviously abandoned. The first man mumbled something about it being strange that an abandoned car be locked, and wondered what might be hidden beneath the blanket they'd seen on the back seat. While the men were climbing out of the ravine, the last discussion Juli could hear was about the value of the car's parts. Then the truck started up and drove away.

When Juli went back to the car, the sun had made it quite warm inside. She sipped from a water bottle that had stayed cool beneath the blanket in the back seat. The wine Lazlo bought at the train station was also there, but she left it unopened. She lowered the windows and sat, as she had earlier, listening for sounds on the road and thinking about the future, but also about the past. She thought of her friend Aleksandra. Recalled the farm wife waiting at the hospital. Aleksandra and the farm wife possessed sincerity. It was in their eyes. Honest women trying to do the right thing in an insane world. Really, they were a lot like Lazlo.

Inside the hot car down in the ravine, Juli kept watch to be certain no one approached. As she waited, she drank water and ate the remaining food Lazlo had purchased in order to keep up her strength for whatever awaited her. There were still many hours to go, and she had not decided what she would do if three o'clock came and Lazlo had not returned.

CHAPTER 31

It was a typical evening in the Ukrainian village of Kisbor south of Uzhgorod near the Czechoslovakian frontier. Ulyanov and Kalinin collective farm workers had returned from the fields. Market workers and workers at the local bell factory had closed shop for the night. By nine o'clock, dinner dishes were put away, and Kisbor's citizens settled in favorite chairs or reclined in bed to watch a weekly variety show. Every television viewer in Kisbor awaited the same show on the same channel, not because they all preferred this particular show, but because there was only one television station available in Kisbor.

The male announcer's voice coming from houses and apartments could be heard from one end of the main street to the other. The announcer said that before the variety show began, there would be an important news program about the Chernobyl accident. Many viewers increased the volumes on their television sets. The announcer's voice echoed in the street, the time delay caused by the distancing of sets making the main street sound like an auditorium.

The announcer began with the obvious. Almost a month earlier, the unit four reactor at the Chernobyl generating facility exploded.

The official death toll now stood at seventeen, and ninety thousand people had been evacuated from a thirty-kilometer radius. The announcer spoke of the bravery of firefighters, volunteers, and bus drivers. He said, although hundreds of thousands were being given iodine pills, this was merely a precaution. The vast majority of Soviet citizens, including those in the Ukraine, were in no danger whatsoever. The news program lasted only a few minutes. When it was over, a light orchestral arrangement signifying the beginning of the variety show began playing very loudly until one volume control after another was returned to a normal level.

The village of Kisbor settled in for the night. At the eight-room Kisbor Hotel, black Volgas recently parked out front were gone. Neighbors of the hotel were relieved because men in overcoats driving black Volgas meant KGB, and the KGB this far from a main city could mean trouble for almost anyone.

Farther away from the village, the sound of the variety show faded. The village resembled a lighted miniature, especially from the side of a hill to the west. It was a clear, moonless night, stars visible to the horizon. Daytime heat radiated, and the temperature dropped. It was quiet on the side of the hill until the music began. The music came from the lone farmhouse beyond the ridge of the hill. Since most citizens of Kisbor were of Hungarian descent, they would have immediately recognized the melody. But the house on the hill was too far away from the village for anyone there to hear it.

From the front of the house, it sounded as though a Gypsy orchestra was playing in the backyard. Although curious, Nikolai remained at his post at the front door. The music was instrumental, a solo violin piercing the night with the rest of the orchestra backing it up.

The violin sounded as if it were crying one minute and dancing the next. Several agents from the Volgas and the van parked out front got out and stood staring at the house.

When the front door of the house opened, the music boomed out until Captain Brovko closed the door behind him. Brovko stood shadowed in dim light from the front window. After a few seconds, he spoke, loud enough to be heard.

"What do you think of our major now?" asked Brovko.

"I don't know what to think," said Nikolai. "Is it the phonograph?"

"Yes. Major Komarov says if Detective Horvath is in the vicinity, the music will lure him. When I told him the noise would make it difficult for our men to hear anything, he opened the windows. I'm puzzled how your routine examination of correspondence in the PK could have led to this. Why haven't other investigative agencies been notified?"

After being reprimanded last night for asking what they should do about Major Komarov, Nikolai felt it would be best to remain silent.

Brovko looked back to the house. "I pity the family. Last night the questioning was relentless. Tonight he blows out their eardrums. The women and children are in the bedroom with the door closed, but the walls are thin. I'll tell the other men the music is not meant to drive them mad. They'll need to be watchful in case Horvath does come, but I don't want them shooting a villager who might wander up the hill. After I speak with the men, I'm going back to the hotel for a container of tea. I have a feeling it's going to be a long night."

While Brovko conferred with the other men, he shrugged his shoulders as if to say he had no idea what Komarov was doing. But Nikolai knew. It was similar to the afternoon in Visenka. There, amateurs were assigned so something other than a routine arrest would occur. Here, their sense of hearing was being obliterated. Perhaps Komarov wanted Horvath to kill another KGB officer. Or perhaps Komarov was simply insane. After Brovko conferred with the men standing at the vehicles, they fanned out, and he sped off in his Volga, heading down the hill to the village. Inside the house, the light went out, and only the flickering light of the television remained.

A new record dropped onto the turntable, the needle finding the initial groove and sending out explosive hisses before the music began. This piece featured a chorus as well as an orchestra. Although a passage here and there resembled traditional classical music, it was soon ruined by a melodramatic violin solo followed by the screaming catcalls of women in a chorus.

The stack of recordings had been in an upper cabinet. When Komarov retrieved them, he noticed a shortwave radio hidden behind them and made a mental note to include this in his report. The phonograph was on the kitchen table, its speakers facing the open windows to the backyard. Komarov had moved the phonograph with Captain Brovko's reluctant assistance. While moving the phonograph, the power cord snagged an icon hanging on the wall and it fell to the floor, shattering into pieces. He'd said something about religion being the ruination of the world, and Brovko had looked at him curiously. He was glad Brovko was gone. Brovko did not understand the need to outshine the tricks at the Hotel Dnieper.

The Gypsy Moth would come, lured by the glow of his music. He would sneak up to the house under cover of darkness and noise. An orderly and efficient capture would be impossible. There were several possibilities. One of the men would put a stream of bullets from his AKM into Horvath; Horvath would shoot another KGB agent, thus confirming his guilt; or Horvath would make it into the house. If Horvath did make it into the house, Komarov was ready.

Komarov's pistol was on the table beside the phonograph and the lights were out. The only light came from the television, which Bela Sandor sat watching with the sound off. Komarov sat behind the glowing television on the dark side of the room.

Bela Sandor had helped Komarov determine Horvath would come tonight. He had done so by acting more nervous tonight than last night, and by hurrying the women and children to the bedroom after dinner. Horvath had contacted his cousin. Perhaps the plan was to have Horvath come in through the bedroom window. No matter, because Komarov was in the shadows against a windowless wall. He had a clear view of both the front and back doors, of the windows, and of the bedroom door. He had ordered Bela to leave the room-divider curtain open and the television on.

Bela's face in the mad flicker of the television made him into a clown. Every few minutes, when he looked nervously at the clock on the wall, his movement was strobed by the television, creating multiple images. After smoking several cigarettes in a row, Komarov watched as Bela coughed violently and went to the bedroom door. Bela knocked, stuck his head inside, seemed to take a deep breath, then closed the door and scowled. Bela began coughing continuously, bending over as if he would vomit. He went to the kitchen sink and spit. He poured a glass of wine and took a sip, but this made him cough even more. Before Komarov could stop him or even pick up his pistol, Bela was out the back door.

"Stop!" Komarov ran to the open door. "Stop him!"

This was it. Horvath was out there! Bela was creating a diversion! Komarov went back to the table where it was darkest and watched the open back door and the closed bedroom door. Outside, above the sound of the music, he heard the sound of running feet.

Then Bela was shoved into the house by two of the men.

Bela kicked and screamed, and it took both men to pin him to the floor. The men struggled with Bela, looking as if they were dancing to the music. Komarov remained seated, aimed his pistol at the doorway, and waited. But the open doorway remained dark and empty.

When Bela finally calmed down, Komarov motioned that he be put back in his chair in front of the television. Above the din of music, Komarov shouted to one of the men to go back in the yard to resume his post and to the other to check the bedroom.

When the first man was gone, the second man took his Stechkin machine pistol from inside his coat. A small flashlight was taped to the pistol barrel. The man switched on the flashlight and went to the bedroom door. He opened it and quickly scanned the bedroom. When the man backed slowly out of the bedroom, Komarov knew this could be it. Horvath could be there. But the man turned and motioned for Komarov to come.

The bedroom was empty. The window was open. Komarov had the man shout search orders out the window and close the bedroom door. While the man stood guard, Komarov slapped Bela's face. But Bela simply smiled.

A few minutes later, a man with an AKM came in and announced that the women and children were nowhere to be found. Komarov told the man to keep watch for them but, more importantly, to watch for Detective Horvath and to shoot him on sight. When the man with the AKM went back outside, Komarov noticed the man with the machine pistol staring at the phonograph. He shouted at the man, ordering him to tie Bela to his chair with rope from the room-divider curtain.

Soon everything was back as it had been, the music playing, Komarov sitting in the dark watching the doors and smoking, Bela staring at the television. Except now the women and children were gone, and this could mean only one thing. Horvath would soon arrive.

The rope holding Bela to the chair was wrapped tightly, and his wrists were tied behind him. His nose bled, and he no longer smiled as he had when Komarov slapped him.

The violin of Lakatos cried its song of despair into the night, and for a moment Lazlo imagined he was back in his apartment in Kiev, lying in bed listening to Lakatos on his phonograph. None of what had brought him to Kisbor on a cool night in May had happened.

In a few seconds it all flashed before him again. Mihaly in the wine cellar; months later the confession of his affair on a snow-covered playground outside the apartment. Tamara with him when he heard about the explosion. The roadblocks and confusion. The news of Mihaly's death from bureaucrats at the Ministry of Energy. Juli arriving in his office at militia headquarters. Had the visit by Andrew Zukor and his wife at the farm had another purpose? Was it possible Zukor had somehow convinced Mihaly to . . .

No! Komarov had created a pretense of guilt out of Mihaly's and Juli's personal lives. Komarov had arranged the circumstances, causing Lazlo to do something he thought he would never do again. He'd killed an innocent man. He'd shot an innocent man and watched him die, resurrecting the image of the Gypsy on the Romanian border. Komarov was obviously trying to create counterrevolutionary scapegoats for what had happened at Chernobyl. But to what end?

With the music playing, with the memories of what he'd seen in the dead agent's eyes and the dead Gypsy's eyes and in Komarov's eyes, Lazlo knew there was more. Komarov needed to destroy him, destroy his family, destroy Juli.

The violin of Lakatos crying out over the plateau gave way to the faster *czardas*, the rest of the orchestra joining in. In the distance, looking like overbright fireflies in Lazlo's night vision, flashlights danced about the house. Lazlo used the opportunity to circle the house. He stayed at the ridge of the hill and was able to count ten men wielding flashlights. While he ran, he thought of the story his father had told, the German troops coming up the hill, only their helmets visible as his father and mother climbed down into the wine cellar.

The faint light of the village was behind Lazlo as he pushed through the weeds approaching the gravel road going up the hill. He held his watch up and saw it was almost ten o'clock. He was about a hundred meters from the house. A flashlight swept across the side of the house, pausing at the open bedroom window.

The open window, Bela's signal telling him Nina and Mariska and the children had escaped into the wine cellar. The men with flashlights were searching for the women and children, searching in an ever-widening circle. It was time. Bela was expecting him at ten, and Lazlo knew Komarov must be in the house waiting for him.

Lazlo considered posing as a drunk walking along the road. He'd stagger up the hill whistling to the music. The men would come, and he'd pretend to speak only Hungarian. But there were too many men. He'd never break free and be able to get to the house without being sprayed by AKM fire. Then he remembered what Bela had told him earlier in the day. A man was stationed on the south edge of the road at the ridge of the hill.

Lazlo crouched low and ran. If the man was at his post, he'd have to disarm him, get the AKM, and make a run on the house. But more likely, the man had left his post and was part of the search. He could hear the men speaking to one another above the scream of Lakatos' violin.

The road was close. Lazlo went down on his hands and knees and crawled ahead, feeling stones digging into his knees, the same stones he and Mihaly had, years ago, hurled from the yard as they helped their father clear a place to plant the private plot.

The men came closer, their legs dragging through dry weeds as they approached the ridge of the hill. Lazlo stayed low, crawled with his face to the ground. Suddenly, near the road, he came upon a clearing about a meter wide. His hand brushed something, a coat on the ground, its inside lining still warm. The man guarding the road had used the coat to stay warm or to sit on. The man was one of those with flashlights. Lazlo crouched low and lay down at the edge of the circular clearing on the side nearest the road. He listened and waited because he knew the KGB agent who had made the nest would soon return.

The stage was set. Everything he had done for the last two decades had led to this. Even times of weakness when the bottle had him in its grasp played a role. He had devoted his life in preparation for this confrontation.

East of the Carpathians, others could easily be arrested to confirm the conspiracy originating in the United States and funneled through here. Anger over Chernobyl would intensify, making prosecution less complicated. Chernobyl traitors would be part of the Soviet Union's future. Whether Gorbachev remained in power or not, Komarov's plan would succeed.

Komarov felt stronger than he had in years. When it was over, he would go to Moscow without the media fanfare used in capitalist countries. It was not the Russian way. By going quietly, he would add to his power. He would accept his medals with dignity and stand with the best of them high above others at the May Day parade. In the crowd, he would see a young blond woman look up to him. Later, at a Kremlin reception, he would meet the young woman, a *Pravda* reporter doing a story on the revival of Russia's superiority over the other Soviet republics. Gorbachev would be no more, and the new president would have befriended Deputy KGB Chairman Grigor Komarov.

After the Kremlin reception, the *Pravda* reporter would return with him to his room at the Hotel Metropole. They would order champagne and speak of their new Mother Russia long into the night.

She is sweet. He can smell her. She puts her head on his shoulder and fingers the buttons of his uniform. She unbuttons his jacket and reaches beneath it. She finds the knife in the inside pocket and asks about it. He tells her the story of Sherbitsky, the murderer. They make love. She becomes his mistress. They meet monthly at his dacha. He does not kill her. Instead, she stays with him as he grows older, wiser.

In the midst of Komarov's reverie, Bela glared at him and spit off to the side. It seemed a provocation demanding action. He imagined rising from the chair and pistol-whipping the brute. But he did not move. Instead, he aimed the pistol at Bela, and this calmed him.

After a few more minutes of thrashing about in the weeds, it sounded as if the men were retreating to the house. Above the din of the music, Lazlo heard footsteps coming closer to the clearing. But instead of one man returning to the nest, it sounded like two. He kept his hand on his pistol as the men approached. The men stopped near his feet. He looked up and could see them facing the house. If one of the men stepped back, Lazlo would be kicked or stepped on, but he dared not move. The two men began speaking, young men.

"Komarov will have a poker up his ass now. When Brovko returns, you'll really hear it."

"This is all quite strange. We're told Horvath is armed and dangerous, we're issued Stechkins and AKMs, and Komarov turns up the music so we can't hear an attacking elephant herd."

"You know what they say about fish."

"Rotting from the head first?"

Both men chuckled, their feet shuffling in the weeds. They continued their conversation.

"Captain Azef is in his glory back in Kiev."

"A lot of the men have been saying Azef will take over. An old-timer in the office said Komarov's been a paperweight the last few years. A serious drinking problem. That's why he's still a major."

"I wouldn't mind a drink now."

"Brovko went for tea. I hope he doesn't spill it when he hears what's happened."

"What do you think of Brovko's closeness with Nikolskaia?"

"He wonders why Nikolskaia was assigned here. His partner was the one Horvath shot."

"I didn't know that."

"Yes. A couple of PK amateurs from Pripyat."

"Ha. I knew Nikolskaia came from Pripyat, but I didn't know he was PK."

"Don't say anything to him. He has enough trouble. He'll get cancer in a year or two from the radiation. My brother and his family had to move, and their place was even farther away. I don't know what the fuck we're doing here. I thought we'd be sent up north or at least to the roadblocks watching for looters."

"I hope we're out of here soon. I met this girl in Kiev."

"I'd rather go back to Moscow. The hell with these Ukes."

The two men were silent for a while, then one of them said he should get back to his post. Because of the music and the similarity of the youthful voices, Lazlo could not tell which man had gone.

Lazlo pulled his legs up to a fetal position. The remaining man moved into the clearing, stood for a moment, and finally settled down on the coat spread on the ground. The man's back was to Lazlo. He could smell the leather of the man's jacket. If he reached out, he could touch the man's back.

Lazlo studied the man, determined the AKM was in the man's right hand, its skinny folding stock against the ground, its barrel upward. He would have to kill the man or disable him without creating a disturbance. Choking him would kill him, and somewhere a brother or even a sister would wonder why. Lazlo recalled the look in the eyes of the Gypsy's sister, the look on the face of the Gypsy when the bullet pierced his head, and finally the look on the face of the dead PK agent he now knew was the partner of a man named Nikolskaia. The music of Lakatos was being played by Komarov to make the confrontation a deadly one. He did not want to kill again. But he would kill Komarov.

The agent stirred, and Lazlo knew he could wait no longer and still take advantage of the turmoil caused by the search for the women and children. When the violin *prima* again changed into a louder and faster *czardas*, he slowly pulled his pistol from his belt. He sat up and, measuring in his mind a blow appropriate to knock a man out without crushing his skull, hit the man over the head with the butt of his old battered Makarov.

After determining the man was still breathing, Lazlo exchanged trousers, coat, and cap to transform himself into a KBG agent. He used his discarded belt to tie the man's hands behind his back, gagged the man with his own scarf, knotted his bootlaces together, and covered him with discarded clothing. He inspected the AKM and found the safety off. He retrieved his pistol from the ground and tucked it into his waist at his back beneath the agent's leather coat. The music continued. Komarov was waiting.

CHAPTER 32

The search through the weeds terrified Nikolai, and he was relieved to be back at his post at the front of the house. But even here with his back to the wall and men sitting in the Volgas parked out front, he had to be watchful, especially with the music screaming inside. Although he had enjoyed Hungarian music on occasion, Nikolai now hoped he would never hear it again. The solo violin reminded him of his friend Pavel across from him in the Pripyat post office, Pavel innocently singling out the letters of Detective Horvath and his brother written in Hungarian.

Nikolai sensed something in his peripheral vision. When he turned, he saw the man positioned out by the road, about fifty meters behind the parked Volgas, walking slowly his way. The man was outlined against the light from the village. Instead of going to the cars, the man turned and headed for the house, his AKM held casually at his side. When the headlights of an approaching car cleared the top of the hill, the man walked faster. The car was Captain Brovko's, bringing tea from the village. Perhaps the man had seen the Volga coming up the hill and wanted his share. But after Brovko parked, the man did not turn to go to the Volga. Instead, he continued to the side of the house, walking still faster, and Nikolai knew something was wrong.

Nikolai gripped his machine pistol, turned off the safety, and aimed it at the man who had now begun running to the side of the house.

"Hey! Stop!"

The man did not stop, and suddenly Nikolai realized he was running after the man. He heard car doors opening and other men running and shouting. When he rounded the side of the house, he saw the man's legs dangling from the window. He aimed the machine pistol at the man's legs but could not pull the trigger. He watched as the man disappeared inside the house.

Men shouted and gathered. One man said his partner was tied up and his clothes had been taken. Another said it was Horvath. Nikolai felt a hand on his arm, a hand pushing his arm and the Stechkin machine pistol down. He was turned around. Brovko stared at him in the shadows.

"Nikolai! Did you see him? Was it Horvath?"

The profile, a moment before he passed the corner of the house. "Yes. I saw him, but . . ."

"Never mind! Come with me!"

The bedroom was warm. He tried to control his heavy breathing. Of all things, he was aware of the smells in the bedroom. The comforting smells of clean linen, the sweet smells of children's bedclothes. If he was going to die, he might as well die here. If only he could be certain the women and children were safe. If only he could be certain Juli was safe.

When the music stopped, it was dead silent, until Komarov

shouted from the other room.

"I wouldn't shoot through the door, Horvath, unless you wish to kill your cousin!"

The sound of a chair being pushed across the floor. Bela shouted, "I'm here in a chair! Shoot high, Laz! He's . . ." Then Bela screamed.

Komarov shouted, "Horvath! Come out now! The knife is at his neck!"

Lazlo aimed the AKM at the door, aimed high, but did not fire. If he fired, men outside would open fire. He could hear their voices, closer, outside the window.

"To prove my point!" shouted Komarov.

Bela screamed in agony.

"Stop! I'll come out!"

Other men joined Komarov. Lazlo could hear them running about the room. No choice. He put down the AKM and reached for the door. His life no longer mattered. In a few hours Juli would be across the frontier into Czechoslovakia, where Komarov could not get her.

When he opened the door, three agents were on him, one grabbing his pistol from his rear waistband.

The goal Komarov had pursued was finally within his grasp. He sent one of the men to the van for handcuffs, rope, and a bandage for the cut on Bela's neck. "After all," he said to his men, "we're not brutes."

Horvath and his cousin were put in kitchen chairs, their ankles tied to the front chair legs; their hands cuffed behind, pulled down tight with rope looped over the cuff-link chains, and tied to the back chair rungs. Horvath stared at Komarov. Bela stared at his lap.

It was clear to Komarov. A conspiracy had been bred long ago, perhaps after 1956, by Hungarians angered by having been made to live like everyone else. Hungarians in the Ukraine Republic instead of in their own spineless province. When Komarov returned to Kiev, he would bring evidence of this conspiracy. If the evidence he brought back consisted only of dead bodies, then the substantial evidence he had already assembled in Kiev and in Moscow would stand. The Hungarians would be found guilty of having used technical expertise and help from the CIA to cause the Chernobyl explosion. It was time to carve his conspiracy into stone.

Komarov began asking questions of Detective Horvath and his cousin. His goal was not to get at the truth, but to create a new set of truths his men, and especially the captain, would substantiate. As Komarov questioned the two, he received the negative replies he expected. Often he received no reply, especially when he mentioned the American cousin, Andrew Zukor. Between questions, Komarov began using the back of his hand. When the back of his hand became sore, he used his palm. When he began using his fist, Captain Brovko, the supposed experienced interrogator, did the unexpected. Captain Brovko questioned Komarov's authority.

"Shouldn't we simply arrest them and return to Kiev, Major?"

Komarov turned to glare at Brovko for a moment, then calmly lit a cigarette in preparation for presenting his case.

"Of course, we'll arrest them, Captain. But as you and I both know, it is KGB policy to gather information, especially while the information is fresh. Zukor visited this farm and spoke with these men last summer. Directorate T confirmed Zukor's CIA ties and his attempt to contact them in Budapest. Unfortunately, before our agents could speak with Zukor about his conversations with his cousins, he had a fatal accident in Budapest's heavy traffic. There exists a trail from the CIA to Zukor to Mihaly Horvath, the engineer in charge at the time of the so-called Chernobyl accident! Simply assassinating their man does not let the CIA off the hook. I will not accept the failure of an investigation into a situation that is ruining the lives of thousands of Soviet citizens! I am in command, Captain, and in my judgment there is more information to gather! Therefore, we will have one more try at it . . . using one of your methods!"

Komarov approached Bela. He took a few puffs on his cigarette, put the cigarette down on the table edge, then spoke softly.

"You're going to be a nice fellow, aren't you, Bela? You're a fine patriot, I know, and you don't want your record blemished. I realize things have changed in our country, but still one can be a patriot."

When Bela seemed to have calmed appropriately, Komarov took the cigarette from the table, puffed it a couple of times to get it hot, blew smoke in Bela's face, made like he was going to put the cigarette back on the table edge, and instead turned back to Bela and pressed the glowing tip of the cigarette against his neck.

The scream from the house was almost as loud as the music had been. Several men who had gathered near the Volgas to console their friend hit over the head looked to the house. But what could they do? They shrugged their shoulders and got into the Volgas to keep warm.

As the hours wore on, the moans coming from inside the house changed to whimpers, which Nikolai could barely hear through the front door. During the last hour, one of the men from the Volgas approached Nikolai, asking him to go inside and ask Captain Brovko if there were further orders. The man said he'd seen Nikolai speaking with Brovko, and since they were friends, he should be the one to ask about the situation. Nikolai told the man he would think about this, and the man returned to his comrades in one of the Volgas.

Nikolai leaned against the wall of the house and held his watch up to the light filtering through the window curtains. It was after three in the morning, and he began to wonder if perhaps he *should* go in the house and ask about the situation.

The last time Juli had driven a car was during the past summer when Marina had borrowed Vasily's car so they could both learn to drive. The Skoda protested fiercely when Juli tried to engage first gear without pushing the clutch all the way in. But she adjusted the seat, turned on the lights, and soon had the Skoda climbing out of the ravine.

All day and into the night she had been frightened the two men from the truck would return to dismantle the car. But she could not leave the place she was to meet Lazlo until three in the morning. Earlier she had taken the wine Lazlo purchased at the train station from the back seat, and placed the unopened bottle up at the side of the road, hoping if the men returned, this would delay them. Luckily, the men had not returned. It was after three as she drove the Skoda down the road in the dark. She stopped at the crossroad.

To her left was the road to the frontier, where the guard on duty near Laborets Castle awaited his bribe. To her right was the village of Kisbor, where, according to Lazlo's description, the farmhouse rested on a hill west of the village. Juli studied the night sky, asked the stars for help. But there was no help there. She would have to betray Lazlo. She would have to deny his last request. Life was short anyhow—words from a Ukrainian folk song. She gunned the engine, slowly let out the clutch, and turned right. A short distance down the dark road stood a sign for the village of Kisbor. She knew her father would have approved of her decision.

"Was it Zukor who bribed Mihaly?" screamed Komarov. "Or did you convince him yourself? Was part of the bribe given to Juli Popovics?"

Komarov smashed his cigarette on the floor and lit another.

"A senior engineer would know about dropping power levels, then pulling control rods to increase power enough to cause a disastrous surge! Technicians at the Ministry of Energy are not fools! Was the plan simply to cause the steam explosion? Did the plan initiated by Zukor spin out of control?"

Lazlo took a deep breath, his nostrils on fire from the smell of his own flesh, his eyes swollen from having been beaten before Komarov started with the cigarette. He stared at Komarov through slits. He thought of the women and children in the wine cellar. Tried to imagine himself and Bela there. Safe. A glass of wine, the smell of wine-soaked wood, bears gone into hibernation. Mihaly there, and perhaps even Cousin Zukor. Everyone dead or in danger hidden alive in the wine cellar. Yes, Zukor there, too. Komarov had said Zukor had an "accident" in Budapest.

When Komarov burned him again, Lazlo was suddenly transported to Kiev. The streets were a mass of traffic. People on sidewalks ran about bumping into one another.

When Komarov burned him once more, Lazlo imagined himself floating a hundred meters above Kiev, its residents asleep below. Close by, as he floated, was the statue of Saint Vladimir. Lazlo prayed to Saint Vladimir for assistance. Saint Vladimir, who performed baptisms in the Dnieper River, could help him.

When Komarov burned him yet again, Lazlo laughed aloud, heard himself laughing and tried to stop. But he could not stop because now, in this place and in this time, laughing was his weapon. Perhaps someone nearby would pay attention to his laughter. Perhaps the captain . . .

For a moment Lazlo thought of his small corner cubicle at Kiev Militia Headquarters. Down the narrow walkway between cubicles, Chief Investigator Chkalov sits in his office. Chkalov's fat face smiling as he piles on yet another case because of the Gypsy's bachelor status. But then Lazlo recalled dreaming this dream in the summer in the wine cellar. Dreaming the dream until he heard the wooden ladder at the entrance creak and saw bare legs and feet encased in red canvas sneakers descending the ladder. Mihaly.

In the village the only lighted window was on the lower floor of the Kisbor Hotel. Juli went into the small hotel lobby and rang the bell. After a few minutes, a tired-looking woman came out of a back room. The woman looked to Juli, looked up at the clock on the wall, looked back to Juli.

"Can you tell me where the Horvath farm is?"

"Horvath? It's not there anymore. Their cousin . . ."

"Yes. I forgot. Sandor. Can you tell me where the Sandors live?"

The woman glanced about the small lobby as if looking for someone, but the lobby was empty. She went to the front window and stared outside. "Why do you want to know?"

"I'm a relative," said Juli. "I know it's late. I had trouble getting here. I was evacuated from Chernobyl, and they're waiting for me."

The woman stepped back, stared at Juli for a moment, a look of concern on her face. Then she pointed west out the window. "Take the street out of town. When it becomes gravel, it will curve and go up a hill. The house is at the top of the hill."

The woman turned back to Juli. "There have been men here. Perhaps you should wait until morning."

"I have to go now."

"Is there anything you need?" asked the woman.

Juli realized the woman was looking at her tattered clothing.

"A drink of water."

When Juli drove away in the Skoda, she could see the woman still standing at the window holding the empty glass.

Juli drove the Skoda to where the main street ended. Ahead she saw the dark outline of the hill against the stars. Atop the hill she could see the faint light from a window.

She parked the Skoda in an alleyway between two shops. She locked the doors and began walking up the road to the house on the hill.

The two Gypsies held their reddened faces high to relieve the burns on their necks. Komarov had allowed them to rest long enough. Captain Brovko sat in the chair across from him. Brovko's eyes were closed, but when Komarov stood, Brovko opened his eyes.

Komarov walked to the center of the room where the Gypsies sat. Bela had pissed his pants, and the room smelled of urine and cigarette smoke. The smell of burnt flesh had diminished. Komarov reached inside his coat, felt his knife there, but instead of taking out the knife, he removed his pistol from its shoulder holster. He carried his pistol to the kitchen table, where he had placed Horvath's pistol beside the silenced record player. He held both pistols, comparing them.

"I see we both carry 9mm pistols, Detective Horvath. Yours is a Makarov, while mine is a Walther West German model. A more significant difference between our pistols is that yours appears to have seen a lot more action. I wonder how many victims there have been."

Komarov put his Walther back in its holster and carried the battered Makarov with him as he approached the prisoners. He kept his questions simple. He asked Bela where the women and children had gone. He asked Horvath where Juli Popovics was. He repeated the questions loudly and clearly. When he received nothing more than a sneer from Horvath, he smashed the barrel of the pistol across Horvath's face.

"Stop!" shouted Bela.

"No!" said Horvath. "Say nothing." Then to Komarov, Horvath said, "You've got me. Let him go. He has nothing to do with this."

"Your accomplice is still on the loose," said Komarov. "These people were obviously prepared to hide you. Was your sister-in-law also involved in Chernobyl sabotage? Did she run away because she has something to hide? Technical knowledge of exactly how her husband caused the accident and how he'd planned to escape? Only he didn't escape! And now . . ."

"You're insane!" shouted Horvath.

Komarov hit Horvath with his pistol again. And when Horvath appeared to lose consciousness, he hit Bela.

"Tell me where they are!" repeated Komarov over and over. "Tell me where they are!"

When Komarov felt a hand on his shoulder, he turned and saw Brovko staring at him.

"Major, I think it's time to stop. It's almost dawn."

"What do I care what time it is?"

"I thought you might have lost track of time. It's been a long night. The men are still outside and . . ."

"The men? You have the nerve to defend idiots who let women and children escape from under their noses?"

"I'm not defending them, Major. I was simply wondering how long this will go on."

"It will go on, Captain, until these traitors tell me what I need to know or until their faces are changed into borscht."

"I'm sorry, Major, I don't understand why we need the women and children. We've got Horvath. Nothing has been proven. We should take Horvath back to Kiev now and . . ."

"Captain! Perhaps you would like to speak directly to Vladimir Kryuchkov at the Lubyanka in Moscow after we leave this cesspool of a farm and find out who is in control!"

Brovko spoke calmly. "I was not aware your authority reached such high levels, Major. Of course, you are in control."

Komarov turned around, saw both Horvath and Bela looking at him. Both had heard his officer question his actions. Instead of shooting Horvath, the men had let him get inside. Then Brovko had hurried in, interrupting his chance to shoot Horvath and have it appear he was defending himself. No one had been killed. But if there were an escape attempt . . .

"You may go now, Captain."

"You don't want me to stay?"

"Correct. Please leave immediately."

Komarov turned, watched Brovko move for the door. He released the safety on Detective Horvath's pistol. As he aimed at Brovko's back, he wondered if he would be able to unlock Horvath's handcuffs before any other men arrived. He wondered if he would have time to make it look like an escape attempt. During his moment of hesitation, the door opened inward, causing Brovko to step back.

Nikolai Nikolskaia stood in the doorway, staring at the pistol aimed at Brovko's back.

Komarov lowered the pistol, spun around, and fired all eight rounds at the feet of Horvath and Bela. When it was over, no one had been hit, but Bela was weeping.

Komarov turned back to Brovko and Nikolskaia. "I hope I did not frighten you. I simply wanted the traitors to know that I am serious!"

Because cars and a van were parked in front of the house, Juli went off the road and climbed the remainder of the hill through the weeds. When she got closer, she saw several men near the cars. There was also a man at the side of the house, and one in back.

Maybe Lazlo hadn't arrived yet. Or maybe he had arrived and had been able to kill Komarov. If so he would have had to escape, unless . . .

No. Lazlo would have escaped. Lazlo would have shot Komarov and run out the door. But where could he go with all the guards and no place to hide? No place to hide except the wine cellar he had told her about.

Juli raised her head and looked through the weeds, but it was too dark to see the entrance to the wine cellar. Lazlo said it looked like a box, most people never knowing it was a cellar at all. If she went to the back of the house, away from the men at the cars, she might be able to see the wine-cellar entrance, or she might be able to see into a back window.

As she crawled, she saw the man at the front of the house go to the door. The door opened, and light swept across the yard. She crawled faster.

Suddenly gunshots erupted in the house, one after another. The men out front and the men at the back and sides of the house ran toward it. Not knowing what else to do, Juli ran into the backyard. Then she saw it, a box shaped like a coffin. She hid behind the box for a moment, felt along its edge, pushed up one side, then the other.

She lifted the edge of the box, glancing to the house, where two men with rifles stood in the doorway looking in. She lifted the lid of the box farther, felt for the ladder, and started down. As she eased the lid closed, she could see the men with rifles through the crack. They turned and spread out, going back to their positions.

The cellar was darker than the night had been, but it was warmer. When she reached the bottom of the ladder, she stepped off onto soft earth. She turned away from the ladder and stood perfectly still. After a while she heard a sound, something like an animal feeding. She thought of rats, and a chill went through her. She thought of Lazlo. Lazlo could be here hiding.

"Is anyone here?" she whispered.

"Who are you?" It was a woman's voice.

"My name is Juli. Have you seen Lazlo Horvath?"

"My God!" whispered the woman harshly. "Lazlo is in the house where the shots came from! He's with Bela! Tell me they're all right! Tell me they've escaped from the madman!"

"I don't know," said Juli. "I was coming up to the house when I heard the shots."

Juli moved closer to the woman's voice. She heard a murmur. A baby! Lazlo had said Mariska had a baby.

"Did Lazlo tell you about the wine cellar?" A voice from Juli's left, a different woman.

"Yes." Juli knew she did not have to ask, but she did anyway. "Who are you?"

"I am Nina Horvath, Juli. You must recognize my voice."

Juli backed away, found the ladder, sat on the dirt floor, and wept.

CHAPTER
33

The cellar, at first warm in contrast to the cold night, soon felt like a tomb. The tomb was damp and cold, conspiring with Nina Horvath to make Juli feel as though she should die. This was the place Mihaly and Lazlo had spoken of, the wine cellar deep in the ground behind the house, the wine cellar with its wine-cellar smell making tears seem bitter and self-serving.

After Juli's arrival, she heard Mihaly's daughters whispering to their mother, asking who this woman was. "She's a friend of Uncle Lazlo," Nina had said. "Now be still, little dears. Try to sleep. Soon it will be a new day, and we'll be out in the sun."

Mariska's baby had been nursing when Juli arrived. Now the baby was asleep. Mariska left the baby with Nina's girls at the back of the cellar. Juli could not see Nina or Mariska, but she could hear them gently shushing the children before they made their way to her, so close she could feel their warmth. The three of them stood near the ladder at the entrance. They spoke quietly, whispering in case one of the guards surrounding the house should happen to walk close to the cellar entrance. While they spoke, Juli felt Mariska's arm on one side and Nina's on the other.

"What could be happening up there?" asked Mariska in an excited whisper.

There was a pause before Nina answered in a more controlled voice, her composure reminding Juli of the night Nina had called her at the apartment and asked for Mihaly. "We have no way of knowing," she said. "At first I thought Komarov was only after Lazlo and Juli. Now I'm not sure. He's insane. I'm convinced of it, and I'm certain Lazlo was convinced of it when he told Bela to have us hide down here. The only reason Bela isn't here is because he provided a diversion. There were too many men to do anything else."

"My Bela," gasped Mariska, choking back tears. "He could have escaped during the day while out in the fields if it weren't for us!"

Juli held Mariska to calm her. Then she felt Nina's hand on hers, Nina also trying to calm Mariska. Neither pulled away, and their hands stayed in contact.

Mariska continued, this time careful to whisper. "I heard the madman threaten Bela before he left for the fields yesterday. He reminded Bela about the well-being of his family. And now, with all that shooting up there . . ."

"I don't think Komarov shot Bela," said Nina.

"Why not?" asked Mariska. "What else has he got to do? You said yourself he's insane. He questioned you in Moscow. And last night he hit you . . ."

"He was trying to frighten me," said Nina, her voice still composed. "He succeeded, and now we have a dilemma. I'll do what I must to stop him from hurting my daughters."

Nina and Juli let go of Mariska, their hands sliding apart in the darkness.

"I'll do what I must," repeated Nina, with determination.

They were silent for a time. Juli felt like telling them she wanted to help. But she sensed Nina needed to say more. Finally, Nina spoke again.

"If we give ourselves up, we might delay Komarov's plan for Bela and Lazlo. But we can't allow the children to fall into his hands. We can only stay down here so long with nothing but wine to drink. You've been quiet until now, Juli Popovics. What do you think we should do?"

"It's what I should do," said Juli.

"What do you mean?" asked Nina.

Juli knew what she needed to say. She took a deep breath and began. "I'm the one Komarov is after. I'm the one who worked at Chernobyl. Komarov is trying to create a conspiracy. Because Mihaly isn't here to defend himself, Komarov wants to build a conspiracy around him by pursuing Lazlo and me as if we are co-conspirators. Lazlo said it's an old KGB trick. If you pursue someone long enough, they begin to take on an implied guilt, especially if they hide, as we have done. Lazlo doesn't know I'm here. I was supposed to escape into Czechoslovakia. I'm not here because I want to be a heroine. I'm here because of my guilt. I am responsible for what Komarov is doing. There is no conspiracy. But if it weren't for my relationship with Mihaly, none of this would have happened."

"Your relationship caused Chernobyl to blow up?" whispered Mariska.

"That's not what she means," said Nina. "Perhaps she is here for forgiveness."

Juli reached out and touched Nina's arm. "No. I want to help Lazlo's family."

There was a long silence. Juli let go of Nina's arm. Then Nina spoke.

"Komarov insists there was a conspiracy. He wants to prove you and Lazlo and . . . and Mihaly were involved. Mihaly is gone. Komarov has Lazlo. Now he wants you. Is that it?"

"There's more to it," said Juli. "A cousin named Andrew Zukor might also be implicated."

"Cousin Andrew?" asked Mariska.

"Andrew is from the United States," said Nina. "I can understand how the KGB might have made the connection. I remember Andrew asking questions about Mihaly's work at Chernobyl."

Juli wished she could see Nina's eyes. She recalled Aleksandra's eyes and the eyes of the farm wife in the hospital. "Komarov wants to capture us. But he also wants to use our capture and the Chernobyl situation in a push for power."

"If this is true . . ." said Mariska.

"Go on," said Nina.

Mariska continued. "If this is true, if his goal is to uncover a conspiracy where there is no conspiracy, he'll want to capture you in order to torture you or kill you."

"I agree," said Nina. "Komarov is a hard-liner. I saw it in him in Moscow. He won't stop until he gets what he wants. No matter who gets hurt." Nina's voice grew somewhat louder as she turned to Juli. "No matter who gets hurt."

Juli was silent, realizing Nina's last statement referred to her affair with Mihaly. Finally, Juli took another deep breath and spoke.

"I want you to understand how Mihaly and I became involved, Nina. I'm not seeking forgiveness, but I want you to know. My father, the only person I was ever close to, died the previous winter. I was quite alone when Mihaly came along. It wasn't his fault. I . . . I needed someone then. It's my fault. Please . . ."

Silence except for one of the children sighing deeply in sleep. One of Mihaly's little girls dreaming of her father and mother and happier times. Juli continued.

"I'm not seeking forgiveness."

"I hear you," said Nina, her voice less composed. "But what else can you do with Mihaly gone and all of us down here together in a hole that may end up being our grave?"

Another long silence, the only sounds the fidgeting of the children at the back of the cellar. Finally Nina spoke.

"Enough about forgiveness and what happened between you and Mihaly. We've got the children to consider. Earlier you said you could help. What can you do? There are men with machine guns up there."

"I know," said Juli. "I saw them. But there's got to be a way. If we knew what was going on up there . . ."

"Perhaps . . ." whispered Mariska. "Perhaps we can spy out the trapdoor without them seeing us."

"It's possible," said Juli. "When I came inside, I saw a small crack where the door doesn't quite close all the way. I know we couldn't see much now. But soon it will be light. Maybe we'll be able to see something during the day to help us decide what to do."

Nina and Mariska and Juli agreed. For now it was the only thing they could do.

They took turns standing on the ladder peering through the small crack at the entrance. The two not at the entrance tried to keep the children warm and quiet.

The hour or so until dawn passed slowly. The crack at the entrance faced the house but was too low to the ground to allow them to see windows beyond the weeds. Only the dark roof of the house and the shadows of trees in the yard were visible. Eventually, when it was Juli's turn on the ladder, the gray of dawn began. It was then that Juli saw a movement against the gray sky. At first she was not certain what it could be, perhaps clouds. But then, after studying the movement, and as the dawn grew brighter, she realized she was looking at the legs of a man, a man standing very close to the entrance to the cellar. As it grew lighter, she could also see, to the side of the man's legs, the barrel of a machine gun.

From below, Nina touched Juli's ankle gently to let her know it was time to trade positions on the ladder.

Before dawn, a man was sent to relieve Nikolai. Nikolai sat in one of the Volgas with the engine running and the heater blowing warm air over his face.

Two hours earlier he had opened the front door to the house and was confronted by a scene he would never forget. Bela Sandor and Lazlo Horvath were tied to chairs in the middle of the room beneath the overhead light. Their faces were covered with welts, their eyes were swollen, their shirts were ripped open, and burn marks were on their necks and chests. Both men looked to the door when he opened it and, with their eyes, pleaded with him for help.

The other part of the scene Nikolai would never forget was Captain Brovko at the door about to come out while Major Komarov aimed his pistol at Brovko's back. The look on Komarov's face was alarming. Time stopped. The men in the chairs stared with pleading eyes. Komarov aimed his pistol at Brovko. Then time resumed and Komarov emptied his pistol into the floor. After this incident Brovko went back inside and closed the door.

The shots attracted the attention of the rest of the men. While Nikolai was on duty at the front door, several held a lengthy conference near the parked Volgas. One of the men approached Nikolai and asked what he had seen in the house. While considering his answer, Nikolai thought of many things. He thought of the look on Komarov's face. He thought of Pavel smiling up at him while blood gushed from his temple. He thought of Pavel's wife at the funeral. Finally Nikolai told the other men that if he hadn't opened the door when he did, he was certain Komarov would have shot Captain Brovko in the back.

Now, as Nikolai sat in the Volga watching the morning sky brighten, he wondered if he should go into the house and tell Captain Brovko what the other men, gathering in small groups before dawn, already knew.

Whenever he moved, Lazlo's face felt as if it had expanded, creating more nerves to send messages of pain to his brain. Although he had lost track of time, he felt at least an hour had gone by since Komarov had stopped his beatings. The last thing Komarov had done was to blow cigarette smoke into their faces.

It was quiet in the room, so quiet he could hear Bela's deep breaths. He hoped Bela would not begin snoring and rouse Komarov, who had apparently settled in the daybed behind them. Earlier, the man he now knew as Captain Brovko had given both him and Bela a drink of water. Now Brovko sat at the kitchen table. The phonograph was off the table and back in the cabinet. When Komarov finished beating them and placed Lazlo's pistol on the table, Brovko had picked it up and tucked it into his belt. Now Brovko sat with his elbows on the table, staring out the window at the new dawn.

Last night, during Komarov's beatings, there had been increasing evidence Brovko did not approve. Brovko attempted several approaches to convince Komarov they should return to Kiev with their prisoners. Each time, Komarov refused, insisting Lazlo knew where Juli Popovics was and Bela knew where the women and children were. After the incident in which Komarov shot Lazlo's pistol into the floor, Brovko was especially watchful, never leaving them alone in the house with Komarov.

Lazlo recalled the man who opened the door. It was the same man he had sent back to Kiev in his Zhiguli after shooting his partner in Visenka. The man who had wept as his partner lay bleeding in his lap. He had heard Brovko call the man Nikolai. And now he recalled the partner's name because it had been repeated over and over.

"Pavel! Don't die, Pavel!"

Again, the question. Why would Komarov send an untrained agent on a dangerous mission? Were there more untrained agents outside? The man he had hit over the head had been young. Were they all fresh recruits primed to kill or be killed?

Lazlo opened his eyes wider and, although it was painful, moved his head slowly from side to side. He tried to get Brovko's attention without speaking out loud, but Brovko continued staring out the window.

As the sun rose, its brightness through the windows overpowered the overhead light. When Brovko stretched and yawned, Lazlo stared at him, motioned with his head, and finally stuck out his swollen tongue and wagged it at Brovko.

Brovko stood and came to Lazlo. "What's that supposed to mean?"

"I was trying to get your attention," whispered Lazlo.

"Why?"

"I thought you might want to hear another Hungarian song. I can sing one for you."

Brovko smiled. "You have a sense of humor." Then Brovko looked over Lazlo's shoulder and frowned. "However, I wouldn't try any jokes on the major."

"I know. My cousin and I didn't laugh all night. Apparently he's sleeping?"

"Your cousin?"

"Komarov."

"He appears to be sleeping."

"Then I'd like to ask you something."

"What?"

"I'd like to ask the same question you did. Why does he want the women and children?"

Brovko stared at Lazlo for a moment. Then he went to the sink and came back with a glass of water. He held the water to Lazlo's lips.

The rooster had crowed, the sun was up, and budding trees surrounding the house were capped in orange. Nikolai reached out and switched off the Volga's engine. He lowered the window slightly and listened to the birds. It was a fine spring morning, and Nikolai relished the moment of peace until, in the distance, he heard the sound of an engine laboring up the hill.

Nikolai left the Volga and walked out on the road. When the bus carrying farm workers topped the hill, Nikolai signaled it to stop. The driver, a heavy man with several chins, looked worried.

"Bela Sandor won't be going with you today," said Nikolai.

"Is he ill?" asked the driver.

"Yes. You can try again tomorrow."

"But tomorrow is Sunday. We won't be working tomorrow."

While the bus turned around, the few farmers on the bus looked out at Nikolai as if he were a monster. When Nikolai returned to the Volga, Captain Brovko was inside.

"I told the bus driver Bela Sandor was ill."

"He's better now," said Brovko. "Komarov is napping."

"What will he do when he wakes up?"

"I don't know. I called two men in to relieve me. If Komarov wakes up, he'll probably chase them out of the house."

A pause, then Brovko turned to Nikolai. "You have something

to tell me about what happened earlier. Something you couldn't say in front of Komarov."

"How did you know?"

"I saw the look on your face when you came through the door."

"I'm sorry to have to tell you, Captain. I wouldn't if I had any doubt."

"Go on."

"When I opened the door, Major Komarov had his pistol pointed at your back."

When Brovko reached into his belt and pulled out a pistol, Nikolai froze.

"Don't worry, Nikolai. I simply wanted to show you the pistol." He held it out for Nikolai to see. "It's an old Makarov belonging to Detective Horvath. The same pistol he used to shoot your friend Pavel. The same pistol Major Komarov emptied into the floor of the house."

"I . . . I don't understand."

"Major Komarov aimed this pistol at my back. Why would he aim Detective Horvath's pistol instead of his own?"

"I don't know, Captain."

"Do you think the major was prepared to shoot me?"

"It's hard to say. He looked . . . like he had lost control."

"The major has become emotional about the case. He can't be left alone."

"What should we do, Captain? You're the officer in charge."

"Major Komarov is the officer in charge."

"But if he's emotionally unbalanced . . ."

"What do the other psychiatrists think?"

"I don't understand . . ."

"The other men. What's the consensus concerning Major Komarov's mental health?"

"Not good, Captain. Not good at all."

On the far side of the room, beyond the Gypsies, Komarov could see the two men who had relieved Captain Brovko. The men leaned close to one another, their faces almost touching as they whispered. They were young men, the same age as Dmitry. Perhaps, while in KGB school, they roomed together . . .

Although the men on the far side of the room stared at him, they did not know he was awake. Rather than sleeping, Komarov had opened his eyes only enough to see out. Back here in the shadows on the daybed, no one knew he was awake. If he had been a little closer, he might have heard everything Brovko said to Horvath. But he'd heard enough—Brovko and Horvath discussing his lack of humor while Brovko played nursemaid with drinks of water.

Komarov knew he could trust no one. Not Captain Azef, who was most likely looking out Komarov's office window this very moment, planning a takeover of Kiev operations. And not Captain Brovko, sent by Deputy Chairman Dumenko to "assist." Obviously Brovko had stood by, allowing Komarov to perform the old-school, iron-fisted work, waiting for the climax so he could hurry back to Moscow and seize credit for the discovery of a conspiracy to destroy Chernobyl. Komarov's anger became so intense he could no longer lie still.

When Komarov sat up, one of the men hurried for the front door. "Where are you going?"

"Outside for a moment, Major."

"Stay here! I want two guards on the prisoners at all times!"

"But the captain asked . . ."

"Never mind what the captain asked!" Komarov stood and walked to the man. "I'm in charge, and I told you to stay!"

The man stepped back from the door, looked to his partner. "Yes, Major."

Komarov walked in front of the prisoners. Horvath stared at him. Bela Sandor was waking up, his eyes blinking.

"A new day has dawned," said Komarov, adjusting his shoulder holster and tucking in his shirt. "Perhaps you've had time to recall where your bitches have gone. Perhaps they've found a stallion or some other barnyard creature with which to satisfy themselves."

Komarov turned quickly, catching the two guards exchanging glances. "Guard them! Not one another!"

It was a sunny morning. Komarov got a drink of water, took a slice of bread from a bread box on a shelf. He chewed the bread and stared out the window. The downslope of the hill beyond the border of weeds made it impossible to see the land between the house and the village. Perhaps, in the dark, the women had been able to find a hiding place only they knew. He wanted to use the children. No one could stand watching a child suffer, not even a Kiev militia detective.

When he arrived the night before last, it had been dark. And although he had inspected the surrounding area with a flashlight, he had told his men to do a more thorough job during the day yesterday. If there had been a place to hide, his men should have been aware of it. But last night, before Horvath arrived, it seemed as though the earth had swallowed them up.

Where would little children hide? Children who might make noise because they are tired and hungry. Unable to play with their toys, they would become fidgety.

When Komarov looked at the stump in the yard with the ax embedded in it, he wondered if his men had adequately searched the chicken coop. Surely a group of women and children would have made an uproar with the chickens if they'd gone in there. Komarov was about to have one of the men search the coop again when he noticed something about the box out beyond the fire pit in the yard. Yesterday the utensils and tin plates had been on the box. Now they were scattered along one side of the box.

Discarded tin plates and forks! An old box for a table! Children's toys! Had one of his men knocked the plates and utensils off the box so he would have a place to rest? Or had someone else cleared the top of the box?

Komarov went to the back door and opened it. When he stood in the doorway looking out at the box in the yard, Bela Sandor whined behind him.

"I'm hungry."

Komarov resisted the urge to go back inside and slap Bela.

"When can we eat? Feed me!"

There was something about the box. Could the Gypsy read his mind? Or had he simply noticed him looking at it? Perhaps there was something in the box.

Komarov threw his remaining bread aside. Ignoring Bela's protests, he motioned for the guard near the back door to go with him. When Komarov walked out into the yard, the guard from outside the back door and one of the men farther out in the yard joined him.

Because the tin plates and discarded utensils were scattered on one side, it appeared as if someone had lifted the box up on end. There was a worn tablecloth draped over the box, but he noticed it was tacked on with nails. Komarov gripped the top edge of the box and lifted. It was surprisingly lightweight. Instead of the entire box tipping upward, only the top of the box with its tablecloth skirt lifted.

Beneath the top, Komarov saw a hole, a deep hole with a ladder leading down into the darkness. It could have been an old well or the entrance to a tunnel or an underground chamber dug during the war so the Gypsies could hide from invading troops. It could lead anywhere!

Once the cover of the hole was tilted back on its hidden hinges, Komarov asked for a flashlight from one of the men. Using the flashlight, he could see to the bottom of the ladder. There was a dirt floor about three or four meters down. On the side of the hole opposite the ladder, about a meter down, there seemed to be an opening. Above the opening there was a wooden timber. A smell drifted out from the hole, a smell like something beginning to go sour mixed with . . . yes, mixed with the faint scent of alcohol. A wine cellar!

Komarov held his finger to his lips so the men would remain silent. He leaned close and listened. Back in the house, he heard Bela shouting something in Hungarian. Komarov had patience now. In what seemed only a moment or two, his patience had paid dividends. Coming from deep in the hole, Komarov heard the unmistakable whimper of a baby.

Rather than tell his men that the women and children were down in what was apparently a wine cellar, Komarov kept listening. He could hear the baby's cries being muffled. He imagined Bela's wife clutching the baby to her bosom, perhaps suffocating the baby with her own flesh. Would the woman kill her own child? But then he heard the whimper again, followed by a clicking sound, and he realized the baby was feeding.

Komarov put the flashlight he held into his jacket pocket and lowered his head even farther into the hole. The sound of the baby suckling its mother's breast reminded him of his wife breast-feeding Dmitry, reminded him of how he had sometimes substituted his finger for his wife's nipple. He recalled the draw on his fingertip as Dmitry suckled it. Then he remembered Dmitry's lover, Fyodor, and a wave of disgust and nausea enveloped him as though the hole in the ground were trying to suck out his insides.

CHAPTER 34

When the front door of the house flew open and two men ran out waving frantically, Nikolai opened the door of the Volga and followed after Captain Brovko. Once inside the house, one of the men who had waved ran alongside Brovko.

"The major is in the yard. He's found something. A tunnel, I think."

When Nikolai followed Brovko out the back door, Detective Horvath shouted after them. "Your major is going insane! You'd better watch him!"

In the yard, Major Komarov was bent over a box Nikolai had seen. But the box was open, its top, with a tablecloth hanging on it, tilted upward. Komarov stood as Brovko approached.

"Get the two Gypsy traitors," said Komarov to the men nearest him. "Carry them out here, chairs and all. Here, give me your gun."

Komarov took the AKM from the nearest man and turned to Brovko. "Captain, a dozen men search through the night, find nothing, yet the women and children are here under their noses. I should have known. The soil on this plateau is high and dry."

Komarov watched the men gathering, trudging through the

weeds. He smiled and waved his arm. "Come, don't be frightened! Women and children cowering in a wine cellar won't bite!" Komarov held up the AKM he had confiscated. "I'll protect you!"

The men sent for the prisoners carried Horvath and Bela outside, the two who were carrying Bela's chair struggling. Bela's wriggling threw the men off balance, and they dropped Bela on his side.

"New recruits," said Komarov to Brovko, shaking his head. "Whichever KGB school they graduated from should be investigated!"

Komarov pointed to the ground near the open box with the AKM. "Put them here."

Because Komarov was smiling, some of the men smiled back. But to Nikolai it was not a contagious smile. It was the grin of a madman.

Detective Horvath and Bela Sandor sat side by side, tied to their chairs, facing the open box. Komarov went to the far side of the box and faced them. Nikolai stood beside Captain Brovko and the rest of the men gathered in a semicircle behind them. They all looked at the box concealing the hole in the ground.

"It's a wine cellar," announced Komarov. "Gypsies drink plenty, the cheapest they can get, homemade rotgut. I should have known there wasn't enough in the house. When I was a boy outside Moscow, legend had it they drank blood when they ran out of wine."

Komarov looked down into the hole. "The Gypsies from my boyhood had a pact with one another. They were clannish, which meant the lives of those outside the clan meant nothing. Neither did the country in which they lived. Some Gypsies ended up leaving the motherland. They'll go to any country foolish enough to let them in. They have a rebellious nature. We've had a taste of this rebellion in Afghanistan."

Nikolai noticed two men who were standing to one side of the box glance at one another and shrug their shoulders.

Komarov stooped down and spoke into the hole. "You may come out now, Gypsies." Komarov paused for a moment, then shouted, "I said, come out!"

Komarov stood up, aimed the AKM down the hole, and fired.

It all happened very quickly. The AKM was on full automatic. At least a dozen rounds blasted into the hole. When the firing stopped, screams echoed from the hole, screams of women and children, making Nikolai want to do something. Off to the side he saw one of the men raise his AKM in Komarov's direction. Behind him he heard a man say, "Don't shoot them!"

The prisoners wriggled in their chairs, breathing loudly through their teeth.

After firing, Komarov stepped back from the hole and shouted, "Will you come out now?"

"Yes!" was the reply, a woman weeping. Nikolai could feel the anguish in his chest.

Captain Brovko broke from the group and approached the entrance to the cellar. When the first woman appeared, he helped her up. It was Nina Horvath, who turned to take the baby from Mariska Sandor, who came out next, causing Bela to call her name. Finally, the two little girls came out.

"Take them into the house," said Komarov. Then he summoned one of the men and gave back the AKM.

After a tearful reunion between Mariska, Bela, Detective Horvath, and his sister-in-law, Nina, Captain Brovko and two other men led the women and children to the house. Mariska was pulled backward, and she looked to Bela, making the sign of the cross.

"Pray to your God!" shouted Komarov. "Instead of joining with our motherland, pray to your icons, your ancestors, your Allah! Idiot zealots! Destroyers of the world!"

The men who had carried Bela and Detective Horvath out began lifting Bela's chair to follow the women and children into the house.

"No!" shouted Komarov, then, more calmly, he said, "Leave them here."

Komarov walked around the cellar entrance and stood before Horvath and Bela. But then he turned suddenly and stared wide-eyed at Nikolai. "Now we will learn something, Nikolai Nikolskaia. When conspirators go into hiding, they confirm their conspiracy. The connection between Zukor and his cousins is established. We need only find Juli Popovics, whose role was to help Mihaly Horvath escape had the reactor not overreacted to his treachery!"

Several men standing to the side looked to one another, wondering whether Komarov's theory rang true.

Komarov turned back to Horvath. "I wonder if the American CIA technical experts knew how the reactor would react when they sent in their Gypsy Moth. Not simply a steam explosion, but a more disastrous explosion endangering many lives! What would they care if the lives of a few Ukrainians and Russians and Hungarians were put at risk? Their goal was to disable the reactor, and they succeeded. Those in the Lubyanka in Moscow knew of the plot. Unfortunately the information they had was not enough to stop it!"

Nikolai listened with confusion as Komarov confronted Detective Horvath. "It's a foregone conclusion, Detective Horvath. I cannot risk the possibility of another CIA plot in the works. You know where Juli Popovics is. She has information critical to us, and I have the women and children."

"They won't let you hurt them."

"What did you say?"

"The men. They have families. You can't expect them to let you . . ."

Komarov took out his pistol and smashed Horvath across the

face. This time, after being relatively silent in the house all night, Horvath screamed. It was an overwhelming scream echoing across the plateau, a baleful scream of release and anger. When Horvath's scream trailed off, yet another ungodly sound began, higher pitched, the shriek of an animal somewhere below ground. Words buried in the scream emerged from the hole in the ground. A woman. How could these words come from a woman?

"Komarov! You have fucked your mother and your father! Is there no one left?"

Komarov smiled an insane smile, turned, and started for the cellar entrance.

"No!" shouted Horvath. "I'll say anything you want!"

When Komarov aimed his pistol down the hole, Horvath shouted something in Hungarian.

Komarov fired all eight rounds. He glared at the men moving toward him. Nikolai felt someone at his back shoving him forward. Brovko came running from the house. Komarov threw the pistol aside, took a large folding knife from his pocket, opened it, and climbed quickly down the ladder. The last thing Nikolai saw was Komarov's insane smile as Brovko ran up to the hole, then turned about with a puzzled look on his face as Horvath shouted in Hungarian. Among the shouts the word *kes* was repeated over and over, and Nikolai knew it must mean *knife*.

Juli's ears rang from the deafening booms of the gunshots into the cellar. The air was filled with the smell of gunpowder. Light from the opening slanted through dust and smoke. No sooner had she stared at the slant of light, and the entrance was blocked by a shadow. The rungs of the ladder creaked from the weight of someone coming down. Komarov or another man sent after her.

She heard Lazlo shouting from above. Something about a knife. Komarov had a knife! When she could see legs on the ladder, she heard another voice, the voice of a man shouting directly into the hole.

"Major Komarov! Wait!"

In the distance, beyond the man shouting down the hole, Lazlo continued. "If you're not going after him, at least keep silent!"

Suddenly, the world above was cut off. The only sounds remaining were the creaking of the last rungs of the ladder and the sound of her heartbeat.

Juli's life, since the day she met Mihaly on the bus from the power station to Pripyat, flashed through her mind as it had flashed through her mind so many times. Small details of what had happened stood out. Other possibilities materialized—Mihaly's parallel world; an island in the South Pacific to which the China Syndrome of Chernobyl has eaten a tunnel; Mihaly and Lazlo together in this other world, united—a seemingly small decision in the past could have prevented Mihaly's death, perhaps even prevented the accident at Chernobyl.

If only she had married long ago, been a married woman with children like Nina when she and Mihaly met casually on the bus. If only she had listened to Mihaly's concerns about the plant and done something, anything. If only she hadn't met Lazlo and fallen in love with him. If only . . .

No! They were depending on her! Everyone up there in the world was depending on her! If Lazlo was willing to die for her and Nina and Mariska and the children, she should be willing to do something. *Do* something!

When the last rung of the ladder creaked, she crawled as quietly as she could to the side of the cellar where she knew the wine kegs rested on a wooden stand, which had felt like a squat table in the dark. She squeezed beneath the stand, spiderwebs settling across her face. It was a tight fit, one of the kegs in its cradle on the stand pressed against her back, another kept the side of her face on the dirt floor. She looked back at the shaft of light from the entrance and saw Komarov standing bent over. Then he disappeared, joining her in the darkness of the cellar.

It was so quiet in the yard Lazlo could hear birds singing down the hill. *Juli! Why didn't you fly away?*

The seconds ticked by, Brovko and several other men standing around the hole, looking to one another. One man took out a flashlight, aimed it at the hole, but Brovko put his hand on the man's arm and the man put the flashlight away.

The birds kept singing, and Lazlo looked down, trying to see through the earth and into the wine cellar. Then he prayed, first to his mother, then to his father, then to Mihaly. He even prayed to the Gypsy deserter on the Romanian border. He prayed that their spirits, knowing the difference between virtue and evil, would tunnel from their tombs. He prayed for them to go into the cellar and take Komarov with them.

Komarov followed the wall for a short distance before sitting on the floor against the wall. Because he held the knife in his right hand, he reached into his pocket with his left hand for the flashlight he had been given by one of the men. He listened for a moment, and when he could hear nothing, he aimed the flashlight straight ahead and switched it on.

She was wedged beneath a low platform holding a row of wine kegs off the floor. She covered her eyes with one hand and tried to squeeze farther beneath the platform.

"I didn't think you had a gun," he said quietly. "Otherwise you would have shot at me as I came down the ladder. This investigation has been a long, hard struggle for me. Even though you may think you are innocent, I know better. Just as I climbed down here on the ladder, I will climb to the top on your back and on the back of your lover. If others try to stop me or take credit for uncovering your conspiracy, I'll climb atop the heap of their remains. I could capture you and say you confessed to me, but I'm afraid there are some who might believe your lies simply because you are a woman."

Komarov switched the flashlight off and put it into his pocket. Soon he would use it once more to look into her eyes the way he had looked into the eyes of Gretchen and Tamara. In his other hand, held down at his side, was the knife he would need to defend himself from an attack from behind.

When the glow of light filtering through her closed lids went out, she opened her eyes and, at the same time, struggled out from beneath the kegs. When she crawled free of her hiding place, she thought her ankles would be grasped at any moment. If she stood and ran to the ladder, he would see her and pull her down before she could climb halfway up.

She crawled slowly to the middle of the floor, pushing her fingers ahead through the surface dirt. She listened for him but could hear only her inhales and exhales. She opened her mouth wide in an attempt to quiet her breathing and crawled against the far wall, away from the entrance where her outline would be visible against the light from above. She crawled a circular path to the place he had been because she was certain he would have moved.

She paused and listened. She heard his breathing to one side. Then she heard nothing and moved forward. Suddenly, her hand touched his shoe.

"I've been waiting for you," he said, his voice seemingly calm, as if he did not really mean to hurt her.

In an instant his hand was at her head, clutching her hair and pulling. She swung out, hit his face. He stood, pulled her up with him, and threw her to the floor. She tried to roll away, but he had her by the arm, twisting her arm until she thought it would break. Her other hand was on the dirt floor. She clutched a handful of dirt and flung it at his face. He coughed and spit, and she was able to pull free.

She ran to the back of the cellar, smashed her shin against a bench. Despite the pain, she picked up the bench, swung it around, and pushed it out in front of her. She hit him with it, but he was quickly back at her, ripping the bench from her grasp and pushing her against the wooden timbers on the wall.

A sharp pain at the back of her head was followed by dizziness. She grasped at the wall, but it moved upward and away from her. She was forced onto her back. She felt his weight on her. Then the flashlight burned in her eyes.

She could hear muted voices from above. Men arguing. They would come down into the cellar to help her. They would drag Komarov away. But Komarov's hot breath blew on her face as he shouted, his voice enraged and insane.

"Don't come down! That's my order! If you do, you'll be shot! She's armed!"

It was all happening too fast. Only seconds had gone by. The arguing from above continued. No one came.

He was behind the flashlight, breathing heavily. She could smell his foul breath. When she tried to push the flashlight away, she felt a sharp pain on her abdomen.

"Lie still." His voice was calm again, a voice seemingly coming from a different person. "I have a knife. I'll push it all the way in if you move."

He turned and again shouted, "Fools! Don't interfere! She's armed!"

The knife was at her. Not inside yet, but pricking the skin of her abdomen. Her baby! What about her baby? She needed something to strike him with. She reached out slowly, not moving, not really. The light stayed in her eyes until she stared above the light where she could now see his eyes in the dim light above the flashlight.

Dirt would be futile. She stretched her arm outward, and this seemed to draw him closer. Then she felt something. Cloth. Damp cloth. A soiled diaper from Mariska's baby. She pulled it in with her fingertips, pulled it closer and dragged it to her side where he could not see it because his eyes were close to hers. He spoke.

"How young you are, and beautiful. I thought you would have reminded me of other Gypsy women. Your hair is lighter than I thought it would be. You are neither Barbara nor Tamara. I'm paying you a compliment when I say you remind me of Gretchen."

She considered pleading with him. Maybe he had made a mistake. Maybe he was really after someone called Gretchen. Maybe if she reminded him she was not Gretchen. No! Reason would not do. He was insane. She could see it in his eyes. And if he was insane, maybe she could make him think she *was* Gretchen, if only for a moment.

She slowly moved the diaper closer and felt more pressure on the knife. When she opened her eyes wide, the pressure lessened. She kept her eyes open wide and forced a smile. She said, "I am

Gretchen. I have something for you."

His eyes narrowed slightly, and he moved his face back when she began unbuttoning her blouse with her free hand. The flashlight lowered, and she could see him looking at her breasts. The look on his face changed slightly. A smile began to appear. As she unbuttoned her blouse, she had his attention. But what would she do after this? And what would he do?

For the first time since he'd held her down, she felt a slight lifting of his weight. Then, when she felt the pressure of the knife at her abdomen ease even more, she pushed the soiled diaper into his face and rolled sideways.

He screamed, and she kicked out her legs, kicked against something. She scrambled to it, swept the floor with her hands until she found it.

When he threw aside the foul-smelling rag, he could still smell it and feel it. Urine, his face soaked, his lips tingling. A sudden image of Dmitry and his lover using the cellar for lechery flashed before him. A wave of nausea threatened to overcome him, but he regained his senses.

He spit and turned in the direction she had crawled. He reached for her. He wanted her beneath him again. But where was his knife? The knife!

Yes. There it was. He found it. He found it! It was . . . in him. It felt hot, as if it had saved up all the heat of its victims.

Were there voices? Did he hear voices? Was it his wife and Dmitry come to see him in hospital? Had time moved ahead faster than he realized? Yes, Grigor Komarov, the hero, taking visitors in hospital. *How did it happen?* asks the visitors. And he tells them how he was forced to kill the woman in self-defense because . . . because Captain Brovko had come down into the wine cellar and been killed by her? Yes, it could have happened that way . . . there were so many ways, so many rungs on the ladder . . .

But the voices . . . the voices. Like being on his back porch in the dark, someone creeping up on him. Was it his father and mother? Had they come to join him in seeking vengeance upon the Gypsies?

Then the voices became a thousand faces, and he tried to scream but could not.

Nikolai saw that Captain Brovko was uncertain about what to do. The captain had started for the hole several times, only to step back. Then, when it seemed he'd made up his mind to go down into the hole and he actually leaned in, he stepped back, his eyes open wide. When Nikolai saw the look on Brovko's face, he stared at the entrance to the hole as if it were a living thing.

A blood-soaked hand gripped the edge of the cellar entrance. There were gasps from the other men as the rest of the bloody arm appeared; then another hand, not bloody; then Juli Popovics climbing out of the hole under her own power.

"Juli!" shouted Detective Horvath.

Captain Brovko stepped back as Juli Popovics saw Horvath and ran to him. She knelt before the chair and hugged him, looked into his eyes as she touched his face with her hands, both of them ignoring the blood on her right hand and arm as they stared into one another's eyes and wept.

Captain Brovko came to Nikolai, handed him a key, and motioned to the couple. Nikolai stooped down behind the chair and unlocked the handcuffs so Detective Horvath could embrace Juli Popovics.

CHAPTER 35

Captain Brovko ordered them to remain in the house. Men were posted at the front and back doors and at all the windows. The three men assigned to stand guard inside the house told Mariska and Nina to care for Lazlo and Bela.

Juli's wounds consisted of a few bruises and a shallow cut on her abdomen. After she was searched, and Lazlo's money along with the keys to the Skoda were taken, she went into the bathroom to change out of her blood-soaked blouse and wash Komarov's blood from her hands and arms. When she came out of the bathroom, both Bela and Lazlo held wet towels to their faces and said they felt much better.

But when Lazlo closed his eyes to rest and she could no longer look into his eyes, the terror in the wine cellar returned. The memory of total darkness, suddenly replaced by Komarov's eyes, momentarily paralyzed her.

She went to the sink in the kitchenette. She gripped the edge of the sink and took several deep breaths. She had killed Komarov! She had killed Komarov, and she and Lazlo had survived. She turned on the faucet and began moistening another towel for Lazlo.

Outside the window, she could see the open trapdoor to the wine cellar; the open lid of the box resembling a coffin had become a coffin. As she watched, Captain Brovko and the man whose partner had been killed in Visenka climbed down into the wine cellar.

It seemed so long ago, yet only a month had passed since the Chernobyl explosion. Juli knelt beside the daybed, applying the wet towel to Lazlo's face. Nina handed her a glass of water. When she took it, Nina looked at her for a moment. Then Nina turned away and wiped tears from her eyes with her sleeve.

The little girls, Anna and Ilonka, came from the bedroom and stood with their mother. The older daughter, Anna, asked, "*Mommychka*, is she going to marry Uncle Lazlo?"

"I don't know," said Nina. "Why don't you ask her?"

Anna came close to Juli, but instead of speaking, she stood silent with her hands behind her and watched as Juli applied the towel to Lazlo's swollen eyes.

At first, because of the way Captain Brovko went into the wine cellar and hurried out in a frenzy announcing Komarov's death and ordering men about, Nikolai thought the brutality might continue. But after Horvath and the others were in the house and men had been posted at every possible exit, Brovko grew calm and asked Nikolai to accompany him into the wine cellar.

Komarov's body was near the back wall of the cellar. He lay sprawled out on his stomach, his head twisted to one side, eyes open wide and glistening wet in the beam of the flashlight. Brovko aimed the flashlight at Komarov's eyes for some time. Even in death, the major's eyes seemed demonic. Because his face was twisted sideways against the dirt floor, Komarov's mouth was contorted into an insane grin, showing yellow-stained teeth.

Below Komarov's waist, a pool of blood extended out in all directions, soaking into the dry soil. Komarov's lower back was arched upward slightly, and when Brovko used his foot to push Komarov over onto his back, Nikolai saw the knife. It was embedded deep in the major's abdomen above the groin. Only part of the handle showed.

Brovko took out a handkerchief, wrapped it about the knife handle, and pulled. There was a liquid gurgle as the knife came out. The sound, combined with the smell of released bowels and Komarov's tobacco, nauseated Nikolai. He backed away to the entrance where the air was better. He found a bench tipped on its side, righted it, and sat down.

Brovko stayed at the body, wiping the knife and inspecting it. Then Brovko placed the knife and handkerchief beside the body and joined Nikolai on the bench. Brovko sat closer to the entrance, and although the flashlight was out, Nikolai could see Brovko's profile against the light from the entrance.

"A lot of blood," said Brovko. "The pressure of his weight pushed the knife in past the hilt. It apparently severed a main blood vessel, and he quickly bled to death."

"It was his own knife," said Nikolai. "I saw him take it out of his pocket before he came down here. A folding knife."

"A large one," said Brovko. "I saw the major with it once before, in Kiev. He threatened an old man playing a violin on Lenkomsomol Square."

"She must have gotten the knife away from him somehow."

"Perhaps," said Brovko. "But it's also possible that in the midst of the struggle, he simply fell onto it."

"I suppose it's possible."

"She was unarmed," said Brovko. "All we found on her were car keys and four hundred rubles. She had it in a sock pinned inside her blouse. She said she left the car in the village. I sent two men after it. A black Skoda, which was originally white. I saw the black paint on Horvath's hands after he was captured."

Brovko was silent, staring straight ahead, his Germanic profile unmoving. Then he turned. "Tell me something, Nikolai. Do you think Major Komarov noticed the paint on Horvath's hands?"

"I don't know."

"He was with Horvath all night, as you know. One thing puzzling me is that he didn't send men out looking for the car."

"I'm not sure what you're getting at, Captain."

"Listen to me, Nikolai. We both saw what happened up there. We both witnessed Komarov's actions, myself more than you. Last night you saw Komarov aim his pistol at me. This morning we all saw him fire an AKM into this cellar when he knew women and children were down here. I've taken over command from a crazy man. Immediately after the Chernobyl explosion, he was told there could be another, even worse explosion, yet instead of investigating this possibility, instead of gathering information about the disaster according to the general directive from Moscow, the major pursued his own investigation. He convinced Deputy Chairman Dumenko he had evidence of sabotage. And I must now decide what to do."

"What do you want from me?"

"I want you to listen to what I have to say. When I'm finished, I want you to tell me what you know. No one can hear us down here. You are the only other member of the KGB who knows vital details concerning this case."

"Very well, Captain. I'm listening."

"Good, Nikolai. There are several factors to consider. The first is the nature of Komarov's interrogation. He immediately began using what we call the active method of interrogation on Detective Horvath and Bela Sandor. He wanted to know where Juli Popovics was, and he wanted to know where the women and children had gone. During the time I was with him, this was the extent of his questioning. Not once did he ask about Chernobyl. Not once did he ask about technical details of the so-called sabotage. He treated Detective Horvath as if he were extremely dangerous, as if the man would try to kill anyone in his path. I found this to be untrue. Horvath was even careful when sneaking up on our men so as not to seriously injure anyone. Doesn't this seem odd?"

"Yes," said Nikolai. "It all seems especially odd to me, because when Pavel and I arrived in Kiev, the major emphasized Detective Horvath's threat while seemingly forgetting what had happened at Chernobyl. When we went to pick up Juli Popovics, we were told to be careful of Horvath because he was a murderous saboteur. Last night, when he arrived here, Horvath could have killed Komarov. And I think he might have."

"Why didn't he?" asked Brovko.

"Because he would have had to kill others. Last night he could have easily killed me and made it into the house. When he climbed in the window, I could have killed him but did not. Yes, he shot Pavel. But Major Komarov was the real killer. Major Komarov was the one who frightened Pavel into aiming his pistol at Detective Horvath and Juli Popovics. Pavel and I were not trained as you were, Captain. I told Major Komarov this when we arrived in Kiev. But he insisted we be put on the case. He made it sound as if he were doing us a favor. Pavel's death was what Major Komarov needed so he could have a more substantial case against Detective Horvath and Juli Popovics."

Brovko touched Nikolai's arm. "Thank you for speaking freely with me. I will return the favor. Komarov left a trail of death in Kiev, and now we are here with his body . . ."

Brovko let go of Nikolai's arm and looked straight ahead again, his profile more exposed because of the brightening light from the entrance as the morning sun rose higher.

"What will you do now, Captain?"

"I'm only certain of one thing at this moment, Nikolai."

"What's that?"

"Major Komarov died in an accident in which he stumbled in a dark wine cellar and fell onto his own knife. Do you agree?"

"I agree, Captain. Are fingerprints on the knife?"

"No fingerprints."

Brovko stood, went to the ladder, and climbed to daylight. Nikolai hurried after him, glad to be away from the smell of wine defiled by the odor of death.

For the remainder of the morning and well into the afternoon, Captain Brovko spoke to each of the men individually. The two men sent after the car returned, saying they found the black Skoda in the village and searched it but found nothing. Late in the afternoon, Brovko sent all but Nikolai and four other men back to Kiev. The men returning to Kiev were new to the KGB, a few on their first assignment. They loaded Komarov's body into the van and took it with them. Nikolai stood at the front of the house with Brovko and watched as the men drove off and disappeared down the hill.

"I told the men to pick up the Skoda on their way back through the village," said Brovko.

"I hope it starts," said Nikolai.

"It will," said Brovko. Then, turning to the house. "Everyone agrees. Major Komarov had gone mad."

The afternoon was quiet, and everyone was tired. Lazlo, Bela, Mariska, and the children slept while Juli and Nina kept watch.

They sat in chairs to the side of the daybed. On the other side of the room, the three guards alternated throughout the afternoon. With Komarov gone, the guards seemed at ease and less threatening.

Juli sat facing the guards at the kitchen table. As the afternoon wore on, she relived the scene in the wine cellar again and again. Even though she knew she had killed Komarov in self-defense, she kept trying to imagine a different outcome. If she had not killed Komarov, he would have killed her, and he might have killed Lazlo and the others. If she had not come to the farmhouse, Lazlo might be dead instead of Komarov. She would have been in Czechoslovakia, and Lazlo would have been at Komarov's mercy. Now it was different. Now they were both here at the mercy of Captain Brovko, whose plans were unknown.

"When is your baby due?" asked Nina suddenly from behind.

The question shocked Juli, made tears come to her eyes as she turned. "The doctor said near the first of the year."

"Ilonka was born the same time of year, four years ago last January. Mihaly wanted a boy, but he was very happy when he saw Ilonka. I hope your child is not affected by the radiation."

Despite her efforts not to weep, tears flowed down Juli's cheeks.

At dusk Captain Brovko entered the house and said it was time to go. When Lazlo asked who was going, Brovko explained that everyone would finally be left in peace, but Juli and Lazlo had to go with him.

During the tearful good-byes, Juli knew there had been no way out of the dilemma from the beginning. Whatever happened to Lazlo and her now was already written down somewhere, perhaps in their own blood. Juli was surprised when Nina hugged her and whispered in her ear.

"Care for yourself and your baby. I have a feeling everything will be all right."

Before going outside, Captain Brovko had Juli handcuffed to one of his men and handcuffed himself to Lazlo. The man handcuffed to Juli led her to the second of two remaining cars and got in the back seat with her while two men got in the front seat. The others, including Lazlo and Brovko, walked to the first car. Nikolskaia and another man got in the front seat of the car, but Brovko held Lazlo back. He led Lazlo to a spot between the cars and spoke with him quietly for several minutes. Although the sun had set and it was getting darker, there was still enough light for Juli to see Lazlo wiping at tears in his eyes.

When Brovko finished speaking with Lazlo, he led him to the lead car, and the two cars drove rapidly away from the house, down the hill, and through the village. Juli watched the car ahead in which Lazlo rode. She hoped she and Lazlo would see each other again before they were sent to prison.

But then something strange happened. Instead of staying on the paved road after going through Kisbor, the lead car turned south onto the same dirt road Juli had taken early in the morning when she drove the Skoda into Kisbor. Only the taillights of the lead car were visible in the dust being raised from the road.

After a short distance, the cars pulled to the side of the narrow road and stopped. First the lead car shut off its lights, then the car she was in shut off its lights. They were in the middle of farm fields with no houses or buildings in sight. In the gathering darkness she saw Lazlo and Brovko get out of the other car. Brovko removed the handcuffs, and she saw Lazlo outlined against the purple evening sky. She imagined Lazlo being shot and left there, or his body taken back, Brovko saying he had tried to escape.

Juli pulled at the handcuffs, tried to open her door, screamed Lazlo's name.

But in a few seconds the terror was over. Her handcuffs were removed, and she was in Lazlo's arms. Then Lazlo took her hand and led her to the front of the cars. The black Skoda was there, ahead of the lead car where she had been unable to see it, the black Skoda looking like a child's toy compared to the Volgas. She got inside the Skoda with Lazlo, and they drove away. When she looked back, she saw the two Volgas turn around on the dirt road and head north, their taillights becoming dimmer and dimmer in the distance.

"Laz, am I dreaming?"

"No. But we've still got to get into Czechoslovakia. We've got to do it soon because Brovko said the militia will be looking for us."

"Why did he let us go?"

"He said he has training in nuclear engineering, and he, as well as others, had doubts about Komarov's claims of sabotage at Chernobyl. He said it would be best for everyone involved if we were not taken back to Kiev. He also told me something else."

"What?"

"Komarov murdered Tamara."

Juli reached out and held Lazlo's hand. "I'm so sorry, Laz."

"Komarov killed his informant first, a poet from Tamara's club. Brovko said he doesn't know why Komarov killed Tamara." Lazlo paused. "Tamara would have wanted us to escape."

Lazlo drove fast along the deserted farm road. When he reached a paved road, he turned north, and Juli saw a sign saying Uzhgorod was ten kilometers away. She remembered the instructions from the woman in Yasinya. First guardhouse to the north. Ask for directions to Uzhgorod, then directions to Laborets Castle. If the guard lectures about Prince Laborets' murder in 903 AD, he is the correct guard.

Soon Juli could see it, a lighted guardhouse well off the road to the left. On the other side of the guardhouse, where the last light from the sun had disappeared, was Czechoslovakia.

Once they were on the main road to Lvov, the second Volga dropped back about fifty meters, and the headlights were not quite so bright. Before leaving the spot where they left Detective Horvath and Juli Popovics, Captain Brovko announced they would spend the night in Lvov and drive to Kiev in the morning. Nikolai drove the lead Volga, with Brovko in the passenger seat. The four other men were in the second Volga.

Brovko turned on an interior light and consulted the map. "About a hundred kilometers more. We'll get there before the restaurants close. None of us has had a hot meal or a night of sleep in two days."

"I'm looking forward to it, Captain. There are supposed to be some fine Polish restaurants in Lvov." Nikolai glanced in the mirror at the following headlights. "I'll bet the others are discussing our dinner in detail, right down to the size and texture of the dumplings."

"They are good men," said Brovko, turning out the light.

Except for an occasional oncoming car causing Nikolai to dim the headlights, the road was dark. It was still farm country, not as flat as the plateau they had come from, but with rolling hills, one after another like the hill on which the farmhouse was perched like a medieval castle.

"One would not have expected such a deep wine cellar," said Nikolai. "Usually they are built into the side of a hill or a mound."

"And surprisingly dry," said Brovko. "It probably never floods because the water table is far below the hill."

"None of the other men noticed the tin plates on the ground?"

"They noticed."

"They did?"

"Yes," said Brovko. "It's one of many things I learned while speaking with them."

"They knew the women and children were down there, yet they didn't tell Komarov?"

"Correct. And they might not have told me if I'd asked them as a group. It's always an advantage to compare individual observations of a situation."

"What about Detective Horvath and Juli Popovics?" asked Nikolai. "Wouldn't it have been better to return them to Kiev?"

"There are overriding factors. I phoned Deputy Chairman Dumenko last night. I was assigned from the beginning to observe the situation and report back. There is concern in Moscow about what Komarov has tried to do and what he has done in the past. Taking Detective Horvath and Juli Popovics to Kiev would have put the KGB in a bad light in Kiev and in Moscow. Dumenko thinks Gorbachev has enough trouble right now."

"So Komarov did plan Pavel's death?"

"Yes. But now, Nikolai, I must give you the order I gave the rest of the men. The order comes directly from Deputy Chairman Dumenko. You are to discuss this incident with no one. When we return to Kiev, all of you, including myself, will be given a final briefing."

"Is this how the KGB eliminates its rotten apples, Captain?"

"Things are changing in the Soviet Union, Nikolai. The KGB must change with them. Even the Chernobyl disaster will change us. Gorbachev realizes this, and so do others on the politburo. For now we should salute the heroes created by the Chernobyl disaster. Men like Colonel Zamyatin, whom I met on my way from Moscow to Kiev. He is in charge of army refugee and cleanup operations. Many have volunteered to help. They are calling themselves liquidators. Perhaps the Chernobyl accident will usher in the new era of openness Gorbachev has spoken of. Everything changes, Nikolai.

Everything."

As they drove, the number of houses increased, and soon they could see a town in the distance. The lights from the town spread before them, taking away the blackness of night for a few minutes. Then they were in the dark again.

"What was the name of the town?" asked Nikolai. "I didn't notice the sign."

"Sambor," said Captain Brovko. "Fifty more kilometers, and we'll be in Lvov, where our dinner and our beds await us."

Back in Sambor, the windows of the houses flickered as residents watched the latest report about Chernobyl. No one had noticed the two Volgas speeding through town on their way to Lvov.

CHAPTER 36

August 1986

It was Sunday. The bells of Vienna's churches had tolled the noon hour. The view from the seventh-floor window of the Vienna Intercontinental Hotel was facing northeast across the city park, where people in colorful summer clothing walked along tree-lined paths.

Juli stood looking out the window, holding her abdomen. Although her baby was not moving now, she had felt it earlier. The baby moved most in the morning, waking her. But now, as she looked out the window, the baby was asleep in its small world. The only feeling Juli had now was the tingling of her newly stretched skin.

According to tests several days earlier in Budapest at the Institute for Radiobiology, everything was normal. The doctors said the baby's growth did not seem affected by radiation. But there were no guarantees. There were never guarantees. The technician asked if she wanted to know the sex of the baby, but she declined. She already had possible names picked out, but she did not want to tell Lazlo, at least not until the baby was closer to being born. If it was a boy, she wanted to name him Mihaly. If it was a girl, she wanted the name Tamara.

After they crossed into Czechoslovakia, several days passed before they could cross farther into Hungary, north of Budapest. Farmers in Czechoslovakia hid them and the Skoda until searches decreased. In Hungary, they abandoned the Skoda, and more farmers transported them south to Miskolc and got them on a train to Budapest.

After the tests at the Institute for Radiobiology, they thought they would have trouble crossing the Hungarian-Austrian border. Instead, a doctor at the institute referred them to Dr. Istvan Szabo at the Hungarian National Atomic Energy Commission. When they told what they knew about the Chernobyl accident, Dr. Szabo began work on temporary visas. During the wait for visas, Juli and Lazlo stayed in a small apartment in Budapest.

It was a strange interlude in Budapest. While she was happy to be with Lazlo, there was always the chance someone processing their visas would recognize them as the man and woman on the run from the Ukrainian militia. She and Lazlo agreed they should make the best of what could be a temporary freedom if Hungarian authorities discovered their identities. While in Budapest, she and Lazlo fell more deeply in love and, with the baby between them as they made love, became a family.

Their assumed name in Budapest was Petavari, Andras and Margit Petavari. The only time they left the apartment was when Dr. Szabo's assistant picked them up to go to the Institute for Radiobiology or to Dr. Szabo's office. If anyone approached and asked questions, they were to say they were brought from an area in Eastern Hungary for tests relating to the Chernobyl accident.

Everything was arranged by Dr. Szabo. They would accompany the doctor to the August meeting of the International Atomic Energy Agency in Vienna and repeat to delegates from the member nations what they knew about Chernobyl. The meeting was to begin tomorrow. Yesterday, at the Parliament Building, she and Lazlo were offered political asylum by the Austrian minister of foreign affairs.

Juli turned from the window, walked across the room, and sat on the ornate sofa. The dress she wore, purchased in Budapest, was already too tight when she sat down. Tomorrow, after a morning session at the Atomic Energy Agency, Dr. Szabo had promised his assistant would accompany Juli to a local maternity shop.

Shopping for clothes! A suite at the Vienna Intercontinental! And all of this after days and nights on the run during which a mildewed tent or a straw-filled barn had seemed precious shelters.

Lazlo was in the bedroom on the telephone. Because there was no telephone at the farmhouse, Lazlo had left a message at the office of the Ulyanov collective's chairman. A few minutes ago, the operator rang with a call from Kisbor. Although she could not hear what he said, Juli heard Lazlo's voice coming from the bedroom, calm and controlled. Lazlo had not asked her to leave the bedroom during the call, but she wanted Lazlo to be able to speak with Nina in private. It was hard enough to talk knowing the PK might be listening.

This morning, when Juli had called Aunt Magda, she had been careful not to mention anything about how she and Lazlo escaped. Aunt Magda assured her everything was fine in Visenka and also gave Juli a message from Marina and Vasily. They planned to marry soon and had moved to a resettlement apartment near Kiev. The news was not all good, however. Vasily's mother and sister were sick from the high radiation they received, and both were being treated at a Kiev hospital.

When Lazlo's voice stopped, Juli closed her eyes. She heard the door open, and Lazlo sat beside her, putting his arm around her. When she opened her eyes, she saw Lazlo smiling. The scar on his upper lip from Komarov's beating made his smile seem crooked. But soon, according to the doctor in Budapest, his smile would be straight again.

"Everything is fine at the farm," said Lazlo. "The KGB never returned after they took us away. Nina and the girls are being checked periodically at a hospital in Uzhgorod. No organ damage, but the girls especially will have to be watched. Nina's decided to stay in Kisbor. Bela wants to help her build a house next to his."

Juli reached out and touched Lazlo's chin with her finger. "Your smile is gone."

"Did I have one?"

"When you first sat down."

"I wish there was something I could do for Nina."

"You did, Laz. You went to your family when they needed you."

"And you came when I needed you."

Lazlo stood and went to the window. He looked east, his profile so sad when he wasn't smiling. "Earlier you mentioned your friend Aleksandra Yasinsky, who was taken away when she spoke openly about radiation dangers. It made me think again about the man named Pavel, and also about the Gypsy on the Romanian border. We've left so many people back there, Juli. I hope leaving is the right thing to do."

Juli went to join Lazlo at the window and held him close. "You said it yourself, Laz. We can help more people from here."

"I know. I simply need to consider these things occasionally. It's part of my melancholy. By the way, before Nina called, I spoke with Dr. Szabo."

"What did he say?"

"He'll pick us up in the morning for the meeting. He said we should consider relocating, perhaps to the United States. He's arranged for visas and contacted a medical facility in New York."

Juli and Lazlo stood together looking east, Lazlo's arm around her, his hand resting on her abdomen.

In the distance, beyond the green of the park and the blue of the Danube, the horizon was a thin line of colorless land and sky. It was like any horizon, a magnet to any Gypsy, a reason to keep moving.

As they stood at the window, they both felt the baby's kick.

Four months after the unit four RBMK-1000 reactor at Chernobyl exploded, Soviet officials joined with scientists from throughout the world at a meeting of the International Atomic Energy Agency in Vienna. For the most part, delegates were pleased with the openness displayed by the Soviets in detailing the causes of the accident. Although there seemed to be many indirect factors leading to the accident, the main cause was reported to have been an ill-planned experiment at the reactor.

Design flaws were also discussed at the meeting, and Soviet officials outlined corrective measures to be performed on the other RBMK-1000 reactors in operation. Although the Soviets said some designers and high-level engineers were at fault, they praised the heroism and bravery of those who were at the site when the explosion occurred.

At the end of August 1986, the official death toll from the Chernobyl accident stood at thirty-one, and hundreds of thousands of people who had been forced from their homes faced a high risk of developing cancer in their lifetimes.

CHAPTER 37

Present Day
Kiev, Ukraine

The Chernobyl Museum (Ukrainian National Museum "CHOR-
NOBYL") is housed in a converted fire station on Khoryvyj Pereulok
Street. The museum is a plain, two-story building with arched fire-
station doors. A garden memorial near the entrance has a single
iconic statue seemingly in prayer. Inside, the museum feels like a
church or funeral parlor, with unhurried footsteps and muted voices
echoing from various exhibit rooms. Some rooms have sections of
girders and metal on the ceiling, simulating the destruction inside
the destroyed reactor. There are photographs of the reactor before
and after the explosion, and photographs of the sarcophagus. There
are photographs of the city of Pripyat and of people who were relocated, especially children. There are photographs of hundreds of
vehicles abandoned in the exclusion zone. And finally, there are photographs of victims, many of whom were firemen and liquidators.

One exhibit area has a display of various protective gear used
during the rescue and cleanup operations. The protective clothing
is primitive by modern standards—rubber gloves, hard hats, face
masks, lead vests, boots, and rubberized suits. Several face masks
hang on the wall, and two are on mannequins in rubberized suits.

The face masks are made of rubber with the pallor of dead flesh. Snouts with downward-pointing screw-on filter canisters make the mannequins into prehistoric creatures not yet ready for the technology assaulting them. Round glass eyes shine like mirrors to the souls inside the suits.

Two caretakers, a man and a woman, walk slowly from exhibit to exhibit, announcing the closing of the museum in soft voices. The noise in the hallways increases as visitors head for the exit, walking briskly on shiny tile floors. In the main hall near the exit is an exhibit of Soviet newspaper stories from the year of the explosion. Most of the headlines concern Chernobyl. But one newspaper from January 1986 has a photograph of the U.S. Space Shuttle Challenger crew killed in the shuttle explosion. The photograph of the crew in black and white, blown up and grainy on the front page of the newspaper, is reminiscent of many other photographs in the museum. Faces from the past full of optimism and trust in twentieth century technology.

Little Ilonka is no longer a little girl. A quarter century has passed since she fled with her mother, Nina, and her sister, Anna, from Pripyat. As Chernobyl Museum visitors parade out the main entrance, several men of various ages glance her way. Perhaps it is a combination of Ilonka's beauty and a reaffirmation of life that makes even women smile at her before heading down the path to the exit gate.

Lazlo and his niece Ilonka sit on a bench near the garden with its commemorative statue and silent bells. The bus from the Chernobyl tour is due in an hour, and they are early. Before coming here, they stopped for a cool drink along Khreshchatik Boulevard. It was hot when they arrived, but the late-afternoon sun has gone lower, hidden by buildings. Although the bench is still warm, the shade is welcome. Lazlo had taken off his jacket and tie earlier in the day, planning to put them back on before dinner. The red, white, and green tie, which Ilonka immediately recognized as representing the Hungarian flag, is draped on his jacket on the bench.

Ilonka is in her late twenties, a professor of mathematics at Kiev University. On their way here, she had admired Lazlo's Sox cap so he bought her one, saying it would not only show she was a fan, but would also protect her head from the sun. Ilonka's hair is very short. At first he worried she had undergone recent chemotherapy, but Ilonka said she had shaved her head, along with several other university staff members, to support a physics professor who had cancer.

Ilonka's whisper-quiet voice is a result of having her thyroid removed years earlier. The surgeon did a fine job on her sister, Anna, but when it came to Ilonka, the surgeon nicked both vocal cords. According to Ilonka, it causes no handicap, especially since she has begun using a wireless microphone and amplifier during her lectures.

Besides the Sox cap, Ilonka wears a short skirt, white blouse, medium heels, and sunglasses. Lazlo is like a proud father as he watches the passing men admiring her. During their walk to the museum, they shared family news. Ilonka's mother, Nina, is happy on the farm in Kisbor. Anna, Ilonka's sister, although married to a farmer in town some years back, has decided not to have children because of her radiation exposure in Pripyat after the explosion. Bela and his wife are grandparents, the mother, Lazlo recalls, a baby during the episode at the farm in 1986. Times are hard in western Ukraine, but it is much better than it was under Soviet rule. The packages Lazlo sends from the United States are appreciated.

Although Lazlo feels more like a proud father than an uncle sitting beside Ilonka, he is not a father. A stepfather, yes, but never a father. During their walk here, he explained the details of his relationships, Ilonka saying she was much younger when she heard about Uncle Lazlo's adventures and wanted to hear the entire story once again, especially since it involved her father, Mihaly.

In 1986, when she was a technician at Chernobyl, Juli Popovics had an affair with Lazlo's brother, Mihaly. After Mihaly's death at Chernobyl, Juli and Lazlo escaped from Ukraine, pursued by a mad KGB officer named Komarov. Juli carried Mihaly's child, a girl born shortly after Lazlo and Juli married in Vienna. Lazlo and Juli named the girl Tamara, after Lazlo's longtime friend who was murdered by Komarov. Lazlo and Juli moved to the United States and lived a happy life until Juli died of cancer at the turn of the new century. After Juli's death, Lazlo visited Ilonka's mother, Nina, several times. Although they were fond of one another, Nina had her life in Kisbor, and Lazlo had his sadness for his loss of Juli. Lazlo also had a life in Chicago. Raising his stepdaughter, Tamara, and watching her grow into a woman gave his life meaning.

After repeating to Ilonka things she already knew about him, Juli, and her father, Lazlo told her something she did not know. She asked how he got his nickname, the Gypsy. When they were little girls, he told Anna and Ilonka his militia friends gave him the name because he liked Gypsy music. Today he told Ilonka the real story about a boy of nineteen in the army, given the job with his friend Viktor picking up deserters near the Romanian border. The deserter who played the violin even as they approached the house in the farm village. The deserter, whose nickname was Gypsy, asking to bring his violin with him, but removing a pistol from the violin case. The boy of nineteen, who had survived recruit hazing with Viktor, shooting the deserter before he could put another bullet into Viktor . . . or into him. Finally, the name Gypsy given to him by others in his unit, the name leaping from the soul of the man he killed to avenge Viktor's murder. The name burdening him with guilt because he should have known better than to allow a Gypsy access to his violin case. Stupid boys. Ignorant boys, with their feet still in their mothers, killing one another.

It was a long walk to the museum this afternoon. After Lazlo told his niece about Viktor and the Gypsy, Ilonka told about a girl-hood friend from Pripyat. Svetlana had settled with her family at another collective a day's drive from Kisbor. She had corresponded with Ilonka for several years, then there was a delay, then a letter from Svetlana's father saying she had died from Chernobyl disease.

While walking to the museum, Lazlo leaned in close to Ilonka so he could hear her whisper above the noise of the street. "I was a very sad little girl, Uncle Laz. How could a little girl understand that Svetlana didn't get enough potassium iodide and I did? At the time I thought about you always seeming sad. I wanted to be like you from then on. It seems I have wanted to be sad my whole life."

"Are you sad now?"

"Half of me is; the other half is not."

"I am the same, Ilonka. The half spending an afternoon with you is content. My contentment will continue into tonight after we retrieve Tamara and Michael from their tour of Chernobyl."

"Where will we dine?"

"I made reservations at Casino Budapest. I wanted to see a striptease or two."

It is after sunset, and the bus from Chernobyl is late. Streetlights have come on around the museum, and other relatives and friends of Chernobyl tourists mill about waiting. With the museum closed, traffic has eased, and it is quiet, allowing Lazlo to hear Ilonka's whispery voice without leaning in close.

"Mother waited until we were teenagers before she told us we were stepsisters to Tamara. Because you were married to Juli, we naturally assumed you were Tamara's real father. Mother said Juli spoke of cancer often, saying many would get it. I was so sorry when it happened."

"Do you remember much about Pripyat?"

"I remember being happy, the playground outside the apartment building, the lights of the Chernobyl towers out our window. I remember you visiting."

"What about the evacuation?"

"We got a ride to the plant in a car, then a bus took us past apartment buildings and away from Pripyat. The bus driver wore a handkerchief over his nose and mouth and drove very fast. I remember looking up at the apartments and seeing bicycles stored on balconies. I remember wondering what would happen to all those bicycles. Anna, on the other hand, always said she remembers dogs chasing the bus. She said dogs chased the buses their owners were on for many kilometers until they gave up or died. Later, the dogs were shot by soldiers because they picked up radiation during their search for food and for their masters."

Ilonka stares past Lazlo and is silent for a time. But then she whispers again.

"There's a man over there I recognize. Wait, don't look yet. He followed me from one of my classes several days ago. When I confronted him, he said he was a journalist doing a Chernobyl story from a conspiracy angle and is also writing a book. He said he's hunting for remaining suspicions. Okay, he's turned away. You can look now."

Lazlo recognizes him. It is the bald man from earlier in the day on European Square.

"He questioned me this morning," says Lazlo. "He said he was a tourist, but he knows too much and speaks too many languages. Why is he still wearing his sunglasses?"

"I think he's an intelligence agent," says Ilonka.

"Whom could he possibly represent?"

"What does it matter?" whispers Ilonka, smiling an evil smile. "We'll confront him. Two against one."

Lazlo shrugs. "What language shall we use?"

"Native Ukrainian," whispers Ilonka.

They stand and quickly walk over to the man, who takes off his sunglasses and backs away when he sees them, almost bumping into the streetlight.

"So what can you tell us?" asks Ilonka, her whisper in Ukrainian harsher than before.

The bald man puts away his sunglasses and eyes them both with a smile, but not really a smile. "About what?"

"Chernobyl, of course," says Lazlo. "The murders. Tell us about the conspiracy and murders at Chernobyl."

The man shifts the sport coat he carries from one arm to the other. "All right. You've got me. I'm here to ask about Chernobyl, but it's simply a matter of cleanup."

"Cleanup?" asks Lazlo.

The man eyes Lazlo's tie draped over the sport coat on his arm. "A side job for Hungarian State Security while here in Kiev. Nothing active. They simply want to know the fate of an American who was doing work for them."

"Andrew Zukor?" asks Lazlo.

The man turns to Ilonka. "How did he know about Zukor?"

Ilonka shrugs and smiles back at the man. They both look to Lazlo.

"You should go to the United States for your research," says Lazlo. "Zukor's widow was quite open with U.S. authorities before her death."

"Unfortunately, they sent me here," says the young man. "For cleanup, you go where they tell you to go, ask predetermined questions, and report back. Have either of you heard of a KGB major named Grigor Komarov?"

Lazlo looks to Ilonka, who smiles back at him, a large infectious smile with one finger to her lips. Soon all three are smiling like old friends who have met beneath the streetlight.

"I guess they sent me to the right people," says the young man. He holds his hand out to Ilonka. "By the way, my name is Zandor."

Zandor continues after shaking hands with Ilonka and Lazlo. "Anyway, Hungarian authorities want to know if Major Komarov had a reason to order Andrew Zukor's assassination in 1986, or if he simply disliked the man. There have been many investigations into Komarov's activities, going back to the cold war. We know Zukor was with U.S. intelligence, and we know a Major Dmitry Struyev in Komarov's office may have given the order. So, my friends, what can you tell me?"

It is an unusual interview, all three of them smiling and talking like old friends while they wait for the bus from Chernobyl. At one point, without realizing it, they switch from Ukrainian to Hungarian. When Zandor asks the identity of the Gypsy Moth, both Lazlo and Ilonka shrug.

"No one knows who the Gypsy Moth was," says Lazlo. "For all we know, he, or she, never existed."

"A fabrication for Komarov's grandiose plan?" asks Zandor.

"A fabrication," says Lazlo. "A name from the past."

After leaving Slavutych, the town built for Chernobyl cleanup workers, they switch from Anton's van to the larger bus at the Dytyatky

Control Point. The evening bus transports both tourists and workers going off shift back to Kiev. It is a comfortable bus with better air-conditioning than the van, as well as ceiling-mounted television monitors. Because it is Lyudmilla's last tour for this shift, she rides back to Kiev with the tourists. She sits across the aisle from the young American couple. At the end of the tour, she noted their names on the tour sheet. The woman is Tamara Horvath, Hungarian. Because of her tears at the visitor center, Lyudmilla assumes she is related to a Chernobyl victim. The young African American man is Michael Richardson. Both are from Chicago. While the driver closes the door and settles in, Lyudmilla leans across the aisle and smiles at the Americans.

"Finally, end of duty for a few days."

"Do you live in Kiev?" asks Tamara.

"With my husband, Vitaly. It is surprising how much I miss him."

"How long have you been married?" asks Tamara.

"Since the fall of the Soviet Union." Lyudmilla reaches across the aisle and touches Tamara's arm. "Tell me. Are you related to one of the victims?"

Michael leans forward and smiles. "She was one of the Chernobylites. Of course, she didn't fill me in on the details until today." He nudges Tamara. "A mystery woman."

"You're too young to have been a Chernobylite," says Lyudmilla.

Tamara touches her tummy. "My mother was carrying me at the time."

"She . . . it must have been terrible for her. Is she . . . how can I say it?"

"She died in the United States in 2000. My father was one of the engineers taken to Moscow, where he died within days of the accident. My stepfather came with me on this visit, but he stayed in Kiev. He was in the Kiev militia in 1986. He says he never wants to visit the plant or Pripyat again."

Lyudmilla shakes her head. "I don't blame him. For me, it's a job. Are you visiting others during your stay?"

"My stepfather is bringing his niece to the museum to meet us, then we'll go to dinner. Tomorrow we're all going into the country-side to visit my mother's roommate from Pripyat and her husband and family."

Michael points to Tamara. "Her stepfather's niece is her stepsis-ter, if you can believe it."

Lyudmilla nods while she tries to decipher the relationship. As the bus begins moving, the overhead television monitors come to life. The volume of the televisions, all tuned to a news station giving the latest statistics on global climate change records, is loud, but not so loud for Lyudmilla to tune out the voice of the inquisitive Ger-man tourist at the rear of the bus.

"Will we get more radiation screening at the museum?" de-mands the German in English. "I wonder if Dytyatky was the last. Can anyone tell me?"

Lyudmilla wishes she could stand and tell the German to shut his mouth. But she is off duty and is not required to respond one way or another. Instead, she closes her eyes and thinks of home, wondering if Vitaly will be there, or if, like the last time they had an argument, he will be away with his friends when she arrives.

The television commentator is also speaking in English. "In Kiev, celebrating the traditional Day of Victory Parade, two elderly World War II veterans who managed to march remain in hospital suffering from heat stroke. In other news, lack of spring rain has caused water shortages on farms throughout Ukraine . . ."

Lyudmilla dozes during the bus ride to Kiev. When she awakens, it is almost dark. A small group of people waits beneath the street-lights in front of the Chernobyl museum, among them a handsome younger bald man talking to an older man and a young woman, both whom are wearing Sox baseball caps. The young woman has short hair beneath the cap, reminding Lyudmilla of how she wore hers when she was young and slender and could wear a short, tight skirt in public and feel good about it.

Suddenly, there is a surprise. Just as she is anticipating the hot evening walk alone to the Metro Blue Line, she sees Vitaly jump out of their car parked across the street. He runs to the bus stop like a younger man. He is smiling. He is carrying yellow spring flowers.

Kiev's Casino Budapest throbs with everything from bump-and-grind to techno to rock and roll to disco, and even some traditional folk music. Tonight, while the striptease bar and the disco pound out their rhythms, the variety show for restaurant guests features a Gypsy orchestra playing traditional Hungarian music.

The restaurant is crowded with tourists. Americans at table twelve, which tonight seats five but can accommodate six, have brought along baseball caps. Two caps, inscribed with the word *Sox*, decorate the center of their table. No one wore the caps into the restaurant, and everyone is dressed casually but appropriately, men in jackets, women in skirts and blouses. The waiter has determined the man paying the tab will be the older, thin-faced man with a prominent nose and who is wearing a garish red, white, and green tie. All five at the table have finished eating, and the table has been cleared.

The two young women at the table are both beautiful in their own way. The young American woman has long brown hair and is buxom. She sits between the older man and a very tall, dark-skinned young African American man. At one point during the

Gypsy orchestra entertainment, she puts her arms around both men and they sway back and forth. The young Ukrainian woman at the table is thin yet shapely with very short hair. She sits with a bald young man who leans very close so she can speak into his ear. She is not telling secrets. Early on, the waiter discovered her voice is a mere whisper and one must lean close to hear her.

After a short interlude, the Gypsy orchestra launches into a Hungarian number. A slow passage is followed by the traditional dance, the *czardas*. While the thin-faced older man at table twelve pays the tab, the other two men stand to pull out chairs. Before standing, the two young women at table twelve each take a Sox baseball cap and put it on. All five laugh as they leave the table. Rather than leaving the restaurant, they move closer to the Gypsy orchestra and the dance floor, where several couples have begun to dance. The tall African American man offers his hand to the long-haired buxom beauty, while the bald young man offers his hand to the thin Ukrainian beauty who, with her short hair and shapely legs, looks like a fashion model.

Both couples watch others dancing the fast-paced *czardas* and try to do the same, but it is obvious they need practice. When the music slows to the solo violin, the couples move closer and sway on the dance floor. The older man in the red, white, and green tie stands to the side, smiling as he plays his own invisible violin.

The soloist is exceptional, reminiscent of Lakatos and his Gypsy Orchestra. The violin cries out on the dance floor, but it can also be heard up and down the hallways of Casino Budapest. As if on cue, intermission is called at other venues within the casino, and the cry of the violin alone travels outside onto the street.

From high on the Kiev hills, this could be any city, the heat of the day making its lights shimmer. The solo violin does not skip a beat as the soloist goes into his final, mournful note. It is as if the violinist possesses a bow of infinite length. This is music from the border regions to the south and west, music from Hungary and Romania. To the north, near the Belarus border, a pair of red lights on the Chernobyl towers blink slowly in the night as if they, too, can hear the violin. The red eyes of the predator, momentarily taken by the music, blinking to clear away its tears.

MICHAEL BERES

Photo by: KB

Michael Beres' experiences during the Cold War and his interest in the environment have shaped his novels. With degrees in computer science, math, and literature, he worked for the government, holding a top-secret security clearance, and in the private sector, documenting analytical software. His fiction reflects our age of environmental uncertainty and political treachery.

A Canadian publisher published Michael's first novel Sunstrike in the eighties when environmental and political conspiracies were considered tall tales. Today we know differently. Medallion Press published Michael's environmental novel *Grand Traverse* in 2005. It presents a realistic portrait of our frightening near future. His 2006 release, political thriller *The President's Nemesis*, was compared to *The Manchurian Candidate* by Library Journal and dubbed "a nail-biting thriller" by Midwest Review.

A Chicago native now living in West Michigan, Michael is a member of the Mystery Writers of America, International Thriller Writers, and the Sierra Club. He has driven a low-emissions hybrid vehicle since the beginning of the technology. His short stories have appeared in: *Amazing Stories, Amazon Shorts*, the *American Fiction Collection, Alfred Hitchcock Mystery Magazine, Ascent, Cosmopolitan, Ellery Queen, Michigan Quarterly Review, The Missouri Review, New York Stories, Papyrus, Playboy, Pulpsmith, Skylark,* and *Twilight Zone*.

www.michaelberes.com

FINAL STROKE

MICHAEL BERES

Retired government agents in Florida cling to a decades-old secret that threatens to wreak havoc on the American political system.

A right-brain stroke victim related to a high profile mobster dies mysteriously at a Chicago rehabilitation facility.

A fellow rehab patient with a left-brain stroke who was a detective in his former life launches his own investigation.

The detective's wife, desperate to help her husband connect to his past, joins the investigation, makes very large waves, and is kidnapped. An environmental activist is murdered while driving his hybrid vehicle to a clandestine meeting. An aide at the rehab facility, who stumbles into the plot while ripping off the health care system, becomes yet another victim. Saint Mel in the Woods Rehabilitation Facility, aptly nicknamed Hell in the Woods by residents and employees, is the last place you'd expect violence on this scale.

The mob, family legacy, health care scams, a troubled environment, crooked politics, and federal agents authorized to commit murder . . . Why is it all zeroing in on a rehabilitation facility?

Final Stroke. The ultimate in stroke rehab . . . Figure it out, or die trying.

ISBN# 9781932815955
Hardcover Thirller
US $24.95 / CDN $33.95
Available Now
www.michaelberes.com

THE FRONT PORCH PROPHET

RAYMOND L. ATKINS

What do a trigger-happy bootlegger with pancreatic cancer, an alcoholic helicopter pilot who is afraid to fly, and a dead guy with his feet in a camp stove have in common?

What are the similarities between a fire department that cannot put out fires, a policeman who has a historic cabin fall on him from out of the sky, and an entire family dedicated to a variety of deceased authors?

Where can you find a war hero named Termite with a long knife stuck in his liver, a cook named Hoghead who makes the world's worst coffee, and a supervisor named Pillsbury who nearly gets hung by his employees?

Sequoyah, Georgia is the answer to all three questions. They arise from the relationship between A. J. Longstreet and his best friend since childhood, Eugene Purdue. After a parting of ways due to Eugene's inability to accept the constraints of adulthood, he reenters A.J.'s life with terminal cancer and the dilemma of executing a mercy killing when the time arrives.

Take this gripping journey to Sequoyah, Georgia and witness A.J.'s battle with mortality, euthanasia, and his adventure back to the past and people who made him what he is—and helps him make the decision that will alter his life forever.

ISBN# 9781933836386
Hardcover Fiction
US $25.95 / CDN $28.95
JULY 2008
www.raymondlatkins.com

BLOOD EAGLE

Robert Barr Smith

A single pistol shot in the night, and an attractive young woman is dead, a suicide. A passing thing in 1931 Munich. Except the dead woman was Adolf Hitler's niece and mistress, the lovely Geli Raubal. The pistol was Hitler's. And the location was Hitler's sumptuous flat.

More than half a century later, despite the facts surrounding Geli's death, surely no one should care. But western intelligence learns someone does care. Very much. Both the KGB and a well-financed neo-Nazi organization. And both are willing to murder to uncover a long-buried secret connected to Geli's demise. A secret important enough to torture and kill to find three elderly Germans.

American Tom Cooper and Englishman Simon Berwick, agents of U.S. intelligence and British MI6, are given the mission to find the three before the Russians or the Nazis. Both men have scores to settle. Both lost their families to terrorist bombs. They have killed for their countries in the twilight war of espionage; they will kill again.

More than one person has already died in the desperate race across Germany. More will die before the search ends in a blinding snowstorm above Hitler's former residence high on the Obersalzburg in Bavaria. And the only reward for the agent who makes a mistake will be a nameless grave.

ISBN# 9781933836102
Hardcover Suspense
US $24.95 / CDN $33.95
Available Now

Flight to Freedom

D.J. Wilson

I KILLED MY HUSBAND, A TOWN HERO, and then called the police and turned myself in. "He's dead as a doornail," I said to the officer and then spit on Harland Jeffers' bloody, dead body.

With my head held high, I allowed myself to be escorted to a squad car outside my house. A house which had been more of a prison than the cell I was headed for.

Cameras flashed.

"Why did you kill Harland?"

Because he needed killing. And I, Montana Ines Parsons-Jeffers did just that.

So begins the rest of what's left of Montana's life. Not that she ever really had one.

Now she's headed for prison. There's no escaping it. It was the ultimate destination in her Flight to Freedom.

But one man might be able to help . . .

ISBN# 9781933836379
Trade Paperback
US $15.95 / CDN $17.95
Available Now
www.doloresjwilson.com

For more information
about other great titles from
Medallion Press, visit

www.medallionpress.com